SHADOWBOUND

DRUADAN LEGACY
BOOK ONE

AMELIA COLE

CONTENT WARNINGS

Shadowbound is the first in an adult, dystopian sci-fi set on a future Earth. It is a 'why choose' romance, where the main character will end up with more than one love interest. It may have triggers for some, including violence, threat of death, blood, sexual themes, sexual acts, harm to animals, death, grief, and depression. It is intended for mature 18+ readers

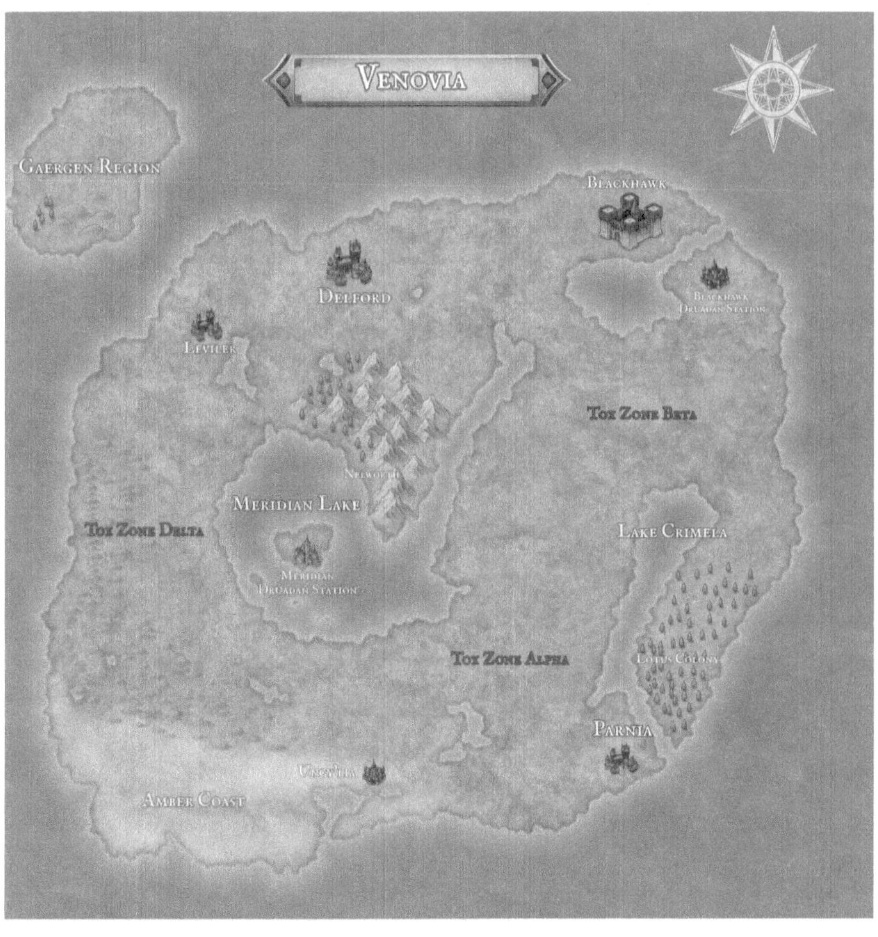
Venovia
Gaergen Region
Blackhawk
Delford
Blackhawk Druadan Station
Leviter
Tox Zone Beta
Newforth
Meridian Lake
Lake Crimela
Tox Zone Delta
Meridian Druadan Station
Tox Zone Alpha
Lotus Colony
Parnia
Uncaville
Amber Coast

Copyright © 2024 by Amelia Cole

All rights reserved.

Interior illustrator: and formatting by Amelia Cole

Book cover by Milbart

This book is licensed for your personal enjoyment only.

This is a work of fiction. Names, characters, pleases, brands, media, and incidents are either the product of the author's imagination or are used fictitiously. The author acknowledges the trademark status and trademark owners of various products referred to in this work of fiction which have been used without permission.

No part of this book may be reproduced in any form or by any electronic or mechanical means, including information storage and retrieval systems, without written permission from the author, except for the use of brief quotations in a book review.

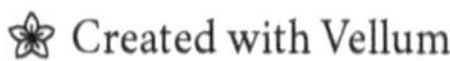 Created with Vellum

To the horse girls who love horse boys

They charge the storm.
Echoes fierce on steeds they ride
With bonds forged of fire and blood,
their fates collide

Blades flash, their enemies fall
Hooves of thunder spark the stone
Vales of night, masks of day
A marked one never rides alone
-Unknown Master Rider 83 PR

One

Trust no one.

Mentally, I chant it like a mantra on the long shuttle ride to Meridian Station. I remember it with every offer of juice or coffee, every door held open, every direction given as I make my way across the stone path to the main house.

No one can be trusted here. Someone is hiding the truth. Any of the staff could know something or be responsible for my sister's disappearance.

And yet, as I wait in the foyer for my interview, my suspicion wanes. I grow tired of sitting and find myself wandering the room, taking in the antiques and priceless art. A statue of a black horse catches my attention. I stare into its glimmering gold eyes, transfixed by their beauty. It's imbued with such vitality that I almost expect the creature to break free from its frozen pose.

The sculpture must be hundreds of years old since actual marble stone is impossible to find these days. Sharice sent me pictures of the paintings and sculptures during her time here, and I told her how jealous I was that her office was equivalent to a museum. This piece is by Bellion, a famous eccentric from the 30th century who was two hundred years dead now. Sharice encouraged me to write a research paper on him and the hidden messages many suspected he concealed on every piece. Sadness seeps into me as I stare at his work. The talented artist is long gone, bones in a coffin somewhere.

I refuse to believe the same has happened to Sharice. I'd know if she was dead, would sense it through some sisterly bond.

I have to believe it.

Moving farther along the wall in the waiting room, I gaze at the display case of paintings, photographs, and sculptures. Everything inside it is old. Like really old. Relics from the station's previous Master Riders and their legendary druadans.

They're probably all dead too, faded into myths just like the battles they fought. The wars have been over for a long time and yet they remain echoes of the once great warriors. Or so the history books claim. Many believe the druadans and their stations are obsolete, which is precisely why I'm here.

Keeping my chin up, I inhale a slow breath, fingering the jeweled bracelet on my wrist. The sapphire-colored stone was a birthday gift from Sharice. The last thing she gave me before she went missing.

I peer at the display of old relics: paintings, photographs, and sculptures displaying famous druadans and their Master Riders. In the glass, I glimpse my long silvery-blonde hair, blue-green eyes, and the smattering of freckles on the pale skin of my nose. So different from my sister's chocolate-brown hair and eyes. I smile into the glass, checking for lipstick on my teeth.

"Miss Corsair?"

I look over my shoulder to see a middle-aged woman approaching me from across the foyer of the old mansion. Her long, red, tightly woven braid sways down her back, a typical hairstyle worn by the Lotisians. She must be from Lotus, a region to the east. "Master Rider Lockwood is ready for you now."

The receptionist opens the door, and I'm guided into an office cramped with bookshelves lining the walls. My gaze immediately goes to the hardbound books inside a locked case. Books are rare, and most are handed down through families as heirlooms or sold at auctions to rich collectors. And here they have dozens of them. Some of them look decades old; I can only imagine their price.

I sit in one of the wingback chairs, pleasantly surprised by the craftsmanship. My thumb strokes the grains, and I fantasize about the expanses of land that used to grow such material. Before the seas rose, the polluted air killed most of the trees along with most of the human population. Now furniture is made from lab-created fibers spun together into slabs or recycled metal salvaged from the ocean.

I rub the sleeves of my sweater together, regretting wearing the thick outerwear. I was warned Meridian has a warmer climate than the more northern city of Delford, but I didn't expect it to be *this* hot. Is it always this hot?

I couldn't believe my good fortune when I saw the posting on the Network. They need a new public relations consultant, and the position fits my resume perfectly. Well, with a little extra embellishment and a three-month internship since my history degree doesn't typically lend itself to marketing. But I can make it work. I have to. For Sharice.

The clock on the matching desk in the room ticks slowly,

and my left leg starts bouncing of its own accord. Several minutes pass, and intrusive thoughts push into my mind.

Get yourself together, Brigid. You need this job. It's the only way you'll get answers.

Just as I approach full panic mode, a door camouflaged by paisley-patterned wallpaper across the room opens. A man steps in and sits behind his desk, ignoring my presence. His white sleeves are rolled up as if he just washed his hands, and he unrolls them meticulously, turn by turn. My breath catches as his rich brown eyes land on me, and I can't help but stare at his clean-shaven face and jet-black hair.

"Miss Corsair," he says, his voice firm and commanding. "Appreciate you coming in today. How was the flight over?"

"It was good. The pilot said it was unusually clear weather for this time of year."

"Glad to hear it. I assume you already know who I am, so I'll skip the formalities."

He's right. I do know who he is. I did my research before coming here. His name is Heath Lockwood. He's a year older than me at twenty-three and one of the youngest ever managers of Meridian Station. He was a Master Rider for two years and then took over station operations when his predecessor, Gilbert Pilchuck, retired.

"I do," I reply, nodding.

"Good. I'll get straight to the point then. I've already reviewed your resume and references, and they all stack up to fit the position's requirements." He lays his hands on the desk and leans forward.

I shift in my seat, aiming to face him more directly. My pencil skirt rides higher up my thigh than I'd prefer, and I squirm to keep it at a respectable level.

"As of late, druadan conservation has been under added pressure and scrutiny," he says. "As I'm sure you're aware, a former employee of ours went missing. The authorities have had no luck determining her whereabouts or any indicators of foul play. However, as we receive the majority of our funding from the Circuit, our reputation must remain impeccable if we hope to continue business."

I press my lips together. I'm intimately aware of the 'situation' since it's my sister who went missing. I dug into Meridian station after her disappearance and have kept tabs on them for the past year, which is why I received the alert when they posted the public relations job on Network. It was the chance I've been waiting for. An opportunity to investigate her disappearance at the last place she was seen.

"Yes," I say, keeping my voice neutral. "I've heard about the… situation, and have extensive experience in managing similar unfortunate predicaments. And you'll find there are no indiscretions with my previous employer, Tritan Strategies. However, I'm not at liberty to give specific details." It's legit, but also a cop-out. My experience is thin, and every project I worked on included a team of more senior staff. If he pushes too hard for specifics, the jig will be up. The truth is, I'm barely qualified for this job, but the authorities failed my sister even after months of investigation.

I won't do the same.

Heath doesn't move, and I feel a tinge of excitement when I realize I've got him. People often tell me I'm the charismatic type and easy to talk to. I suppose that's true. I was the one at university the drunk partiers would sidle up to and spill their life story. Sharice said it was because I have an innocent face, which I took as a compliment at the time, although later, it felt more like a subtle jab. I don't want to be perceived as innocent. I want to be seen as strong, someone with depth beyond what meets the eye. But there's power in being underestimated, in having others let down their guard around me. I lick my lips, folding my fingers as if speaking such high praise is small talk. In truth, talking about my career is easy. My life? Not so much.

"Well, Miss Corsair—"

"Brigid," I interject. "Please, my department director at Tritan encouraged the marketing department to be on a first-name basis. The more casual and comfortable everyone is, the more likely they'll share a potentially genius idea instead of holding it back."

Heath laces his fingers together, contemplating my words. "Very well, Brigid. Looking through your resume, I see that you only minored in communications."

"Yes, that's right. My major is Venovian history, but the college mentor I worked with suggested I select a more employable minor just to be safe."

Heath taps the screen, which I'm assuming has my resume on it. "Your mentor was probably right. The filtration centers need chemists and biologists more than historians, unless of course you wanted to continue working at the University?"

I shake my head. "Teaching isn't off the table, eventually, I suppose. But after graduation I wanted to travel around Venovia, maybe even off the continent for a while."

Heath taps his chin contemplatively. "Tell me a little about why you chose Venovian history."

I sit up straighter in my chair, mentally sifting through my rehearsed notes for these very questions. "When I was in elementary school, my mom bought me a history book for my birthday. It was used, and some of the pages were torn, but I was fascinated by the pictures of animals that went extinct after the air turned and how entire cities were submerged in a day when the seas rose." It was one of the few actual real bound books we owned and stuck at the research station with mom working round the clock. I read through it again and again to stave off the boredom. Even now, I remember how it smelled and how it felt to run my finger over the pages and feel the printed letters. "Believe it or not," he continues, "a history background would prove beneficial in this position."

He scrolls further, then sets the tablet down. "I understand you aren't able to divulge any information regarding your previous work, and I suppose their stellar reputation is almost entirely due to your part."

I flash him a tight grin, and his eyes dart to my lips, remaining there a fraction longer than what I'd consider acceptable for a job interview. I can't help but fight the fear that my choice of burgundy lipstick was all wrong. I should've gone with the neutral pink or peach, as Laura suggested. I tuck a loose piece of hair behind my ear, and his eyes shift upward again to study my face.

I clear my throat. "No. I laid out a series of plans and contingencies that I believe would not only cleanse Meridian of its somewhat tarnished outlook but rejuvenate enthusiasm from council members and supporters alike."

His left eyebrow twitches. Most people wouldn't notice it, but I do. Subtle actions speak louder than words, exposing hidden emotions. He clasps his hands together on his lap and leans back in his chair. "I'm sure you're aware we've had other applicants with their own agendas and strategies."

Working at Meridian is a coveted position. It's one of the few non-military installations run by Circuit, the closest thing to a government Venovia has. Since it's at an isolated location hours from the city of Delford and still has living plants and animals, it would make half my graduating class envious. We read the history books, theorized the authors' experiences, and discussed the philosophies people had before the floods, but here...

Here, I would be living it.

You can't mention any decade of Venovian history without including the druadans in the same breath. Druadans are intertwined with our history, so much so that Circuit portioned off millions of credits every year to keep their legacy alive.

"So, Miss... Brigid," he says again, correcting himself. Damn if my name doesn't sound like honey slowly running off his tongue. "What makes your strategy different from all the other ones I've heard?"

I squeeze my thighs, frustrated at the amount of control he holds merely by speaking my name. It has been quite a long time since anyone had that kind of effect. Coby was the last, and our relationship ended when Sharice disappeared. I threw myself into searching for her and threw out any future with Coby. I begged my old professors for a stack of gleaming recommendation letters in order to secure an internship at a company I knew would position me to align with Sharice's old job.

I raise my chin, preparing to launch into my rehearsed speech. "The druadan stations are considered obsolete by many. There are more pressing matters that Circuit needs to handle, such as the toxic air and filtration plant strikes. The druadan and their riders provide a morbid fascination at most and an idle curiosity at the least. Not to mention the various animal rights activist groups and anti-Circuit organizations that believe the stations are a waste of Venovian tax dollars."

He narrows his gaze, and I momentarily worry I went too far by speaking the harsh truth. But this is it. The toughest part of the job. I am supposed to play the Devil's advocate, lay the shortcomings of a company in plain sight so I can swoop in and save them with the answers to their problems. "I propose in my seven-part plan that you expand outward from your daily tours and shift to allow more personalized experiences." Heath doesn't move, but I see a slight tick in his left jaw. I know he's listening intently, weighing my proposal against the others. "If you allow me the privilege of working here, I will work to guarantee a unanimous vote on next year's budget, along with double that from generous benefactors."

He narrows his gaze. "It's been a while since I've met someone else who is as good at bluffing as I am."

"I assure you, Mr. Lockwood, I am not bluffing. Excellent at my job, yes. Bluffing, no. When I set a goal, I meet it."

He studies my face, looking for any cracks in my facade. He won't find any. I mean every word. When you're the face of a business or a company, confidence comes with the job, but so does authenticity. I've been around enough public relations professionals to know they can spot a lie as fast as anyone. During my internship observing the seasoned pros, I learned to bend the truth just enough. I call it 'Brigid's no bullshit approach,' and in the three months I've been at Tritan Strategies, it has worked.

He stands abruptly, and I suddenly worry that he's ending the interview.

"Let's go for a walk."

Without waiting for me, he strides out of the room. I quickly but carefully get out of my seat to follow him. He leads me out of the waiting room where the receptionist is keying something in on her computer.

"I'll be back in a bit, Carla," he says as I follow him. As we pass her, he keeps his eyes forward but adds to me, "Before you commit to anything, perhaps you'd like a tour. Then we will discuss whether you're a good fit here."

Instead of going out the front door leading to where the shuttle dropped me off, he takes me out the side door and down some stairs to exit the side of the building. We walk across the artificial grass and I'm given my first view of the station. Two enormous barns form a V-shape at least three hundred feet long in the center, flanked by rows of fences and various pieces of farm equipment.

He slows his walk as he starts down a narrow path leading next to one of the fences.

This is a good sign, right? Or maybe I'm reading too much into it. Maybe he just wants an excuse to get out of his office and get some fresh air. Maybe everyone gets a tour. Either way,

I can't contain the tiny flicker of excitement inside me. Very few people get to see the behind-the-scenes at druadan stations without knowing someone on the inside or paying for them.

I follow him under the enormous archway, entering the barn, a monstrous metal thing crafted of polished steel and stone. Rows upon rows of artificial green lights hover above me, and I'm sure they give my skin a ghastly appearance. My heart quickens when he stops in front of one of the enclosures.

"Have you ever been to a druadan performance?"

I nearly laugh out loud. It would've taken a Circuit-issued order to force my mom to leave the research station in Uncy'lia. But even if she was willing to take a break from her work, the price of the ticket would've been only half the issue. Waitlists for druadan exhibitions are months long, typically booking up the day they release the season's schedule.

"No," I reply. "I'm sorry to say I haven't."

Heath's hazelnut brown eyes glint at my response. "Shame. Even if you don't end up taking the position, I'll see what I can do to get you a pair of seats."

I sigh a little wistfully, unable to help myself. Laura and Vince would have a field day if I told them I got tickets to a druadan exhibition. Like many, I grew up with stories of the druadans and their riders, fearless soldiers in ancient wars. I'm standing next to what most people would consider a mythical creature. However, I can't let my focus waver. This job is more important than tickets to a show. Finding Sharice is the priority, and I need to make sure this tour ends with him offering me the position.

Heath slides open the top railing, and an elegant white horse sticks his head over the bars.

No digital image, no matter how high-resolution, could capture the intelligent cat-like glowing orbs peering back at me. They're fringed with shimmering translucent eyelashes that almost look like tiny icicles. The white fur covering its body looks velvety, and its black mane is thick. My fingers itch to touch it.

"This is Shadowmane," Heath says proudly. "He's mine."

Shadowmane looks similar to a horse, but the genetic manipulations have left parts of him slightly off. Bony ridges run down between his ears, over his forehead, and stop just above his nose. His extra-long ears are nearer to a rabbit's than a horse's. However, the weirdest thing about him is the low hum coming from him. Like a giant cat's purrs, it vibrates against my chest. It isn't painful, just different.

"You get used to it after a while," Heath says when I press a hand against my breastbone.

"What is it?"

"He's talking."

"You can understand him?"

He nods. "Yes."

Before I can stop myself, curiosity forces the words from me. "What's he saying?"

Heath's face curves into a smirk.

I suddenly don't know if I trust my knees to hold me. He is devastatingly handsome. All tall, dark, and broody with jet-black hair falling perfectly over his forehead and that cleanly shaved face that accentuates his square jaw. But it's his eyes, with that piercing dark brown gaze, that unsettle me the most. Every time I look at him, it's as if I'm drawn in, unable to resist their allure. A tendril of fear slithers down my spine as I'm suddenly afraid my eyes will betray my true intentions.

"It's...incredible," I say, meaning it and willing myself to look away from him and back to Shadowmane. Information about druadans is limited to the public, so I only know what the few searches on the government-maintained Network produced. Sharice frequently warned me not to trust everything in the shared data system. While most of what's there is accurate, everything is filtered through a Circuit positive filter. A common theme, however, is that druadans and their riders were a symbol of Circuit's initial rise to power during the ancient wars. They were innovations the government achieved centuries ago and a testament to the safety and security of Venovia.

Heath rubs the druadan's nose, and the creature blows out steamy puffs of air.

I reach out to touch him, and the stallion snorts, taking a step back. His lip curls slightly, exposing a set of pointed teeth. Heath quickly pushes my hand away. "Wait." He takes a padded glove from the hook next to the stall. "Put this on."

I slip on the insulated glove.

"You should be safe now. Their temperature is around 110 degrees Celsius. It's like touching a hot stove."

Don't touch. Got it.

Heath's mouth moves silently, and the vibrations increase. Shadowmane moves closer, hanging his head over the stall again.

Fear seeps into my veins. "What's he saying?"

"I told him you're a friend," Heath says. "He'll behave."

I stretch out my gloved hand, and the stallion lowers his head just enough for me to stroke the side of his jaw. Warmth permeates through the glove, and although I can't feel anything, my hand glides over his smooth hide. I imagine it being quite soft, like a cat's or a rabbit's.

A thousand questions bombard me. Why doesn't their blood boil? What do they eat with those teeth? Do they ever get cold? And most of all, how can a person safely ride something that hot?

Footsteps behind us draw my attention before I can voice any of them.

Another man walks toward us wearing jeans and a collared shirt with the Meridian logo. "If I'd known you were giving tours, I would've come down here earlier and got the place cleaned up for you guys."

Holy crap, I thought Heath was good-looking with his dark eyes and hair, but this guy is *the* definition of hot. He's over six feet tall like Heath but has longer sandy-brown hair with light curls falling around his ears. It's tousled like he's just been for a run on the beach. His short beard only adds to the rugged charm of hazel-green eyes that could easily be straight out of a girl's fantasy.

Okay, okay. *My* fantasy.

While Heath's toned muscles are evident even under his shirt, this man's body is that of a true athlete, with sculpted shoulders and defined arm muscles.

I take a step back and pull the glove off, trying to quell the heat pooling low in my core.

Whoa, lady parts. Let's keep focused, please.

Heath gestures to me. "This is Brigid Corsair. She's applying for the public relations position, and I thought about giving her a quick tour before offering her the job."

"Nice to meet you," I say, smiling. Then his words hit me, and I blink in surprise. I was so caught off guard by the crazy sexy new guy's appearance that I completely missed the part that I passed the interview. I start to stammer a thank you when the other man interrupts.

"Glad it's you doing the interviewing," he says, his eyes sweeping over me. "I wouldn't have waited this long. I'd have given her the job on the spot."

My cheeks flush with heat as his eyes return to my face. I might have regretted the burgundy lipstick earlier, but now it feels like I made the right choice.

He holds out a hand. "I apologize. I haven't introduced myself, and it sounds like we're going to be working together. My name is Carter. Carter James. I run the tours and demonstrations here at Meridian." His accent is thicker than the one I picked up from my four years at DU. He is a true Delford native.

I shake his hand. His fingers are warm as they gently caress the inside of my wrist. "Nice to meet you."

Heath clears his throat. "I've got to run to another meeting. Carla will email you the formal offer with the salary and the list of benefits. Please take all the time you need to read before deciding, but I hope you take it."

"Thank you," I manage to say, and the joy in my voice is genuine.

"If you'd like to see more around," Carter says, leaning forward and lowering his voice, "it'd be my absolute pleasure to show you the hidden secrets of the place."

Heath's eyes darken, his eyebrows bunching together in Carter's direction. "You sure you're able to take over the tour?"

The smile on Carter's face widens. "You wouldn't believe your timing. I actually do have a free hour until Logan needs help with the novices."

Heath turns to leave. "Very nice meeting you, Brigid," he says, smiling briefly, then clicks the com inside his ear and answers an incoming call. I only catch a snippet of the one-sided conversation, something about a supply delivery update, before he leaves the barn. My heart does a little somersault at the interview's success, and then the intrusive thoughts start in. My stomach sinks.

Getting my foot in the door is only the first step. Now comes the hard part: gaining everyone's trust and integrating myself to find the answers I need.

I'm not here for a paycheck or because I give a damn about druadans or their riders. Sharice went missing last year, and I'm here to find out what happened to her.

I won't leave until I do.

Two

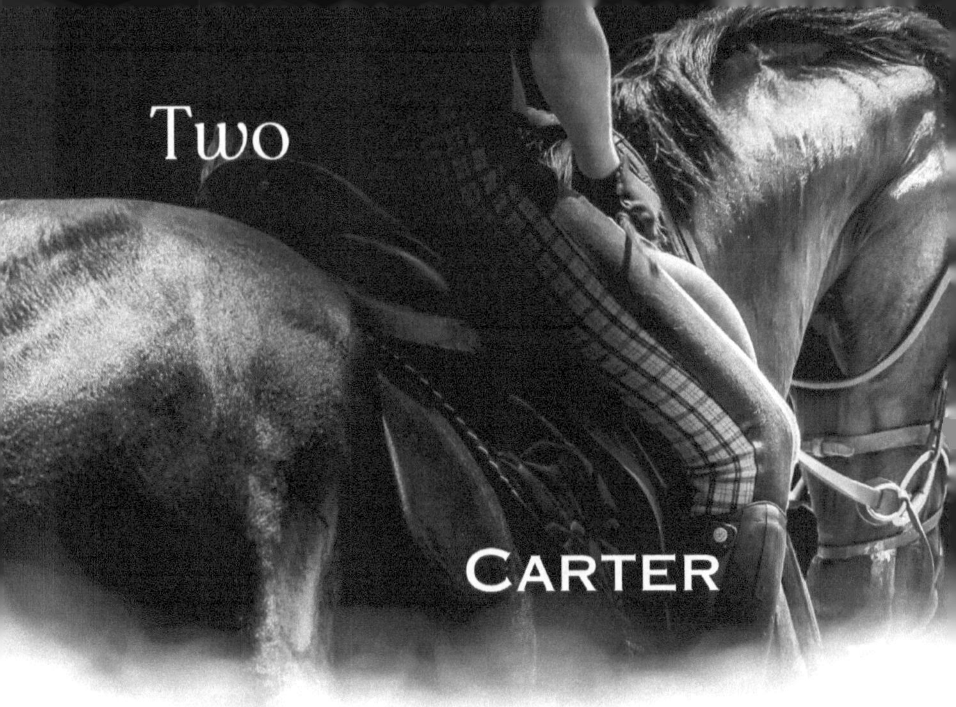

*W*ell, damn. Heath hit it out of the park with this new hire. Holy fuck is she hot. Between that tight skirt that hugs her ass and that blouse with the top button undone so I can glimpse the tops of her gorgeous tits, this woman conjures all sorts of naughty workplace fantasies.

Logan and I were drilling maneuvers with the novices when I overheard the shuttle pilots talking about some hottie from Delford they'd brought in for an interview. And although it didn't take much for me to ditch morning lessons, my day improved when I ducked out early to see what all the fuss was about. Being the first to escort her around here would be well worth the earful from Logan.

"So, are you a whiskey girl or a champagne girl?" I ask.

She looks more than a little confused since Heath left so abruptly after offering her the job. Typical behavior for him these days. The station manager bullshit has him so wrapped up in his own thoughts that he rarely stops to check on anyone else's. Truth is, the station has been running just fine without a

PR person, but with the gala twisting Heath's briefs more than usual, it's good timing that he finally filled the position. I wasn't sure how many more of his long-winded meetings discussing the gala invitation design I could handle.

"Uh, what?" she asks.

"You know, to celebrate your coming on here at the station."

Her eyes widen. "Ah, oh, right." She purses her lips as if thinking. "I guess I have to pick whiskey. I'll admit I've never had champagne." A faint blush touches the apples of her cheeks.

"You're joking."

She shakes her head, smiling sheepishly, and the workplace fantasy evaporates in my head, shifting to more of a girl-next-door at her first frat party. Equally hot.

I clap my hands together. "That settles it, then. If... no, *when* you accept the offer, I'll get us a bottle. We can open it together, and I'd be honored to"—*pop your champagne cherry*— "help you experience one of the perks here at the station."

Her blue eyes brighten at the promise. "Since I am still deciding, maybe you could convince me by telling me about some of the other perks?"

I push aside the hundred dirty thoughts that come to mind. Heath trusts me to be professional, and with as moody as he's been lately, it'd be shitty as fuck for her to run back and file a sexual harassment report on her first day here because I can't bite my tongue. "Absolutely," I say. "Besides the fine selection of alcohol, we have an extensive library in the main house, a full workout facility, and round-the-clock medical staff."

The two of us continue down the aisleway, and Brigid turns her head, looking at the stallions in the stalls. Her eyes narrow with genuine interest. It's somehow different from the usual touristy apprehension. Intriguing. It's almost like when the novices are first introduced here at the station and shown which stallion they might potentially bond with.

"This way," I say as she leans toward Shadowmane. The gray

stallion is Heath's and as wound-tight as his rider. When she doesn't react, I cough loudly.

Brigid pauses, her gaze drifting to mine as if she's forgotten I'm here. "Hmm? Sorry, did you say something?"

"I said I'll show you some of the more private areas, the ones that the regular guests don't get to see."

"I'd like that," she says, following me. "I should know this place well if I'm going to work here."

"That's true," I reply, glancing over my shoulder at her. There it is again. That weird feeling hit me again. It reminds me of two years ago when I guided Sharice, Brigid's predecessor, just like this. Sharice was reserved and cautious, while Brigid seems more... something. Bold. Ambitious. Not to mention, she doesn't seem to mind showing off her curves. I never saw Sharice in so much as a tank top.

"So then," I say, leading her out of the barn and into the open air. "Tell me about yourself. Blackhawk station has more amenities and benefits, with the fortress being right next door. They're also hiring, so why pick Meridian?"

"It sounds super cliche, but I just wanted a fresh start," she says. "Away from the busyness of Delford."

I nod. The station is quieter and does offer a slower way of life. "Is that where you're from then? Delford?"

Brigid shakes her head. "No, I went to DU but was born in Uncy'lia." When she tucks a strand of hair behind her ear, I can't help but watch. She catches my eye and clears her throat. "Before Lannet Corp bought up the restored land, of course."

"Figures," I say. Lannet and Circuit have always jerked each other off. Circuit's officials turns a blind eye to Lannet's often illegal land rejuvenation practices while Lannet portions off a chunk of all newly obtained land to Circuit.

"I couldn't help but notice your Delford accent, though," she says.

My fingers go to the tattoo on my neck. "I'm from the

Gaergen region, but soon after I was born, I went to boarding school in Delford. Unfortunately, the accent stuck."

We move out into the afternoon sunshine, and her eyes scan the hundreds of acres that make up the compound, barns, housing, and exhibition hall. Now *this* look I recognize. Her face mirrors the awe I've seen on so many first-timers. Meridian Station is one of the few areas on Venovia that doesn't need filtration—a pocket of clean air for miles in every direction.

I point to the south at the perimeter wall and the rectangular building and concrete pad. "That's where the shuttle dropped you off. We have our own craft available to take you to Delford for your time off, but just a heads up, we get some storms that can cause delays."

I lead her across the courtyard to the exercise facility. It's late in the afternoon, so the gym is full. We pass by the rows of treadmills, the free weights, and the wall of punching bags swaying like they're itching for a fight. Strolling the grounds with her by my side, I've got to admit, she's not the worst person I've given a tour to. She seems to be absorbing everything, asking the right questions, and not openly staring at the shirtless novices sparring on the mats.

"Whoa," she gasps as Danner kicks Stefensen's feet out from under him, and he lands with a hard thud on the mat.

I snort.

"You guys don't hold back, do you?"

"Why should we? The holograms we fight won't."

"You really can get hurt?"

I rest my arms on the railing. "Not if you're good. Which comes from hours spent in here."

Danner is bigger than Stefensen, but he's also slower. This time, when the two novices square off again, Stefensen sidesteps to Danner's weak right side, shoulder-checking him. He grunts as he's sent backward.

Brigid raises her eyebrows, clearly impressed.

"That's nothing. As a novice, I could take both down blind-folded and with one arm tied behind my back."

"Really?" she says, sounding skeptical. "That's quite the claim. They're not exactly slacking down there."

"Maybe not, but if there were a contest, I'd win hands down. It's all in the technique...and a bit of natural talent."

"Natural talent, huh?" she asks, her eyes alight with humor. "Does that include the talent for modesty, or is that one still in training?"

I can't help but grin at her comeback. "Since we've only just met, I guess I should tell you *modesty* is my middle name."

She smirks. "Is that so?"

"Sure," I say, sniffing. "I just keep it in reserve for special occasions. Besides, a little friendly competition never hurt anyone. It keeps things interesting around here."

She laughs, shaking her head, and I soak in the sound. Making people laugh, especially someone as captivating as Brigid, always gives me a thrill.

"I'll have to remember that," she says. "Care to demonstrate?"

Brigid's challenge sparks a fire in me. The thought of showing off, of proving my boasts weren't just hot air, tempts me more than I care to admit.

Yet, as I weigh her request, part of me hesitates. Sure, I could easily humble the novices. But there are more pressing matters at hand. I still need to show Brigid the exhibition hall, and time's ticking away before my dinner meeting with Heath and Logan. I'm already on Logan's shit list after playing hooky this afternoon, and I can't afford to be on Heath's too.

"Some other time," I say, injecting a regretful tone into my voice. "We've got a schedule to keep, and I promised to give you a full tour. Plus, I have a meeting with the other riders tonight that I can't push back." I continue walking. "Over there is the sauna, an ice bath, and a laser therapy room. Keeping our bodies fit is our main priority, so if we ask for it, Circuit sends it."

Brigid looks over the facility, only slowing to take in the massive floor-to-ceiling windows that look out to the north at the expanse of rust-colored sand, rocks, and dirt. "The gym is open to all staff?"

"Yeah, except for the hours the riders reserve it for combat training."

"Combat is just for demonstrations," she says. "You don't *actually* fight anything, do you?"

"It *is* considered a demonstration, so there's no real combat. We only fight holograms. However, there is a danger since we're working with live animals and weapons."

She blinks. "Holograms of what?"

I swipe a hand through the air, gesturing for her to hold the thought. "It's easier if I just show you."

At the back of the gym, there's a designated area with padded walls and foam-covered beams, and I guide her to it. "This is where the real work happens."

With a few taps on the control panel, a hologram of the last recorded image of a mystyl, a bizarre, gigantic spider-like creature, appears in mid-air. Brigid's eyes widen in amazement, and she flips up the cap on the comm on her wrist to take a photo.

I quickly step in front of her. "Naughty, naughty. Patented Circuit military tech."

She lowers her wrist. "Sorry. I didn't realize there was an NDA. Anything else I shouldn't put on the Network?"

I laugh. "I can think of a few more things."

"Care to enlighten me?"

Shit. This girl is walking right into it, and I'm not about to ruin the game. "Isn't half the fun in discovering things on your own?"

She scoffs. "I hardly consider being fired for being ignorant of what needs to be kept a secret here, *fun.*"

"Fair point. Carla has a file full of photos the last PR person took. I'm sure you could use what you need from there and hold off on any new pictures for now."

She nods, seemingly satisfied.

With a few more button presses, I cycle through a series of forms we can spar against. "Mostly, we work with the Mystyl since that's what we use during performances, but you can make it look like whatever you want." I end on my personal favorite, a dog-sized squirrel.

"Okay, you can't be serious. What *is* that?"

I thrust a thumb at the hologram. "They live in burrows on the island. If you ever see one, don't underestimate the fucker. They might look cute, but they're crazy territorial and have sharp teeth. I'd trust an un-bonded druadan more."

"Good to know," she says with a laugh.

We step out of the training facility and circle around the short distance to the front of the exhibition hall. Her amazed expression gives me a little jolt of pride. It's like taking someone on their first shuttle ride. The massive structure with arched hallways and intricate stone architecture is a fantasy for the Delford elite and never fails to impress. This piece of ancient Venovian history managed to survive centuries of floods, violent weather, and political fighting over dry land when the old world collapsed and continents shrank or drifted apart. Majestic chandeliers, dripping with crystals, hang from above and cast brilliant prisms of light across the space. Fluted columns of ivory marble rise tall, punctuating the room's perimeter, while sunlit patterns dance playfully on the perfectly groomed arena below.

The grandeur of the place—the ornate moldings that frame the walls and ceiling, the stone statues, the life-sized paintings, real wood doors, beams, and paneling, along with the marble staircases has become just a part of the backdrop of the life we lead here at the station. However, every time I bring someone new here, it's like I'm seeing it through their eyes again for the first time, and Brigid is taking it all in. The rows of seats, the giant statues of druadans performing various maneuvers, the immaculate white sand in the arena. I can't help but watch her jaw drop as those big blue eyes gaze at her surroundings.

As we move away from the grand entrance, her gaze lands on the gilded glass display hanging on the wall. She leans closer, looking at the gleaming medals and ornate plaques. "I can't believe it. Some dates here go back three hundred years."

"Meridian's an original station," I reply, running my eyes up the giant display case. "Older than Blackhawk even. No one really knows how old." The case isn't just a trophy shelf. It's a memorial. A haunting one. Every shiny piece of metal, every finely etched name—they all belong to riders long dead. Gone but immortalized in brass and glass. The names resonate like echoes in my mind.

"It's like a whole other world," she whispers.

"They're an inspiration for us, I guess. Awards and recognition for riders that pulled off some amazing maneuver or another."

"Look at their ages. They're all so young."

Smart *and* sexy. I was wrong. Heath didn't just blow it out of the park with this one—he scored a grand slam. "Legally, riders can bond at eighteen, although most have to spend months working with a druadan before it chooses them."

"How old were you when you…?" she says, trailing off.

"Bonded?" I finish for her. "A month into my novice training. Ember initiated the bond." Warmth radiates through me, remembering how the fierce, red stallion called to me.

"A month? Is that fast?"

"Set a station record, if that's what you're asking." Heath might be bigger-brained than me, and Logan just goddamn bigger, but I have them at this. I got my mark before the other two and smashed a three-hundred-year-held record, and I never let them fucking forget it.

"A week later, I turned nineteen with rider bars on my jacket, a tattoo on my chest, and this scar on my hand." I show her the faded half-moon scar on the back of my hand. The bite mark every bonded rider bears.

She winces. "Did it hurt?"

"Like a fucking lightning bolt to the arm."

"And you chose this… this life?"

Her question catches me off guard. Usually, I get asked about being a celebrity and getting all the ass, privileges, and fame that comes with it. But no one has ever asked me if I actually *wanted* this life. "Like most riders, I didn't have much of a choice. I'm a fifth-gen military family and the first-born son, so here I am."

"That's not really an answer."

"Sure it is." I scratch the back of my neck. "What do you want me to say? That I wanted to uphold the legacy? Make a difference in the world? Any rider who tells you that is bullshitting you. It's all about the lifestyle, babe. The 'travel anywhere, eat anything, *do* anything or anyone' lifestyle."

She blinks, and her face pales, warning me I overshared. *Shit.* She hasn't even decided if she wants to work here yet. Still, what fucking difference does it make if she knows the truth? I'm a rider. Why should it matter how I started out? It is who I am now, and it's not like I could just fucking walk away. It's about more than just a scar on my hand and a tattoo on my chest. There's an invisible tether to the core of my being, a shackle that can only be broken by death.

Her eyes hold mine, softening with empathy. Not pity, I realize, but genuine understanding. "That's it? Because you were unlucky enough to be born first in your family, you had to become a rider?"

"Yeah. It's a dumb tradition, I know. It could be worse, though. Living the good life as a rider is better than going blind and having my lungs burned to a crisp at one of the filtration plants. Am I right?"

What I'm not saying is that I'd live longer doing *literally* anything else. However, I'd rather live a short, fucking glorious life than die facedown in some tox zone after an extended laborious one.

"And Heath?" she asks. "Why did he become a rider?"

"Same as me. Oldest son. Founding family. The choice was made before we were born."

She sighs, and I get the sense she wants to ask more but is holding back. It's not something I honestly like talking about. Sure, the choice wasn't mine initially, but I don't regret it. Not the academy, meeting Logan and Heath, or bonding with Ember.

I continue onward, leading her past the display cabinet, and we walk the perimeter of the exhibition hall encircling the arena. Her eyes drift up to stare at the elevated pedestals behind me. "Are those what I think they are?"

Without turning, I know what she's caught sight of. "Yep, that's them."

"Wow. The last three druadan eggs. They're bigger than they look in the pictures."

I don't usually dwell on them, but her fascination makes it impossible to look away.

"And they're such pretty colors like they were hand-painted." She tilts her head toward me. "I think it's sad that they'll never hatch."

"Yeah," I say and glance away, unease settling in my gut. We need to leave. I shouldn't have brought her here in the first place.

The clatter of hooves and the low hum of voices signal the arrival of riders entering the arena. I gesture to the groomed expanse of sand behind us, and Brigid turns away from the eggs. "Looks like practice is about to start," I say, eager to change the subject. Two fellow riders enter the arena. Shane rides his black and white Obsidanyx, and Jack comes in with the sandy brown Gemindusk.

They're riders like us, but only Heath, Logan, and I are Master Riders, which means we call the shots.

Heath wants Shane and Jack to open for the next performance, but anytime there's a shift in the lineup, there has to be a unanimous vote from the master riders, which include Logan and me.

I rest my elbows on the marble wall next to Brigid. The novices ask their stallions to trot, manes flowing like liquid, hooves barely making a sound on the ground. They weave around each other in an attempt to keep their strides matched.

"Beautiful," Brigid murmurs, her eyes following their every move.

I don't reply because while she's watching them, I'm watching her. The glimpse of skin on the side of her neck, the light sprinkle of freckles on her nose, the way her silk blouse drapes down between her tits... *Shit.* I'm getting hard already. Better put a rush on that order of champagne bottles. That'll still give her a few days to settle in. Then she's *mine*.

She's fresh from DU, and as gorgeous as she is, she's probably picked up a few skills at dodging cheap come-ons. She's going to make me work for it, I just know it, and God if that doesn't make me hard thinking about it. Logan might try to claim her, but it's doubtful. He doesn't have the patience to pursue any woman for longer than a night. Sex, for him, is a means to an end to stave off brimming. For me, it's a meal to be savored and enjoyed, and it always ends with them begging for seconds. And thanks to the bond, I'm more than happy and *able* to satisfy their request.

The thought draws me back to reality. My dick is going to be left high and dry if she doesn't accept the job offer and goes back to Delford. The sooner she signs the paperwork, the sooner I'll get to see what's underneath that blouse instead of fantasizing about it.

I slap my hands on the low wall. "Well, we should get going. Carla wants to meet you at the cottage."

Brigid nods, then reluctantly turns away from Shane and Jack, who are galloping along the perimeter as they shoot the targets on the wall with the training guns.

"This is nothing," I say, stepping back. "Ember and I will blow your goddamn mind."

She smiles. "Is that so?"

"Guess you'll have to accept the offer and find out for yourself."

She laughs as she follows me out of the exhibition hall, down the front steps, and back into the sunlight.

"The senior riders' apartments and offices are in the main house," I say, "but you'll get a house all to yourself if you take the job."

She laces her fingers through her hair, realigning one of the curls as we walk. "If I take the job?"

"It's your decision, but I wouldn't think too long about it. Heath isn't known for his patience." We move around the side of the stone storage building, then down the stone path to one of the staff's cabins. "So, what do you say? Was my tour a success?"

Her eyes meet mine, and she inhales before smiling. "Yes, I accept the offer."

"Happy to hear it." I tap twice on my comm with my fingers to bring up Heath's info, letting him know she agreed. "This is where you will stay."

We stop in front of one of the cottages, and Brigid eyes the small lilac-colored stucco wearily, eyes narrowing on the bright yellow door.

I snort. "Don't like bright colors?"

She presses her lips together, suppressing a grin. "I didn't say anything."

I shake my head. "We understand how isolated Meridian can be and have learned that letting employees have a little freedom makes everyone happier when we're all cooped up together. If the colors bother you, you're welcome to paint it any way you'd like." I punch in the executive universal number on the door, and it swings open. Then, moving to the side, I gesture with a grand sweep of my arm for her to enter. My comm buzzes on my wrist, and a pissed-off message from Logan flashes on the small screen. "I have to run, but feel free to look around. We'll have to make plans to celebrate later. I'll let Heath and Carla know, and she'll be by with the paperwork."

Brigid surveys the interior of the space and then flashes me a timid smile. "Thanks, Carter. It was nice meeting you, and I look forward to working with you."

"I look forward to working with you as well," I say, turning my back and stepping down the stoop onto the pathway. "I'll be by this evening with the champagne to celebrate."

She smiles and waves before closing the door. As I return to the main house, my thoughts are preoccupied with the night ahead. Her arrival is a shining light in the mundane routine of my days. Her interest in the station and inquisitiveness are as intoxicating as her body. The thought of raising a glass of champagne with her will sustain me through the dull upcoming meeting.

I slide my sunglasses back on and quicken my pace.

If I play my cards right, Brigid Corsair will expose herself to me in more ways than one.

Three

BRIGID

I tug the curtain aside and peer out the window. When Carter turns the corner, disappearing from sight, I breathe a sigh of relief and re-enter my new living space. The cabin is small, encompassing a living room, a kitchenette, a bedroom, and an adjacent bathroom. I take the free moment to freshen up in the bathroom. The encounter with Carter has given me a massive boost in confidence that I don't let dare go without savoring. He's ridiculously hot, and sure, he knows it, but so what?

He made his intentions very clear.

I groan. It's been an embarrassingly long time, *months* since I'd slept with a guy. Holy shit, I wished I could take him up on it. But it was too risky.

Until I had proof, I had to be cautious of everyone. I had to believe he was somehow tied up with Sharice's disappearance, and the thought of sleeping with someone who had hurt or possibly killed my sister was enough to keep my hormones in check.

The sooner I get used to the idea that my dry spell won't be quenched anytime soon, the better.

Feeling more composed, I re-enter the living room just as there's a light knock on the door. I open it to see the petite woman with red braided hair standing on the stoop.

"Sorry to keep you waiting, Ms. Corsair. We met earlier at the main house but weren't properly introduced. I'm Carla Danby, the HR director."

She has a file folder in one arm and a tablet in the other. She's still wearing her green blazer with the Meridian Station logo, a black knee-length skirt, and leather boots. An odd combination that I must've been too focused on the interview to notice. Vince would like it. Since I've seen so few paved pathways, I imagine trudging through the dust and mud would ruin expensive heels, not to mention difficult to walk on.

"Carter informed me of the exciting news that you're taking the PR position. I have all the paperwork in order for you to look through and sign. We can do it here if you'd like, or we can return to the main office."

"Here is fine," I say, moving out of the way to let her inside. A few loose wisps have tugged free of her braid to frame her face. Freckles cover the bridge of her nose and cheeks, and she's wearing the barest amount of makeup. Makes sense in this heat. I'm sure it melts right off.

She moves with quick, efficient steps. Her posture is ramrod straight, even in the bulky boots. Everything about her style and demeanor screams professionalism and competence, yet there is a softness in her brown eyes, and she flashes dimples when she smiles.

She keeps smoothing her hands over her blazer, as if self-conscious about looking polished enough, and a pearl bracelet glints on her slender wrist. She's pretty in an understated way. Sharice would like the way she dresses. My sister always appreciated stylish women.

Carla goes to the center of the room while I close the door.

"Can I offer you something to drink?" I ask before realizing I haven't even looked to see if there's anything in the fridge.

"No, no. Thank you." Carla lays her file on the table. "I'm so excited you accepted the position. Now, as I'm sure you've figured since we are so isolated, there are a few logistical hurdles to get you moved here." She pauses, pursing her lips as if hesitating about what to say next. "Normally, we allow new employees to get their own belongings. However, Master Lockwood is concerned about a storm system developing over Leviler to the north and insists you stay here until it passes. It is out of the ordinary, but our staff's safety is top priority. The storm shouldn't last more than a few days, and then the shuttle can take you to Delford to pack up your belongings."

I weigh my reply. Part of me wants to head back to celebrate with Vince and Laura. It feels right after a win like this. But logic kicks in. Staying could play to my advantage. No wasted days flying back and forth or packing when I could be getting answers. And really, there's nothing in my apartment I can't live without. I'll just have Laura pack up my stuff. This unexpected turn might not be such a bad thing after all.

"That won't be necessary," I say. "I have a roommate that will forward any mail, and she can meet a courier with some of my stuff."

Carla's eyes brighten as if delighted by this suggestion. "That would be wonderful. We really appreciate you being so proactive. I don't want to overwhelm you so soon, but we do have a fundraiser event coming up, and I was so relieved to hear Heath has hired someone for PR. I've been having to cover both positions, and I'm glad someone with your skillset will be able to take over and help me with the planning."

"Event planning has always been a favorite of mine," I say, remembering the holiday office party I helped coordinate that ended with a coworker proposing to his girlfriend and a video of our boss doing karaoke he'd never live down.

"Excellent," she says, then hesitates before pointing to the front door. "You can change the door's key code to whatever you'd like as long as it's six digits and easy for you to remember."

I nod, barely listening. This woman worked closely with my sister. She must know something about what happened to her. I clear my throat, choosing my next words carefully. "Carla, I hope you don't mind my asking, but how much did you work with the previous publicist?"

Carla's eyes widen at the question, and she brushes over her hair with her hand, clearly buying herself a moment before responding. "Oh yes, Sharice and I crossed paths frequently. She was a lovely girl."

"It's just so troubling what happened to her," I say, watching Carla closely for any reaction.

Carla shakes her head, her gaze falling to the floor. "It didn't make sense to any of us. She gave no indication anything was wrong." She looks back up at me with a sympathetic smile. "I wish I had more to offer, but Sharice kept to herself outside of work matters."

I clasp my hands to keep them from shaking. Carla's response seems genuine, but my gut tells me she knows something more. I'll need to gain her trust if I'm going to get to the truth. "I appreciate you letting me ask about it."

Carla nods, her expression softening. "Of course. I understand." Her gaze swivels to the kitchen, clearly wanting to change the subject. "There are some staples in the cupboards and the fridge. I'm afraid most of what we have out here is Circuit standard issue like the beans and goat milk, but I can try to accommodate any special dietary restrictions or requests."

Don't worry about having to keep track of your hours since you're on a salary. You'll be paid bi-weekly by a direct deposit into your account. We have a shuttle that comes twice a week."

Carla flips open the file, and I spy my name at the top, along with my birth date and a paper copy of my resume.

"This is a copy of all your orientation paperwork, but I'll send you a digital version too," Carla says, swiping a button on the com in her hand. "There will be an assessment of our regulations and practices once you've had time to study."

My comm chimes with the message receipt from Carla, and she hands me the tablet.

"This will be yours for the duration of your employment." She taps the screen, bringing up the digital paperwork. "I know this is a lot to take in, but look through it, and there are three places to sign and initial."

She watches me, a pleasant smile on her face.

Oh, shit. She means now. I bite my lip and stare at the screen, scanning the pages. First is an agreement saying my contract will last a year and then will be auto-renewed upon annual review by the station manager and Carla. Second, is a waiver and liability form informing me that the station has limited access to medical resources and that I will be working in a region with unpredictable weather, wild animals, and, of course, druadans.

Third is the non-disclosure agreement Carter had warned me about. It is indeed long, and I skim through the boilerplate jargon that boils down to me keeping my mouth shut. In the end, I see that all information and proprietary secrets must be kept private for up to ten years after the termination of my contract for the safety and security of all druadan stations. Easy enough. I don't give a shit about their secrets, nor do I want to reveal their coveted training technology; I just need to find out what happened to my sister.

I swipe my finger in the signature boxes. Once I've signed, I look back up to Carla's awaiting gaze. "Done."

Carla beams. "Great. As always, if you have any questions or need help with getting acquainted with the station, don't hesitate to find Heath or me."

"Also," Carla says, taking off her blazer and laying it over her arm. "The sun here is no joke. It's more intense than in the city. Make sure to respect it. You'll find most of us keep our outside work to morning and late evening, avoiding the mid-day sun, and it'd be smart of you to do so."

"Thanks for the tip," I say, not bothering to mention that Uncy'lia has some of the hottest summers in all of Venovia. My heritage from Uncy'lia is one of the things in my history that can connect me to Sharice, and the less I bring it up, the better.

Carla walks to the door and then stops on the threshold. "I'll send over the staff directory and weekly agenda. We've got a big gala fundraiser coming up, and you're going to have a pretty full plate organizing it. I'll forward you all the details so you can familiarize yourself with them before our morning meeting tomorrow. If you think of anything else, don't be afraid to ask."

"Got it," I say, and Carla pats me on the shoulder.

I thank her and close the door behind her.

Holy shit.

I did it. I actually got the job at Meridian Station. Once Carla had left, I fist-pump the air and let out a small squeal. The whirlwind of the past two hours has left me exhausted, my mind reeling with the conversations.

I collapse into one of the cushioned chairs and bury my fingers into my hair, lowering my head between my legs.

Okay. Next step: actually *do* the job and try not to get fired before I get answers.

I clench my teeth together, fear lashing at the sides of my mind, threatening to spill over into full-blown panic. Imposter does not come close to describing how I feel. I don't have a fucking clue how to do public relations for a druadan station. Sharice spent four years at DU learning marketing and spent her summer internship at Blackhawk. The only true experience I had was managing politicians who'd been caught in an affair or planning some B-list celebrity birthday party for their dog. But apparently, it is enough. Or at least Heath thought so, which is all I needed.

Because I am here, walking the last place Sharice walked. Talking to the last people Sharice could've spoken with.

Sweat drips down my forehead, the heat almost unbearable. I fan myself with my blouse and undo another button, hoping for some relief. I reach over to the window where a small fan sits and flip the switch. It grumbles for a moment, triggering a flash of irritation in me, before finally starting to spin its plastic blades slowly.

The fan feels amazing, and I lean back, closing my eyes. I need to prepare myself for what I'll find. No matter how much it might hurt. I need answers not just for myself but also for Mom and Sharice's friends, who are still left wondering what happened.

Leaning forward, I tap my comm and stare at Sharice's face on the contact list. Out of habit, I hit call and let it ring and ring. When a minute passes with no answer, I end it.

My comm bracelet buzzes right after, with my friend Laura calling as if she could sense my gloomy mood. I answer.

"Hey!" I say when her brown eyes and round face appear on the screen. Due to the two-hour time difference between here and Delford, fading rays of sunshine from between the buildings cast a golden hue over her. She's outside walking and guessing from silver hooped earrings, her bright yellow low-cut halter top, and face full of makeup, she's heading out.

"Hey, B," she says, "Vince is here with me." She pans over to my other friend. He's pulled his shoulder-length brown hair into a low ponytail and is wearing a crisp white shirt with a purple vest. It's adjacent to what a host at a classy restaurant would wear, but somehow, as usual, he makes it look casual.

A drawback of my DU friends pursuing fine arts friends while I'd been chained to a desk in the research section of the university library was that they both have more fashion sense in their pinky fingers than I ever will. One of a multitude of reasons that having Laura and Vince as roommates and friends was advantageous for someone like me who would just as well fill a closet with nothing but jeans and white t-shirts.

Vince smiles and waves.

"So, how'd the interview go?" Laura says, her face filling the screen once more. "I'm assuming you got the job because you look gorgeous in that blouse I loaned you, and everyone loves you that meets you, and they'd be idiots if they didn't hire you."

I roll my eyes, pretending like I don't appreciate the compliment. Laura is my biggest confidence booster, and just hearing her voice loosens the tension I'd built up from the interview.

"Yes, as a matter of fact, they did offer me the job, and I accepted it."

They both cheer on the other side, and another group of clubgoers cheer along with them, swept up in the excitement. A bittersweet tang coats my tongue. I'd flat-out lied to Carter. I didn't hate the bustling city. I loved it.

I've only been here half a day, and already I'm missing it. The energy. The vibrancy. The spontaneity of who or what you might find around the next block. The thought of returning to my apartment to pack up everything overwhelms me with dread.

This is a temporary situation. I remind myself. I only need to keep this job long enough to find out what I can about my sister, then get the hell out and return to my life with friends, going out, and midnight wandering the streets of Delford looking for street cafes that are still serving greasy food.

"I'm not sure when I'll be back," I say. "Can you throw some of my clothes and things in a suitcase for me? They said they have a courier that will pick it up if you can unlock it for them?"

She pouts. "Of course, whatever you need."

"Thanks. I appreciate it."

"Congrats again," she says. "Hope you get the answers you're looking for, but know that we miss you. We'll be here waiting for you when you get back, so don't stay too long."

I hear a murmuring from somewhere off-screen. "All right, we really got to go," she says. She presses two fingers to her lips and then the screen. "Love you, B, be careful."

"I will," I say, and then the call ends.

My wrist comm buzzes almost instantly after. It's an alert from Carla confirming all my paperwork and background checks passed. No surprises there. I had no criminal record. Nothing that would've tipped them off. Sharice's last name was our mom's middle name and I didn't know of any criminal background checks that looked as close as siblings.

I swipe close the notification and glance into the bedroom, seeing the edge of the full-size mattress and carved plastic headboard.

Tonight, I'll be sleeping in the last bed Sharice slept in. Tears well in my eyes. It's been a year since I've spoken to her, sent pictures to her, or heard her laugh, which she so rarely did.

Does, I remind myself. The police never found proof she'd been harmed or killed. She is still alive. Somewhere. I have to believe it.

These people, Heath, Carter, and Carla, all seem so nice. Kind, considerate, and welcoming even. But I can't let their politeness cloud my judgment. They are the last ones Sharice was with when she vanished.

One of them must know something. Something they hadn't shared in their testimonies to the police. They'd all had air-tight alibis. There'd been no sign of foul play, no blood, no indication she'd had a mental breakdown or anything unusual.

With pressure from Sharice's friends, Mom had hired a private investigator. A month later we'd gained a single still image from security station footage in the case file from the police, and a steep bill. I'd been living off the scraps of my savings during my senior year at DU, and so had nothing to contribute to the endeavor but a few tense lunches with my mom trying to comfort her when the investigator had come up short. I'd graduated, and Mom had returned to her research in Uncy'lia, convinced Sharice had left of her own accord and would return when she wanted to.

She was an adult after all, she'd said as if trying to convince herself as much as me, and if she felt she needed to take a break getaway, then so be it.

I had been less than convinced. Sharice wasn't some free-spirited adventurer. She was a studious, careful planner like mom. If either of her daughters were more likely to spontaneously up and leave their job, it would have been me.

I freshen up in the bathroom and peruse the drawers and cupboards. I tell myself it is to take stock of what has been provided, but the reality is, I secretly hope Sharice has left something behind—a notepad with a secret message for me. Toiletries are arranged in a certain order to spell out a hidden code—anything for me to grasp onto and give me a clue as to where she could have gone. But my search has proved fruitless and has left me feeling even more hopeless than before.

I know it won't be that easy. I'd read a dozen books on why people disappear. No matter what the scenario, kidnapped or absconded, there is rarely time or the foresight to leave behind any clues. The outlier is ransom notes, of course.

As the cool air from the fan wafts over my hair and face, I start making a mental checklist of everything. The student instincts left in me encourage me to write notes and store them on my comm for review and organization later, but it's too risky. No. This isn't some exam I'm trying to cram for. This is so much more important. Potentially even dangerous. Everything I learn, every clue I obtain, I'll have to memorize.

I start with the few people I interacted with today.

Carla Danby: She seems very nice. Helpful. Sharice would've liked her. Trusted her. She could've easily manipulated Sharice into leaving without warning or trusting someone she shouldn't have. But for what reason? And if she *had* done so, why stay here at the station where she could potentially get caught? That didn't seem like the smart thing to do, and from my brief interaction with her, it seemed quite intelligent.

I don't cross her off the list entirely; instead, I push her to the bottom of the mental stack.

Next up is Heath Lockwood. Old money. Master Rider. Position of power. Overachiever. He seems proud of the station. He was friendly, but I also felt like he didn't get close to people. My director at Tritan had been like that at first. I wouldn't have excelled at that internship if I didn't have at least some skills in knowing what people wanted to hear. Heath gave the impression he was all business, especially toward coworkers. If he knows more, he'd be the toughest to crack.

And finally, there is Carter *'Modesty'* James. I smirked as I recalled the private tour he was so keen on giving me. Cocky. Egotistical. And also *way* too hot, which is good but also bad for other reasons. Sharice didn't like men, so while his charms might've worked on becoming her friend, there wasn't a risk of anything romantic happening. However, his fondness for the ladies could work to my advantage.

I scroll through the personnel list Carla sent over. Thirty-nine in total, so once I'm added, it'll make an even forty.

Thirty-nine people could've lied to the police. Could've done something to her. Could've seen something they didn't report.

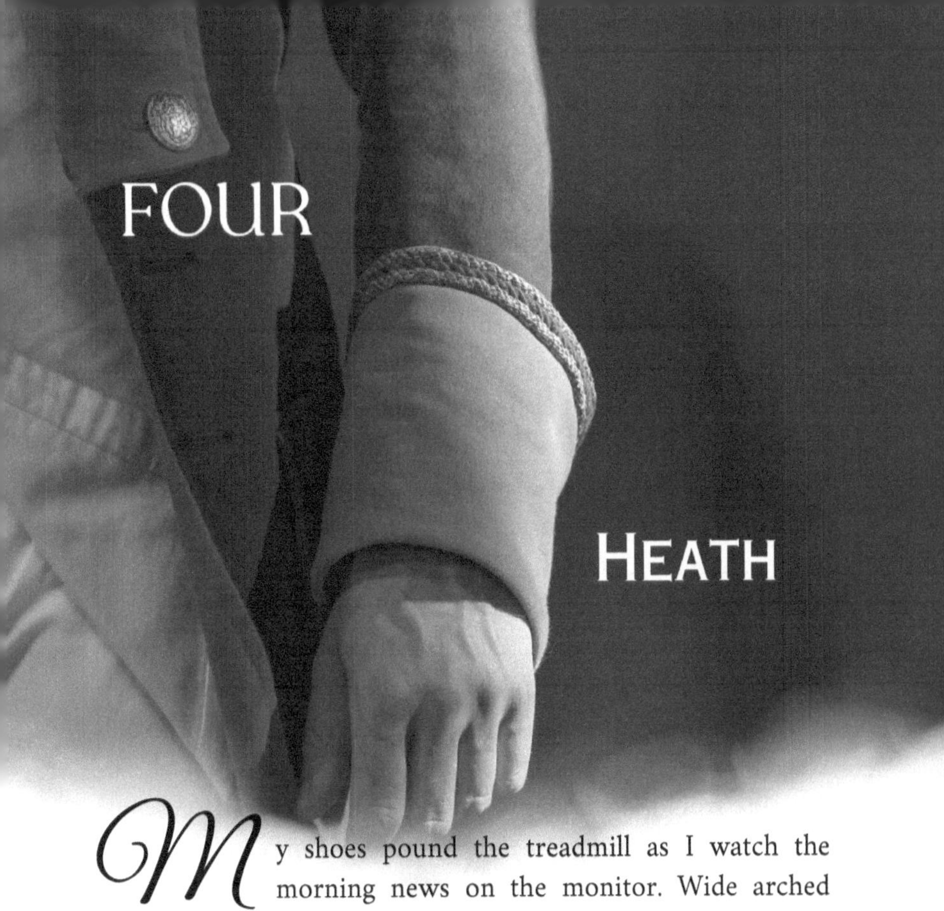

FOUR

HEATH

 y shoes pound the treadmill as I watch the morning news on the monitor. Wide arched windows overlook the northern part of the property and flank the screen. The gentle sunlit rays of dawn illuminate the red rock formations, scattering the dark gray landscape of yellow sand. I tap my earbuds to switch from the audiobook about increasing cohesion in the workplace to the TV channel.

The news anchor, a black woman with purple lipstick and matching eyeshadow, finishes her two-minute set highlighting a new restaurant opening in Blackhawk and is replaced by a Caucasian middle-aged, balding man discussing an accident at a cleansing plant that led to a worker's death last night and three others being hospitalized.

"The plant owned by a subsidiary of Drakeford Enterprises will remain temporarily shut down while Circuit's inspection authorities conduct an investigation."

A grin pulls at the edges of my mouth. Preston Drakeford

must be having a field day with that. I should reach out to Jess. It would be expected of me to consider my fiancée when her family's company has had an incident.

I switch off the treadmill and head to the shower. The gym is quiet this early, and I have it all to myself.

My pounding heart and heavy breathing had drowned out the irritating thoughts of the annual contributor's meeting and charity gala in three days, and I can't fuck this up. Every choice I've made. Every dollar I've spent. Every person I've hired or fired during the past year as Meridian's manager will be evaluated, scrutinized, and inspected to see if their money has been put to good use.

I hang my head under the cascading water of the shower, pressing a hand against the ceramic tiles on the wall to brace myself. I'd call her later, after the staff meeting. I dread the calls since they often lead to discussions of the wedding plans. The pressure from Jess's father to set the wedding date is something I don't want to deal with right now, and I am running out of excuses. I grab the washcloth, scrub it with a bar of soap, and rub the side of my face. I can feel the heat loosen my tired muscles. I'd pushed myself this morning by adding a sixth mile to my routine.

My hand moves lower, stroking my partially erect cock. It twitches at the touch, and I close my fingers around it, feeling it harden and lengthen with each stroke. I focus on Jess, her auburn hair, and imagine her manicured nails are gripping me, but immediately I feel myself deflating. I grit my teeth, determined to see this through. I need this. My bond needs this. I have to clear my head for the upcoming meeting.

I stroke faster, keeping my eyes closed as I tap into the most recent memories of Jess and me together. It'd been two months, and the memories were foggy at best. Our last shared night had been unremarkable and rushed. She'd had to leave first thing the next day, and I, too, had an early morning.

My thoughts slip, replacing Jess's brown hair with nearly white cascading locks. Smooth skin that's so soft and delicate, I can imagine the silky way it'd taste on my tongue. The woman turns, and two striking blue eyes hold mine.

Brigid.

I grunt the word, feeling my thighs clench as I crest over with climax.

I open my eyes, watching my wasted release swirl in the water and disappear down the drain.

Soon afterward, the water turns cold.

"Fuck," I mutter and flip off the shower handle. I wrap a towel around my waist and move to the sink. I wipe the fog from the mirror and examine my dark hair and eyes, looking unsettlingly similar to my father's.

For a long time, I'd been resentful and despised my father for forcing me out of the family business, but that was before I came to the station. Before I'd met Carter and Logan.

Before I'd bonded with Shadowmane and sealed my fate.

After quickly drying off with a towel, I exit the gym through the side door. The journey back to the main house is brief, but the chilly morning breeze nips at my still-damp hair. The sun has just begun its ascent, creating long shadows across the ground. As I walk, I see the staff bustling about with their daily tasks, signaling that the estate is awakening with the dawn.

A familiar feeling tugs at my chest - it's Shadowmane. In my mind's eye, I can almost see him being fed by whatever novice was assigned morning barn duty. My own stomach grumbles in agreement.

Upon entering the main house, I make my way up the stairs and into my room, straight to the bathroom. Satisfied with the best shave achievable with Circuit-issued razors, I move to my closet. I take a pressed white collared shirt and khaki pants from the dresser. The air conditioner hums pleasantly as if unaware of the strain on the electric grid.

Damn. It's barely into September it's still hitting triple digits.

The solar modules work well enough but are aging. They, along with a dozen other items, are on the ever-growing list to be purchased or repaired this year.

I sneer at my black leather loafers and slide on canvas boat shoes. I'd have to wear the hot rider jacket soon enough; I might as well be casually comfortable when I can.

I pass the door to Carter's room, spying on a perfectly made bed.

He didn't come home last night, which means one of two things: he is hooking up with staff, or worse, he, like me, isn't keeping his bond in check.

Neither of which is good nor something I have the time to deal with right now.

I down the green smoothie Carla has left for me, along with a printed daily schedule including druadan training, rider evals, supply shipments, and requests for leave.

Outside, I walk the short hallway lined on either side with more apartments. These are all empty as they're reserved for elite guests. I descend the curving carpeted stairs to the first floor, where the living spaces have been converted into office space.

I find Carla, Carter, and Brigid all waiting for me in the meeting room.

Brigid sits in the middle chair wearing a pale blue dress and her hair in a loose side braid over her shoulder. The straw of her smoothie rests against her full lips as she studies the tablet. Instantly, the image I'd cultivated of her not an hour before in the shower barges forward in my mind. I try to focus elsewhere, catching Carter tapping his dirty boots together on the table while leaning back in his chair. I give him a pointed stare, and Carter continues tauntingly. "I didn't have time to change," he says.

I frown but don't argue. The smell of whiskey hovers around him. He'd either been at the barn all night or at Logan's.

Carla moves to the head of the table, slides into the closest seat, and begins taking notes on a digital tablet.

I clear my throat. "I know we've got a lot to do today, so I'll keep this brief." My eyes sweep the room once more, narrowing my brow at the empty chair to my right.

"Carla, where's Logan?"

Carla stiffens. "I told him this was a mandatory meeting and at that he—"

But before she can finish, the door opens, and Logan enters. He is wearing his usual black shirt and pants and has recently shaved his head, revealing the scar that runs up the side of his neck and above his ear.

"Appreciate you gracing us with your presence, Logan," I say.

"If I knew sleeping in was an option," Carter says, faking a yawn. "I would have brought my pillow and made this a slumber party."

"Slumber party?" Logan snaps. "Any excuse to wear a frilly nightie, James."

"You would fantasize about me wearing one, wouldn't you?"

"Enough." I bark. "We have lots to get today and I don't have the time, or the patience to listen to you two." I gesture to the empty chair next to Brigid. "Please, Logan, take a seat."

His eyes pass over Carla and Carter before settling on Brigid. There is an irritated twitch in his jaw muscle, but he doesn't say anything. He hated newcomers at the station and had been the only one to voice concerns about her before we brought her out for an interview. Concerns I felt were justified and reasonable. However, I'd chosen to look past them. As much as Logan wanted to protect the place, he'd have nothing to protect if we didn't have a publicist to keep stations on the politician's and voters' good sides.

Logan leans against the wall and crosses his arms. "I won't be here long."

"All right then," I continue, ignoring him. "Let's get to it." I tap my tablet, and an illuminated projection of the Meridian station property appears on the table. "First things first. The donor's visit on Saturday is the top priority for all the staff." I flick my wrist, zooming in on the exhibition arena and guest houses in the center of the property. "Carla, I'm going to need maintenance to bring in fresh sand for the arena floor, clean the benches, and pull down the faded banners to replace them with new ones."

Carla nods, her fingernails clicking on the tablet's screen.

"Carter and Brigid, I'd like for you to get some photos and videos to put together for the guests to view during the meeting. They'll be touring the facility, of course, but it'd be ideal if they saw a polished product to highlight the best Meridian has to offer." I pause, waiting while they both give me confirmation noises that they understand what I am asking.

"Got it," Carter says, dropping his boots off the table so he can twist in his chair closer to Brigid. "You get your camera ready, and I'll show you *all* the good stuff."

"Master Rider James," I say. A warning.

Brigid appears unfazed by the come-on, tossing her braid over her shoulder. "Sounds like a plan. I'll be sure and bring the zoom lens."

Carter's eyes sharpen like a hawk zeroing in on its prey. "I guarantee you won't need it."

She tilts her head as if intrigued. *God dammit.* She's been here fucking day and he's already trying to get in her pants. I swear there was nothing that guy wouldn't stick his dick in. I need to put a stop to this before he proves his point right then and there in the meeting room.

"Next on the agenda," I interject. "Budget concerns." I have a list of items to get through and am not about to let things derail.

I switch the projection from the layout of the property to a series of financial charts and graphs. "As you all know, our budget for this fiscal year is on shaky ground. I have meetings lined up next week with donors and local council members. The council is considering reducing our budget for the next quarter, which would seriously affect our operations here."

I scan the faces around the table. Carla seems concerned, her fingers no longer tapping on her tablet. Carter leans back and rests his hands behind his head, clearly displeased but unsurprised.

When my eyes land on Brigid, however, she appears to be deep in thought, her eyes narrowed as she looks at the projections.

"This isn't just about maintaining the station," I continue. "It's about the druadan riding program. The community outreach work we do and genetic research. A cut in our budget means scaling back, perhaps even shutting down some of these essential programs."

The tension in the room seems to sink a little deeper, each person absorbing the gravity of what I am saying. "I'll be arguing against any budget cuts. However, the council tends to respond better to results rather than rhetoric, which is why the donor's visit this Saturday is so crucial. We need to put our best foot forward—show them that Meridian isn't just a line item in a budget, but a vital part of Venovian heritage and community."

Carter breaks the heavy silence. "So, no pressure, huh?"

I offer a tight smile. "Pressure is a privilege. It means we've got something worth fighting for."

Brigid's eyes lock with mine. She's watching me. Studying me with a curiosity I hadn't seen before. It's a brief look, almost imperceptible. But as soon as I see it, it's gone, her face instantly returning to its usual passive-attentive look.

I clear my throat and switch off the projection. "All right. Any questions before we adjourn?"

There are none. The stakes are clear. As everyone disperses, I stay behind to review my notes.

After the meeting, I retreat to my office, a modest room with a large desk cluttered with stacks of paperwork and book-keeping ledgers next to my computer monitor.

I sink into my leather chair and swipe my tablet awake, pulling up my packed schedule for the week. Donor meetings, employee reviews, training sessions—each appointment weighs heavy like a stone in my pocket.

I gaze out of the window. Carter is escorting Brigid down the path back to her cottage. Their laughter carries on the breeze, and I find myself swept back to our shared days at the Vanguard. Barely eighteen, Carter, Logan, and I dreamed of the future that awaited us. We were riders-in-training by day, but come nightfall, we were just friends, laughing, joking, and tasting the freedoms that went without any worries except what sadistic exercises the drill instructor had planned for us the next day.

I remember the long walks we'd taken to the only town nearby to buy liquor from the one store that didn't ask too many questions. We'd return to the barracks, bottles stashed away, grinning like we'd stolen a druadan egg. And then, there were those nights by the campfire when the world seemed to narrow down to the flickering flames, the night sky, and the camaraderie we shared. Sometimes, we'd invite girls from town, wrapping up in blankets and sharing whispered conversations punctuated by laughter and the clinking of bottles.

Life was easier then. We'd been caught in the freedom of the moment without the burdens of leadership and responsibility.

I sigh and run a hand through my hair. Since then, every-thing has changed. At twenty-two, I had become the youngest Head rider and Manager of Meridian Station in history, a distinction that came with an unyielding load of expectations and judgments. Carter had followed me to the station, as had

Logan, but the levity of our academy days seemed to dissolve in the responsibilities that now enshroud us.

I look back out at Carter and Brigid, still laughing, still seemingly unburdened, if only for a moment. I refuse to envy them. I'm the one sitting at the manager's desk of a druadan station, after all.

There's a knock at the door, and without waiting for me to answer, Logan strides in, his tall frame and broad shoulders nearly grazing the doorway,

"Are you fucking kidding me?" he shouts.

I grind my teeth together and give him a false smile. "Language, Logan. Or do I need to get out the employee handbook again for you to—"

"Oh, fuck off," he snarls.

I sigh, glaring at the open door, and push back from my chair. I move past him to shut it. Carla is used to Logan's temper tantrums, but Pete and Tim were working on a project in one of the other offices, and unlike Logan, I liked to keep a modicum of professionalism around here.

I return to my desk but remain standing. Riders are the definition of Alpha males, and while he might have a height advantage over me, he'd have more if I was seated.

"What is it, Logan?" I ask.

"That girl you hired," Logan says, thumbing the wall separating us from the meeting room. "Did you even read the background report I sent you?"

"Yes."

"And you still hired her?"

"Obviously, I did." I keep my voice low, not betraying the irritation underneath. Carter and Logan are like brothers to me, closer than brothers, but holy shit, do they like to test me.

"What the hell? Why would you hire her when you know she's her sister?"

I fold my arms. "For one god-damn second, Logan, use your

brain. Think. We can't let her leave. We need her here to keep a close eye on her."

The crease on his forehead deepens. "Does Carter know?"

I despise keeping secrets from the other two, but it's one of the many tough choices I have to make as station manager. Besides, I'd already burned them with the biggest secret of all. The one that, if it got out, could ruin everything.

"No. And let's just keep this between us for now."

Logan's jaw shifts. "He should know."

"I'll tell him. Soon. The longer she thinks we don't know, the longer we have to see if she's going to make the same choices her sister did."

His upper lip curls as he bares his teeth, reminding me of one of the stallions when you're too slow with the feeding bucket. "I hope you know what you're doing. If this goes sideways, she'll be the ruin of us."

"Just keep an eye on her," I say, my tone reassuring. "I'll let you know if I need anything else."

Logan grumbles something under his breath about blondes with perky tits, then adds, "Training arena. One hour."

"I'll do my best to be there," I say, and we both know we're lying.

Once he's left, I sink into the chair at my desk and force myself to focus on the screen before me, on the numbers and tasks that dictate my life now. His speculation isn't unfounded and, in fact, appreciated. His overprotective instinct is valued for his position as head of security. I'd never regretted giving him that role.

Subconsciously, I run a thumb over the mark. Keeping it concealed under the desk, I glance down at the crescent-shaped scar, seeing the telltale iridescent sheen and feeling the tingle signaling a surge in the bond I'd been neglecting.

Well, why the fuck not? It's not like I don't have enough to worry about. I need to get a handle on this, or I won't need to worry about keeping the station running through the next year since I'll be dead.

The stronger the bond, the more difficult it is to manage. Every day you're away from your druadan and don't ride, the bond intensifies like a fever in your blood. Go long enough, and your heart will give out.

However, when travel or illness, or in my case, a busy work schedule, keeps a rider from their stallion, strenuous exercise helps take the edge off.

Drinking more so.

Sex is the best.

None of which I've been doing nearly enough of.

I stare at the spreadsheet on my tablet. The numbers blur into an indistinct mess, and I pinch the bridge of my nose, trying to draw some focus back into my tired eyes. After a moment, I glance again at the screen. The numbers remain just as unintelligible as if mocking my attempts to give them meaning.

Fuck it.

The burning sensation from the mark flares, and I hiss in pain before slamming the tablet down onto my desk. I rise from my chair and go to the wardrobe in the corner of my office. I pull out my riding boots, still flecked with dirt from my last ride, and my riding jacket, smelling faintly of leather and the meat slurry in their feed. Every single time I slip into the boots and jacket, I feel like I've found a part of myself I'd temporarily misplaced—a part that is integral, familiar, and comforting. I leave my office and descend the stairs out of the main house.

I make my way across the central courtyard to the barn.

The stalls on either side of Shadowmane's are empty, and I know Carter and Logan beat me here.

The stallion looks up as I enter his stall, his rich garnet-colored eyes meeting mine.

My Shadowmane. Instantly, the bond flickers like a light

switch, reigniting the shared consciousness, and I inhale, feeling like I'd been holding my breath for days. There it is.

The sensation is euphoric. Nothing compares to the raw understanding, the intuitive connection that seems to transcend the complexities of human emotion and speech. The burning sensation on my hand vanishes as I pat the horse's arched neck.

"Hey, big guy," I murmur, smoothing the thick black mane that contrasts his silvery gray coat. The stallion snorts softly, leaning into the touch, and the slightest vibration buzzes the air around him, and the familiar phrases I'm used to are voiced in my head.

"You come."

"I am here." While I've spoken the words out loud, no sound escapes my throat. At least not one unbonded human can hear. Through the bond, the frequency of my speech is lowered to a pitch only druadans can hear.

"Too long."

"I know," I say, apologizing. It's been a week since I was here. Whirlwind meetings, calls, and shuttle flights back and forth to Blackhawk have kept me away from him.

"Run?" he asks, as he always does when I greet him. My heart soars with the excitement in his voice.

"Not today," I reply.

"Eat?" he asks.

"You've been fed."

Shadowmane perks his narrow ears and tosses his head, signaling the third question I know he'll ask.

"Mate?" he asks expectantly, even though I tell him the same answer.

I laugh and scratch the space where his neck meets his cheek.

"You know that's not possible."

He stomps a foot. There are no females, not anymore. Every

living druadan stallion today is a clone of a previous one—generations and generations of only stallions.

Disappointment bleeds into the connection. Shadowmane is old, and I will most likely be his last rider. The instinctive urge to mate is especially intense with him, pressing him to pass on his genes before he's out of time.

Which, in turn, passes through the bond and leads to the constant urge for *me* to mate. It never fails to demand my attention at the most inopportune moments, like, say, during important budget meetings when an attractive silver-haired blonde sits across from me in a sundress.

I pat the smooth lines of his face, where the coarse silver fur covers the bony ridges on his nose.

"Fight," he says as I slip the carbon fiber bridle over his ears. The tether between us soars with excitement.

"Fight," I confirm, bringing him out of the stall to saddle him. My increased internal temperature means that it's safe for me to touch him. However, the saddles are specially designed with thick layers of carbon fiber and leather to prevent burns from prolonged exposure. Once saddled, I lead him to the practice arena and climb onto his back.

Heath and Carter are already mounted and waiting for me.

The lights are off. The hair around Shadowmane's hooves begins to glow in anticipation of what's next.

"Look who's decided to finally join us for some fun," Carter calls out from the shadows.

"So nice of you to join us," Logan says, mocking my words from that morning's meeting.

Shadowmane and I walk to the center to join them. Our stallions' hooves and only the two red security lights in the corners are all that punctuate the blackness of the indoor arena. "I figured I'd give you guys a head start," I say. "You know you'll need it."

"Wait till you see what I cooked up for us." Carter taps his wrist comm and projections of three giant squirrels appear. Bushy tails twitching, they squat down as if ready to pounce.

Logan barks a laugh. "When you said squirrel, I didn't expect it to be so big."

"Funny, your mom said the same thing last night," Carter says.

Shadowmane paws impatiently. "Ready?"

They both stop laughing and look at me.

"Ready," They say in unison.

Shadowmane lunges into the fray, centuries of selectively bred instincts activating, and the weight of budgets, donors, unmet expectations, and unsolved problems—evaporate.

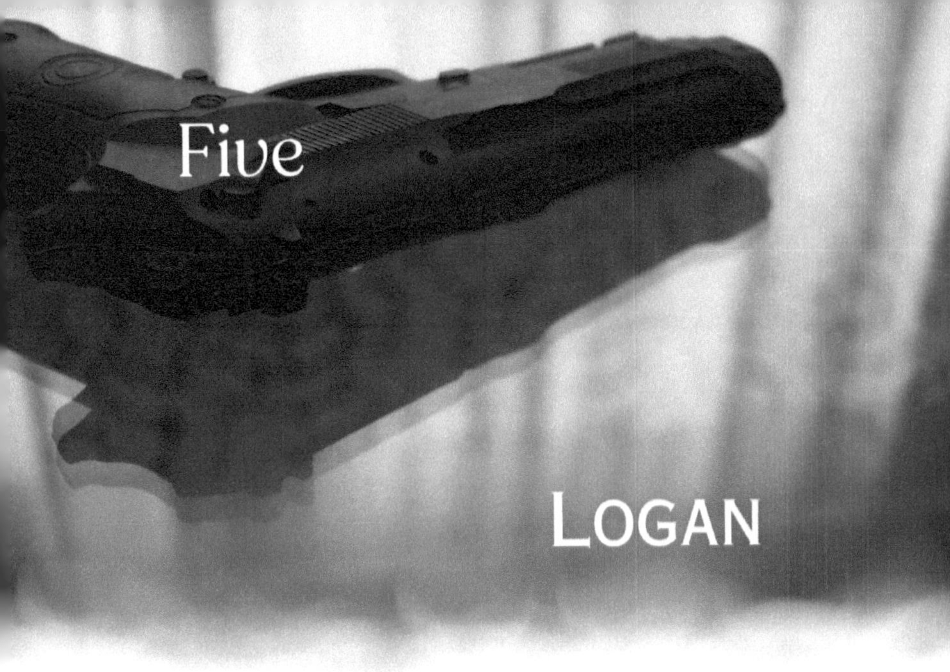

Five

LOGAN

"**F**ucking novices," I curse under my breath. Vanguard really thought they were sending us the best this year, didn't they?

The next day, Carter is already up on Ember, running drills with the novices for the afternoon's training session. The musky scent of sweaty druadans permeates the air in the practice arena. I pull on my gloves, snapping the last buckle into place, and look around.

"Quit fucking pulling, Danner," I bark as my eyes scan the indoor training arena. Carter and Ember lead the way, demonstrating the correct way to canter over the poles on the ground. They're unbonded, so they can't phase, but the idea is the same for when they will.

"Lighten your hands, dammit," I call out to the group. "Keep pulling the reins like that and see how long it takes them to toss your skinny bitch asses onto the ground and stomp you into a bloody pulp."

Danner's hands loosen on the double reins of his gray unbonded mount, Wraithwind. They've been working together for weeks, and still, it looks like he's a first-year at Vanguard.

His seat is all over, his focus is lacking, and Wraithwind might as well be a chair for as much movement as he's giving him. However, what concerns me more is they're overdue for their bonding, and if it doesn't happen soon, it'll never happen.

Three months of intense training down the drain.

Gone.

Danner will either be demoted or sent packing to Blackhawk or another station for a second and final attempt.

The problem is, if they send him away, the academy has no one to replace him, and it'll be another year before they send anyone, which leaves Wraithwind, at a peak bonding age of three, without a rider.

My attention shifts from the novices when I spot Brigid walking around with that camera of hers, taking pictures of everything, including the training arena. My hands form fists, feeling the tug of the leather over my knuckles. This is supposed to be a closed practice. No outsiders. Period.

And Brigid is more than that though, she's Sharice's sister. She's a goddamn liability and Heath brought her right to our doorstep.

I swing my leg over Galaxian and guide him to the stone wall of the indoor arena, where Brigid is seated on one of the wooden benches, looking like she intends to sit there all day.

Galaxian snorts beneath me, perhaps picking up on my mood as I pull him to a halt in front of her.

"Brigid, is it?" I call out, stopping a few feet from where she's perched, camera in hand.

"Yes," she says, flashing me a smile. "And you're Logan? We didn't get formally introduced at the meeting earlier."

I don't have the time, nor do I need to make small talk. She's admin. I'm a Master Rider. The less we interact, the better. "No pictures," I start to say, as my kneejerk reactions take over. Fuck me. Heath had *wanted* me to keep an eye on her and what better place than right in front of me?

"Look, lady, so you know this isn't a public performance. This is a closed practice where we work free of distractions."

"Is that what I am? A distraction?" Under the arena lights her eyes glimmer with defiance.

"Not yet," I say. "So, don't become one."

"I'll do my best," she says, crossing her legs and sitting a little taller. "I wanted to include some candid photos of the training here in the invitation package." She gestures with her camera. "Everyone sees the polished performances, and it's creating a gap in your audience. The world thinks you're all just a bunch of well-rehearsed circus acts. They need to see the dirt, the effort, the actual hours of work that goes into this."

Well, shit. Blondie has a point. "Fine. But you can't drop in unannounced. From now on, you will let me or one of the other Master riders know if you're going to be in here," I say, but my tone has lost some of its edge.

She peers up to where I'm sitting, her piercing blue eyes locking with mine. "Deal. I assure you I'm not here to disrupt. I just want to add another layer to the narrative. Pull back the curtain so the people out there get a better, more authentic picture of what happens behind the scenes at this station."

Blondie is good at keeping up her little act. I'll give her that.

"I promise you won't even know I'm here," she says, pressing a finger to her lips to reinforce her words.

She bends to look at the viewfinder on the camera, and her ivory-colored hair catches the light. For a moment, it's like seeing a ghost. Sharice. Irritation coils in my gut, my fists clenching on the reins, and Galaxian tugs against them.

I don't reply. Fucking Heath and his obsessive need to control everything and everyone. *Keep your enemies close.* As much as I hate to admit it, that son of a bitch was right. It still pissed me off that her sister got away with what she did. But I have to shove those thoughts down and focus on the task at hand: whipping these novices into shape so they don't fail at bonding or fall off during a live performance.

It's never happened at Meridian, and I'll be goddamn right it doesn't on my watch.

I shake off the thought, focusing on the present. Boredom trickles into the bond, and Galaxian's chest vibrates. *"No more talk. Time run."*

"Okay, slap-dicks. Break time's over," I call out, causing Brigid to flinch. I grin, pleased that my shouting was able to break through her composed exterior.

Galaxian and I move back to the center of the arena. "Arrow shaft formation, now! And for the love of God, make it precise. No dragging or moving off the lines," I command, hoping these guys get it right this time.

As I lead them into the pattern, I'm more demanding than usual on them, calling them on the slightest errors until they get it right.

Better than right. Perfect.

A performance has never had so much pressure on it before.

We have one performance before the Gala, and then, it's fucking on. Make it or break it.

We can't just put on a show; we have to blow their fucking minds and leave them speechless. Prove that we're still relevant, and they'll be compelled to keep the money flowing.

It's not just entertainment—it's a goddamn fight for survival, and I'll be damned if we don't give it everything we've got.

Six

BRIGID

inally, I am alone.

Excitement bubbles in my stomach as I slip on a sports bra, exercise shorts, and tennis shoes. I glare at the portable computer and digital tablet they'd issued me on the table. Those were totally monitored. My own personal comm, however, is not and is password protected. Any evidence I find, I'd store on it and demand they be proof enough for Circuit to reopen the investigation.

The photo from the PI's case file that was pulled from the Meridian station security system is burned into my mind. It'd been timestamped at almost midnight on the last night Sharice had been here. I close my eyes, recalling the grainy image that I'd seared into my brain.

Sharice is standing by one of two gates leading out of the station. Her hand was outstretched like she was touching the keypad to open it. Or to close it. The gate is halfway open, so either could be true. A true Schrodinger's cat situation. Both can be true. My philosophy teacher would be proud.

In my mental image, the angle of the camera is centered on the gate, so there's no way to tell if there is someone beside her, out of view, or on the other side of the steel gate.

Sharice was calculated, meticulous, and a control freak. Now that I think about it, she was damn like Heath in that regard. I'm the impulsive one. The one who stole bolt cutters from the research lab to cut fencing and set off alarms just to play soccer with the kids at the neighboring filtration plant. I'm the one who walked away from a career, friends, and a life because I wasn't satisfied with the answer Circuit had given me.

I'd stared at the photos for days. Convinced I was missing something. If the roles had been reversed and I had disappeared, Sharice would've found me by now. I know it. Her meticulous eye for detail had earned her more than a few awards in school and the rare praise of our mother. What would Sharice have noticed that I'm not?

Just then, my wrist comm buzzes with a message from Carla, reminding me of the video conference call we had with Blackhawk's PR team. I tap away the notification, and I'm struck with an epiphany. I shut my eyes again, focusing on her right hand hovering near the keypad.

Holy shit.

Her wrist comm is missing.

Authorities hadn't mentioned finding it among the belongings she'd left behind, so she had assumed she'd taken it with her. I kick myself for being so stupid. Sharice wasn't stupid. She knew she could've been tracked with it. Or the person that forced her to leave had made her take it off. Whatever reasons she'd had to leave it behind meant that there was a possibility, albeit small, that it was still somewhere here at the station.

Circuit had all but eliminated crime, and their guards and detectives were jokingly lazy in their investigations. But had they truly missed this? My stomach somersaults. Or what if they hadn't? What if someone had paid them off to omit that little detail from the report? Someone with money, connections, influence.

Someone like a station manager with ties to one of the richest families in Venovia.

I exit my cottage, determined to make use of the moment I have to freely snoop around the station. Carrying a metal water bottle and towel, I cross the empty courtyard and head to the main house.

Heath, Carter, and Carla are an hour away in Nelworth to meet with a new produce supplier.

Now is my golden opportunity to dig a little. The main house is all to myself.

I push open the front door and hesitate at the bottom of the stairs. The knowledge that the house is supposed to be empty wrestles with the irrational fear of being caught. My ears stretch for the faintest noise, seeking reassurance in the quiet. The silence, thick and confirming, emboldens me. With each step upstairs, my heart picks up speed, thumping against my ribs at a frantic tempo. I reach Heath's door, its slight opening like an unspoken invitation. I cast a wary glance down the hall, ensuring it's still just me and the shadows. Then, with a breath held tight in my chest, I nudge the door wider, stepping into the unknown.

I leave my water bottle in the meeting room. An alibi of sorts in the off chance someone catches me here, I could lie and say I was going to exercise at the training center and had forgotten it here.

The door to Heath's room is ajar, and after glancing down the hall, I push it open.

Inside, his room is a professional organizer's wet dream. The epitome of organization. All the furniture at the station was government-issued and fit Circuit's motto to a tee. 'Built to last, not to enjoy.' Value was in the things of use, not in aesthetics. Art was only valuable if it doubled or tripled as something else. An engraved mirror. A bright-colored plastic lamp. Manufacturing was too expensive if the thing's sole purpose was to look pretty.

And Heath's room is no exception. His bed has a gray headboard and is made, looking as though it'd never been slept in. An uncomfortable, hard, cushioned-looking couch houses a throw blanket folded over the top with a pillow in front. Shoes are lined perfectly up against the wall. No dirty clothes on the floor, no empty drink containers. It's hard to imagine any secrets hiding in a room this pristinely clean.

I move swiftly, examining the two paintings of druadans hanging on the wall. One I recognize as Shadowmane, caught in a graceful rear, and the other appears to be a skyline view of the station at sunset. Several plaques are arranged on his dresser. 'Top Marksman.' 'Junior Team Leader Achievements.' 'Swift Curriculum Advancement Award." So, he'd been a rock star at the academy. No surprises there. I could've guessed as much by how uptight he is. I search inside the dresser, finding only neatly stacked piles of clothes. My eyes lazily trail over his large bed, imagining his head lying there, hands tucked behind his head, eyes closed and at ease.

Nope. I can't do it.

Even in my imagination, he still looks untouchable and guarded.

I side-step to the nightstand with a single drawer and open it. A neat stack of granola bars, earplugs, and a dog-eared book on the biography of a blues musician. Frowning, I close it and drop to the floor to look under the bed. It's ridiculous how spotless it is. No socks, no garbage, nothing but a small metal box. Bingo. I have to kneel to reach under it and find it bracketed to bolts under the bed.

"Dammit," I curse. Obviously, there's something good in here or else why would he go through the effort to secure it like this? My fingers find the lid and flip it down. I'm half-expecting to find nothing more than credits of nude photos. Instead, I find a comm bracelet.

Not just any comm-bracelet.

Sharice's.

Fingers trembling, I pick it up, inspecting the laser-engraved lily flowers that run along the perimeter of the metal ring. Lilies were her favorite. It had made gift buying easy for me and Mom. Gold lily earrings? Done. A lily-scented perfume? Sold.

So, someone *had* found it here and lied to the authorities. Had it been Heath or another staff member? Either way, why did Heath hide it from them?

I sink to the floor, resting my back against his bed. The screen is locked. My fingers hover over the keypad, punching in different passcodes. My birthday? No luck. Our mom's birthday? Nope. After several failed attempts, my mind went blank. What was I missing? *Think.* Mentally, I sifted through the handful of conversations I'd had with my sister. What had she been interested in? She was smarter, smarter than me, although I'd never admit it to her. I swipe through my comm for the last things she'd sent me, pausing when I see the picture of the black horse statue. *Hidden messages.*

Bellion, I type, and the screen rewards me by illuminating. Her background is the two of us standing in front of the Uncy'lia coastline. We'd visited Mom a week before I'd started at DU. My hair had been shorter then, and that trip had been the first time I'd seen Sharice happy since her girlfriend and she had broken up.

A warmth spreads over me as I remember something happy from our last years at the station together for a change.

Instead of the blood and pain and the haunting expression he'd worn before I'd made a choice. A choice that had led to someone losing their life and me being sent away from the research center at eighteen. Whatever tenuous relationship I'd had with my mom before then worsened. She never looked at me the same after that. Not like a mother to a daughter, but like I was a specimen under a microscope, scrutinizing for flaws, and never quite trusting what was seen on the surface.

Only Sharice had treated me the same. She'd stood by me even when no one else had. Assured me that I'd be okay after everything.

I scan through the old messages, heart aching at the year-old conversations my sister had with her friends, including some from me, all ending the same approximately eleven months ago. "Where are you?" "Are you okay?" "Call me!!!"

Six down from the top are a few unfamiliar numbers with no names attached, and then—my pulse skyrockets. A recent one. Three days *before,* the station had reported Sharice missing. It has no words, just numbers. But it's enough. Sharice had received a payment transfer for a shit ton of money. Enough to buy a house in Delford with a view of the ocean kind of money. The kind of sum that might as well have had 'blackmail' in the comment line. Had Sharice gotten this money and then decided to disappear?

My finger hovers over a voice message dated two days before she disappeared when—shit.

A door creaks open downstairs. My heart lurches. I'm not alone.

Adrenaline surges as I shove the comm bracelet into my pocket. The door eases open, and Heath steps inside, locking eyes with me.

Well, shit.

Seven

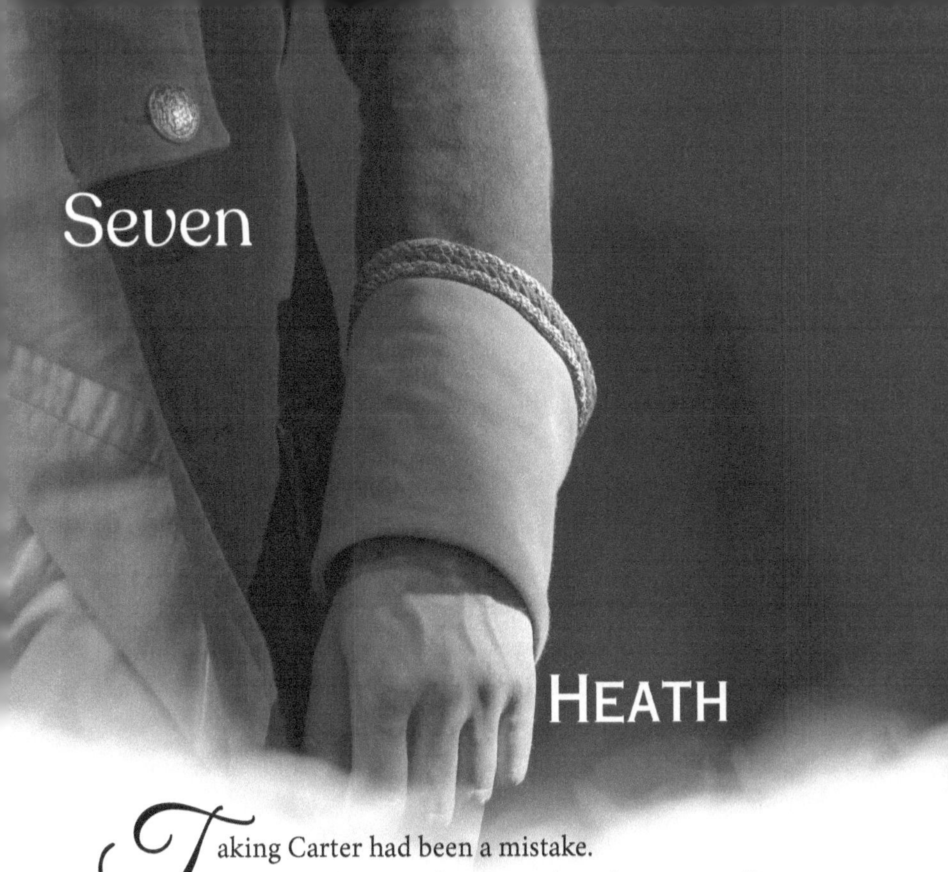

HEATH

$\mathcal{T}$aking Carter had been a mistake.

Now, the one fruit supplier that was willing to ship weekly to the island backed out because he had some *history* with the guy's wife. The second he'd laid eyes on him standing next to me, the man had backed out. I tried offering him double his fee, and still, he refused.

It'd been close. I'd nearly lost my cool. Had Carla not intervened, my response might have veered into regrettable territory. *What the hell is happening?*

The shuttle ride back had been tense, and as if some sense of self-preservation had finally blessed Carter, he'd kept his mouth shut.

I push open the door to my bedroom, the one place where I can find solace and isolation. I stop, however, upon seeing Brigid kneeling next to my bed. Her round ass sticks out from under tight black shorts and reveals her toned bare legs. My mouth goes dry. Finally, my brain races to catch up. The spark of irritation I'd been harboring since Nelworth ignites.

"Why the hell are you in my room?" I snap as Brigid scrambles to her feet. "No one comes into my room uninvited. And I am damn sure I'd remember if I'd invited you."

Her nipples press against the thin cotton of her sports bra, and I avoid lingering them too long. It's an invasion—her presence, her attire, all of it.

She'll be the ruin of us. Logan's warning echoes in my head.

Her eyes are cold and unyielding. She lifts the silver bracelet as if it were a prize that she's won. "Why do you have this? This belonged to my sister, Sharice."

"I know." I hold her gaze.

Her jaw drops in disbelief. "What? You knew?"

I close the door and move closer.

She stumbles back, but the bed stops her from retreating any further.

"Yes."

She shakes her head, dropping her gaze. When she looks up again, recognition dawns on her features. "That's why I got the job," she stammers. "Not because I was qualified, but because you wanted me here."

"Yes," I reply simply, my voice calm and measured. She's scared. I'd anticipated she would be when she inevitably found out. Finding her comm within a matter of days here is impressive, and clearly, she's as smart as her sister.

Still, there is no way she can fathom the precariousness of her position; how close she is to being escorted to the next shuttle off this island and dumped off at a filtration center. With a single comm call, I could destroy her life. This wasn't on today's agenda, not in the slightest.

After the disaster in Nelworth, I had planned for an afternoon of isolation in my room with a glass of scotch and the new Etta Langston album and how to salvage the relationship with the vendor. Yet here I am, wrestling with a situation that threatens to unravel the delicate balance I've fought so hard to maintain.

Brigid's body tenses, and she lifts her chin. "You can't keep me here." She's putting on an act, trying to act tough, but the tremor in her voice gives her away.

"Sure, I can."

She taps on the comm on her wrist. "I'll call..." Her voice trails off, her face going as white as my bedspread.

"You can call whomever you like, but it won't do you any good."

Tears stream down her face, but I don't relent.

"Please," she says, her voice cracking. "I just want to find my sister." She sinks to her knees, defeated.

My fists curl into hard balls, steeling myself against the wave of sympathy. I push back against it. *Hard.* She'd thought she was clever enough to deceive me. That I wouldn't recognize the last name from the exhaustive background searches I'd ordered on her, not to mention did she think I was blind? Sure, their hair is different, but the resemblance is there. The sooner she learns that I control the station and everything in it, the better.

Silence stretches between us, and I find myself moving closer to her. She shrinks away as I reach down to help her up, and it's like a dagger has pierced my side.

"Then we want the same thing," I say, softening my voice.

She peers up at me, her blue eyes wet with tears. "You..." she murmurs. "You don't know where she is either?"

"No."

Brigid sniffs, and lets me help her to her feet. Our bodies close, the scent of her is overwhelming, and I can feel my carefully constructed walls crumble. The walls I've fortified in my mind to resist Shadowmane's urges through the bond are under siege. I drop her hand and quickly distance myself from her.

The screw-up from Nelworth has left my mental strength weakened, and arousal causes my cock to twitch.

"If you want to find her, then why keep this from the authorities?"

"In truth, I'd forgotten I had it," I say. "Shortly before she disappeared, Sharice told me she was having problems with her comm connecting, so she brought it to me to have it sent to Nelworth to be repaired. The company we used for Tech repairs went under, and I never got a chance. You can't accuse me of hiding anything because I didn't know I still had it."

I shift my gaze to the window behind her, trying to distract myself from how vulnerable her presence makes me. I inhale, feeling the effects of Shadowmane's urges easing before returning to her face.

Her eyes study mine. "Fine. Who else knows about me?"

"Just me and Logan." I pause, pressing my lips together. "I think it'd be better in both our interests if we keep it that way. I presume you're here doing your own investigating, which I applaud, and if people knew your connections, they might not be as honest as you'd like."

The tension leaves her shoulders, her face visibly relaxing. "You're okay with me looking for her here?"

"Of course. So, long as it doesn't interfere with your job or the other employees."

"So, then, what happens if I find out where she is? Will you let me go then?"

I lace my hands in front of me and tilt my chin up. I'd anticipated this very question from her and had an answer at the ready. "You find out where your sister is, I promise you'll be on the next shuttle out of here."

Her eyebrows raise slightly, no doubt wondering what motivation I have to find her sister. She's wise to be suspicious and I doubt she'll back down without a reasonable answer for my intentions. I sigh, pretending like I'm conceding to her. "You, of all people, should know scandals like this damage companies. And I'll be dammed if I don't keep Meridian's house as clean as it was when I inherited it."

Brigid's forehead furrows as she nods. Slowly, understanding flickers in her eyes.

Smart girl.

"All right. But I'm keeping this." She presses the comm to her chest, and strides past me, her footsteps whispering on the carpet.

As the door slides shut behind her, I'm left standing alone, the room feeling even emptier than usual. I'd lied to her about the comm. I'd never lose track of something as important as that. But I couldn't have Brigid thinking I wasn't on her side. She was too much of a risk, of liability, and even though I *did* have the sway to nudge Circuit from re-opening the investigation if she scratched the itch too much, it would bring them back for a second look.

And the risk was too great.

I sit on the loveseat and drag my hands over my face. Once again, the bitter taste of guilt stings my tongue as I struggle to fight off the fear that I somehow could have been responsible for Sharice's disappearance. The last cruel words I'd spoken to her. How scared she'd been. Of course, she'd been shit-faced drunk or even possibly high on something, and I'd written her off as a paranoid person, telling her to go sleep it off.

The next day, she was nowhere to be found, and Carter, Logan, and I had made a solemn pact to protect the station. A shared secret that we'd take with us to our graves.

Eight

BRIGID

$\mathcal{H}$e knew.

For the last three days, he'd been lying to me. Well, okay, technically, it wasn't a lie, more like withholding information, but still, the betrayal stings all the same.

He'd known Sharice was my sister and had *wanted* me here. God, I'd been such an idiot. How could I have honestly thought I could sneak past the background check by using my mom's maiden name and checking the 'no' box, asking about other family members? This was a Circuit controlled facility, for shit's sake. They knew everything about everyone.

I'd taken a leap of faith, I guess, when I'd applied incognito and had landed firmly on my face when Circuit's overreaching records of people had cut the lines to my parachute.

After leaving Heath's room, I beelined it back to my cottage and locked the door behind me. I fall face-first onto the bed and scream into the pillow.

I'm stuck in this place with no way out. How long will I be trapped here? Until I found my sister, or until he deems me useless? Didn't he understand that if I had any valuable information, I wouldn't have spent three months of my life doing an internship for a career I didn't want and applying for a job I had no interest in?

Angry thoughts consume me. I hate him. The fucking, control freak asshole. Who does he think he is that he can just force people to do whatever he wants? When the tears finally stop, I roll over. If I'm going to be stuck here, then the only way out of here is if I *do* find my sister. In that one aspect, we are on the same side.

I scoot to the edge of the bed, tears streaming down my face as I clutch my sister's old comm device. My fingers tremble as I access her private video files - her personal diary entries that the police somehow overlooked.

One by one, I play them, soaking in her voice and her mannerisms. Her hair is a dark brown. She'd dyed it. But why? She'd always loved her blonde hair like mine. It was the one thing we had in common when the rest of us was so opposite. Her timidness, her freckles that she hated, the way I loved chocolate, and she couldn't stand it. How she strove to earn perfect grades and extra credit in the small school on the research base, while I was proud of myself for turning in an assignment on time.

I play the first video and quickly can tell it's her first day at the station. I can tell from her expression that she was a bundle of nerves but excited as well.

"And here is my bedroom," she says, spinning around the very same room I'm seated in. "Today was my first day at Meridian," she says into the camera with a smile. "The buildings are so old, and it's so hot out here, but the desert is beautiful." The video swings around to her face again, and she has a wistful expression as she stares out the window. "I'm looking forward to seeing what this place has to offer."

She goes on to talk about Heath, and a tightness spreads across my chest. *"He's old money." "A real control freak" "Commanding."*

Yeah, sis, you don't know the half of it.

She comments on Carter flirting shamelessly with her and laughs that it took him several failed attempts to hit on her, and only when she'd admitted that she preferred girls did he finally back off. *"He sure likes to have fun and is probably the best rider."*

As she chats away in front of me, I feel like I'm in the room with her again, like no time has passed at all since we last talked. I wipe the tears from my face as I watch her speak about her excitement for what lies ahead. The optimism and joy from getting to work around druadans and their riders.

As I watch the recordings, they begin to space out further and further until three weeks go between her making a new one. Sharice dyes her hair again a darker brown, then cuts it, and soon I don't recognize her eyes and realize she's wearing contacts. She doesn't wear her blazer and slacks anymore and when several months have passed, she's wearing the station-issued jumpsuit the maintenance staff wear.

Suddenly, I feel lightheaded. It's almost as if before my eyes, she's become two different people— the one I grew up with who first arrived at the station and this other...more impassive, detached one.

She's all business now and isn't wearing any makeup anymore. All she talks about is the monotony of her day and what she ate for lunch. How many emails she'd replied to? How many miles she'd clocked on the treadmill?

Suddenly, I don't feel safe here. I glance at the locked door, wishing I could flee this place. Wondering, not for the first time, if coming here was a terrible idea. I haven't been here more than thirty-six hours, and already two people know my secret.

My hand trembles, my finger hovering over the play icon for the next entry. Sharice looks nervous, eyes shifting back and forth. *"I've found something. Something big,"* Her voice shakes, and she pauses for a moment. *"I'm afraid to say it until I have more proof, but I think a lot of people are going to get hurt."*

A dozen ominous fates my sister could've met flash through my mind, each one more horrific than the last. Could he have hurt my sister? Threatened her? Forced her to run? Assault her? Feed her to one of the druadan beasts? They are omnivores. I didn't know much about them, but at least I knew that.

Maybe it was subtler. Slow poisoning at shared meals. An "accident" was staged with one of the wild stallions. Or simply a bullet to the back of her head, her body dumped down an abandoned mine shaft miles from here.

I glance anxiously at the locked door, unable to shake the feeling that I'm being watched. Monitored.

I swallow down the rise of paranoia coating my throat. If Heath had been responsible for Sharice's disappearance, why would he want me? Why not make me disappear too the first day I'd arrived? Unless he was toying with me.

Or was he protecting someone else?

Another employee here, perhaps.

Another rider.

But I can't give in to fear. Not now. Not when I had the first real viable clue in my hand. I start the next video, steeling myself. Sharice was close to the truth when she was silenced. It's up to me now to find answers, no matter the risk.

Her whispered words again fill the room.

My sister reaching out, begging for justice. I strain to listen for any clue amidst her ramblings. Any hint about these men and what they are hiding? Her face is the color of ash as she ends the recording.

By the time just four recordings remain, I'm shaking uncontrollably.

"I didn't think they were serious, but they are," my sister says in such a fearful tone that the hairs on the back of my neck stand up. *"They're connected to very powerful people. I don't know how they found me, but they know I work here. They're sending threats to me and have said they'll move on to my family if I don't cooperate. I don't know what to do."*

My heart races, frantic in my ear drums. I close my eyes to stop the room from spinning. I'm unable to turn away or shut it off.

"I don't want to take it," Sharice continues, her voice cracking. *"But it's just one egg, and they..."* her words trail off. *"They said they'd kill my family, make it look like an accident at the research center where my mom works, and then Brigid..."* Her voice falters again, and tears stream down her cheeks. My heart thunders at the mention of my name.

"They said they'd do terrible, awful things if I go to the police. I don't have a choice. I don't know if anyone will ever see this, but please know I didn't have a choice." The video ends, and I'm left with my thoughts, a swirling storm staring at a black screen.

What did my sister stumble upon? What if she'd refused? What if that was why she was missing? Perhaps they'd sent someone else to finish what she wouldn't do, and so took her, possibly killing her to cover it up? There were dozens of employees here at the station they could have their pick from. What if she had fought back, and they'd moved on to blackmailing someone else?

I clutch the comm device to my pounding heart.

Had Heath found out about this? Is that why he wanted me here? Surely, he wasn't the type to get his hands dirty, or maybe he was? *Do the job yourself if you want it done right.*

The room continues to spin. Any one of them could have ended her life. Snuffed out her light because of what she uncovered. Heath, Carter, Logan. Did I actually believe they could be killers? I'd seen the ways they'd trained. They were skilled fighters. All had military training, and if the rumors were true, they were top of their class in marksmanship and combat. If anyone could do it, they could.

Still, pretend killing with holograms was one thing; really going through with it was another. It took a certain type of person to end someone's life. I should know.

It takes someone deranged or desperate. And even with my limited interaction with Logan, I didn't see any of them as deranged, which meant they needed to keep her quiet.

As much as these videos have given me clarity, they're only the start. I need more. It wouldn't be my word against some mentally ill serial killer; it'd be mine against three of the most influential and adored men in the country.

Me—the daughter of a low-level Lanett scientist —versus them. Three Master Riders. They were as untouchable as anyone could be in Venovia. They had the fame and fortune of rock stars and the political connections to go with it.

If I had any chance at all against them, I'd need rock-solid proof. Something tangible that even their unrivaled reputations couldn't match, which means I have to stay strong.

I *will* unravel whatever secrets took my sister from me. For her, I must finish what she started.

The truth is here. Hidden in this place that forced her to flee, or perhaps took her life.

I can feel the secret lurking in the shadows, just out of sight, and I won't stop until it's found.

Nine

*T*his is fucking living.

The crowd roars, and my fan section is decked out in red, chanting Ember and mine's nickname: "Jamber! Jamber!"

The atmosphere in the exhibition arena is electric. The house is packed with people eager for a show they won't forget. And I am more than ready to give it to them.

This is the last show before the gala, and the pressure is on more than ever. I soak up the roar of the crowd as I settle into Ember's saddle. The thick, carbon fiber riding pants and boots dampen the intense heat radiating against my calves and thighs. He's sensing the excitement, too, and the bases of his braided mane and tail are glowing brighter than I've seen in a while, and I know my boy is ready to kick some ass.

The music kicks in—a throbbing beat sets the tone for the mock battle—and the spotlight hits us. Multicolored lasers dance across the stands as the crowd screams in anticipation.

A holographic projection of earth — back before the continents were broken and split — spins slowly, hovering in the center of the arena.

"Thousands of years ago!" the recorded announcer calls out. "The ocean rose, and the world was plagued by a terrible alien scourge that left our air poisoned and governments in ruins." The earth shifts to the present-day form, dotted with dozens of smaller land masses, before zooming in on Venovia, one of the largest. "The Mystyl were vicious, brutal creatures." The earth disappears, and there are shrieks in the crowd as the projections in the corners skitter over people's heads and between the aisles. "Humanity, however, found hope when the first druadan was born!"

The crowd gasps in awe as the holographic projection grows in size before splitting in two, and a young druadan emerges. Oohs and ahhs emanate from the audience as the projection staggers to their feet before taking a few timid steps. The hologram shifts, showing the druadan growing rapidly to full size into a prancing black stallion.

"With their natural resistance to Mystyl's venom and their supernatural ability to move lightning quick, it allowed them to avoid the Mystyl's attacks and form an unbreakable bond with their riders. The druadans finally rid the land of mystyl once and for all." Logan, Heath, and I move as one, our druadans responding to each nudge and shift of our bodies as we communicate to them through our minds.

When we hit the center of the arena, I command Ember to rear and then leap into the air. At the peak, he kicks out, and I maintain the center of my seat, executing the difficult maneuver perfectly. "But the most fascinating feature of a druadan is their ability to bond to a single rider," the announcer continues. "A mysterious connection so powerful that death itself is the only way to sever it."

As I bring Ember around behind Heath, his voice comes through the earpiece molded into our helmets. "Pincer two maneuvers."

A grin spreads across my face as I nudge my heels into

Ember's flanks. We race past, flanking Heath and Shadowmane, while Logan and Galaxian mirror us on the other side. The novices, Danner, Nelson, and Ve'loth, ride charge from the other side, trying to keep pace. As we circle back, the music changes to a heavy metal remix that shakes the arena floors. I grip the reins tighter as the beat pulses through my body. My heart soars, thrumming loudly in my ears. This is it—the high-stakes game of chicken that always gets the crowd going wild.

As we rush toward each other, Ember's mouth opens wide, gnashing teeth at invisible enemies with fangs that gleam like daggers. A collective gasp surges from the crowd. My pulse quickens, adrenaline a wildfire in my veins.

"Shift," I whisper. Sweat beads my brow, and I feel the heavy pull in my chest, like a vice clamping as I force the command through the bond.

In a blink, the world fractures, pulling apart—there's a brief, disorienting moment of weightlessness, nothingness. Time pauses. The world fades away to infinite blackness, except for Heath, Logan, and their stallions beside me come into razor-sharp focus. Their souls, their fears, and their desires lay bare for me. For a split second, we share a collective consciousness. Their faces show the strain and the intensity of the maneuver, and then, out of the corner of my eye, as Ember's body moves, I see a flash of silver-colored hair. Like a beacon in the darkness, then my vision returns, and the sounds of the crowd and music slam me back into reality.

We reappear at full gallop to the left of the novice riders, who shoot past us, wide-eyed, a little shaken, but grinning like idiots.

The music changes, signaling Act II of the performance. I can't shake the thought of what I saw—or better, what I *thought* I saw. Ever since our bonds have been acting up, weird things have started to happen. The insomnia is bad enough, but now I'm seeing things during phasing.

I shake my head, hoping to clear it. I need to focus. I can't afford distractions, not when we're doing maneuvers that have zero room for error. A skewed shift could mean half of me goes with Ember, and the other half stays behind. There's a reason riders dedicate their entire life to training.

The announcer initiates the next part of the performance, and holographic Mystyl monsters materialize around us, tentacles poised. They're meant to mimic the mind-numbing speed of the ancient aliens, but with the druadan's shifting ability, they're nearly matched. Ember and I weave through them, each dodge and feint perfectly timed. My lance, with its laser cord tether, cuts through the virtual enemies, each hit erupting in a shower of light, eliciting cheers and whistles from the crowd.

Heath and I flank each other, the tension building. We've come to the climax. Weapons poised, a tornado of swirling tentacled holograms flutters around us, and the music reaches a shattering crescendo. With a final battle cry, we charge the remaining holograms. Right on cue, the audience loses their fucking minds.

I feel like a warrior god as I slash through enemies, and Ember snaps angrily at them as if they truly were attacking.

As the smoke clears, Heath and I stand victorious, our druadans rear up and shift in and out in time with the music. The crowd is on their feet, the deafening roar shaking my bones. My name echoes through the stands, and I lift my arms, drinking in the electric energy. This is what we live for. The Mystyl holograms regroup for a final assault, and we charge, our weapons slashing through them as if they're smoke.

With a final flourish, we dispatch the last of the holograms and ride to the center of the arena. A rush of heat slithers up my spine from Ember, and my pulse ratchets higher, feeling the delicious surge of energy from the bond. I reach down and stroke Ember's glowing mane, and he paws the arena floor as if saying he'd only warmed up. I'm grinning like an idiot. Our bond has never been stronger.

It's all in my head. Nothing more. Fucking Logan and his bleak outlook on our future is messing with me. The cheers reach a deafening crescendo, and I lift my arms in triumph as if I actually had won a battle. *This* is what I live for—the rush, the adoration, the sheer exhilaration of being in the spotlight and owning it. Of being one with Ember. Of sharing the same mind.

As the applause fades, my eyes scan the crowd until they find her—Brigid, camera in hand. She's smiling. Damn right, she is. We're magnificent. We're God damn rock stars.

"THANK YOU ALL FOR COMING TO THIS SPECIAL EVENT AT Meridian Station," the announcer's voice rings through the arena. "Become patrons to experience stable tours, attend VIP parties, and enjoy exclusive behind-the-scenes access and meet and greets with our talented riders!"

With Ember back in his stall, I give him his evening feed and a well-deserved pat. Once he's content, I go to my locker in the changing room. I unfasten the buckles on the black carbon fiber jacket and put on the dark blue dress coat with gold buttons signifies me as one of Meridian's Master riders. Unlike my daily riding jacket, it's made of natural fabrics, so not meant to ride in, and is only for show. As I'm leaving, I pass by the two of the novices, still wearing their plain khaki gear as they finish sweeping and hosing down the center aisle of the barn.

"Gym workout first thing tomorrow," I say to them.

Danner and Nelson look up from their brooms, their eyes widening in surprise. "Yes, Master James," Danner says.

I say goodnight and exiting the stable, make my way to the roped-off section of the stands where fans and VIPs await. The mingled scents of perfume and cologne fill my nostrils. Two girls — both wearing sequined halter tops and tight skirts— motion at me to gain my attention. *Here we go.*

One has a pixie cut and a shade of chocolate brown hair, and the other has curls of red hair in a high ponytail. Between their makeup and clothes, they're here for the post-performance party. And as I approach them, the shine in their eyes that's from more than arena lights confirms it.

They hold out the glossy printed program. "Thanks for coming," I say. "Who should I make it out to?"

They giggle. "Victoria and Alliya." The redhead says, handing me a pen. "We're from U of D."

"Oh yeah," I say, feigning interest as I scribble a generic plati- tude. "What are you studying?"

"Mom wants us to go into politics like her, but I've picked Venovian history as my major," Victoria says.

"And I'm studying environmental impact," Alliya adds.

I hand them back the program, and take another look at their faces, immediately recognizing them. "You're Vicky and Alliya Jameson. Senator Jameson's daughters."

Vicky's smile fades. "Yeah, so?"

I swallow hard. Son of a bitch. "No, nothing. Just thought I'd recognized you, is all."

Alliya takes the program and tucks it into her purse. "So, we're staying at one of the guest houses tonight. You should come by."

The temptation tugs at me, resting on the tip of my tongue, and for a moment, I'm so damn close to saying yes. But Heath's still pissed about the fruit vendor bullshit, and now might not be the best time for me to be fraternizing with politician's daughters. I force a smile and thank them for the offer, catching the flicker of disappointment in their eyes as they walk away.

Heath is nearby, swarmed by journalists, answering ques- tions with that effortless way of his. Logan, predictably, is a no-show; the guy never sticks around for autographs or anything after a performance.

Feeling the pull of post-exhibition exhaustion, I head back to my house and change out of my riding clothes. The adrenaline has fizzled out, leaving me in a state of drained contentment.

After changing out of my riding gear at my apartment, I'm too wired to sleep.

I decide to wind down at the hot springs reserved for staff, located behind the exercise facility. The night sky stretches above me like an inky canvas specked with stars.

That's when I hear it—a splash, followed by a soft, contended sigh. From the edge of the stone basin, a halo of pale hair glows in the moonlight, and I blink my eyes, attempting to clear my vision.

Brigid.

Okay, so this evening just improved significantly. A flicker of anticipation awakens inside me and between my legs. Maybe, just maybe, this could be a *different* kind of relaxation altogether.

"Didn't expect to see anyone else here," I say, shrugging off my robe until I'm only wearing the black pair of swimming shorts.

Brigid's head spins around as she pushes off from the seat on the edge.

Brigid startles, her hands clutching her chest. "Oh," she says, her eyes landing on my bare chest, as I do the same, and realize her tits are barely beneath a light blue halter top bikini. "I can leave if you want."

"No, it's cool," I say, eying the large oval-shaped stone basin. "How about the show tonight? Fucking wild."

"Yeah," she says, "Carla had tried to prepare me for how packed it'd be, but I still was amazed. I had to keep moving to get better angles around since so many bodies kept blocking me. I took a lot of pictures and videos. I think they will work out great."

"Mostly of Ember and me."

She rolls her eyes and laughs. "I took a few, yes. I'll have to show you them when I've had a chance to edit them."

I wade into the milky blue water, my muscles sighing in relief as I sink into the underwater benches lining the perimeter. The water glows a pale green from the underwater lights. I sneak a glance beneath the surface, catching a glimpse of Brigid's bare legs. She's twisted her silvery hair into a braided bun on top of her head, and her teal blue eyes—mirroring the spa's lights—watch me intently.

"That was some performance tonight," she says, breaking the silence. "I've only ever seen recordings on the Network."

"Nothing beats live," I reply dryly and lay my head back on the ledge.

She murmurs in agreement.

Time stretches as I relax in the hot water. The distant sounds of laughter and music from the exhibition hall drift are direction, as does the occasional low hum of shuttles taking off.

Finally, I feel the movement of the water against my chest and open my eyes to see Brigid has moved closer.

"So, tell me about this water? Why does it look this way?"

I shrug. "Honestly, I don't know much. The original station builders piped off a nearby hot spring. That jar over there," I point to the low shelf set in the brick wall, "has some sediment that's supposed to be good for your skin or something."

Intrigued, Brigid climbs out of the water, grabbing one of the clay jars. I watch her, captivated by her movements. Her feet step lightly on the stone, and her matching bikini bottom sits low on her hips as they sway. I drop my gaze lower, landing on the curved shape of a tight ass, and my dick twitches between my legs.

She returns, carrying the glass jar, and sits back down, her eyes meeting mine as she begins to apply the clay mask to her face. Her fingers glide slowly, reverently across her cheeks, the bridge of her nose, and her forehead. It's hot as fuck, and my cock is rock-hard. She hasn't even touched me. *What the hell is with this girl?*

"Could you put some on my neck?" she asks, holding out the jar.

I grab it and hesitate for just a moment. She's staff. New staff, sure, but still not off-limits, at least according to Heath's rules. However, just cause Heath wouldn't care didn't mean it was a good idea. Staff relationships—at least in my experience— have chances to get messy. Fucking around with the station meant fucking with the druadans.

Don't fuck where you eat. As Logan would so eloquently put it.

But it's too late. I've already committed, carefully spreading the clay along the nape of her neck. She twists to give me better access, and I'm fully aware of the tension building between us and not wanting to assume this is anything other than platonic. I keep my touch light, not lingering more than I think is necessary.

But when my thumb grazes just beneath her earlobe, she lets out a soft moan, and my dick strains even harder against the fabric of my shorts.

Once her face is covered in the gray clay, I hand the jar back to her.

The corners of her mouth creep into a sly smirk. "Now, it's your turn."

"What? No, I'm good."

She giggles, a delicious sound in the night air. "Come on. It's good for your skin. You're a celebrity, right? You have to keep your moneymaker looking good."

"My moneymaker is just fine."

She arches an eyebrow. "What? Are you afraid someone is going to see you?"

"I don't give a shit."

"Then what is it?"

I scour my thoughts for a reason and find none. Well, except one. Her hands on me and the thousand ways this night could end. Nine hundred and ninety-nine of which my dick is eager to participate in.

"Fine," I say, letting out a sigh.

She moves closer, inches separating us. Her blue eyes shimmer in the dim light, and even under the gray clay mask, she is stunning. "Great, now hold still." She dabs her fingers in the pot of clay, and I feel the sandy bits of cool liquid stroke my left jawline.

"So, have you ever done this before?"

"The face mask? No." I lie. I totally have. It's just been in the privacy of my bathroom when I'm sure Logan is either out or asleep. She isn't wrong. I do have a certain appearance to uphold. Even if gray hair and wrinkles weren't in my future, it didn't mean I shouldn't take care of the body I have. Best benefit of dying young? Never growing old.

She laughs. "I meant the hot springs. Alone. With a girl."

"Oh, that." I try to sound casual, but it's hard with her so close and her fingers caressing my chin. "This hot spring is like the Delford Shuttledepot of Meridian. It's seen everything from terrible first dates to emergency staff meetings."

She wrinkles her nose, an endearing gesture that sends a rush of warmth through me. God, I want to lean in and kiss her, but caution whispers in the back of my mind. I barely fucking know her, and my past spontaneity has led to misunderstandings more than once.

But the way she looks at me, with those blue eyes sparkling like the lake at sunrise and the grin tugging at the corners of her lips, makes me want to forget all reason and just do it.

Better to let her take the reins. Fewer chances for mixed signals that way.

A comfortable silence settles between us, and she sighs. "I don't think I'd ever get used to this view." She stares up at the sky, blanketed by stars.

"No stars in Delford," I say.

She shakes her head. She turns to face me again and her eyes land on my chest.

"That's a cool tattoo. Does it mean anything?"

I tap the inked 'U' with the red and orange flames that encircle it on the right side of my chest. "It's the mark of the Inferno line. Ember is a descendant of it."

"Do all the riders have one?"

"Most, yes. But they're all different depending on their stallion's lineage."

She squints at it, and she reaches out to touch it. "May I?"

I give a subtle nod, and she inches closer. I fill my lungs with her scent, a sweet aroma that lingers in the air. Her fingers graze over the tattooed skin on my neck and chest with a gentle touch, eliciting a shiver down my spine.

"Tell me, Carter, Do you believe in fate?" she asks softly, her fingers still resting on my chest.

A chuckle escapes from deep within me, and her gaze meets mine with a serious expression that remains unchanged. "Shit, you're serious?" I take a deep breath, unsure of what to say. "I'm not sure," I reply honestly. "I think sometimes things happen for a reason, but other times it's just luck."

She nods thoughtfully, her hand still lingering on mine. "I used to believe everything happened for a reason, but then something happened that made me question that belief."

The familiar flicker of discomfort washes through me, the weight of her words pressing against my limits. The unease of venturing into such personal territory tugs at me, but I relent. No one else is around, and there's some easy way about her that I like. The way she looks at me like I'm just a man. Not a rider.

"What happened?" I ask, my voice wavering slightly.

Sadness clouds her eyes, and she looks away, staring at the water. "A long time ago, I was forced to make a choice I didn't want to make. A choice I still doubt was the right one."

Her words instill an ache in my chest as I can't help but imagine losing Heath or Logan. Both are integral to my life. And together, the three of us are a force. Without one another, we'd be a shell of ourselves.

"I'm sorry to hear that."

She smiles wistfully and stares up again at the stars.

We sit in silence again for a few minutes, listening to the gurgling of the hot water circulator before she speaks again.

"You know, I've been here for three days, and I still haven't got the part of the off-the-books tour you promised me. I did the employee orientation and read the station manual. Give me the juicy stuff?"

I shift in my seat, glad the mood has lightened. The water sloshes gently around me. "I doubt you're ready. Meridian is one of the oldest stations on Venovia. There are secrets here you couldn't even imagine."

Her lips part, and a flicker of curiosity sparks in her eyes. "Is that so?"

"It is," I say a little smugly and rest my arms on the stone wall behind me. "Druadan riders are privileged. All sorts of secrets are taken with us to the grave."

She twists her face in thought. "Okay, fine. No druadan rider secrets. So, what about the rest of the station? The other people that work here? Any sordid affairs or secret gambling problems? In case you didn't know, it's actually in my job description to present the station in the best possible light, which means sometimes doing damage control when shit happens." She pauses, cupping the water in her hands and letting it spill back into the spa. "Say like staff members disappearing."

I feel a lump lodge in the back of my throat. She is talking about Sharice. I lower my arms, letting them slip back into the warm water. "Sharice, yeah. It was really weird how she just left like that. The Council police were involved, and Heath had Logan limit the number of shuttles coming and going along with a background check after we had a few nosy fucking journalists posing as guests sneak through."

"That's awful," she says, and it sounds genuine. "Did you know her very well?"

I shrug. Trying to recall any details from the few conversations we'd had. Every meeting, she'd been early, sat in the same place, and rarely asked questions. Then she'd take her meals to the cottage and only would come out for exhibitions or, later, to have secret meetings with Heath in the main house. "Not too much. She was nice. Looked kind of like you, actually."

Brigid's eyes widen. "Really?"

I tilt my head and squint. "Sort of. She has brown hair, though, and her eyes—" I pause, suddenly realizing I couldn't remember her eye color. "I don't know what color her eyes are. Guess I never paid much attention." I laugh dryly.

Her hand goes to her hair, and a slight tinge of pink appears on her cheekbones as if suddenly self-conscious.

"Truth was," I continue, feeling like I'd made her uncomfortable. "Sharice kept to herself. She didn't cause problems, and I never once heard Heath complain about how she was doing her job, which is the oddest thing of all because he doesn't handle someone being lazy or half-assing their duties here. His employee reviews are brutal."

I feel the clay working, tightening on my face, along with a slight tingling. Suddenly, Brigid's thumb lowers from next to my nose and brushes over my bottom lip. My eyes settle on hers, and that's when I see it. The widening of her pupils as they fill with desire. A momentary flicker that says she's as caught up in this magnetic pull as I am.

"And the sordid affairs?" she whispers.

"None that I know of currently." The temptation to act, to

close the gap between us, becomes nearly unbearable. Still, I hold back, giving her the space to decide what comes next. She seems to understand, her eyes meeting mine in silent conversation.

"Good," she finally says, her voice so soft it's almost drowned out by the gentle lap of water against the edges of the spa. "Because I'd hate for this…" Her hand slides down my chest, painstakingly slow, until landing on my hardened dick. Her fingers stroke it gently through the fabric, and I feel it grow harder, lengthening further at her touch. She leans closer, giving me a better look at her, more than ample cleavage spilling out of the top of her bikini.

"…to be more than it is," she finishes.

My heart races with anticipation as I drink in the glorious sight of her. I catch my breath at the electricity that sparks between us, a sensation I know all too well.

She leans closer, her lips brushing against my ear as she whispers, "Do you feel it, too?"

My body responds as I feel my cock grow even harder, pressing against my suit, yearning for more of her touch. I can't help but lean into her, my fingers tangling in her hair as our bodies press together.

Her laughter rings out, musical and carefree, as she pulls back to look into my eyes. "I'm going to take that as a yes," she says with a devilish grin.

I want more from those fingers. I want to feel them exploring me without restraint, without the fabric barrier.

I stifle a groan of pleasure, moving to unlace my shorts. "And what is this—"

"Master James," I hear a voice from behind me. Brigid and I lurch away from each other, the water slapping the tiled walls surrounding the spa.

I whip my head around, fully prepared to rip the head off whichever fucking novice interrupted us.

But I stop the second I see Logan standing a few feet from the edge.

His hands are on his hips, eyes locked on Brigid. "Heath called a meeting. *Now.*"

"A meeting? What the hell, Logan? It's almost midnight."

"Don't care," Logan says, his eyes moving from Brigid to mine. "Get out. Get dressed. Meeting in ten."

Then Logan leaves, his massive form disappearing into the darkness beyond the security lights.

I return my gaze to Brigid. Her cheeks and chest are flushed skin, both from embarrassment and the heat of the water. Her wide eyes and full lips tempt me to linger, to blow off Logan and Heath and finish what we had started, but I shake my head, thinking better of it.

"Fuck." Frustrated, I slap the water, and it splashes the both of us.

She giggles. "It's fine. I understand. But um…" She trails off, pointing to my face, "You might want to…"

My hands go to my cheek, and I feel the dried clay mask. Well fucking fantastic. Not only did Logan catch me getting handsy with the new hire, but I'm also wearing a face mask like some sort of Delford douche.

I splash the warm water on my face, doing my best to scrub it off, then climb out. Brigid doesn't move from her corner of the spa, but I can feel her eyes watching me as I grab a towel from the bin.

"I'll see you around," I say, turning to leave, then pause. "Rain check?"

"Yeah," she calls out, smiling. "Rain check."

Ten

BRIGID

The scent of Carter on my skin and the steam of the hot springs lingers after he leaves.

My fingers have turned pruney, but the water's warmth is hard to say goodbye to. Finally, I drag myself out, wrapping up in a plush towel before I transform into a human raisin.

As I walk to my cottage, I notice the stable is pitch black, and the exhibition hall lies in darkness. But there's one light shining from the main house in the distance. It must be Heath, Logan, and Carter at the meeting. Logan had summoned Carter, too. Curiosity lifts its head, and for a moment, I'm tempted to sneak over and do some spy shit, but then I begin to shiver. The reality of trying to be quiet while freezing to death in just a bikini and a towel firmly grounds me.

Once back inside my cottage, I turn on the shower. The hot water washes over me, but it can't rinse away the thoughts swirling in my mind. Carter had been so cagey about Sharice, my predecessor. He'd given me tantalizing crumbs but held back the loaf of bread. And yet, despite the omissions, he'd offered more than anyone else since I arrived.

I'd been avoiding Heath like he's a landmine in my path, even ducking out early from the performance to skip the post-performance meet and greet. But I know it's only a matter of time before we cross paths and have to address the last conversation we'd had where I'd angrily accused him of hurting Sharice.

Which is why I'd had to take advantage of the opportunity Carter stumbling upon me in the hot springs had provided.

As I lather the floral soap across my skin, my mind drifts to our conversation. Carter has a way of making me lower my guard despite my better judgment. My stomach flutters, remembering his bare chest and broad shoulders. The guy was insanely hot. And ripped. God, it'd taken every ounce of my willpower not to gawk at them. If I hadn't been seated when he'd arrived, I'm positive my knees would've buckled.

Guilt flits across my conscience like a restless bird, pecking at my thoughts. I'd overheard one of the maintenance staff talking about how Carter often went to the spa after a show and had hoped it'd give me an opportunity to pry a little more.

Of which I'd been successful.

At the same time, the fooling around with Carter had not been the original part of my plan and had been a bad idea, one that would surely add to my ever-growing list of regrettable decisions. However unplanned my approach was, it had worked. Carter *had* opened up, sharing more about Sharice.

Not much, but more than I'd had before. Sure, he could've been lying. I didn't think so. He had such an easy, uncaring way about him. Like he truly loved his life. Unlike Heath, who got off on regulating everyone and everyone, or Logan, with a permanent look of disdain on his face, as he'd just got back from having to shoot a puppy.

As the hot water cascades over me, rinsing off the sulfur scent of the hot spring, I'm reminded of all the showers my sister took in this very cottage before me. I imagine her standing here, letting the water wash away the grime of the station.

The floral scent of the shampoo fills the steamy air, masking the musty odor of old pipes in the walls. I close my eyes, recalling our hands on each other in the spa. Holy shit, was he handsome and charming and funny, and if we hadn't been so rudely interrupted, I might've gotten to know him even more.

I'm not sure what would've happened if Logan hadn't interrupted us. Carter seemed more than willing, and I, too, was seconds away from hopping on the poor-decisions-to-make-with-your-coworkers bus.

If Logan hadn't stopped us, could I have trusted myself to stop before things went too far? And just how far is that? I'm an adult. He's an adult. So, what is wrong with mixing pleasure with business?

My hands squeeze the water from my hair, and I sigh.

Because that wasn't it at all. I was using *him*. Manipulating him into telling me more about my sister.

Fine, it's wrong, but so is whatever happened to Sharice. I re-lather the sponge, scrubbing harder. Still, the residue of guilt remains, no matter how hard I scour.

The secrets lurking here cling to everything like moss. I'm tangled in a web I can't even see the threads of.

After toweling off, I make some tea and sit at the desk where Sharice likely sat countless nights. Her presence is palpable as I open the computer. My body is relaxed from the soak, but my mind is buzzing. Might as well take advantage and get some work done. I draft a few memos for the staff set to go out end of the week. Check the station's PR inbox. A high school wants to schedule a visit and tour. A dozen girls ask for Carter's, Heath's, and Logan's phone numbers or addresses to send fan mail. One includes a photo attachment, which I promptly deleted.

Eventually, the mouse drifts to Sharice's old files on the computer. I'm certain they've been looked through by both Heath and Carla, as well as the Council police, and are only pertinent to the station, but still, I can't help but click through the digital files, imagining her sitting in my place, doing the same.

As I suspected, there's nothing out of the ordinary—budgets, schedules, old memos, mundane reports about staff training and supply shipments. The clock flashes 2 am, and I'm about ready to call it a night when a folder catches my eye at the bottom.

It's labeled 'banquet seating chart' and, as I immediately find out next, is passcode protected.

My pulse quickens.

Bellion is my first try, and I secretly hope I'm wrong. I sigh with relief when it doesn't work. My passwords were the same three combinations of my favorite flowers, sometimes capitalized with different numbers. Next, I try birthday combinations, her college graduation date, and anything tied to her or this place.

Nothing.

I click open the folder's details, hoping to glean something from it. It's big. Probably pictures or videos. It's also encrypted, proving once again that Sharice had always been smarter than me, and as scared as she looked in the last of her video messages, she'd felt a need to figure it out. Had the police missed this somehow? Assumed an upcoming seating chart would be of no interest to her disappearance? My stomach clenches at the police's incompetence. No one knows my sister better than me. This file, whatever it is, is important. As I'd suspected, Sharice *was* onto something - and it may have put her in danger. Finally, I close my laptop and check the lock on my door and windows. I head to the bedroom and sliding under the cool sheets, I'm more confused than ever. My thoughts are a chaotic mixture of half-truths and fragmented secrets.

And I fear it'll only get worse.

Eleven

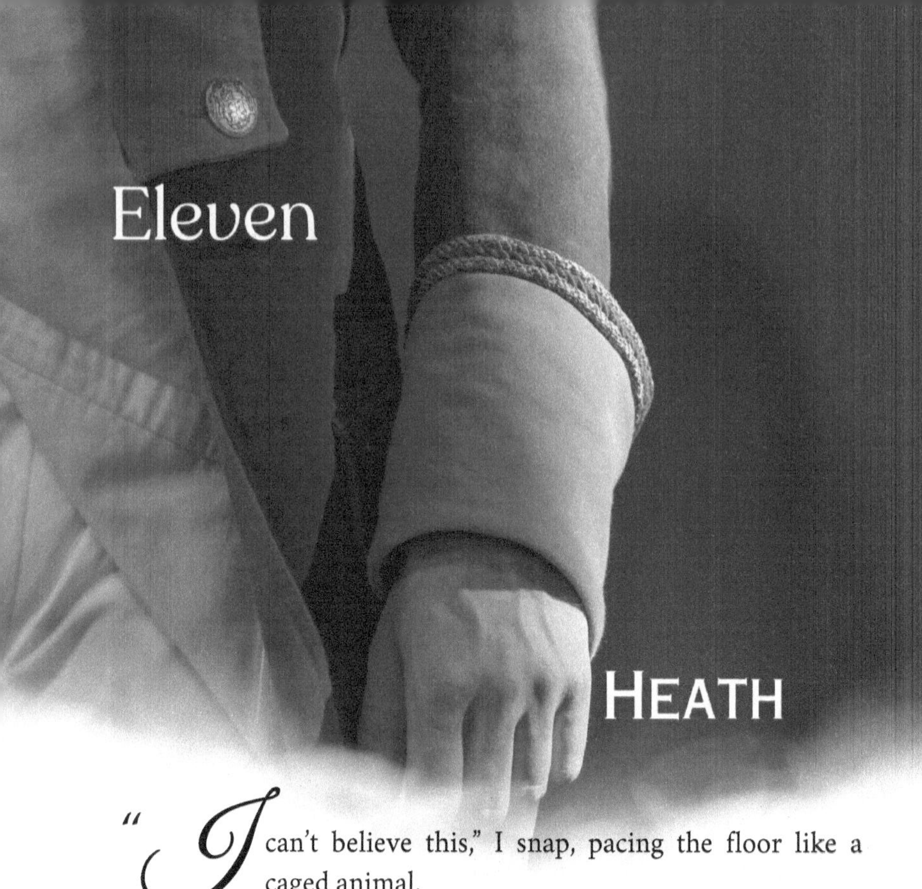

HEATH

"*I* can't believe this," I snap, pacing the floor like a caged animal.

"First, the supplier changed the formula for the protein pellets, and now Gemindusk is sick."

The three of us are in my office, and it's been one hell of a day. "We don't have a fucking choice, Heath," Logan says. "Dr. Gideon needs the herbs from Leviler to make the salve."

Carter pushes off the bookshelf and steps toward me. "Look, we can handle this. Since the herbalist says they're too fragile to ship, we'll have Dr. Gideon take the shuttle to pick them up. You need to—"

"Don't tell me what I need," I cut him off, my voice tinged with more anger that's typically reserved for Logan.

Without warning, Carter reaches out and places his hand on my shoulder. The touch sends a warm, soothing sensation through me—the bond awakening between us. Before I can shake it off, Logan adds his hand to my other shoulder. The power of the bond intensifies, filling me with a heady rush that temporarily numbs my senses.

A distant hum reverberates through the night, and I know it's Shadowmane voicing his form of support as the ripple of our combined energies surges.

I take a deep breath, letting the wave of calming energy ground me. "Fine. But Dr. Gideon should stay here. Send a novice to get the order from Leviler."

Carter removes his hand, and the intense connection is severed. "We'll sort this out, Heath. We always do."

Logan nods, his gaze meeting mine. "Stefensen will be the least likely to fuck it up."

"And you should know, I caught Brigid in the practice arena during training. She claimed you gave her permission." Logan glances briefly at Carter before looking back at me.

He'd told me about finding them in the spa together, and it's overdue for us to bring him in the loop. Carter is one of us. *Part of us.* It isn't fair to make him play a high-stakes poker game with only half the cards.

I run a hand through my hair with a frustrated sigh. The timing of a sick druadan couldn't be worse. It'd been two days since I'd caught Brigid in my room and revealed I knew she was Sharice's sister, and I'd put off talking to her in private again longer than I should.

She had free rein of the station to investigate her sister, but rules needed to be put in place. "Her proposal high-lighted an attempt at showing a more authentic side to the station, but I should've been clearer on limits about where she can and can't go. I'll talk to her first thing tomorrow morning," I say, making a point of keying in a memo on my comm.

"If it counts," Carter says, smirking. "I didn't mind her watching us practice."

"Nobody fucking asked," Logan says, then fixes me with a

narrowed gaze, silently challenging my authority. The hairs on the back of my neck stand up, and my hands flex into fists.

Neither of us moves, neither wanting to break eye contact. "If she keeps sticking her nose where she shouldn't," Logan says, keeping his voice low. "Then all the staff will think they could do whatever they want. There is a reason certain places are off-limits here, and if anyone gets hurt, it won't be on me."

I release the breath I'd been holding. "Agreed. The last thing we need is another disappearance on our hands."

Logan's eyes darken, and he stands up, the tension leaving his body slightly. Beside him, Carter's playful expression sobers. "You don't think Brigid is in danger, do you?" It's a genuine question and is filled with concern. Out of the three of us, he's the good one.

Sure, he'll sleep with anything that moves and has two legs, but he's not as jaded as Logan and me. Carter actually gives a damn.

"No," I reply. "We know why Sharice left and why she won't be coming back. We've learned from our mistakes and have taken better precautions. Brigid is perfectly safe here, so long as she remains ignorant of her sister's real reason for leaving."

The instant I realize I said too much, Carter's eyes widen, and at the same moment, Logan scoffs.

"You're kidding me. Her *sister*?" Carter exclaims. "How the—"

I hold up a hand. "Yes. We only just found out yesterday."

Carter pins Logan with a fierce glare. "You knew, too?"

Logan's jaw clenches, and his steel-gray eyes deepen a shade. "It's my responsibility to be aware of any potential threats to this facility."

"And you waited until now to tell me?" Carter says. His words are hard with betrayal and anger, and I feel the pinch in my chest. The remorse I knew would be there when we'd finally come clean. I purse my lips. "I didn't think it was relevant until now."

Carter runs a hand through his hair and begins pacing. "So, what do we do now?"

"Nothing." I say, "We go on as normal, keeping tabs on her, and then wait and see if her sister reaches out.

Carter stops his pacing and looks up. "She could be here to finish what her sister started, you know?"

I shake my head. "I know. But we've learned from our mistakes. All outgoing and incoming calls are recorded, and we've installed more cameras with round-the-clock monitoring. She might be wondering where her sister is, but she can't go anywhere or do anything without one of us knowing." I pause and tap on the tablet on my desk. "With Brigid here, we can keep a better handle on the situation. She has Sharice's comm and computer. If she hasn't figured out how to unlock it, she will soon."

"Fine. Then what happens?" Carter asks.

"Unless you say something, she'll assume you don't know her relation to Sharice, and you can get her to reveal what she knows."

Logan crosses his arms, a grim expression resting on his face. "A close enemy gives you something to aim at. A distant one gives you something to worry about." He turns to Carter.

"You've already got a headstart. Why don't you put that mouth of yours to good use and get her to confess."

Carter's lips twist into a sneer and his back tenses. It's been more of a struggle than usual lately to keep their egos in check, and I hope they can keep their shit together long enough to get through the gala.

"She's not the fucking enemy," Carter snaps, his eyes pinned with Logan's. "Are you even hearing yourself? She's just someone looking for her sister. What if it was one of us that went missing? Wouldn't we be doing the same? Looking for answers no matter the risk?"

"That's just it," I say, diffusing the situation before Logan can answer. "It is a risk to the entire station having her here. She could expose everything." My voice hardens. "Destroy *everything.*"

Carter's throat moves, and while the crease between his brows stays, he gives a submissive nod and steps back. Logan's lips form a thin line, and he retreats to the corner of the office, where he assumes his usual stance with his arms folded.

"We need her to stay here at the station," I continue, my words softer now. "Keep her doing her job so as not to raise suspicion to anyone."

"And we're just supposed to let her have the run of the place?" Carter asks.

"Within reason, yes, which, as I said, I will relay to her."

"For how long?"

"Long enough for her to learn that there's nothing more here connected to Sharice, and then she'll either drop it or quit on her own. Or until she finds out where Sharice is and they contact each other."

The back of my hand burns, and I rub it to stop the itch. The movement catches both of their attention.

"How bad?" Logan says, his voice low.

The overcharged bond churns inside me, threatening to split open my chest. On a scale of one to ten, it's probably a solid eleven. "I'm fine," I say.

Logan levels me with his gaze that's intense enough to make most men either wet themselves or rethink their life's choices, usually in that order.

Carter shifts closer, a flicker of worry in his mossy-colored eyes.

"How long?" Logan asks.

"A week," I say. "Ten days, maybe."

"Holy shit," Carter says. "Have you spoken to Marshal?"

"No." If I reached out to Marshal, it would arouse suspicion of my condition and seed doubt in my ability to be a manager. My age already was a barrier, and while I trusted the guy, I didn't trust the rest of the assholes at Blackhawk, where he worked.

"For fuck's sake," Carter snaps. "Heath. You're going to have to—"

"I know," I snap back. "I will, okay? I just haven't had the time, and with everything else going on, I just thought—"

"Thought you could handle it?" Carter cuts me off, moving forward. "You're going to die, Heath. Your blood is going to boil, and you're going to burn up and die."

"Don't worry. I've got it under control."

"You just rode Shadowmane, though," Carter supplies. "That had to help?"

"I'm still breathing," I grumble. It had, but not as much as I'd hoped. It wasn't a full reset, not like it'd been in the past. But it had been enough to keep me going even if I still felt my control slipping.

Pilchuck didn't have this problem. A few odd meetings a week, an interview once a year, and the circuit annual review. That was it. Aside from those obligations, he was with his stallion or his girlfriend. Since the new wave of elected board members had shifted their attention from filtration plants to extraneous Circuit spending, they'd directed their sights on the stations.

The meetings, trips, and ass-kissing politicians consumed my days.

If I wanted to keep this station going, every free minute I was with my stallion was a minute the death grip I had on this place loosened.

We sit in the shared silence until Logan asks, "What about Jess?"

I shake my head, sinking into my chair. "Vacationing in Gaergen," I tell them, but it didn't matter, anyway. The sex with her wasn't helping.

Not anymore.

This meeting wasn't supposed to be about this. In fact, I hadn't intended to tell them at all that I was brimming. I'd dealt with it before. Alone, I could do it again.

Or maybe I was broken.

Finally, when no one has said anything for some time, Carter speaks, "Look. These two sisters are staying at the guest cottage, and before you say no, hear me out."

"No," I say.

"They're hot, fun, and want some rider company," he continues, "It'd be like our own branch of public relations. Extending the station's warm hospitality via our dicks."

A dry laugh escapes me, and even Logan cracks a smile.

"I know who you're talking about," I say, "And the answer is an even more a no."

Carter frowns. "Alright. If you don't go to the party, we'll bring the party to you." Swiftly, he dashes out of the room before I have the chance to stop him. I hear the downstairs door open and close, and irritation bubbles up inside me that he'd ignored me and gone to fetch the girls anyway. However, a few minutes later, not nearly long enough to make it to the guest house and back, I hear the door open and close again. Carter reappears in the doorway with an unopened bottle of Gaergan port.

"Been saving this since my mom sent it to me for my birthday," he says, catching his breath. He wrenches off the cork and takes a swig from it, not bothering with the glasses Logan has retrieved from my adjacent office.

He smacks his lips. "Hell yeah. That'll do just fine."

Logan takes the small square bottle from him and then pours two glasses to the brim. He keeps one for himself and slides the other across the table to me.

"May our bonds never break," Logan says, holding up a glass.

"And may we burn until the last breath," Carter and I echo the old druadan soldier's blessing.

I tip back the glass, draining it in two gulps. The heat emanates through me, coalescing with the excessive surge of the bond I've neglected to satisfy.

The burn of the sweet wine is nothing compared to the cooling sensation radiating from the connection that links me with the others. My eyes drift to the back of Logan's hand as he sets down his glass to refill it. Unlike Carter and I, two crescent scars overlap each other on his hand — one older and gray, the other fresh and pink.

He catches me staring, and he passes me a silent warning: tonight's discussion is about my bond, *not* his.

In the distance, the deep rumble of the stallions vibrates the air; the bond, like a thin string, tugs at my chest, and I know Shadowmane is leading the haunting chorus. It's a sound I've grown to love, as familiar and reassuring as the hills that absorb their calls. The stallions are like us, bound to each other and their collective strength, yet each fiercely their own.

For a moment, I savor their company. Logan and Carter don't need to say anything; their presence is enough. Most riders share a collective bond just from their druadan, but because the three of us were friends before we'd been marked, it means ours is uncharacteristically strong. It's also the reason I'd been able to brim for as long as I had without flaring out.

Still, a strong bond only tempered it for so long. I needed to get a grip on it. I'd request a meeting with her in the morning first thing. Then, I'd have Carla clear my schedule and be with Shadowmane for the rest of the day. The storm isn't over, far from it, but for the first time in a long time, I feel like maybe, just maybe, I can weather it.

Twelve

Sitting in Heath's office, I try my best to look fierce in the station-issued navy blouse and black leggings.

The morning sun streams in through the large windows behind him, and I'm acutely aware of how hot it's going to get. I've messed up. I know it. We'd avoided each other almost entirely except for the few exchanges during meetings since I'd snuck into his room. Perhaps he'd had a change of heart? Perhaps he *was* going to fire me and send me back to Delford. *Why* else would Heath call me for an early morning private meeting?

"Breaking into another staff member's room is a violation of security and privacy, Ms. Corsair," Heath begins, his voice steady but weighted with an undercurrent of warning.

I bite the inside of my cheek. He'd said, Ms. Corsair, *not* Brigid.

Yep, totally getting fired.

"This station is small. There are thirty-nine full-time employees, and we're a tight-knit community, even bordering on family, yet boundaries still exist. While I understand your desire to play detective regarding your sister's disappearance, invading another person's personal space is a violation of our rules here. Consequences must be enacted."

I tilt my chin, feeling like I'd been called to the principal's office and was about to get expelled. That was it, four days I'd last here. Four goddamn days.

I've failed you, Sharice.

Heath lets out a heavy sigh, his dark eyes intensely studying my every move. I can feel the weight of his gaze on me as he speaks. "Which is why I'm going to extend your probationary period by another thirty days."

The breath whooshes from my lungs, and it's a struggle to keep my body perfectly still. I keep my face a mask to hide the flood of relief coursing through my veins.

"You will not receive your raise or be eligible for any additional bonuses until the thirty days have transpired."

"I understand," I say. No raise? No bonuses? Fine. I can handle that. I still have my job and access to Sharice's computer, her comm, and the station. It's not good, but it could be so much worse.

Heath looks visibly relieved that I'm not challenging him. "Additionally, the training arena is off-limits to you during private sessions. The novices are on the verge of forming bonds. Outside presence can be a distraction."

Fucking Logan. "All right," I say, smiling sweetly. "I'll be sure to do so." Curiosity piqued, I ask, "Am I allowed to photograph any of the bonding?" In truth, it's a professional concern for the sake of answering questions and posting on the Network without violating the NDA. "What makes you think it'll happen soon?"

Heath's posture stiffens. "This group of novices has been with us for three months. Bonds will form within the three to six-month window. If not, the rider will be matched to a different mount. After two failed attempts, they're dismissed from the station—with a severance package, of course."

Two tries. That's it. Damn. I wonder what happened to the riders who washed out? Did they go back to school? Marry? Or perhaps counted it as a sign that they were destined for a long life doing something else, like accounting.

Sensing the shift in conversation from Heath reprimanding me to back to actual business, I press on. More than ever, I need to get back on his good side and show him that while I might have taken this job initially to find my sister, I *was* capable of doing both. "So, say, they *do* bond. Is there any warning before? Like signs or indications?"

He sniffs, almost as if he's weighing whether to trust me with this information. "Riders just know. It's different for everyone, but usually, they'll awake in the middle of the night, drawn to their mount. When we think a mark is about to occur, we set alarms on their doors to be there for support."

"Support?" I press.

Heath's eyes appraise me as if deciding on how much to reveal before he shows me the back of his hand with a similar half-circle scar as Carter had shown me. "Sometimes riders see things, feel things—visions of friends or long-dead relatives— that can lead them into danger."

"So, you'll be there to stop them from jumping off a cliff because they saw the ghost of their grandfather?"

"Yes. Something like that," he says. "So, it's up to the rest of the other riders to sense the initial stirrings of the bond and guide them safely—to their druadan."

The new employee orientation had provided more information than the general Network could, explaining the ten-year life expectancy for riders after bonding and the reasoning behind there never being girl riders. Druadan stallions only bonded with men.

"You said before one of the novices is close? I'd love to do a profile interview and showcase with him for the newsletter if it's alright with you?"

Heath laces his fingers together on his desk. "I'll speak with him first, and if they agree, I'd prefer the Novice trainer, Logan, to be present, but I don't see why it'd be a problem."

I plaster a grin on my face as if pleased by the idea that I'll have to spend more time with the asshole.

Heath stands, apparently ending the meeting. While he's a presence when sitting, when he stands, he's the embodiment of authority. His dark hair falls gracefully over his strong brow, framing his piercing brown eyes. His black collared shirt hugs his toned shoulders and highlights the chiseled lines of his jaw and trim waist. The morning light plays upon his features, further emphasizing his striking profile, and I find myself stammering as I fight my way free of the chair.

"Okay, then," I say, copying him and getting to my feet. "Thank you again for..." I hesitate, trying to find the right words. "For giving me another chance."

I step behind the chair and toss my hands, and a nervous laugh escapes me. "Guess my dreams of being a cat burglar are officially dashed, huh?" *Stop talking, Brigid.*

The corner of his mouth twitches, and for a fraction of a second, it almost looks like he's going to smile, but then it's gone. "Sorry to disappoint you," he says.

My hand rests on the doorknob, and I'm almost out when he says, "I am sorry about your sister. Truly. I hope you find the answers you're looking for."

The metal of the handle feels cool against my hand, and I

glance quickly at him. His steel-gray eyes lock with mine, a sincerity swirling in them.

"Thank you," I say and leave.

OUTSIDE, THE HEAT IS STIFLING, AND THE DRY AIR SNATCHES breath from my lungs. By the time I make it back to my cottage, I'm drenched.

I swap my work attire for a sundress dotted with tiny violets. The last of my freeze-dried meals lingers in the cabinet, and I add water and heat the pasta and veggies for a mid-morning meal. Outside, the wind begins to pick up, carrying reddish-brown dust along with it. Perfect. Looks like I'm bunkering down with my laptop. I pour myself some lemonade and bring it and my bowl of steaming noodles to the kitchen table. I set up a workstation with my computer and switch on my favorite music to keep focused, determined to make the most of a hot, dusty day.

"Thank you so my for your inquiry." I type in the message to a druadan rights activist with the grammar skills of a kinder-gartner. "We appreciate feedback from all of our supporters. The health and welfare of our druadans is our highest priority, and your request will be forwarded to—" But before I can complete the sentence, the screen goes black. Dammit. I knew I shouldn't have trusted the battery indicator. I shove out of my chair to fetch the charging cord from the bedroom when the lamps and light fixtures flicker. Once, twice, then go out.

The power cuts out. No music, no cooling fans—just silence and growing darkness. I grab my comm off the table to call Carla, but it's as dead as the lights. Great.

I move to the window, peering out into the bleak dust storm, unable to see more than a foot beyond. What if something happened at the main house, a fire or something, and that's why my comm wasn't working? I slip on my short, ankle-high boots and step outside, peering through the dust-choked air to assess the situation. I squint, feeling the grit pummel my face.

I can barely make out the dark outline of the main house and see no flames or smoke. Next, I hold a hand against my mouth and nose and look at the exhibition hall and, finally, the barn, which is closest. A bright yellow maintenance truck is parked by the southern wall, and a guy in a yellow jumpsuit is wrestling with a broken post, apparently attempting to fix a gate.

From the haze, a dark form emerges a few feet from him. It's smaller than the others I've seen, and I assume it's one of the younger, unbonded druadans. It has a coat of melted chocolate with white spots dotting its legs and neck.

The man turns, shouting at it and waving his arms to keep it from going through the opening, but it's no use. The young druadan charges, forcing the man to leap out of the way or be trampled.

I stand frozen, unable to process what is happening. A druadan is loose. Freed in this fucking storm.

Without thinking, my legs are already propelling me through the dust storm.

The wind viciously whips as I fight my way through the brewing dust storm, each step an immense effort. I pull my scarf up over my nose and mouth but still end up choking on the swirling grit assaulting my lungs. My eyes water from the stinging particles, blurring my vision.

I stagger onward, focused only on putting one foot in front of the other. The howling gusts batter me from all sides, threatening to knock me off balance. I have to lean into the powerful wind just to inch forward. Strange noises seem to come at me from all directions - roaring, whining, groaning.

I'm nearly blind in the brown haze, forced to rely on four days of memory.

South - the colt ran to the south. But it's impossible to get my bearings without any landmarks. What if I'm walking straight toward one of the treacherous rocky outcroppings along the perimeter? One misstep could break an ankle; another could break my neck.

Fear surges through me. I could easily get lost out here, swallowed up by the raging storm. The stinging sand burns my skin, but I don't dare stop moving. If I stumble or fall, I may never get back up. The only thing keeping panic at bay is the thought of reaching the relative safety of the base.

The instant I see the colt, everything seems to happen in slow motion. Fear roots me in place, even as my mind screams at my legs to run. I try to will my frozen muscles to move, but it's no use—I'm paralyzed as the wild colt stalks toward me.

It circles, eyes feral, teeth bared and gleaming. I've become prey, and I can already feel its hot breath on my skin. Adrenaline finally overrides my paralysis; I stumble back, heart hammering, as the colt snaps its teeth and charges.

I open my mouth to scream, but the sound dies in my throat, swallowed by the angry roar of the wind. Dust swirls around me, blurring my vision.

This is it. I'm going to die here. I was a fool. I didn't belong here.

Out of the haze, a figure appears, rushing toward me— Carter. Before I can even process what's happening, he throws himself between me and the raging colt. I watch in stunned disbelief as he grabs the leather halter, wrestling to gain control as the colt thrashes and kicks up debris.

A strange humming noise amplifies around me, vibrating through the very core of my being. Disoriented, I push through what feels like a swarm of buzzing bees in slow motion and scramble to my feet.

The humming intensifies. There's a rhythm, a pattern, and for a second, I swear I hear the word *'Danger.'*

I blink, shaking my head as Carter turns to face me, the whites of the colt's eyes visible as it jigs sideways under his grip.

"Are you hurt?" he yells over the howling wind.

I shake my head.

"Okay. Stay close and follow me."

He leads the colt into the storm, and I keep my steps in time with his, ensuring he separates me and the colt.

Slowly, the adrenaline recedes, leaving me shaken and unsteady. The world around me feels muted and distorted.

Carter leads the wayward colt into one of the empty quarantine stalls of the barn, securing the latch tightly. I lean against the stable wall, still overcome with shakiness now that the adrenaline surge has faded.

Heavy footsteps echo down the corridor as Logan storms in, looking angrier than I've ever seen him. His face is tight with fury, eyebrows drawn together, and the muscles under his broad jaw are clenched. "What the actual fuck happened out there?".

I stand my ground, even as my knees feel like jelly. "One of the colts escaped, so I ran after it."

His nostrils flare as his towering form looms over me. He almost never attended meetings, and besides the few times I observed training, this was the first time I'd been this close to him. He rarely looked at me, and when he did, his gray eyes cut through me with a mixture of disdain and annoyance, as if my very presence was a minor inconvenience he preferred to avoid

I look up from where I only reach his chest. Heath and Carter are undeniably fit, muscular, and wildly attractive, but Logan is a giant. I knew that his hands could easily snap my neck. I clench my fists tighter, my nails digging into the tender skin of my palms, refusing to show any sign of weakness in front of him.

"God dammit, blondie. Do you have a fucking death wish? You could have been killed."

"I was thinking that a druadan was in danger and that I could help it!" I shout back. Our eyes lock, neither willing to back down.

Carter steps partially in front of me and rests a hand on Logan's chest. "Easy, Logan. It was spooked and near the canyon's edge. What Brigid did saved it."

Logan glowers but seems to accept the explanation. He mutters something about recklessness as he storms off and knocks an empty feed pail out of one of the novice's hands. It goes clattering across the ground.

Carter watches him disappear around the corner as the tawny-haired teen hurries to pick up the pail.

Carter's forehead creases in concern. "Don't worry about him. Logan takes the safety here very seriously."

He puts a gentle hand on my shoulder. "You're okay, though? That was a close one out there."

I nod, still a bit shaken by Logan's outburst and the whole ordeal.

Carter gives my shoulder a comforting squeeze. "Come on, let's get cleaned up and something to drink."

I nod, and as we head out of the barn, I have to shield myself against the relentless wind.

We hurry to my cottage, which is blessedly not far from the barn, but I can't stop thinking—Why did that colt hesitate? It had me flat on my back; it could have easily trampled me and ripped out my throat, but it didn't. Why? Maybe I was imagining it. Everything had happened so fast, and the dust made it hard to see things clearly.

All I knew for sure was—whether it be fate or luck—Carter *had* been there in the nick of time to save me.

Thirteen

I brush the dust from my hair as I follow Brigid into her cottage. My heart is still pounding from our run-in with that damn yearling tearing through the canyon in the middle of a dust storm.

Since Obsidanzia is unbonded, there was no way to communicate with him, but it'd been obvious something had spooked him.

We were lucky to capture him without any injuries to him or us, but the chase had left both of us caked in grim and a layer of crimson dirt.

The storm knocked the power out, and a lone battery-powered wall sconce in the kitchen is all that lights the interior of her cottage. The dim light casts Brigid's face in shadow, and I can see a weariness in her eyes. I can't stop replaying those seconds when the yearling charged past Brigid, nearly trampling her. I can't help but feel awe in her presence, the way she didn't hesitate, driven by a need to help even against her own self-preservation.

I close the door to the howling wind, and the two of us stand in silence.

She peers up at me, and a red dust tints her pale lashes and hair.

"Thank you," she says, her voice a whisper in the near darkness.

"I've never seen anyone do what you did today," I start, my voice breaking the silence that envelops us. "You ran into that storm without a second thought."

Brigid laughs softly, and I feel that stirring deep inside me. The way I want to capture that sound is so I can replay it over and over again. "I couldn't just stand by," she says. "It was clear he was scared and frantic."

Her words, so simple yet profound, draw me in further. I find myself moving closer, compelled by a growing fascination I've tried to ignore. But here, in the dim light, with the adrenaline still coursing through me, I can't hold back. "There's something about you, Brigid," I confess, my heart racing. "Ever since I first saw you, I've been drawn to you. I can't seem to get enough."

Her sapphire blue eyes meet mine, holding a depth of emotion that takes my breath away. I brush my thumb against her lower lip, marveling at how perfect they feel under my touch. "I wasn't sure before," I confess. "But after today, I can't ignore it anymore."

The space between us diminishes until there's no distance left to close. I kiss her, a gentle press of lips that speaks of the days I'd fantasized about this moment. She leans closer, deepening the kiss and fueled by the intensity of the moment and the undeniable pull between us.

When we part, the air between us is charged with the release of pent-up energy of the bond. I sense Ember's presence, his consciousness awoken by my arousal.

I cup her cheek, refusing to break our connection.

Brigid's gaze is steady on mine, her voice soft but firm. "Carter, you made me feel welcome here, like I belonged, from the very first day. What you said about being unable to get enough…" she pauses, biting her lower lip, and my already half-hard cock, turns to iron. "I feel it, too."

Hearing her admit her feelings, the echo of my own, it's overwhelming. A mix of relief and exhilaration floods through me. "Brigid, I—"

She presses her finger to my lips, interrupting me. "When I was the dust storm, I acted on instinct. I knew it was right. And it's the same way I feel when I'm with you. I don't want to over-think. I just want to be in this moment with you."

Her words, so fearless and mirroring my own emotions, sweep me over the edge, and I find myself kissing her again. This time, we're not gentle, and our lips collide. Grit coats our lips, but neither of us cares. Her lips are soft yet unyielding. A spark ignites, like electricity where we touch, and I curve a hand around the nape of her neck, drawing her closer. She moans into my mouth, and I growl in response. With my tongue, I coax her to part her lips. When she does, I swipe my tongue carefully across her lower lip, tasting her, feeling her. Suddenly, her tongue meets mine, and we are intertwined, bound together.

At this moment, there's nothing more I want. The power outage, the storm, the dirt on our skin, all of it fades into insignificance.

But it's not enough. God, how I want more. I *need* more. The bond hums in response to my erect cock. Soon, I'm not going to be able to stop if this continues.

The overactive bond causes me to snarl as I break the kiss.

She stares up at me breathlessly. Her lips are swollen, and she has a questioning look in her eyes.

"What is it?"

"Tell me you want this."

Even in the ambient light, a faint blush touches her cheeks as she nods.

"No," I say. "I need to hear it."

Her blush deepens. "I want this."

My pulse thunders in my eardrums. The shred of self-control I'd been clinging to shatters, and I draw her to me.

She bends to my touch but then braces her arms against my chest. "We're filthy." she laughs.

"I don't mind."

She rolls her eyes. "I do," she ruffles the front of my hair, and I feel the dirt shake loose.

"Fine," I say. "But without power, there's only the reserve tank of hot water."

"Are you implying we share?" she says skeptically.

"What happened to not overthinking things?" I ask with a sly grin, unable to resist teasing her. Her gorgeous blush deepens.

Her mouth twitches as if she's trying to hide a smile. "You're impossible."

Then, we're kissing again as we make our way in the dark to the bathroom. We barely have time to kick off our shoes before we're both standing in the stone basin, still fully clothed. My hands roam, exploring, touching. She reaches behind me, and instantly, cold water douses us.

She gasps, and I press her face to mine, drinking it in. Cold transitions to warm, and her body relaxes. The water clings to our clothes, making them stick to our skin, and suddenly, the playful atmosphere is charged with an intense, urgent kind of intimacy.

My hand slides down her neck to the tops of her breasts, and I ease lower, gently cupping it through the wet fabric.

This needs to come off. *Now.*

Trying to peel off the wet fabric becomes our challenge. Our laughter at our struggles echoes around us as our fingers fumble with the clinging clothes. Every accidental brush of skin, every shared look, sends waves of anticipation coursing through me.

Anticipation between us keeps us from rushing, savoring each success. Her adorable wriggling out of her leggings that we toss aside. Then her fingers run across my stomach, helping me lift off my shirt. I drop the soaked fabric to the ground and can see the desire in her blue eyes as they trace over my bare chest and arms.

"Your turn," I murmur, and my hands eagerly work to untangle her wet shirt, exposing her breasts adorned with a pink-laced bra. Her nipples harden under my gaze, and I can't resist tracing them with my fingers. Her giggles dissolve into breathless moans, and I pull her face to mine, wanting to capture the sound. We stand there, looking at each other.

Coyly, she slips the straps of her bra down, and I get my first full glimpse of her exposed breasts.

Smooth skin, and her rosy pink nipples. They're the most perfect set of tits I've ever seen. Master Rider's honor.

They're perfection.

"Like what you see?" Her voice is laced with amusement.

"Fuck yes, I do," I growl.

She takes my hand and presses it to her chest. My fingers caress them, cupping them as I tease her nipple. I'm nearly panting with want. Fuck. I want her.

I adjust myself, the growing erection becoming uncomfortable in waterlogged jeans.

I reach down to undo the fly when the lights in the bathroom flash on.

Soon after Heath's voice draws both of our attentions.

"Brigid," Heath calls out. "Power's back on. I heard about the incident with the yearling and wanted to check if you're all right?"

I hear her mutter, "Shit. Shit. Shit."

"We can invite him to join us?" I ask.

She gives me a playful swat, but I don't miss the mischievous glint in her eyes.

Babe actually considered it.

"Yeah," Brigid says, sounding a little breathless. "I'm okay. I—" Before she can finish, I drop my hand between her legs and gently rake a finger across the thin fabric of her panties, feeling the delicious heat of her. She bites her lip, stifling a moan.

"I'm just…shower," she stammers, "Give me a minute."

From between her legs, I see her looking down at me, trying to hold back laughter by biting her lip. "Do you have any shame?"

"When it comes to you? Not a single ounce." I lean in closer, letting my hot breath whisper over the increasing heat between her legs.

Brigid sucks in a sharp breath and purses her mouth into a tight line. "We should stop. Rain check, okay?"

Reluctantly, I ease my hand away. I caress her cheek, enjoying the flush of her skin.

"Promise?"

She grins. "Promise."

Hastily, she turns off the shower and steps out. Taking a towel from the shelf, she then wraps it around herself. The skin on her neck and shoulder are flushed with the heat of the shower, among other reasons.

Panic drains the blood from her face as Heath calls out her name again.

"I've told you before," I say, comforting her. "Heath won't mind if that's what you're worried about." Well, under normal circumstances, he wouldn't mind, but in Brigid's case, he might have a few opinions regarding it.

"No," Brigid says quickly, then changes course. I study Brigid's eyes for a moment, wondering if she's still playing me or if there's a genuine feeling between us now. I'm not an idiot. I know this whole thing between us, starting from the hot springs, is a ploy to gain my trust and try to get me to reveal some secret about her sister, but Heath had wanted us to keep a close eye on her. And I definitely was keeping her close.

"If you're okay, Carla and I have some things to discuss with you that can't wait," Heath says, sounding impatient from the other side of the door. "Since the power is back on. We want you to weigh in on the entertainment itinerary and promotional interviews for the fundraiser if you have time this evening?"

She glances at me, still standing in the shower. "Persistent, isn't he?"

"You have no idea."

A deep crease forms between her brows. "Please, can we keep this secret, just for now?"

I flash her a grin, scratching my stubbled cheek. "All right. But just for now."

"Thank you," she says. "Just stay here, and I'll try and get him to leave."

She tightens the towel around her and steps out of the bathroom.

Soon, silence hits me, and I'm left standing half-dressed in soaked clothes and a flagging erection like some gardener hiding from the husband who came home early.

What the actual fuck is happening right now. Women in Delford practically crawled over each other for the privilege of telling their friends they rode the Master Rider Carter James train.

I'm a trophy, a goddamn badge of honor they can brag about over brunch or cocktails.

But with Brigid, it's *I* who is vying for her attention. There's something about her that I can't figure out, and it's driving me crazy. It's like reading a book with half the pages ripped out. One minute, she has the "it's-just-a-job" attitude, and the next, she's charging headlong into a dust storm, trying to catch runaway druadan colts as if her life depended on it. *Who does that?*

"Ah, sorry," Heath says, his voice muted through the door. "Logan told me about the yearling during the storm and wanted to see if you were okay."

She's just fine, bro. Well, she was until you got all controlling.

"I appreciate it," I hear Brigid say, "I'm good. Just a little shaken is all."

There's a long pause. My ears strain to pick up any of their conversation. Maybe she's coming up with some excuse that she'll be running late and joining him later? Or wants to call it a night? Whatever she needed to, so she could stay, and I could finish what I damn well wanted to.

What I knew she wanted me to.

There's the click of the door closing, then more muffled words as I imagine her leading Heath away from the bathroom.

The voices fade, and I hear the front door opening and closing.

Are you kidding me right now?

She left.

Just fucking left me. Standing half naked, nearly freezing to death in her bathroom.

But the minutes tick by without her returning. Feeling like a complete tool, I finally step out of the shower. The cold tiles press against my feet, driving home the chill of my own confusion. "You're losing it, man," I mutter to myself as I gather the soggy mess of a shirt, socks, and shoes.

I make my way through her tiny living room and out the front door. If they're still on the front porch, I don't give a shit. I'd promised to keep it on the down low, but that didn't mean I'd bend over backward. If she was ashamed of me, or embarrassed or whatever the hell it was, she wanted to keep Heath from knowing what we were doing, fine. But I wasn't going to play that game. I wasn't into bullshit.

However, there's no sight of them when I step into the chilly evening air. I pick up my pace, heading to the main house. The bushes that line the pathway rustle in the wind, and the moon casts a soft glow over the buildings of the station, but as I hustle through the biting wind, all I've got to look forward to is a night alone and a head full of questions, which, in my case, is never a good thing.

I change course and go toward Logan's cabin by the front gate.

He'll be out most of the night checking the perimeter fencing and any downed power cables, so he wouldn't mind if I borrowed something from his liquor cabinet.

Fourteen

BRIGID

he fundraiser is two weeks away, and my schedule's already threatening to implode.

I literally can not make any more hours in the day to get everything done in time. The meeting with Carla and Heath still buzzing in my head, I leave the main house.

A charity auction with druadan antiquities, old weapons, and commissioned art of legendary druadan and their riders. It's a logistical nightmare and a PR dream all rolled into one.

My thoughts flicker to the file on my sister's computer, still sitting there like a stain I can't get out. I used to think the station held answers, clues to... *something*. But now? Now it feels like I'm chasing ghosts.

The trail's gone cold, and my frustration is hitting boiling

120

point. Maybe this whole thing was a colossal waste of time. Maybe after the fundraiser, I should resign and learn to live with the truth that Sharice is gone and never coming back.

My thoughts drift to Carter and me in the bathroom. Okay, so maybe I didn't need to rush the resignation letter so fast. There were other perks to working here.

Him being a very big one. A pulse of heat burns between my legs. He'd smelled amazing, like the fresh air, not the filtered kind with the artificial scents added, but true, pure air. I shiver, hugging myself as I recall the feeling of his lips against mine. The heat from his breath. God, it had been hot. Turn on hot, yes, but also physically, like *hot* like hotter than the steam in the spa.

I shove my hands in the pockets of my dress and keep walking. I felt awful leaving him in the shower like that, but after I had gotten dressed, Heath was insistent that I meet him and Carla for the meeting. Since I'd already been reprimanded once for sneaking into his room, I didn't feel like I had the option to tell him no.

I look up at the sky at constellations and stars you never see in Delford. Memories of Dane and me laying in one of the fishing boats, staring up at them drift forward. We'd spend hours lying together, and we'd call out the names of them.

On my seventeenth birthday he'd told me he loved me and that night he'd been my first.

And how *fucked* up that all had ended.

Up until that time, my childhood was never this hectic, never *this* complicated. It was just the southern coast, and every day had been the same. Network schooling in the morning. Tide came in. Lunch with Mom and Sharice or chores around the lab. Tide went out.

I wonder if I should call Mom. Just a casual chat, nothing heavy. Sharice and her shared a stronger bond. Their conversations about air purification and hypothesis testing lasted hours into the night when they thought I was asleep.

I remember the sunny, windswept beaches and the cries of gulls wheeling overhead. My sister Sharice and I would spend our free time after the makeshift school they'd set up for the other researcher's kids, combing the sand for shells and polished stones. Further down the beach sat rows of domed enclosures—small transparent habitats where Mom would carefully monitor air and soil samples, collecting data for her ecology projects.

While Sharice was always eager to help Mom with her experiments, I'd preferred to explore on my own or lounge on the shore, reading and daydreaming about traveling to other continents. The rhythm of the waves had been hypnotic, and I'd stared endlessly at the horizon, imagining the beaches the ocean touched.

As I walk, it hits me. Maybe the only answers I'm looking for aren't in Sharice's computer but in the very ground, I'm walking on, here at the station. Maybe she'd left a clue, a sign, something that she knew only *I* would notice.

I quicken my pace. There's a night security team patrolling, and I'd learned that it took about twenty minutes for them to walk the perimeter.

A prickle of alertness dances up my arms. It's so strange. It's almost like I can *feel* them, the unsettling hum of the druadans in the barn, like a magnetic pull—a shared anticipation hanging in the air that draws me to them.

My shoes crunch on the gravel as I approach the giant building. The closer I get, the more my senses go on alert. The hairs on my arms stand to attention as if charged by the air.

I shouldn't do this. It's the middle of the night, and I *should* go back to my cottage.

I'm already here, and what if I'm right? What if Sharice did leave a clue here for me? I'd never get another chance like this to be in here unescorted and alone. I'll make it quick, five minutes tops, then leave.

Decision made, I push open the heavy door I step into the dimly lit barn. A few of the stallions stick their heads into the aisle, their eyes meeting mine. Since my first day, I'd been timidly curious about them. However, after getting up close and personal with the dagger-like teeth and mind-numbing speed they could move during the duststorm, I am *extremely* wary of them now. I keep to the center of the aisleway, giving them a respectful distance.

As I walk further in, my mind starts to wander to Sharice, my sister. She was the scientific one, analytical, grounded. If she felt something was off, what would she notice that I'm not seeing? What would she leave for me—some sort of message or sign that only I would understand? I'd cracked her comm with Bellion. I can do it again.

Stepping as lightly as I can, I pass by the colt that had escaped earlier Obsidanzia and see his head in the corner as if asleep. Here in the dark, with his head down and tail slowly swishing, he looks nothing like the crazed creature with bared teeth.

I continue down the aisleway, seeing more of the stallions are all in similar positions while they sleep. My eyes scan the wooden walls of the barn, half-expecting to see some obscure writing etched in the stone, but instead, I hear the creak of a door opening. Heart leaping into my throat, I slip into one of the empty stalls and crouch down in the shadowy corner.

It's probably a maintenance person or a novice out doing late chores, but still, I don't want to get caught. There are too many questions I won't have answers to that will make them suspicious. First and foremost is why I, the PR person, am in the stallion barn in the middle of the night.

I crouch, holding my breath, and listen. The barn is a hollow of shadows and silence. No distant call of the desert jackals. No rustling of hooves in the sandy bedding.

Just stifling emptiness.

Something's off.

I'm not losing my mind; I *know* I heard something.

Shit. I should go. I've stayed here too long.

I cautiously stand up and check the coast is clear. That's when I see them—two eyes, like shards of emerald, peering at me from between the metal bars of the stall. My skin prickles at the sight, like someone's marching a row of needles down my spine.

The stallion stares at me. I'd seen them at the performances, in training, and out in the storm. Druadans are unfathomably strong and fast, and I have little faith in the aged brick wall and metal bars separating us.

Watching me with those eerie green eyes, he breathes slow, rhythmic puffs that fog the air between us. There's a momentary vibration, a pulse that ripples through the space like a tuning fork striking a shrill note I didn't know existed.

I pull back, instinct forcing me to put distance between myself and it.

A droplet of something wet lands on my cheek. First, it's cool, then searing hot, like a wasp just stung me. I hiss in pain and wipe it away. The burning sensation lingers, a red-hot stamp that makes my head swim for a moment. I look at my hand. A clear, sticky liquid with glowing particles coats my finger. With every second, the burning worsens, and I quickly wipe it on my dress. The bio-luminescent glow fades as the fabric absorbs it. Pulse hammering in my ears, I do the next thing I'm most terrified to do.

I look up.

Suspended on the ceiling ten feet up is a gelatinous creature, with no eyes, no mouth, only a shifting form of tentacles speckled with the glowing gel that dropped on me.

I scurry backward and press my back against the wall, but I'm not quick enough. The thing falls from the wooden beams and lands with a plop in front of me. It's fast, and I barely have time to blink before one of the arm-sized tendrils whips out and wraps around my ankle, pulling me down. Pain erupts from my tailbone as I land on the floor, and an uncomfortable tingling sensation shoots up my leg from where the tentacles contact my bare skin.

I scream, clawing at the sand dragging me down, desperate for any way to escape. The burn intensifies, and another tendril lashes around my right wrist, lurching me forward and nearly pulling my arm from its socket. I'm five feet from it.

Four.

Three.

Two.

The air vibrates, rattling my eyes in their sockets, and I have to clamp my teeth down to keep them from chattering.

Suddenly, an enormous dark form materializes in front of me.

Galaxian.

The stallion rears, mane and tail glowing as it slams its sharp hooves down, hard, onto…nothing. There is nothing, and yet I hear a squelch, like the sound of boots in mud.

Preparing to bolt out of the barn, the already strong vibrations intensify further, growing to a skull-splitting bang, bang, bang. Ozone tinges the air, prickling my nose, and something invisible takes shape between Galaxian's front legs. A multi-legged, strange thing appears for a split second before Galaxian rears up again.

Again and again, the druadan stomps at the ground, each strike sending splatters of bio-luminescent gore until the walls, its front legs, and I are coated in it.

Galaxian lowers his head, lunging at the open air with bared teeth, and the high-pitched squelch grows louder as pieces of the translucent goo smear his face and mouth.

Something whistles in the air beside me, and there's a wet smack of something landing in the alleyway. The humming subsides as Galaxian's belly heaves from the assault, apparently after having either killed the creature or fled. I collapse to my knees. My wrist and ankle sting like I've fallen into a hornet's nest while the rest of me feels drained. My head swims, and the world shifts to the left like a drunken bender.

The ground rises to meet me, and I collide face-first with the pink sand bedding. Four tan-colored druadan legs, splattered with glowing green slime are the last thing I see before the black speckles in my vision coalesce, and then I see nothing.

Fifteen

LOGAN

The buzzing alert on my comm jerks me awake.

Bleary-eyed, I scan the message: Motion detected in the barn. I sit up on my bed and flip on the video feed, cycling through the views of the aisle way, the turnout pens, and then the twelve stalls. Everyone is accounted for until I get to Galaxian's. It's empty. No, that can't be right. I know I put him in the barn for the night. A sinking feeling settles in my gut. My right hand flexes, testing if I'd detected anything through the bond.

Nothing.

Heath is brimming, and here I am, getting barely a whisper. A second bond is always weaker, but we'd hoped it'd balance out since Galaxian is a descendant of my first.

Apparently, we'd been wrong. Marshal had told me to be patient. It'd only been a few months, and it would take time for the old bond to fade and allow the new one to take root.

I, however, am not a patient man.

I pull on a black shirt and cargo pants in record time, adrenaline replacing any lingering drowsiness. Obsidanzia's escape yesterday, and now Galaxian?

If he was hurt, I *should* have felt something. Which meant

one of two things: either he wasn't hurt, or my bond was too weak to pick up on it. I grit my teeth and take the steps two at a time down, passing by Carter's room. He's sprawled face down on the unmade bed, his snores loud enough to wake dead. At least one of us has our bond in check.

I burst out of the apartment, crossing the station grounds at a sprint. The night is a blanket of darkness, punctured only by the dim lights scattered around the property. My boots hit the ground in a rhythmic thud, each step amplifying the urgency of the situation.

I skid to a halt as I reach the barn. A clear, gooey substance streaks the stones on the aisle way. My initial thought is that some novice is going to get their ass chewed for spilling the special spray wax we use to shine the druadan's hooves, but when I see Galaxian sauntering down the aisleway — glowing splatters marring his chest and legs like he took a dive into a pool of iridescent mud—all bets are off.

"What the fuck?" The words escape my mouth. Through our bond, I reach out to Galaxian, scanning for any signs of injury. I rest a hand on his face, pushing into the tether that links us. The air in my lungs vibrates. *"Bad worm,"* he says. *"I fight. I kill."*

"You kill what?" I whisper, my voice mimicking the frequency.

"Bad worm," he repeats with a stomp of his hoof.

"Bad worm did this?"

Galaxian tilts his head sideways, giving me one of his 'Are you stupid' looks. His predecessor, Galaxyla, was the poster boy for respect. He'd never questioned any of my commands. But he's gone now, and from the looks of it, I'd nearly lost Galaxian, too. I run my hands over his legs.

A tingling, almost burning sensation prickles my fingers as I touch the glowing spots.

"Are you hurt?" I ask and sense a gentle tug on the bond that indicates no.

Satisfied, I move to the center of the barn, intending to take a halter from the rack, so I rinse Galaxian off and put him away, but then I see her. Brigid, her white hair gleaming like spilled moonlight around her face from where she lay on her side in one of the stalls. Her eyes are closed, her body crumpled in a way that shoots panic straight through my veins.

For a heart-stopping moment, I fear the worst—that Galaxian's 'kill' referred to her, and the 'worm' is a poor translation on my part of 'woman.' Abandoning the halter, I dart to Brigid's side and kneel, checking for signs of life. Her pulse is there, thankfully, but her face is twisted in discomfort like she's battling demons in her sleep.

I gently shake her. *Please don't be fucking dead, blondie.*

She doesn't stir, and my throat cinches closed. Glancing back at Galaxian, I catch his eye as he stands outside the stall.

"What happened? Is she 'the bad worm'?"

Galaxian twists his head to the right, staring down the aisle way, and perks his ears. Another gentle tug on the bond. *No.* My eardrums vibrate, hearing his low voice reverberate in my head. *"Bad worm gone."*

My fingers skip along her arms and face, examining for any signs of injury. There's a red welt on her wrist and a similar but deeper one on her ankle. They *could* be a druadan bite. I sigh and rest my hands on my thighs, hating the question I'm about to ask next. Because the yes or no answer could be the end for Galaxian and for me. Druadans are dangerous, and accidents are frequent. Kicks, bites, and scrapes are all risks anytime we work with something that had been originally created to be a predator.

However, if a druadan kills a human, no matter the reason, they're immediately euthanized, along with any living progeny. Their DNA samples are also incinerated, removing the line forever. And their rider? Dismissed and disgraced. No pension, all records wiped clean.

I grind my teeth together and whisper the hardest question I've ever asked through the bond. "Did you hurt her?"

Galaxian snorts, tossing his mane, a clear sign of agitation. *"No, touch her. I fight. Hurt worm."*

I sigh, relief washing over me but still leaving a residue of new questions. What the hell could be a 'bad worm'? And how could it have made those wounds on Brigid but not harmed Galaxian? And why was her hair glowing like that? For now, though, the questions have to wait. I've got a potentially injured druadan and an unconscious employee to deal with.

I maneuver out of the stall, take the halter off the wall, and toss it over Galaxian's neck. Then, I lead him to the neighboring stall and, once secured, release him. "I'll be back soon to clean you," I whisper through the bond, leaning my head close to his ear. Hot breaths waft over my hand where he'd marked me three months ago.

Then I slide the door shut and return to Brigid. Her hair still glows, more faintly, though, like a battery that's slowly dying. Easing my arms beneath her, I lift her. She's surprisingly light, or maybe I'm just used to scooping novices off the arena floor when they had a disagreement with their stallion and lost.

I rush out of the barn with her, heading to the med bay before thinking better of it, and instead toward the main house. As I carry Brigid across the station grounds, her unconscious form cradled against my chest, my mind is a storm of conflicting thoughts and emotions. Dr. Rajesh will have to report this incident. That's non-negotiable. I hope to hell there's no severe damage to her. The welfare of the entire station has to come first. Serious staff injuries always bring in Circuit investigators to follow up, and the last thing any of us want is those pencil-pushing bureaucratic assholes shoving their noses where they shouldn't.

I swear to god, the station won't shutter because of me. I know my part, and I'm goddamn good at it. The burden of the station's future falls squarely on the station manager's shoulders. Heath had wanted to be the manager with the golden shovel. Then he gets to shovel all the bullshit.

I look down at Brigid's face, and the security lights on the corners of the buildings cast her face in a blueish glow. *Like this bullshit right here.*

Her eyes are closed, like she's asleep, and her body is warm against my chest, a gentle weight that's as unsettling as it is reassuring. The scent of lilies drifts off of her.

I haven't held a woman like this in— if I'm being fucking honest— well, ever. I'm rarely at risk of brimming since I can spend nearly every day with Galaxian. So, between that and the physical training I push on my team and the novices, my bond doesn't need any *additional* assistance.

Still, she does smell nice.

A sudden burst of white-hot anger flares inside me. What the hell was she doing in the barn after hours alone? Had Obsianizya not been enough to scare her?

I'd told Heath what she'd done, and here was the proof that Blondie had a goddamn death wish. Heath had promised he'd make the safety rules clearer at the meeting.

If a druadan is loose, leave it the fuck alone.

Clearly, she hadn't listened. No one except riders was allowed in the druadan barn unescorted. Annoyance digs its claws into the sides of my skull. She's been a wild card ever since Heath hired her, and it's long past time she understood the rules here aren't for us but for her. To keep this very thing from happening to *her*.

As I continue up the path to the back of the main house, simmering just under the anger and annoyance is fear—raw and unyielding. What if the wounds left permanent damage? Or was it a toxin of some kind? My pulse ratchets higher. My eyes reflexively scan the darkness around me as I walk, half-expecting some vile creature to leap out from the shadows.

What if she'd been attacked and Galaxian hadn't intervened? Not to fucking mention, he'd shifted out of his stall.

A call to Marshal would happen as soon as the sun was up. They weren't supposed to be able to do that. Not unless a rider commanded them to.

I run through all the things Galaxian could've been referring to, trying to make sense of it all. Most likely, it was some sort of snake, considering his terminology. But would a snake explain the glowing splatters on his body? Or the goo in the aisle? I scour my mind, coming up empty.

When Carter had crashed at my place earlier, we'd gone back and forth about what could have spooked Obsiniaiza as it had. We'd concluded after three glasses of Delford gold that the storm had been the reason. He was young and had only been here through the winter.

My grip tightens around her limp form as I near the main house. What if we'd been wrong? What if something else had made him bolt? Something that was still lurking around.

The lights grow brighter as I get closer to the house and supposed safety. But safety feels like an illusion right now, a fragile construct that's cracking at the edges.

At the back door, I punch in the code and push the door open with my foot when I hear the mechanism click. Balancing Brigid in my arms, I step into the dimly lit interior. The only light comes from a lone lamp in the living room, casting long shadows across the floor. My boots thud softly on the hardwood as I head for the staircase, each step taking me higher, three flights up to Heath's door.

I knock twice.

It takes a minute before the door swings open, revealing Heath in nothing but shorts, rubbing sleep from his eyes. Then he blinks like he's trying to process the scene in front of him.

"Logan?"

"She's hurt," I blurt out, my voice tinged with desperation. "I don't know what else to do."

"What the hell?" Heath's sleepy gaze drifts down to my arms, and his eyes widen in horror. He steps aside. "Get in. Put her on my bed."

I move past him and lay her unmoving body on the covers. Heath takes a flashlight from his dresser and flips it on. Then, kneeling on the bed, he leans over her, pulls open her eyelids, and inspects her pupils. They react to the light, but she remains unconscious.

"I need to call Dr. Rajesh," Heath mutters, switching off the flashlight. He pulls out his phone and presses the speed dial for the med bay. It takes longer than it should for the doctor to answer, but soon, Heath exchanges a brief conversation and hangs up.

Heath flips on a few lamps on the opposite end of the room and then grabs an extra blanket from his closet. All the while, I'm pacing, my boots soundless on the thick carpet, my mind a whirlpool of what-ifs and how-comes. Should I leave? Go back and check on Galaxian? He's alone and rattled. He needs that shit rinsed off him, and what if the thing that attacked him is still out there? My boy did a number on it, but that only means it couldn't have made it far if it was injured. Now is the best chance to find it before it finds some hole to crawl into and die.

I make a move for the door, but Heath's voice stops me. "Thank you," he says, and the words do little to comfort me. A creature is on the loose at the station, hurting people, and he's thanking me. This is my fault. The security of the station is my responsibility, and I have work to do.

"Yeah," is all I manage to say. I take one more last look at Brigid and stalk out of the room.

Sixteen

y eyes blink open, and for a moment, the world is a blur of shapes and colors. Soft, silky sheets brush against my cheek and the smell of antiseptic tickles my nose. I raise my head, and the room spins, forcing me to squeeze my eyes shut again with a low groan. Behind the throb pulsing in my skull, I gradually become aware of noises— hushed voices reach my ears, too indistinct to interpret. I try to call out, but my tongue feels clumsy and dry against the roof of my mouth.

I peel my eyelids open again, nearly exhausted by the smallest movement. I try to move, and a sharp pain sears through my wrist and ankle. Looking down, I see they're both bandaged, wrapped tightly in white gauze. I let out a breath, a mix of relief and confusion. Someone's taken care of me, but how did I end up like this?

I shift my gaze and find Carter sitting in a chair beside me. He's wearing only shorts, his elbows resting on his knees, eyes fixed on something down the hallway.

Then he senses my movement, or maybe he just feels my eyes on him. The lamplight casts a warm glow, catching the green flecks in his hazel eyes as he focuses on me. A deep v appears on his forehead, and his sandy brown hair — which I'm intimately aware of how soft it is between my fingers — is tousled like he's just woken up.

"Finally, Sleeping Beauty," he says, his voice heavy with relief.

His words pull a reluctant grin from me, even as my mind races. What's he so worried about? What happened that's got him looking at me like I'm a ghost?

"I feel more like a zombie than a princess," I manage to say, wincing at the dry rasp in my voice. "And for the record, watching people while they sleep is super creepy."

"Just doing my job," he says, leaning back and resting his hands behind his head, inducing a flurry of butterflies in my belly as I get an unobstructed view of his bare chest and toned abs. My tongue works as I try to force down a swallow in my very parched mouth. I tear my eyes away from his chiseled torso, searching for a drink.

As if reading my mind, he hands me a small steel bottle with a screw top. I eye it warily.

"It's only water, promise. If you want something stronger, I'll see what I can sneak past, Heath."

"Buzz kill." I take a sip from the bottle.

Carter laughs. "That's exactly what *I* said."

I take two more swigs of the water, feeling the wariness slowly subside from my limbs, and move to a sitting position. A dull ache radiates from my ankle to my leg, and I toss off the covers to get a better view of the injury. My cheeks flush with heat when I realize that someone changed me into my pajama shorts and tank top.

"Where's my dress?" I whisper.

Carter nods to the doorway. "Sorry, but Heath tossed it. There was some sort of chemical all over it, and the doctor didn't want to risk it getting on anything else." He pauses, his eyes dragging lazily over my body, sending a ripple of shivers up my arms and neck. "So did you—?" I let my question hang in the air.

He laughs, leaning back in his chair again. "I'm crushed you think I'm anything but a gentleman. Carla helped the doctor change you after Logan brought you here."

"What...Logan? Wait, what happened?" I stammer, my gaze returning to Carter's.

Concern tightens his temples as his eyes search mine like I somehow have the answers.

"Logan brought you here after he found you lying in a stall in the barn. An animal attacked you. He's got the whole security team out there looking for it. Do you remember anything?" he asks, and I wish I could give him something solid, something that could iron out the worry lines on his forehead.

My head feels like it's stuffed with cotton, and my thoughts drift lazily, unable to latch onto any one thing. I try to piece together the shards of memory—vibrations in the air, a burn on my cheek, iridescent eyes—but it's like trying to catch smoke with my fingers. "I remember... bits and pieces," I admit, my words halting. "But it's all a jumble right now. My head's a mess."

He leans forward, whispering in my ear. "You don't know how much you scared me."

The skin on my neck tingles from the warmth of his breath.

"Don't do that again, okay?"

I tilt my head toward him, our faces inches apart. "I'll try not to."

A pair of footsteps draw our attention to the door, and Carter pulls back into his chair. Heath and a man I don't recognize enter from the hallway.

Heath looks like he's barely slept. He's dressed in workout shorts and a sleeveless shirt from Vanguard Academy, a change from his usual black collared shirts and slacks. My rebellious gaze takes in the defined muscles on his arms and legs, a sight I've never seen before.

The man next to him has brown skin and is middle-aged, with the start of a receding hairline. He's wearing a blue sweatshirt, jeans, and a wide smile as he approaches the side of the bed.

"Good to see you are awake. How are you feeling, Miss Corsair," he says.

I manage a wry smile through the discomfort. "Fine. A little tired. How long was I out for?"

"A good twelve hours, I'd say. I gave you a pretty heavy dose of pain meds last night once we learned there was no serious internal damage. His brown eyes hold mine as he holds out an electric stethoscope above my chest. I nod, giving him consent, and he presses it gently to just above my left breast. He asks me to take deep breaths, and I do so as he slowly positions the stethoscope in different locations on my front before moving to the back.

"I'll let Logan know you're awake. He'll want to be here to hear if you remember anything," Heath says, his eyes first on me, then moving to Carter. He taps twice on his wrist com, and there are two taps in response.

Dr. Rajesh removes the stethoscope and pats my hand. "I'm going to prescribe an antibiotic, just to be safe," he says, peeling back the edge of the bandage to trace his finger over the reddened area on my wrist. "And some mild painkillers for the discomfort. Come to the med bay, Miss Corsair, and we'll change the bandages every day for a week. Nothing is broken or serious, but I suggest we do some blood work to rule out any toxins."

I nod. No use in putting up a fight. Heath knows Sharice is my sister. The cat is out of the bag, so my blood flagging any connections to her wouldn't be a surprise to him.

The doctor wastes no time, and I grit my teeth as the needle pierces my skin.

By the time he's drawn two vials, Logan appears in the doorway wearing fatigues, boots, and a laser rifle strapped to his back.

He exchanges looks with Carter and Heath, and an unspoken message passes between them.

Heath rests his hands on his hips. "At our meeting, I thought I made the rules very clear about interacting with the druadans without a rider present."

"I know," I say, tilting my chin so the doctor can press on my lymph nodes and ask me to swallow. "I thought I heard something." It's a lie, but not a big one. I *had* heard something, but after, I was already in the barn.

"Tell us why you were in the barn," Heath says.

"Please," Carter says, getting to his feet to stand beside Heath. Seeing the two of them side by side like this at the foot of my bed, they look like Greek gods come to life. The sight of their toned bodies and chiseled jawlines sends a shiver down my spine. Damn, they make for a sexy pair.

Maybe it's the trauma from almost dying or the painkillers, but my lusty thoughts are out of control today. Maybe it's the way their arms are crossed and the concerned looks on their faces as they stare at me, but I could almost imagine them as my bodyguards. My two big, strong protectors that—

Dr. Rajesh stands, interpreting my runaway fantasy. He

mumbles reassurances, and moves to the other side of the bed, where he types something into a digital tablet.

"I heard a noise," I say, answering their question once Dr. Rajesh is done examining me.

"What kind of noise?" Carter says.

I frown. "Like someone else was in there."

"Did any novices have the night shift?" Heath asks Logan.

"No, they were all accounted for in their bunks."

"Maintenance staff, then? Or security?"

Logan shakes his head.

Heath's lips press into a hard line, waiting for me to continue.

I suck in a nerve-steeling breath, choosing my next words carefully. I had been in there looking for a sign or message from my sister, and I was keenly aware that I was walking a very fine line here, and unfortunately, the pain meds were making the tightrope wobble. "I know it was stupid, but when I heard the noise, I hid in an empty stall." My hands go to my cheek, fingers brushing the raised, sensitive patch of skin. "Then something stung me." I close my eyes, willing the memories to solidify. "I looked up, but it was dark. And after, there was a druadan, and then it's all a blur."

I open my eyes and stare at where my hands have balled the sheets into a death grip. The fear, the pain, that's what I remember most. Then…*nothing*. The desire to sleep for eternity. I had been so very tired. At the thought, my eyelids sag.

"I think that's enough questions for now, don't you?" Dr. Rajesh says.

Heath turns to me. Worry tightens the corners of his eyes. "For now." He firmly says, as if it were his idea. "Rest. We'll be back to check on you later."

My sluggish mind shoves its way to the surface over the pain meds as I remember the upcoming banquet and fundraiser, and worry gnaws at me. "But what about the event? I need to work on the seating chart, confirm the menu with the caterers, and—"

"Carla and I can cover for a few days," he says, interrupting me.

My stubborn streak flares, but the medicine has taken full effect, and I give in.

Rest *did* sound nice.

Heath's eyes darken. "Also, I'd feel better if you stayed here in the room next to mine."

Surprised by his protectiveness, a warm feeling blooms in my chest. "Alright, Heath. I'll stay," I say, my words slurring.

As Heath and Dr. Rajesh exchange a knowing glance, I settle back into the comfortable bed. Despite the pain in my wrist and ankle, the only thing worse was the void in my memories. The not knowing plagued me, even as I drifted to sleep, through shifting images I didn't understand, memories of tentacled creatures, and glowing eyes filled with rage.

Seventeen

My gaze lingers on Brigid's sleeping face.

No matter what I do, I can't look away from her. I don't care if she thinks it's creepy, I didn't want to let her out of my sight.

Not after almost losing her...*again.*

I couldn't believe it. *What the hell had she been thinking?*

Dr. Rajesh gently pats my shoulder as he leaves the three of us with her. He reassures me she'll be fine and he'll be back later to do another check. Just the three of us are left in the room with her.

She looks so different asleep—at peace, a vivid contrast to the fierce and driven persona she projects when she's awake. She'd been so playfully bold in the hot springs and the shower. But now, here in peaceful repose, she seems vulnerable, her defenses down. A surge of protectiveness washes over me. It almost overpowers me, instilling a desire to climb into the bed beside her, wrap my arms around her, and breathe her in.

This morning, I'd awoken with my mind filled with silvery hair, soft skin, and a hard-on like I hadn't had since I was a teenager and had caught a glimpse of two female cadets getting busy with each other in the mess hall storage room. As much as I hated to admit it, she was doing something to me. Pushing her way into my thoughts during the day and now in my sleep.

Fuck. She could still be a danger to us. Logan and Heath and the station came before everything else. I didn't have the privilege of letting her all the way in.

Not yet. Not until I knew she had nothing to do with her sister.

Logan's gruff voice breaks through my thoughts. "Meeting. Now."

"Agreed," Heath says. When I don't move, he adds, "Carter, are you with us?"

Reluctantly, I turn my back to her and find them both staring at me. "Yes. I'm with you."

"Good," Heath says, moving to the hallway. Logan and I follow him out of the room and down the stairs.

Once inside the meeting room, Heath shuts the door.

Logan slams his hands on the table with a bang. A mug that had been left by one of the other employees skitters off and falls to the floor with a thud.

His gray eyes blaze with emotion. "I want her gone, Heath," he shouts. "She needs to go."

Logan is royally pissed. Like more than his usual state of perpetual agitation, and I venture a guess that some of this rage isn't all because of Brigid's actions. There is a danger here, a real threat, and the fear of losing Galaxian, his second mount, is ripping him apart.

Tension hangs in the air between us.

They're too alike, too controlling. Both vying for power. In a way, it works, as they push themselves to their limits like some damn competition, but other times, like now, for instance, it's a cluster fuck.

"No. Nothing has changed," he responds with a calm voice. Contrasting Logan's shouting. "We still need her. She can't leave until we know she isn't connected to Sharice in some way. You know what will happen if she finds out what her sister did."

This was it. There were no more second chances for Logan.

Logan clenches his fists. "She broke your rules and put the entire fucking station at risk," he pauses. *"Twice."*

Heath's eyes sharpen. Of course, Logan would hit him right where it hurts most. Heath and his God damn rules. And Brigid blatantly ignoring them was shaking the very foundation of his command.

"I am aware of her actions," Heath finally says. "However, you know what they'll do if word gets out what happened here. The station will be shut down. For years, the Blackhawk assholes have been itching to get their hands on this place. We'll lose everything."

His words linger, and I know he means more than our positions as riders. Our druadans will be killed. *We* would be forced to kill them as punishment. The very thought of living a life without Ember squeezes my heart like a vice. There is no moving on from such pain, no living an ordinary life with an office job and fenced yard. Such pain would break a man, and if it didn't, a laser pistol pressed to my forehead would.

"So how long are you going to let her just run around defying your orders? Since she's been here, it's been one fucking crisis after another. Druadans escaping, and now an attack in the barn. Don't you see the connection? *She* is the one causing all the problems."

I know Brigid's choices have put the station at risk, but I can't help defending her. She's been here a week. She might be looking for her sister, but I don't believe she's purposely sabotaging the station.

"No, she isn't," I say. The others look at me, obviously surprised at the fierceness in my tone. "Why am I the only one thinking that maybe she *saved* Galaxian? Or have you already forgotten that she ran *into* a dust storm after Obsidanzia? And now, again at the barn, she said she heard something, and instead of wasting time to come find us, she knew she needed to act quickly and went in. Yeah, she was being reckless, but it was also brave as hell. Her being there could've been the warning Galaxian needed to escape his stall. *She* could be the reason he's still alive."

Logan's stony expression flickers with doubt, and I know my words have gotten through to him. He knows I have a point, even if he's not ready to admit it. "You're playing with fire, Carter, and she's going to burn you."

"Don't worry, your pretty little head, big guy," Carter says, flashing him a toothy grin. "I can handle the heat."

Logan growls and— pulling his classic response—storms out of the room.

The door slams behind him.

"I'm going to get dressed," Heath says, sighing. "I'll do rounds, make sure everything is good at the barn with Galaxian and Dr. Gideon. Dr. Rajesh should be back soon. Stay with her, will you?"

"I will," I reply.

After Heath leaves, I return to his room, where Brigid is still asleep.

I take a seat in the chair beside her. I grow bored and swipe open my comm. Reading fan mail always brightens my mood, and today, of all days, it's a perfect distraction.

Pictures of women and men wearing transparent nightgowns or various styles of lingerie flicker on the screen, and I close it out only when Dr. Rajesh re-enters. His nurse follows, pushing a wheeled stretcher alongside him. He checks her vitals again, and then we move Brigid onto it. She stirs but doesn't fully wake, lost in a world between consciousness and dreams. He leaves a list of instructions and confirms she doesn't have any brain trauma and is mostly just experiencing drowsiness from the pain medicine. He and the nurse then leave, the soft click of the door punctuating the room's silence.

I look at her lying there in the guest bed and feel a pang of emotions I can't fully identify. Anger at her recklessness and frustration at the questions still unanswered, sure, but also relief that she's here, still breathing.

Her eyes flutter open. Her full lips curve into a soft smile. "You going to sit there all day?"

"Sure am," I say.

"Don't worry about me, I can go for days."

She lets out a small laugh. "Is that so? Well, if you're going to insist on watching me, why not make yourself more comfortable?"

Before I know it, I find myself slipping off my shirt and climbing into bed beside her. The fresh sheets suddenly take on the warmth of intimacy as I lay there beside her.

I close my eyes, pulling her gently towards me. This is wrong, and Heath would have a few choice words to say if he caught me like this, but I don't give a shit. Her body fits so perfectly against mine. Her warmth radiates into me, and I rest a protective hand on her arm, this fierce desire to shield her from all harm washing over me.

In the stillness of this room, with only the soft sounds of our breathing, I feel something shift inside me. I press my face into her hair, inhaling her scent, unable to deny this connection between us. For in this quiet moment, she is exactly where she belongs— here in my arms.

Eighteen

"Please, Sharice?" I continue pressing my sister. "It's a clear day, and the tide is low. We'll find the best shells. I promise I'll give you any of those rare blue clam shells you like so much."

The rising sun casts a warm, golden glow over the black sand, and the tide is low, promising a treasure trove of seashells. The salty scent of the sea tinges the air, and my hair whips wildly around my face from the constant breeze.

But Sharice, busy with waiting for the soil sample analysis to finish, seems annoyed with me. Her voice carries a hint of irritation as she replies, "No, Brigid. I'm busy."

Disheartened, I turn and leave, my footsteps carrying me through the plastic-framed research tents and onto the beach.

There, my gaze is drawn to a shuttle landing not far away. Three figures emerge from the craft, and I approach them slowly.

An adult man and two younger boys stand before me, and the shuttle pilot waves, introducing me to a new geologist, Dr. Nunson, and his sons, Dane and Elton. Elton is older than Sharice, nineteen years old, but Dane is my age, fifteen.

Lydia, the shuttle pilot, suggests that I give Dane a tour of the research station, and I'm eager to have another kid around. Dane is tall, with nearly black hair, dark eyes, and pale skin. He's cute, in a boyish way, as if he hasn't quite filled into his frame yet and could use a bit more time under the sun.

I happily lead Dane around, pointing out the school stream we watch every morning, showing him the mess hall, and asking him what he likes to do for fun. Soccer and games on Network.

I glance at the ocean, and his expression reflects pure awe. "You've never seen the ocean before, have you?"

He shakes his head, his eyes fixed on the vast expanse of water. "It's bigger than I ever could have imagined."

My heart fills with a sense of pride for the place I call home. "It is. I love coming out here every day and seeing what treasures the ocean has brought me."

Dane's voice interrupts my reminiscing. "I should go find my dad. He said there was a safety orientation I needed to do. But could we meet up later, Brigid?"

My heart flutters with excitement. "Yes, I would like that very much."

"Great," he says. "See you then!"

SUDDENLY, I AWAKEN IN AN UNFAMILIAR ROOM. THE DREAM fades, but a warm, secure feeling remains. Every muscle in my body is stiff, and it feels like a hot poker has been stabbed into my ankle joint. I wiggle, trying to get comfortable and feel a warmth pressed against my back. My eyes snap open just, and my pulse quickens as I realize that someone is in bed with me.

I freeze and listen to the steady breathing behind me, all while slowly sliding my eyes around the room. The blue-striped wallpaper and gilded light fixtures tell me I'm still in the main house, just no longer in Heath's room. So then, who the hell is lying with me?

Carefully, I shift my head. The arm resting over my waist tightens, but not before I glimpse the sandy-blonde hair and unshaven jawline.

Carter.

My pulse pounds in my ears as I process the situation. We are in bed...*together*. Me, the PR person, and a rider, no, not just any rider, Master Rider Carter James.

Okay, okay. *Just think this through.*

Fact: I was still fully dressed

Fact: Carter is shirtless but has shorts *and* was on top of the covers

Fact: It'd been a year since I'd shared a bed with anyone.

I bat away the fog of sleep mixed with pain medication and remember how I'd asked him to join me.

As embarrassing as that memory seems, the truth is, it's nice. I feel comforted and safe snuggling against him. My fingers idly scratch at the bandage on my wrist, noting that it had been recently changed. The grogginess that clings to me slowly dissipates. The warmth, no, *hot* form next to me, and not just because of his chiseled abs or gorgeous face. The dude was actually hot. Feverish. And I recall how hot his lips had been when they'd been on mine.

It must have something to do with the bond. A rider thing.

I wriggle under the comforter to get cozier, feeling a hardness press into my lower back. His voice, gravelly from sleep, whispered in my ear. "Here I am, trying to be a gentleman, and that's not making it easy."

A smirk tugs at my lips as I shift to face him.

Eyes still closed, he says, "You snore, you know."

I scoff. "I do not."

"I'm not saying it's bad. In fact, I kind of like it. It's cute."

"Cute? Really?" He laughs, finally opening those gorgeous green eyes of his. The light in the room seems to dance in those irises, momentarily taking my breath away. He is undeniably sexy in a way that stirs something inside me. He is a Master Rider.

There have to be so many things he should be doing right now instead of lounging in bed with me. Either he's taken a vacation day, or there's something else...

My breathing stills, my blood turning to ice in my veins.

Shit. He knew. Heath must have told him that Sharice was my sister. I draw in short, shallow breaths as panic floods me.

I can't let it show, or he'll think something's wrong. Instead, I keep my cool, maintaining the facade. I am an assignment. A duty. Carter isn't being chivalrous. He's here to spy on me.

The realization is like an icy dagger has been thrust between my ribs.

I have to be careful. Maybe I can slip out without him knowing... My stomach lets out a low grumble. *Thank you, stomach.*

"You want something to eat?" He whispers. "It's the afternoon, but there should be something in the kitchen downstairs."

"You read my mind," I say through clenched teeth.

Carter climbs out of bed and walks to the door. As he reaches it, he glances back at me. "Don't run off now," he says, smirking.

My eyebrows raise as I point to the bandage on my leg. "Don't think I could even if I wanted to."

Once he's gone, I seize the opportunity to assess my situation. Carefully, I ease out of bed, testing my injured leg on the floor. A sharp pain shoots up, and I hiss. I clamp my jaw, biting down to suppress the sound. *So much for making a break for it.* If Carter really is spying on me, then the only option I have is to continue doing what I was doing. Act totally normal and don't do anything to raise suspicion.

I draw in a shaky breath. Easy enough.

First, I need to pee.

With tremendous effort and a lot of muffled cursing, I managed to make it to the bathroom.

I relieve myself and then splash water on my face. Leaning on the counter to take the weight off my leg, I witness the state of my face in the mirror.

Bags have formed under my eyes, and there's a small purple bruise on my left cheek. My hair is a disaster.

I rummage through a drawer and find an array of perfectly organized toiletries, makeup, soaps, and a brush, like a hotel room. I tear off the paper sanitary packaging and brush my teeth, then run a comb through my hair.

As I stare at my reflection, I shuffle through the rapidly dwindling list of choices. I can barely walk ten feet to the bathroom. Do I honestly believe I can just scale the perimeter wall and flee into the desert?

Okay, running into the wilds of the island is out of the question, at least until my leg is healed.

I'm too vulnerable here. I need a new plan, a way out of this situation, that doesn't involve me doing a lot of walking or having another face-to-face with that slimy *thing*. It is possible I could climb into a shipping crate and hide during a shuttle departure, but I have no idea when the next shuttle would leave, and it could be days of hiding. Slowly dehydrating to death in a metal container in the heat, yeah, no thanks.

I feel like a wild animal trapped in a cage, and Carter will be back soon, likely with Heath and Logan in tow, demanding answers. My mind races, searching for a way out of this unexpected and dangerous predicament.

Since there is no way I can escape, I need to get my thoughts in order to prepare myself to answer their questions in a way that will sway them to see my side. They aren't brothers by blood, but it's not a secret that they care about each other. Which means I might be able to use this, somehow, to convince them to let me keep looking into what happened to Sharice.

I pause, my hands resting on the bathroom counter as I stare into the mirror. That is unless *they* were responsible for it.

The revelation detonates in my mind, sending waves of fear through my body, causing my legs to almost give out beneath me. Could they be the ones responsible for Sharice disappearing?

Heath and Carter had both sworn they didn't know where she was or what happened to her, but what if they'd been lying?

Or covering up for Logan.

My mouth goes bone dry. Had I so readily forgotten the promise I'd made myself the day I got here? Anyone here could be a suspect. Anyone here could be responsible. I'd gotten complacent, charmed by Carter's sweet talk and Heath's façade of integrity.

Had I been living, working, beside those responsible the whole time?

Any second, I could be trapped in the room with the same men who had done something to Sharice.

And there will be no one to save me. As far as my mom thinks, I'm still in Delford interning at Triton, and it will be weeks before she notices before she finally realizes that I haven't called.

Fuck that. I refuse to go down without taking one of those egotistical pricks with me. Just because they are riders doesn't mean they can do whatever they want and hurt whoever they want without consequences. I open another drawer and find a pair of scissors nestled between the tweezers and nail clippers. They are small and used to trim hair and beards, but the end is exquisitely sharp.

They'll have to do.

Just as I'm about to slip the scissors into the top of my ankle bandage, I hear Carter's voice calling from the other room. Startled, I hadn't even heard the door open. He says he's made me a green smoothie and found some bread squares and cheese.

Reluctantly, I stash the scissors away and move out of the bathroom.

Carter has returned, and to my relief and displeasure, he's put on a T-shirt. He holds a metal tray with half a sandwich and a cup filled with green liquid. "I told the doctor you're up, and he says he'll be in once you've had a chance to eat."

He grins upon seeing me, and my traitorous heart flutters. *Swoon.*

I'm intoxicated by the way he looks at me. We've been apart a handful of minutes, and yet he's staring at me like I'm the sunshine after climbing out of a cave.

No. I can't let myself slip.

He's in on this. I'm certain of it. He waits for a response from me, but I don't reply. Then, as if he's remembered something, he reaches into his pocket and holds out my comm. "It fell out of your pocket when you were attacked in the barn."

I take it from him, smugly convinced that they've searched through it and found nothing incriminating. It's all work-related, college friends' photos, and baking recipes. Carter encourages me to eat, and I sit on the bed, taking a cautious sip of the green smoothie. It tastes like fresh grass with a sour bite, but then it turns sweet and silky.

"You like it?" he asks.

I give him a timid nod. It's good. Different, but good.

"It's brewed from Liton leaves."

I raise an eyebrow. "Isn't that what you put in the protein pellets?"

A mischievous smirk appears on his face. "Yep, good enough for them, good enough for us."

I squirm under his playful gaze, emotions warring inside me. Can I really defend myself against him? Carter is physically strong, and I've seen his skills with weapons during the exhibition, but I can't just push away the feelings I have for him. The memories of us in my cottage during the storm were too fresh, the feel of his kiss on my lips, his hands on my body, too vivid, clouding my judgment and my mind.

Before I have a chance to decide, though, the door swings open, and Heath, dressed in his typical work attire of an ivory shirt, a black jacket, and pressed khaki pants, enters. Logan, in navy fatigues, follows closely behind. The atmosphere in the room shifts so fast I'm nearly lightheaded.

Carter stands, moving to the back of the bed so he can face them.

"I'm glad to see you up and eating," Heath says, but his words lack conviction. "There are some matters to discuss that are rather urgent."

He pulls a chair from the desk, its heavy wood scraping softly against the floor, and positions it with deliberate precision in the room's center, only a few feet from me. Logan, like a stalwart lieutenant, follows him silently, coming to flank his right.

Exhaustion tugs at the corners of their temples.

Good. Bet it's the guilt making you sleep like shit.

Heath sits. "Securing the safety of Meridian Station is paramount," he says, his words measured and precise. "Logan and his security team are meticulously combing every crevice and corridor, searching for any traces of the mysterious creature that attacked you and Galaxian. Our veterinarian, Dr. Gideon, is extracting samples from Galaxian's wounds. Oddly, the station's surveillance cameras were malfunctioning precisely at the moment of the attack, leaving us without visual evidence."

A lead weight sinks to the base of my stomach. "Are you serious? You can't actually believe that *I* did this."

Heath's mouth forms a thin light. "Like I said, we're just trying to fill in some blanks. We're just looking at all the possible scenarios."

I shift on the bed, feeling the need to sit taller. "Oh, I get it. And one of those scenarios is that I'm somehow responsible? That it was me who let a wild animal on the grounds?"

"No," Carter says, his voice as hard. "We would never think that."

Fury blazed inside me like an awoken dragon. "Then what? That I made all of this up?" My voice reaches an octave higher. "What about this? Huh? How do you explain this?" I rip off the bandage from my leg, revealing the angry red lines of the wound, and the tiny scissors go skidding across the floor.

Fuck. I dart for them, but I'm not quick enough. Logan's hand is lightning fast, lashing out to snatch them before I'm barely off the bed.

He holds them up, a sly smirk resting on his lips, and twirls them proudly on his finger.

Another hand clamps down on my right wrist, firm but gentle. "Don't," Heath says, his voice laced with warning. "It is a very, *very* bad idea to threaten a rider with an injured stallion, Ms. Corsair."

I stop struggling, feeling the rage slowly recede as if his touch is a siphon, drawing the heat from my veins.

I chew the inside of my cheek, feeling like a toddler who got caught with candy stuffed in her pockets, and lower my other hand, still glaring at Logan.

Apprehension gnaws at my core. I'd showed my hand. That was it. There was nothing else I could do. I was at the mercy of three men with military training, combat skills, *and* the sole authority on an isolated druadan station. I'd have been better off using the scissors on myself, slitting my own throat before they did whatever cruel and twisted acts they intended to do. Whatever they'd done to Sharice.

My chest heaves with a shuddering breath, and I lower my gaze to the floor, feeling like I'd just submitted to a pack of wolves. My mind races with happy memories of my life.

There are so few, which makes them all the more precious. The best ones are with Sharice and my Mom, a few with Laura and Vince, and coworkers at Triton.

I squeeze my eyes shut, anticipating the butt of Logan's gun or a fist that will knock me unconscious. Would I cry out when I died? People sometimes do that when they die.

Dane had done that.

My stomach twists into a tight knot. This is what I deserve. This is what happens to people who kill other people. Karmic balancing is on the docket, and I have a front-row seat.

However, as I stand there, body stiff, bracing for the attack, nothing happens. No blow to the face. No bullet to the temple.

Nothing.

Tentatively, I pry open my eyes and see Logan's glare locked with mine. I feel the weight of Heath's gaze on the side of my face, neither of them moving. Were they playing with me? Wanting me scared so they could get off on their sick game?

"Ms. Corsair," Heath says, "Please sit down."

A small, frantic laugh escapes my throat. "Why? Is the blood easier to clean up on the sheets?"

Logan's gaze hardens and flicks almost imperceptibly to Carter's before settling back on me. "What the hell are you talking about, blondie?" he says.

I bite my lower lip, feeling the tension slowly melt away from between my shoulder blades. "My blood, you know, from killing me?" God, this was some sadistic shit making me say it out loud.

Carter's laugh cuts through the tension of the room, and Heath and Logan join him.

"What drugs did Dr. Rajesh give you?" Logan asks. "Cause I think I need some."

Carter moves and takes a step closer. "We aren't going to kill you, Brigid. Why the hell would you think that?" The frantic beat of my pulse eases slightly as I suck in a breath.

"It's just I thought—"

"We don't make it a habit of killing women, I can assure you," Heath says, interrupting me.

"But getting rid of them? Making them disappear? That's another matter entirely, right?"

"You're referring to Sharice," Heath continues, and when neither Logan nor Carter reacts, my suspicions are confirmed. The bitter taste of betrayal coats my tongue.

I don't nod, don't move, my body as still as the statues of the druadans in the foyer downstairs.

Heath purses his lips, and his throat bobs as he swallows. "There is a lot we should talk about. It would be better if I didn't have to go back on my argument against Master Rider McCelroy's suggestions on using lead straps to restrain you, which he adamantly insisted on before our little meeting here."

Logan's eyes search mine, but I don't back down. Not again. If they aren't going to kill me, fine. That still doesn't mean I trust them, or they aren't planning to do something *after* our 'little meeting,' as he'd called it.

Finally, I turn and limp back to the bed. Carefully lowering myself onto the edge, I wince at the throb of pain as I'm forced to pivot on it.

Carter leans down and picks up my unfinished smoothie. I fix him with my hardest glare, not moving to take it, even as a reassuring smile tugs at the corners of his mouth. I don't buy it. *Sorry, handsome. It was nice while it lasted, but you picked your side.*

"Now," Heath says, returning to his chair. "I think we should start from the beginning to clear up a few things."

"I agree," I say, crossing my arms. "You first."

The muscles beneath Heath's square jaw tense, and I worry if I've pushed him too far. I loathe this feeling of being made the bad guy. The accusatory looks. The doubt. However, answers are the very reason I'd come here to begin with.

I am willing to play along so long as he is.

"Everything I've told you about your sister is true," Heath says. "Sharice was a great employee. She kept to herself, got along with the other staff, and always met the deadlines we'd set for her." He hesitates, indecision flickering in his eyes, and I find I've got a death grip on the sheets. "However, the comm bracelet you found in my room. I lied to you about my having forgotten it was there. The day before Sharice disappeared, she gave it to me in confidence. She made me promise to hide it from anyone, including the police."

"But why?" I ask, the question slipping from me.

"I have no idea. She seemed scared, on edge, and told me that I was the only one she could trust." He pauses again, his gaze steady as if assessing me for reactions. My tongue sweeps the backs of my molars, but I maintain my composure. All of this I'd learned from the last videos on her comm. This still didn't explain anything.

"Then, when she didn't show up to work the next day, Carla went to check on her. Her cottage was empty except for some of her belongings. It was like she'd just vanished. The rest you already know. The Circuit police investigated. They interviewed all the staff. Took swabs in the cottage and combed the surrounding area for footprints or indications of where she'd gone. Nothing."

"I spoke to the shuttle pilot myself," Carter adds. "No one had come in or out, and they'd run the crates through heat signature detection when they'd unloaded in Delford."

Heath laces his fingers together on his lap. "You see, Ms. Corsair. We cooperated to the utmost extent with the authorities to help them find your sister. We are not the monsters you think us to be."

I maintain the white-knuckled grip on the sheets, his words having little effect on my paranoia. "So then, why keep me here?" I snap. "Why not let me leave?"

"For fuck's sake, Heath, just tell her," Logan barks.

My eyes dart between the three of them. "Tell me what?"

Heath sighs, a heavy sound full of regret. "The day after Sharice left, a novice interrupted a security staff meeting. He said he'd been cleaning the exhibition hall when he'd noticed something amiss."

He stops speaking, his gaze dropping as if dreading the words that he's about to say. "A druadan egg was missing."

Silence fills the room for a long while. I squint at the three of them, confused. "But there are three? Carter showed them to me."

"There *were* three before," Carter says softly. "One's a fake. There are only two now."

My heart slams into my ribcage, adrenaline spilling into my veins. This is it. This is why they want me here. No. It can't be. Sharice wouldn't.

As if sensing the battle raging inside me, Heath leans closer, his dark gaze locking with mine. "It's the same day your sister went missing. It's not a coincidence."

The revelation is like a punch to the gut, forcing me to recalibrate everything I thought I knew about my sister. My head is a swirl of confusion and betrayal. Each thought was a biting wind in the storm of my emotions. And them—Logan, Carter, Heath —they're not the enemies here.

So, if Sharice stole a druadan's egg, what does that make her? And what does it make me to search for her?

Nineteen

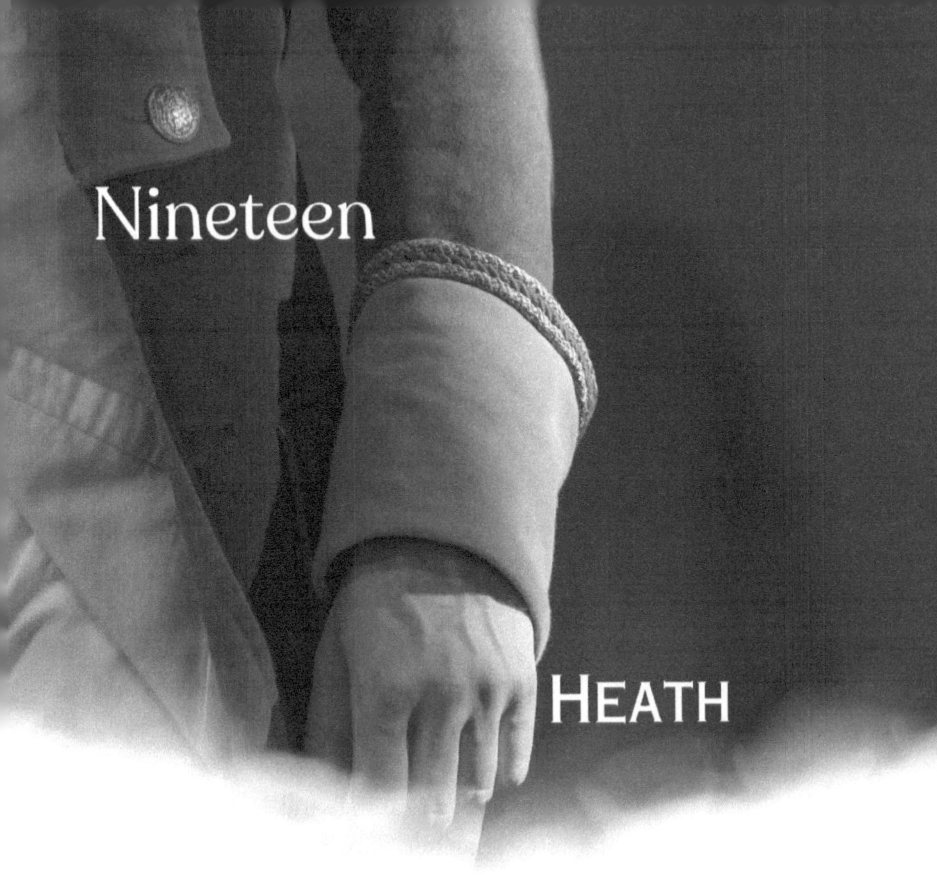

*I*t had been I who had broken our oath.

Logan's pressuring me to tell her, and the fear in her eyes had forced my hand.

Each inhale draws in the acrid taste of guilt and regret. But it's done. The three of us that once knew it had become four.

If Brigid thought she was in danger before, she has no idea what she's done now.

"We assumed she was going to sell it, so we have been keeping tabs on auction houses and black markets," Logan says, his words laced with a sharp edge.

Brigid bolts upright, eyes flaring. "You don't know a damn thing about my sister!" I take in the fire blazing in her eyes, the defiant set of her jaw. Even with her injured leg, she stands toe-to-toe with Logan, unafraid of his imposing height and muscular frame looming over her. One hand curls into a fist while the other trembles ever so slightly at her side, the smallest indicator betraying her bravery.

"Fine. You want proof? I have proof," Brigid says, "Come to my room. I'll show you."

Without waiting for a response, she hobbles to the door. Her movements are wobbly like a fresh-born colt. Before I have a chance to react, Carter's beside her, his hand darting out to catch her elbow and steady her. A silent, unspoken look passes between them, and the way his body angles toward hers churns my gut.

Dammit Carter.

If they haven't fucked yet, they will soon. I had explicitly told him to stay by her side, and it was apparent that he actually listened to me for once. A slight twinge of jealousy creeps in as I watch him pull her closer. She's stunning, and I can't imagine Carter finding anyone better than her. I just hope he realizes that.

Logan and I follow Brigid and Carter out of the guest room into the hallway before slowly descending the stairs that lead out of the main house.

Carter assists her down the path to her cottage. This is a mess, a damned mess, and I'm the one who has to clean it up. All because of secrets. All because of lies. Isn't that what the druadan legacy was built on, though? Secrets layered in myth. Truths are too dangerous for the common people to know. Ancient whispers that died with the riders of the past.

Logan and I step inside, trailing just behind Carter as he assists Brigid through the living area and to her bedroom door. She pulls away from him before he can follow her into it. "Thank you, but I'm fine. I'll be fine." With firmness in her steps, she retreats into her room and closes the door behind her, leaving the three of us in the confines of the tiny house.

I glance around, taking in the surroundings. It's evident she hasn't personalized the space. No photos, no keepsakes, just a few stacks of papers I recognize as guest lists and caterer's menus, as well as an empty vase sitting on the counter.

Maybe Carla can arrange for some flowers to be sent here on the next shipment. After all, we'll need Brigid's cooperation if we have any semblance of hope of finding her sister and recovering the egg. A peace offering might smooth things over, especially given Logan's abrasive behavior earlier.

The door creaks open, drawing my attention. Brigid steps out, now wearing loose pants that sit low on her hips and a crop top that teases a peek of the bare skin of her flat stomach. An unexpected heat rises in my throat, and I swallow, averting my gaze to the floor.

Control yourself. You're engaged. For shit's sake, I silently scold myself, annoyed at my body's reaction. It's just the bond. That's all. Shadowmane's overactive libido seeping into my consciousness. A thirst needing quenched. No, that was an understatement. *More like a forest fire needing a monsoon rain.*

She holds up the wrist comm. "*This* is the proof that they coerced my sister into taking the egg," she declares, her finger pressing the play button with a force that mirrors her resolve. "Just listen, okay?"

Silence envelops the room as Sharice's panicked voice fills the space. As her confusion and desperation play out on the screen. My chest tightens upon hearing the anguish in her voice. I think back to the nights I'd laid in bed, grappling with how to hack into her passcode and uncover her messages.

In the end, I'd had no luck. And I couldn't risk sending it to a tech person who might happen to see the incriminating evidence of what had happened here. But now, seeing this video, I wonder if I should risk it anyway. If I had access to this video, could we have found her and the egg already? Could we have asked the right people the right questions? A hollow guilt burrows in my chest.

For a full year, I had to come to terms with the fact that Sharice had taken the druadan's egg with her. We couldn't search for it openly, and our efforts on Network yielded limited results. I had accepted the possibility that she'd sold it to a curator who would hide it away in some basement, or even worse, to a wealthy individual with ambitions of becoming a rider if they could figure out how to hatch it.

"They said they'd do terrible, awful things if I go to the police," Sharice says. *"I don't have a choice. I don't know if anyone will ever see this, but please know I didn't have a choice."*

The recording ends.

Logan's jaw muscle works under his stubbled cheek.

"She came to me about it," I say, my voice low. "I should have done something."

"Yeah, you're right," Logan says. "You should have."

Carter bristles beside me, preparing to defend me, but I hold a hand up, stopping him. "I regret not taking her more seriously and not notifying the police about her comm. However," I pause, pinning Logan with a glare. "Dwelling on the past errors will not help us find Sharice or the egg."

Logan watches me, the ever-present challenge flickering in his eyes. He knows his place, and I know mine. We might butt heads, but we have a deep respect for each other. Lately, our bond has become more complicated, but if push came to shove, we wouldn't hesitate to sacrifice ourselves to protect the other two.

"Sharice was always very good at keeping secrets," Brigid says, breaking the tension. "I don't think there is anything else you could have done to make her tell you the truth.

Her blue eyes meet mine, and I see understanding rather than accusation in her gaze. "My sister is stubborn. Once she makes up her mind, nothing can change it." A slight crease forms between her eyebrows as if speaking this evokes a specific memory from her childhood. "I know if she was bound and determined to keep this from you, nothing would have swayed her."

"Fine," Logan grumbles. "So, what do we do now?"

"We work together," I assert, trying to regain some semblance of control. "Ms. Corsair," I say, looking at her. "You and Logan see what you can find here at the station using the station's record logs and security cameras. Whatever clearance you need to access, I'll authorize it."

Brigid blinks up at me as if she'd misheard, and her eyes flick to Logan before going back to mine. "Uh, are you sure?"

"Yes," I say. I turn, directing my gaze to Logan. "Cooperate. We're on the same team now, so I expect there will be no issues."

Logan stares at me, cooly.

"Excellent," I say, taking his silence as an answer. "Carter," I say, and notice he's standing a little too closely behind Brigid. "You can come with me to Delford. Now that we know someone was coercing her, we might be able to better direct our search. We'll see what we can discreetly dig up. Surely you have some Circuit contacts through your folks? I'll see what threads I can pull in rare artifacts and antiquities possibly being wanted by extremist groups."

"And then what?" Brigid asks. "What happens when we *do* find out who was threatening Sharice and where she is?"

I sniff, tilting my chin up. "Then we track down them down and make them regret the day they ever fucked with Meridian Station."

Twenty

BRIGID

As the door closes behind Heath and Logan, a surge of emotions floods me.

The hope of finding Sharice, the shock of her involvement with the stolen egg, and the monumental secret Heath had shared with me consumed my thoughts.

Genuine concern is evident in his eyes as Carter rests a hand on each of my shoulders. His touch grounds me for a moment, and I resist the urge to lean into him, press my head against his chest, and cry. "I know Heath said he wanted me to go to Delford," he says softly, his green eyes gripping mine, "but I can tell him no if you want me to. If you want me to stay?"

A warmth blooms across my chest at the sweet gesture. "No,

go. I'll be fine. I just need time to process *everything*," I mumble, finding the pain meds are making it hard to formulate thoughts.

Carter searches my eyes, and I try my best to steel them, block off the whirlwind of emotion inside me. "I'm so sorry for all of this. I promise we can talk more, and I'll make it up to you when I get back." He kisses me on the forehead. "Get some rest. We'll be back as soon as we can."

And then he's gone.

Left alone, I try to find solace in the quiet of the cottage, but the revelation about the egg is a painful reminder that Sharice and I have never truly been as close of sisters as I'd thought. Though we share blood, we are opposites in so many ways. Like our mother, Sharice prefers spending hours alone, lost in books, or losing herself in ongoing research projects. I've often suspected she'd kept parts of her life locked away from me.

Now I have proof.

After the accident with Dane, she'd protected me. She was the first person I went to after it happened. Without hesitation, she'd shielded me from the wrath of the Nunsons, powerful people who could have destroyed our family's future. She'd convinced Mom to send me away to the private school in Delford and give me a fresh start before I could be tangled in the scandal.

In her own distant way, she cares about me as I do for her. She'd protected me then. Now, it's my turn to help her. Save her.

As I head to the shower, a slight ache pulses in my left ankle with each step, though the pain has dulled to a manageable throb. Peeling away the bandages on my wrist, I'm relieved to see the angry red welts have faded to a soft pink.

The hot water is soothing as it cascades over me, washing away not just dirt but the weight of this endless day. I stand motionless, letting the heat relax my sore muscles until the water starts to cool.

After drying off, I run a brush through my long hair, savoring the smooth feeling as I work out each tangle. I braid it neatly, securing the end with a hair tie. I slip into my short-sleeved shirt and shorts for pajamas, and exhaustion washes over me. I feel like all I've been doing is sleeping, yet it somehow feels like it's not enough.

I can't remember the last time I'd been this tired. I'd been strapped to the front seat of this emotional roller-coaster powered by the conviction that Heath, Logan, and Carter were behind Sharice's disappearance. And then, in an instant, it'd all changed. Now we were working together. Now, we trusted each other. Okay, fine, not trusting them but trying to. And it seemed that they were beginning to share their trust in me as well. Not that I deserved it after accusing them of so much.

Settling into bed, I power on my digital tablet, knowing I should try and get some rest, but I find I'm unable to ignore work completely. My eyes scan Network messages about the fundraiser, and I'm pleased I have something to do to keep me busy, some way to help the station, at least in my own small part.

After emptying my virtual mailbox, I get lost in the professional photo images taken around Meridian and do a search for the island's native flora and fauna, eventually ending up on predators, specifically snakes. I cycle through the images, looking for any familiar patterns on their scales, shapes, or sizes, hoping something will trigger my memory. However, fatigue weighs down my eyelids, and the glow of the screen dims as sleep becomes impossible to resist. I lean back against the headboard and drift off, the tablet's light fading into darkness.

A loud knocking pounds my thoughts, snatching me away from the fitful sleep of invisible monsters and eyes glowing in shadows. I jolt awake, a cold sweat clinging to my skin. The darkness of my room is pierced by a repetitive, insistent knocking. Heart pounding, I push myself up, the weight of the day's mental strain pressing down on me.

"Brigid. You up? Carla's voice calls through the door, urgency threaded through her words. "It's happening tonight," "Danner and Wraithwind. They're bonding."

My mind buzzes to alertness. The bonding ceremony. *Holy shit*. This is huge. I push off the covers, swinging my legs over the edge of the bed. My fingers fumble as I pull on black leggings, followed by a loose t-shirt. Spotting my camera on the bedside table, I snatch it up, already hearing Heath's argument about allowing me to share these pictures with the public. Still, even if they never see the light of day, I can't risk missing the opportunity. It's easier to ask forgiveness than permission.

Once dressed, I hurry to the front door. The door softly creaks as I open it, and Carla's excited gaze meets mine. "It only just started. You haven't missed anything yet, but sometimes things move fast," she says.

"Thanks for getting me," I say, stepping outside. Stars sprawl across the vast expanse above, and the full moon bathes the landscape in a silvery glow. The warmth of the night air wraps around me. There's electricity in the air like before a storm. The night is alive.

"What's it like?" I ask Carla as we hurriedly walk to the barn. "The bonding, I mean."

"It's... hard to describe," she replies. "I've only ever seen one and have heard all of them are a little different." She purses her lips, and I notice she's wearing a full face of makeup.

"How'd you find out the bonding was happening tonight?" I ask.

Carla's eyebrows lift slightly. "Since Heath is in Delford, I'm the temporary manager of the station and am one of the comms Danner's alarm goes to."

"That has to suck waking up in the middle of the night—"

She makes a sound caught between a chuff and a laugh. "Oh honey, I wasn't asleep. Dale and I were…on a video call."

A small smile forms on my face. That's the reason she is all dolled up at 1 am.

"Heath mentioned you were engaged?"

A blush touches the apples of her cheeks. "I am."

"At Blackhawk station, right? Is he a rider?"

"God no," she says, laughing. "I would never date a rider, let alone marry one." We turn the corner around the edge of the barn, and as we approach the field, I can see others already gathered by the fence. "He's in administration, like me."

We approach the field, and I can see figures gathered by the fence. In the center, a man wearing only sweatpants and a lean-looking gray druadan stand twenty feet apart, facing each other, their forms silhouetted by the moonlight.

Carla leads me to an opening along the stone fence, and I rest my elbows on it, camera-ready. This moment, right here, is pure magic. I snap photo after photo, focusing on the dark shapes of Danner and Wraithwind as they stand perfectly still. The blanket of stars, the full moon, capturing the stillness before what I assume will be a storm. Flanking either side of me, staff members wear a mix of pajamas and hastily thrown-on robes, buzzing like they're watching the season finale of the lunar reality TV show.

A chilly breeze washes over me, forcing me to shiver, and I regret not bringing a jacket. I'm tempted to ask how long these usually take, but I feel it'd be rude, especially considering I'm still considered new here.

"A hundred bucks says Wraithwind, takes a bite out of him in the first go," Henry, the shuttle maintenance lead, mutters to my left.

"Nah, I've seen Danner at the gym. He might be short, but he's fast. Bet another fifty, he dodges it," an older woman with gray-streaked black hair counters. Sandra, her name comes to me. She helps Petyr with station maintenance.

"I'll take some of that action," Carla says, tapping her wrist comm. "Best guess about what skill they'll bond over?"

"Shifting," Henry says. "It's common with full moon bonds."

"Speed," Sandra argues. "Has to be. I've seen another from the Ghost line at Blackhawk, and that stallion was quicker than a hare caught in the shadow of a hawk."

The chatter dies down as Danner takes a hesitant step forward, his gaze never leaving Wraithwind. The gray stallion snorts, a little puff of misty air billowing from its nostrils, and his luminescent eyes glow brighter, two white beacons in the dark.

Wraithwind's form shimmers like waves of iridescent mist arising from him that I recognize at once as the first phase of a Shift. My heart pounds with excitement as Danner, barefoot and shirtless, runs full speed towards the druadan. I fear they are going to collide, the energy in the air electric, but at the last second, Wraithwind shimmers and disappears, reappearing close to where I stand by the stone wall. I feel the gust of his sudden arrival, the power radiating from the tall stallion the color of ash.

Danner appears momentarily disoriented, and it takes a second for him to locate him, but then his eyes lock-in, and he sprints again. This time, I swear his fingertips nearly touch the druadan's smooth hide, but he's a second too slow, and as if punishing him, the druadan lashes out with his front legs, throwing Danner backward. The novice lands on his back and winces as he clutches at the side of his chest, where the front of a hoof probably broke a few ribs. Danner slowly sits up and forcefully coughs up a mouthful of blood before standing.

Dr. Rajesh murmurs something to his nurse, but neither

move. If that's not enough of an injury to justify their involvement, then what is?

My nails dig into the stone, unable to look away from this dangerous game of tag as Danner turns his gaze once more to the stallion. His head is held low, snaking back and forth, and the blue shimmers from the sweat coating his hide.

And so, it continues. Danner charging at full sprints, Wraithwind shifting.

Every eye along the fence is glued to the pair in the grassy moonlit field. Screw reality TV, this is a thousand times better. Finally, Danner hunches over, catching his breath.

"He's too young," Henry says, shaking his head. "Wraithwind is only four. Maybe he isn't ready to bond tonight."

Carla nods, her forehead creased in concern. "Heath sure picked a perfect time to be away from the station."

"Should call this off. Danner may not be ready either." Someone else asks an older man with dark skin and a tan sweatsuit that makes him look like he just finished a stint at an aerobics class.

I try to ignore the others, my attention focused on Danner. I barely know the guy, and yet I'm rooting for him. I understand the drive to be good at something you've worked hard for. To finally accomplish that lofty goal others said you could never achieve.

My fingers clutch the camera's body, and I find I no longer want to take pictures. Something about this feels intimate, and the thought of taking photos of it feels like an invasion of personal moments. A wrongness. They'd never do it justice, anyway.

This whole event is an experience. Capturing the lightning is beautiful, sure, but it's the thunder immediately after that is the true drama.

Danner is growing tired, and a sheen of sweat glistens off his arms and back. He's returned to the center of the field, and Wraithwind is thirty feet away, appearing calm and steady.

Something changes in Danner's posture, his shoulders straightening, his chin lifting as if scenting the air. Then, as if mimicking Wraithwind, he lowers his head, his eyes never leaving the druadan's, and slowly advances to him. There is no eagerness to his steps, no hurry, just a careful stride forward. Wraithwind's body shimmers as he readies another Shift to evade him.

Twenty feet from him, the druadan shifts. The second he does, Danner spins with startling speed and bolts to space to his left, where Wraithwind suddenly reappears. With mind-numbing speed, he reaches out and places a hand on Wraithwind's shoulder.

The druadan trumpets an excited squeal, echoed by the others in the barn. My heart races like it's me out there alone with a possessed creature looking like he's poised to kill. But Wraithwind seems to mull it over before lowering its head, allowing Danner to touch it.

As their contact solidifies, a ripple of energy sweeps across the field. It hits me like a wave, tingling from the soles of my feet to the tip of my head, and I can almost hear their thoughts intertwining, becoming one unified consciousness.

"They did it," Sandra breathes out, her voice tinged with awe.

Wraithwind rears back, bellowing a sound that shakes the very ground we stand on. I feel the reverberation in my bones. Then, when the stallion's front hooves touch the ground again, Danner grabs a fistful of Wraithwind's mane and leaps up onto his back. Wraithwind doesn't wait for him to get fully seated before charging ahead. His long strides cover the length of the field in a heartbeat, and it's like watching a streak of light, too fast to be real but too vivid to be a dream.

A security worker standing near the gate swings it open as

they race through it, and just like that, they vanish into the misty desert, leaving us all in stunned silence.

Henry breaks it first. "Well, damn. That's gonna be hard to top."

"You owe me," Sandra grins.

"What happens now?" I whisper to Carla as the crowd dissipates.

"I'm not sure. A rider and his stallion run are a private thing, and there's some archaic code about how the secret is the bond, but all I know is they'll come back in a day or so, tired, dirty, and Danner will have a fresh bite mark on his hand."

"Really? No food or water. Just the two of them out in the desert for days?" I feel gross when I go three days without a shower, and hell, Danner didn't even have shoes.

"Yeah," Carla says as she slaps the top of the stone wall. "But they've prepared for it. Vanguard first, then a novice here. Danner's a smart kid. He'll be fine."

I worry about my bottom lip. My ankle still ached, and the longer I stood here, the more it hurt. I had zero interest in following him out there. I'm sure Carla was right. He'd been here nearly a year. The other riders had trained him, prepared him for the bonding, or the Run, as she'd said it was called.

"Do they ever *not* come back?" I ask.

Carla chuckles dryly. "I'm sure it has happened on a rare occasion, but I've been here eight years and have yet to see it. Don't worry. I've been told it's all part of the forming of the bond. They need a moment to forge trust between druadan and the rider. In regards to the snakes and oversized coyotes out there, I wouldn't worry. He's got Wraithwind with him. They'll be fine."

The tension leaves my body just a little at her words, still not entirely convinced, yet she has seen more of these than me, so she has to be right. I can't deny the fear that the creature that attacked Galaxian and me is still nearby, but there's no controlling when a bonding will happen. And even if Heath *had* been here, I guarantee he wouldn't have tried to intervene, even with the risk.

She tells me good night and reminds me we have a virtual meeting with the VIP guests for the fundraiser in the morning and heads back to her apartment in the main house. Others return to their own beds, or the handful that have to resume their night shifts, but either way, I doubt many will get much sleep tonight.

The energy in the night air is palpable, and I find myself reluctant to return to my cottage. Under the soft glow of the exterior lights, the purple of the cobblestones and the ivory of the moon all seem a little more vivid. Every sound is brighter and sweeter. I catch the edges of laughter and chatter from the staff apartments nearest mine filtering through the air, mingled with the sound of music from a familiar singer.

My footsteps lead me, and I find myself, once again, drawn to the barn.

The barn door is open, and two other riders, Shane and Ben, are sorting through storage crates in front of the stalls, which means it's okay for me to go in.

See, Heath, I *can* follow the rules.

"Evening, Brigid," Shane says, waving.

"Good evening," I say.

"Hell of a bond tonight, eh?" he says.

"It sure was. I swear I'm too wired to sleep."

"Why do you think we're here organizing?" Ben says, holding up two handfuls of an assortment of leather straps and buckles.

I laugh. "Mind if I walk through?"

"Be my guest," Shane says, shrugging. "Just be careful. They're just as jumpy as you are."

I move past them and pause to take in the serenity. Blanketed druadans pace in their stalls, their luminescent eyes all are alight, brighter than I'd ever seen. Carter's red stallion, Ember, stamps impatiently in his stall, his knee banging loudly against his feed bin.

It's hilarious how alike he and Carter are, and I wonder if it's something that starts that way or a side effect of the bond, like a married couple who finish each other's sentences or end up dressing alike without intending to. I continue deeper into the barn, passing by several druadans before stopping in front of Galaxian's stall.

"Hey there," I murmur, leaning on the wooden frame of his stall. My voice is tinged with an almost giddy energy, and there's a soft glow to the edges of my vision as if I'd drank several glasses of Gold Coast red. "How are you doing? Lots of excitement these past few days, huh?"

The sand-colored stallion doesn't look up from where he's faced the corner, and I can't help but smile. "Right, you can't understand a word I'm saying. But figured I should check on you and should say a thank you."

The stallion lifts his head, and his right eye — a glowing emerald green—peeks out between the curtains of his black mane. I don't need him to speak to know he's giving me one hell of a side-eye. He's a few feet away now, and I reach for the padded glove, eager to touch him.

"I wouldn't do that if I were you," Logan says behind me, and it takes every ounce of my will not to startle.

I pull my hand back and slowly turn to face him, keeping my face neutral even as my pulse thrums in my eardrums.

Logan is leaning against the opposite stall, eyes locked onto me like I'm prey.

"Do what?" I say, tilting my head to the side as if his sudden presence didn't send a hundred alarm bells off in my head. Had he followed me in here? If so, how long had he been standing there?

"Touch a druadan on a bonding night," he says, holding a

bottle of beer. "It's the quickest way to lose a few fingers, if not a hand."

I lace my fingers together as if reassuring myself they are all still fully attached. "Good to know."

His gaze is unwavering, as if he can see right through me and know what I am thinking.

The temptation to flee overtakes me, and I take a step to my left. Within a heartbeat, however, Logan's pushed off the wall and is in front of me, blocking my path.

Something clouds his steel gray eyes as he peers down at me, and there's a smile on his face that I'm not used to, and it leaves me breathless. "Chatting up druadans now?" he says, setting the beer down on the closest storage bin. "Run out of people willing to listen to your lies?"

A shiver runs through me, but I shrug it off. If Logan thinks he can unnerve me, he's wrong. I cross my arms and hold my ground.

"You're drunk and don't know what you're talking about."

"Hate to break it to you, blondie," he continues, his voice low. "But Heath's not here. Neither is your Carter."

"He's not *my* Carter," I snap.

Logan smirks a wickedly handsome thing that does even more wicked things to the space between my legs. "If you say so." The tension in the air between us is thick enough to cut with a knife. I don't know why Logan is here, but one thing's for sure: I won't let him see that he's getting to me.

"Look," I say, feeling my temper flare. "Get it through that thick skull of yours that I'm not lying? If I really wanted to take the other egg, 'finish what Sharice started' as you so evidently think, wouldn't I have done so already? I've had plenty of opportunities to sneak into the exhibition hall, grab it, and hitch a shuttle ride to Delford without any of you knowing."

"I would've known."

"Oh really? And why is that? Are you watching me every second of every day?"

His jaw ticks.

Oh shit. He *had* been. Thoughts surge to the front of my mind of the showers I'd taken, and the late nights I'd struggled to fall asleep, the singing sessions while I'd made food in the kitchen.

As if reading my thoughts, he says, "There are no cameras inside any of the staff's apartments, only the exteriors of the buildings."

A rush of cool air inflates my lungs.

"I'm *not* sorry for suspecting you," Logan says. "It's my job to be suspicious, especially since one of the eggs was stolen. And let's not forget, you're the new face around here and Sharice's sister, no less."

"So, guilty by association? That's your play?"

"It's not a 'play.' It's goddamn due diligence. I have a responsibility to be thorough, and yes, that means I don't trust easily."

I roll my eyes. "Wonderful. So, what you're saying is, I should feel honored that I've caught your attention?"

His gaze narrows. "You have definitely caught my attention."

The air evaporates from my lungs, and I'm suddenly hyper-aware of how close he is to me. The wood of the stall presses against my back, but I refuse to move, refusing to show him just how much he affects me. Dammit. How did this night end up like this? I was supposed to just snap a few photos of the bonding ceremony and get back to bed. Now, here I was in the druadan barn, alone, with the one person I most definitely *did* not want to be alone with.

The conviction I'd clung to a few minutes ago that I wouldn't submit to this man and his accusations was growing alarmingly weaker by the second.

For what feels like an eternity, our eyes lock, neither backing down nor conceding. The tension crackles between us like live electricity.

The heady rush of intoxication causes my head to sway, and I recognize that he, too, is feeling the effects of the night. The pent-up tension reverberates in the air. Without warning, he leans closer to me, and his warm breath caresses my ear. "I need to know one thing. One fucking thing that is the truth."

"What?" I breathe the word.

That intense heat radiates from his body. So, I'd been right. *It* is a rider thing. He rests a hand on the slope of my neck, his fingers lacing into my hair and the base of my skull. I tip my head back, giving in to the touch.

"Your hair," he whispers. "Why did it glow like that?" He's close enough that I can smell the malty scent of the beer on his breath, proving that he was feeling more than the effects of the night.

"My hair?" I stammer. "What are you talking about? Logan, I—."

"Dammit," he says, slamming a hand on the stall behind me. "Don't lie to me."

My eyes widen, but I don't flinch. I'm not getting the sense he'll harm me. Of course, I could always be wrong. "I'm not lying. I swear it's just normal hair. I don't know what you're talking about."

Emotion blazes in his eyes, the flecks of silver in the gray catching the dim overhead lights. "When I found you. When you were hurt." His voice sounds strained like it's taking an effort to speak. "Your hair was glowing. I *know* what I saw."

My back hits the wooden planks of the stall, a jarring thud echoing in the tense silence. Logan's face is inches from mine, eyes like storm clouds, unreadable and dark.

"You know more than you're telling me," His voice is a low growl, his arm braced against the stall above my head, effectively trapping me.

"The fuck I do. I've told you all I know," I shoot back, pulse racing. I've faced challenges before, but this feels different. Dangerous on a level I can't quite articulate.

His other hand slams against the stall, boxing me in even further. The scent of him, leather and earth, is overpowering.

Suddenly, the air begins to vibrate like a plucked string. A low, guttural warning sound emanates from the stall behind me. I dare not move, dare not breathe as I feel the incredibly hot breaths of Galaxian on my neck.

Twenty-One

LOGAN

My eyes flit from Brigid's face to Galaxian, my usually composed stallion, now sending a storm of emotion through the bond.

I snarl. *"What the hell are you—"* I say to him, but he interrupts me before I can finish.

"Don't. Hurt. Female".

His voice buzzes the air at a frequency that grates on my nerves, and I grind my teeth together to keep them from rattling in my skull.

A boiling mix of anger and confusion roils inside me. *"Back off. "* I respond in my head. He curls an upper lip, revealing a pair of sharp canines. Why must he constantly test me?

Bonds are supposed to be a union, not a battle, and yet every time I try to get Galaxian to bend to my will, he defies me. Brigid is trapped between me and the stall door. Her heart pounds against my chest as the tense moment stretches. He won't hurt her, not on purpose anyway, but that doesn't mean he won't attempt to bite me and accidentally get her instead. I need to end this now before anything unforgivable happens.

"I'm not going to hurt her," I say in my head. *"I am just talking to her."*

I pull in a shallow breath, attempting to slow my pulse that's drumming a frantic rhythm in my eardrums. Shithead's senses are better than mine, and I'm sure he can hear it.

Galaxian remains frozen, clearly not convinced.

Brigid whimpers, and I can feel the fear wafting off of her, which means Galaxian can smell it. It's no surprise he's in defense mode.

"What's happening?" she whispers. "What's he doing?"

"It's okay," I say, not taking my eyes off my stallion. "The bonding night has him especially anxious, so it's important you *exactly* do what I say."

She gives a timid nod, and her eyes fixed on me.

"Step slowly this way. No sudden moves." I place a hand on her shoulder and carefully guide her toward me and away from the stall. Galaxian's left nostril flares, and he stamps a hoof as if bothered by a fly.

However, he doesn't charge as I'd feared he would. Instead, he allows me to tug Brigid into my arms and away from him. The heavy blanket he's wearing has battery packs that send out micro-currents, preventing him from shifting and escaping his stall. As soon as I'd gotten the alert from Carla that Wraithwind had called to Danner, I'd followed standard protocol and made the novices blanket all the druadans.

For the most part, they behave when stalled, only shifting when commanded to by their rider, but after what had happened before with Brigid and Galaxian, all bets are off.

Once we're a safe distance away, I drop my arms, releasing her, yet she stays next to me, her head pressed lightly against my chest. The closeness induces a fresh wave of energy from the bonding ceremony, and it takes every ounce of my willpower not to tear off her clothes and bury myself inside her. The thought is enough to get me hard, I swallow and take a full step back. It's the bonding ceremony mojo, fucking with my head. It has to be.

I *can* resist it. I just have to get away from her.

Put distance between us. That's what I need. Distance from *her*. This was at the top of the fucking list of bad ideas to follow her in here. A bad idea to be alone with *her* on a bonding night.

What the hell was I thinking?

Truth is, I hadn't been.

I didn't know why I followed her into the barn.

"Okay," she whispers. "What now?"

"Now, you leave. Get the fuck out of here as fast as you can."

Confusion and hurt cloud her eyes, but I refuse to yield.

"Go," I bark, causing her to wince.

Our eyes lock for one more intense second before she breaks it and strides past me and out of the barn. I keep my eyes fixed on the ground as the unsettling realization lingers in her wake. This isn't over. Whatever the bonding night is doing to me is only the beginning. Something has fractured inside me because of her. Galaxian's bond with me is decaying faster *because* of her.

And I'll be dammed if I let it break.

OUT OF THE BARN, I STEP INTO THE MUGGY NIGHT AIR. THE constant thump of music coming from the staff's houses drifts across the courtyard to me as I take the long way back to my apartment. I pass by the exhibition hall., the circle around the back side of the gym.

Figure it is as good a night as any to check the perimeter wall for cracks that need fresh mortar. Just as I pass the shuttle pad, I catch one of the shuttle attendants outside, taking sips from a bottle of beer. She's a decent-looking brunette about my age. Has to be one of the shuttle crew's temps since one is out on maternity leave.

She looks up, her hazel brown eyes glinting in the lone security light above her.

"Hey," she calls out. "I know you. You ride the brown one with the teal mane, right?"

I stuff my hands into my pockets and keep walking.

"I watched you guys a few nights ago. He has to be my favorite, you know? So pretty."

"I know," I say. Galaxian is a damn fine-looking stallion, although my perception of him is currently tainted by my most recent encounter, where he was a snarling asshole with Brigid standing between us.

She pushes off from the side of the building, and I hear her footsteps lag behind me. The muscle between my shoulder blades tightens.

"I'm just staying for the night," she says, stepping up to my shoulder. "And the bunk in there is flat as a board. I might as well be sleeping on the ground out here." She laughs, the sound breaking through the night air.

"I'm sure riders have comfortable beds. It'd make sense, right? You're the stars, after all."

I stop, and she has to catch herself a step ahead before realizing we are no longer walking. The heady rush of the bonding power surrounds me as if I'd momentarily outran it, but the second I'd stopped, it collided with me. The edges of my vision swim as I turn to look at the woman next to me. With a mischievous grin on her face, she holds up the half-drunk bottle. "I'm really good at sharing."

I clamp down my jaw, indecision warring inside me. I should go home, take a cold shower, and pop some of the leftover sleeping pills Dr. Rajesh had prescribed me after losing Galaxyla.

But why? So, I can go home at watch the cameras? Every

employee here is at their house, partying, drinking, and fucking. It's a bonding night.

Besides, she's a temp and will be gone in a few days. My dick is half-hard already. Inwardly, I cringe. Holy shit, I've been around Carter too much. I flex my hand, feeling the tightness of the scar.

Scars.

The power influx tonight is ridiculously strong, and I'm an idiot to think I can shrug it off with a cold shower and pills.

If I don't find a way to release it, I'll be in the early stages of brimming in the morning. At the academy, they'd warned us about bonding ceremonies. There were only two ways to survive the night with your dignity intact: One, leave the station entirely, and two, if that was not a possibility, find consenting other people to share your bed. Whether that be another rider or, in this case...

"I'm Jaquie, by the way," she says sweetly and presses the bottle to her lips. Her tongue darts out seductively, tracing the rim.

Fuck me. I adjust myself as my dick fully hardens.

I'm not going to make it to my apartment.

I guide her into the bramble bushes that grow along the base of the twenty-foot-high perimeter wall. Once positioned in a way that makes us mostly secluded, she lets out a throaty giggle. "I've always wanted to do this. Riders are so freaking hot." Her hand goes to my crotch, her fingers tracing along the shape of my dick in my pants. "Is it true you can stay hard even after...?" She trails off.

"Why don't you find out," I say.

She drops to her knees and peers up at me with a suggestive smirk as she undoes the four buttons of my jumpsuit. My erect cock springs out, and she grabs for it eagerly, pressing it to her lips. A groan escapes my throat, and I twist my fingers into her hair, gently coaxing her to take all of it.

She swirls her tongue around the head before taking more of me into her mouth. She moves expertly up and down my length as I arch toward her, my opposite hand resting on the wall behind me for stability.

My body trembles with pleasure, the pent-up energy from the ceremony being finally allowed to satiate me fully as she works me faster and faster. I squeeze my eyes shut, and flashes of iridescent silver hair cloud my vision.

Her nails dig into the backs of my thighs, and I move harder, faster inside her mouth, thrusting deep while keeping a steady rhythm. Finally, I crest over, spilling into her warm, wet mouth. She sucks me dry, her movements slow and careful, almost reverent, before rocking back on her heels to gaze up at me, her face flushed, eyes darkened with desire.

She wipes her chin, and I slip still hard dick back into my fly before helping her up.

"What about that bed?" she asks, eyeing the bulge in my pants.

"Thanks, but I've changed my mind," I say and start to walk past her.

"Are you fucking serious?" she yells. "Asshole!"

I keep walking, feeling the lingering effects of the orgasm fading rapidly. I'd die before ever admitting it to him, but the truth is, I envied Carter, who seemed to have a never-ending rotation of women at his beck and call. He could have his pick of the litter, indulge in short flings, or repeat hookups without any consequences.

But for me, one-night stands always left me feeling empty and unsatisfied. Enough to ease the strain of the bond but nothing else.

I'm sure there's something broken in me that a therapist would love to pick at. But after sex, I felt a hollowness.

Like I was settling for an appetizer when what I really wanted was a four-course meal.

The desire to find someone who would truly fulfill me was a fucking fantasy. What was the point of dwelling on something that could never exist? It would only lead to disappointment and heartache in the end.

Say if I did find someone who could fulfill me in every way possible, it wouldn't change the fact that I had eight years left. Eight years to devote myself to someone and have them do the same. Sure, I could be selfish. Take what I wanted, screw their feelings, but as much as Heath would argue, I wasn't that big of an asshole.

I shake my head and push those thoughts away as I make my way back to my secluded cabin.

My home for the rest of my life.

It was better than a lot of the kids back at the filtration plant I grew up had.

It could always be worse.

Twenty-Two

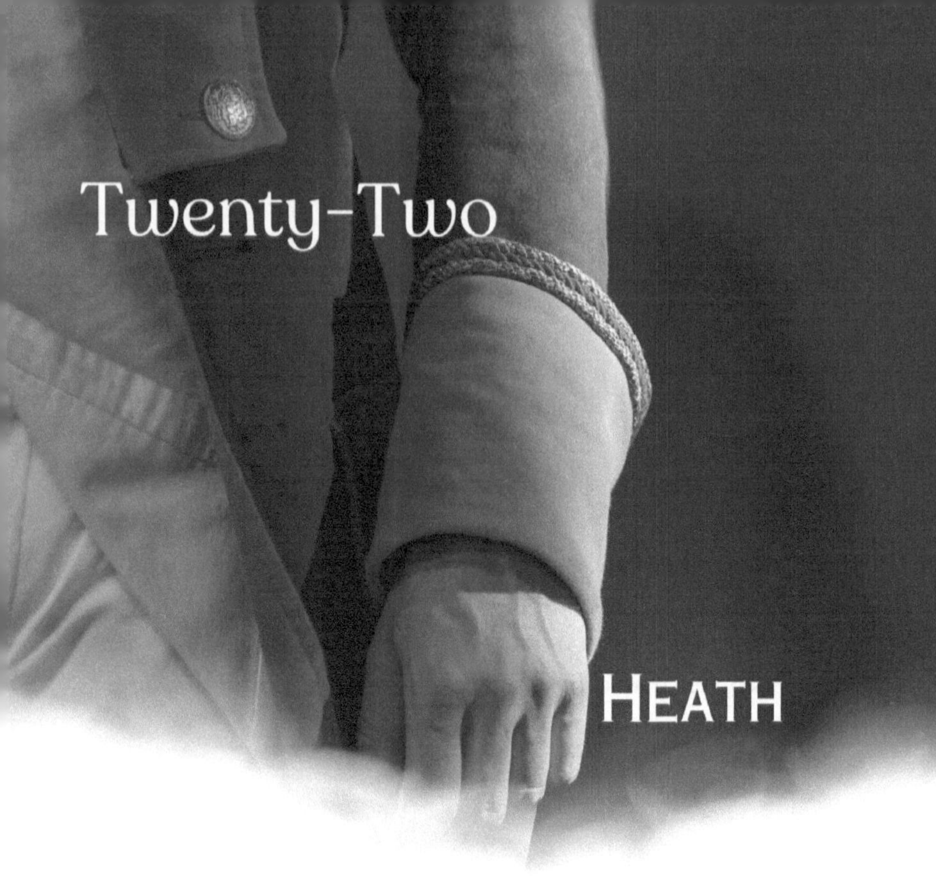

"Heath, I swear, the lobster bisque here will change your fucking life," Carter says, peering over the digital menu hovering in the center of the table.

"I've had it before," I say, "It's passable, but no one does it better than Mauricios."

Carter shakes his head. "Well, for us downtowners, it is delicious." He swipes a finger through the floating ivory paper, spinning it to view the other side. "Looks like they're out of that scotch you like. My choice?"

I shrug and let my eyes drift around the restaurant. It's moderately crowded for a Thursday night. Nicely dressed couples line the long bar out for post-work cocktails, and their chatter and occasional quiet laughter carry to where we're seated at a booth.

I could've had that life, I think. A life unscripted by legacy and social standing. But being the eldest Lockwood son has its expectations. The tradition is archaic; the firstborn son in powerful families joins Vanguard Academy as a rider to protect and serve. A grand gesture stemming from centuries ago in an effort to display to the continent that Venovian duty and safety are held above all else.

Cadman, our server, comes over, and Carter orders two glasses of mid-shelf whiskey. It's not my usual, but after the day we've had, I'd drink shuttle fuel. We'd split up upon landing that morning and knocked on every door, made every phone call, and crashed every auction house for information on black market druadan's eggs.

All had come up dry. Dinner here was our last chance.

Soon after, the server returns with our drinks. "Since we are so seldom graced by your presence," he says after setting our drinks in front of us. "Gentlemen, please enjoy. Our house specialties, compliments of Chef Peitzman."

He snaps his fingers, and two other servers rush over, laying down a parade of dishes in front of us. A platter of artfully arranged tuna and microgreens, the slices of a fruit splattered with honey, and two bowls of dark orange soup with a spiraling white cream floating on the surface.

"Thank you, Cadman," I say, and he and the other servers bob their heads before backing away.

Once alone again, Carter samples a puff pastry drizzled in something caramel-adjacent. "Think he'll ask for two or three tickets this time?"

"Two. His son was accepted to Vanguard." I admit, picking up my spoon.

"No shit? I never pinned that kid as rider material, but what do I know," Carter leans back, gesturing to himself. "They picked me, didn't they?"

"Mistakes happen," I quip, provoking a snort from Carter.

"Look at that. He made a joke."

"If the occasion is right, yes, I am quite funny, actually."

"Too bad being the big boss man doesn't allow for such occasions."

My mood darkens. "Not very often."

Whenever I was away from the station, I loved the moments I'd be swept away by the bustle of the city or taking in a show or musical performance, and for those fleeting hours, I'd forget I was a Master Rider. Forget I was a manager, and the aftershock of guilt would slam into me. I could never have a life outside of the station. And no matter how much I enjoyed myself, I could never run from the cold, hard truth. If I stayed more than a week away from Shadowmane, I would die.

A cruel, twisted Cinderella and her enchanted pumpkin carriage. There would always be a limit on the allowance of my time away from the station.

Carter dabs a napkin on his lips and suddenly locks eyes with a middle-aged woman wearing a black dress that is two sizes too small hovering by the bar. "That's my cue. Be back in ten—actually, make it twenty. Dessert's calling."

He rubs his hands together and flashes me a toothy grin. "Wish me luck. She's a talker." He pushes back from the table and saunters off. The woman's giggles drift across the restaurant, and from the corner of my eye, I see her lace her arm in Carter's. The two wander off to the back of the restaurant, where the private rooms that can be reserved for birthdays and celebrations are.

I sip the late summer vegetable soup. It's good. Sweet and savory, and just the right amount of seasonings to offset the earthy tones. I used to come here when my dad was working in the city and decided to bring me. Back then, it had a different name and a different feel.

"Master Rider Lockwood?" a man says, forcing me to set my spoon down.

Looking up, I see an older man standing before me, gray hair neatly combed, glasses perched on the bridge of his nose. Beside him is a young girl, maybe school-age, with brown hair, pulled back into a ponytail. "I'm Bernard, and this is my granddaughter, Isabelle. We're huge fans. Can we take a photo?"

"Sure," I say and get to my feet.

The elderly man and his granddaughter flank me, scooting in close as she taps twice on her wrist comm. A second later, a light flashes over the three of us, and the image appears on her comm screen.

"My late wife always dreamed of seeing one of your druadan shows," Bernard says as I return to my seat. "But we were never lucky enough to be picked from the wait list for tickets."

The man rests a hand on the young girl's shoulder. "Isabelle is twelve today, and since her parents are working a week-long shift, I decided to treat her to a special dinner here."

The words dig at me, scratching at a sense of guilt I can't easily ignore. With a small sigh, I pull out a business card from my wallet and scribble Carla's work number on the back.

"Call this number and tell them you're on 'Shadowmane's tab,'" I say, handing him the card. "She'll make sure you get tickets to one of our upcoming shows."

Their faces light up like they've won the lottery, which, in all honesty, they have.

"Thank you, thank you," Bernard says, and Isabelle jumps up and down, her ruffled dress fluttering around. "The kids at school are going to be so jealous," she says and swipes on her comm, already sharing the exciting news.

As they walk away, their eyes alight with excitement, I sink back into the chair. The mark stings on the back of my hand as if I'd dribbled the scalding soup on it, and I rub my thumb against the skin, attempting to dull the mild ache. The downside of being hundreds of miles from your druadan is the bond is weaker, which, in my case, on the verge of brimming, is actually a good thing. I'm less feverish and less irritable, and my appetite has returned.

The separation is risky, though, like taking morphine when you're actively bleeding out. The symptoms are important. A constant alarm that something is terribly wrong and your body is failing. However, it's only a day, and after the last three fitful nights of sleep, I'm optimistic I might sleep tonight when we return to the station.

There's a murmured greeting from the maître d' at the entrance, and I look up to see Jess striding toward my table. Multiple heads turn in her direction, as elegance and grace personified. Even if she's not readily recognized as heir to the Drakeford name, she looks like she belongs in this establishment where the cheapest bottle of wine costs the average person's weekly salary.

I stand and kiss her cheek. "Good evening, Jess. You look well." I help her with her coat and pull out a chair.

"Thank you," she says, sliding into her seat. The server appears, and she orders the cobb salad with dressing on the side.

We pass the time with small talk. End of Summer weather. Her grandmother's health. When her salad is brought, she picks at it, also pausing between chewing to talk about a business partner of her father's selling their shares so he can retire. Arousal drifts through the bond from the back of the restaurant. My cock hardens, straining against my pants, where it's pressed against my thigh. Oblivious to my mental state, she continues to talk. My eyes drift up from my drink and I stare at her mouth as she forks cherry tomatoes into her mouth.

The thought of inviting Jess to join me in one of the backrooms flits across my mind. I could use the release, and there's no denying the appeal of a shared experience with Carter. However, as quickly as I consider the idea, it's snuffed out. Jess knows that sex relieves an overcharged bond, but she'd choose to let me suffer rather than do anything as impulsive as having sex in a restaurant. If we were caught, it'd lead to a scandal. The damage to her reputation as a Drakeford and a businesswoman would be irreparable. At least, that's how she'd justify it.

Sex with her involved candles, champagne, and a king-size bed in a penthouse suite. It was a goddamn production to get her to take her imported silk panties off.

I drain my glass of scotch and ask for another as the waves of arousal continue to assault me. A painfully long thirty minutes later, Carter returns then with his hair a little more disheveled, and tie slightly askew, and a shit-eating grin on his face.

He settles back into his seat. "Hey, Jess."

"Hello, Carter," she says, blinking as if she just realized he was there. She sends a loaded glance to a woman adjusting her hat near the door, standing in the direction Carter had just come from.

"Ah, Carter," Jess coos, "I saw you talking to that older woman. Have you finally run out of women your age?"

Carter grins, unfazed. "Haven't run out, just diversifying the portfolio. Speaking of age, still using that cream for your dry scalp?"

Jess's eyes narrow into icy slits as she glares at me. "I see you two still share everything."

My face grows warm, and I clear my throat. "Sorry, Jess. You know how the bond is. No secrets between riders."

Jess's mouth tightens into a thin line, her disdain for the bond as subtle as a sledgehammer. "How convenient for you."

Carter chuckles, reaching for another spoonful of the caviar in the gilded dish. "Don't worry, Jess. Your secrets are safe with us. Mostly." He shoves the spoon into his mouth, a satisfied grin on his face, lightening the tightness forming between my shoulder blades. He drives me crazy sometimes with his care-free attitude, but damn if he can't make me laugh.

"You're lucky I was in town," Jess says, turning her attention away from Carter. "I just brokered the deal for that building on Ninth and Cedar."

"Congratulations," I say.

Jess beams. "Delford classified it as a historic site since it was a hospital a hundred years ago, so the negotiations were a night-mare. Imagine going to a hospital and having strangers poke and prod you with needles to 'cure' you. So medieval. Med apps are so much more hygienic, not to mention discreet."

She peers at the empty whiskey glass on the table and waves for the server to bring a Riesling. "Speaking of wines," she continues once he leaves. "There's a boutique vineyard in northern Gaergen that I visited last weekend with Laycen and Heather, and they had the most divine merlot. We should mark them down on the list for the caterers. I'd love to feature wine from all the regions of Venovia. Wouldn't that track well in the media?"

My mind falters at the mention of the media, and I suddenly feel like I'm sitting across from Brigid discussing PR. I chew the inside of my cheek, worry flooding my senses. Had this been a mistake to leave the station? To leave her alone after she'd been hurt?

No. She isn't alone. Logan's there with her. Logan.

My teeth clench together. He's been even more unstable than usual, his connection with Galaxian only exacerbating his already unpredictable behavior. But I have to trust that they can handle one day together without destroying each other or the station. When I return, everything at the station hopefully will still be intact.

I nod absently, my eyes darting to the look of sheer boredom on Carter's face before returning to hers. "Yes, it would."

"Oh, and for the flowers, I've decided they *must* be Parnian orchids. They'll be in season in time for our wedding, well in southern Parnia they will be. We can have them flown in specially."

My stomach sinks. The wedding. Shit, that's two months away. "Sounds...exotic."

She brushes a strand of hair back, her eyes sparkling. "It is. They have this lush, deep purple hue that'll match the bridesmaids' dresses perfectly. So, it all ties together."

"Very coordinated," I murmur, and Carter conceals a snort of laughter, transforming it into a cough.

"You have no idea," she says, folding and refolding the napkin on her lap. "A friend of mine just honeymooned at a resort in Lotus. Can you imagine? Waking up to a sunrise with all those trees. Can you believe the whole peninsula has clean air? No filtration systems anywhere. I hear land developers going wild right now selling lots for second homes."

I'm barely listening now. Every moment I spend here, chatting about flowers and honeymoons, is a moment wasted searching for clues to where Sharice might've taken the egg. If Jess knew that we'd had an egg stolen under my watch, she'd leap at it. Using it to craft a loophole that might grant me an early exit from my rider duties. Anything to make our scripted life play out on her terms.

Regret fills me, clawing up my insides. Why did I think I could juggle this dinner, Jess, and the mission?

I rattle the ice in my empty glass, and the server returns with a tray, switching it out for a fresh one. I feel Carter's eyes on my face as I sip. His mild concern filters through the bond from him to me. Jess stabs at her salad with a fork, still talking about seating arrangements and live bands versus DJs. But her voice fades into a distant echo as the weight of my two worlds—the one I'm chained to and the one I'm born for—pulls me apart.

"Heath, did you hear me?" she asks, clearly annoyed.

I blink at her, suddenly aware I'd missed her question. "Sorry, what?"

She arches a perfect eyebrow. "Have you settled on your groomsmen?"

"Logan and Carter," I say, my eyes darting briefly to Carter across from me. Boredom dulling his eyes, he's absentmindedly stabbing at the ice in his drink with his straw as if trying to drown out the drone of wedding talk by taking it out on defenseless cubes of frozen water.

"I've picked Logan and Carter," I repeat a little louder, gesturing subtly toward Carter as if to say, 'See? He's already thrilled about the role.'

Jess's lips tighten. "Two won't balance out for the photos. I want my cousin McKenzie and my brother Nathaniel in the bridal party, too. Otherwise, it's going to look lopsided."

"Oh no," Carter feigns a high-pitched voice. "Can't have it lopsided, now, can we?"

Jess rolls her eyes.

"Of course," I tell her. "That'd be fine."

Carter's comm buzzes, and he pulls it out, glancing at the screen. "Ah, would you look at that," he says, getting to his feet. "Looks like a thunderstorm is rolling in. If we don't head to the shuttle pad now, we'll be grounded for a few days. Duty calls, you know?"

I get to my feet a little faster than I'd intended, garnering a raised eyebrow from Jess. "Sorry to cut our dinner short, but we should get going."

Jess looks slightly bewildered. "Okay. I'll see you next week at the charity fundraiser."

Dammit. Of course, she'd be there. Drakeford was one of the platinum sponsors for the event. "Great. I'll see you then." I lean down to kiss her, and it's as awkward and stilted as they always are with her. No fireworks, no passion—just a hollow gesture that feels more like a contractual obligation than an expression of affection.

Carter and I leave. The whole meal is comped, so there's no need to stop and pay. Our private car is waiting for us, and we request it to take us to the shuttle station. As we speed through the neon-lit streets, Carter turns to me with a mischievous smile.

"Fine. Tell me," I say once we're seated in the back. He's as restless as a druadan who's been stalled for three days. "When you got back from 'talking' to Mrs. Welch, you looked like you'd been through the wringer."

"You have no idea," he replies, taking a sip of the drink the restaurant let him bring when we'd left. A Gold Coast sour whiskey with a twist of lemon.

"Did you know she used to be an alternate for the DU swim team?"

I narrow my eyes.

"I know, right? Sure, it was like forty years ago, but still, the things that woman can do while holding her breath—"

"Any luck on learning about the items that will be at her auction?" I interject before he gets sidetracked with vivid descriptions of what was accomplished in the coat closet.

"Do you want the good news or bad news first?"

"Bad news." Always bad news first. Why put off the inevitable?

He frowns. "Nothing about the egg from any of the black market auctions. There's the usual druadan and anti-rider chatter with the extremist groups, but nothing specifically about an egg. She also said the Delford auction house hadn't heard any rumors about a seller wanting to move it. She also said it hasn't been a topic of conversation among the bidders, which, if there is a demand, it will often pull in a seller."

"Damn," I mutter, taking a sip of my drink. "Our list of leads is shrinking by the minute."

"Yeah, I get it," he says. "But at least we can cross a few more off. Process of elimination, right?"

"I suppose so." It's frustrating to have to handle these leads in person, taking us away from the station and adding to my already mounting responsibilities. "Let's keep making calls once we're back. But be discreet. I'd hate for rumors to start to circulate." He lifts his glass in response, smirking. "Ah, yes. Here's to Network, always spreading disinformation for our safety and well-being.'"

We clink glasses, the sound echoing in the air of the shuttle long after. I sigh, feeling the disappointment weigh heavy on my chest. That lead was one of our last hopes for finding the missing egg in time.

"You forgot to ask me about the good news," he says cheerily.

I tilt my head in question.

"You survived a dinner with Jess."

I chuckle. "Small victories, huh?"

"Sometimes that's all we've got," he says as the car pulls up to the shuttle pad.

Twenty-Three

The shuttle hums softly around me as I stare out the window, lost in thought at the sight of Lake Leviler below. The familiar dinosaur-like shape of the lake soothes me, and I find I'm anxious to get back to the station.

For one obvious reason. Fragments dart across my mind of her nearly naked body in the steamy bathroom. The softness of her skin beneath my fingertips. The intense desire smoldering in her gorgeous blue eyes. The memory alone is enough to make me instantly hard.

When I'd been between Mrs. Welch's legs, my mind had been elsewhere, distracted. When we'd switched positions, and she'd gone down on me, I'd nearly lost my arousal. It wasn't her fault. The woman was skilled and enthusiastic. However, it'd been the thought of Brigid being the one on her knees that had been enough to get me through. It hadn't been my proudest moment. And while Mrs. Welch had left more than satisfied, this unfamiliar feeling of guilt clings to me.

I'd done what I had to, what Heath had ordered me to do.

Everyone has their skills. Their talents. Mine just happens to be getting ladies to spread their legs for me and scream my name as if their lives depended on it. It'd been a means to an end. I'd done what I needed to in order to find more information about the egg. So why the guilt? Why did it feel like I did something wrong? A strange mix of emotions leaves me feeling confused and conflicted.

Because of Brigid. Because she consumes my every waking thought, and just thinking about seeing her soon makes me smile. She has a playful side to her when she lets her guard down. I want more. I want to make her smile and hear her laugh every day. I didn't know this was possible to want someone so badly.

Well, fuck me. I've never felt this way about anyone before.

Heath's comm chimes from where he sits in the chair across from me in the private shuttlecraft. "Hello, Mother," he answers, and it's as if he tossed a bucket of ice water on me.

I gnash my teeth at the agitation in the bond and lean back.

"Yes, I'm sorry," he continues, giving me a suspicious look. "Yes, I was in town but it was a quick trip, and I am needed back at the station." He pinches the bridge of his nose, assuming the same frustrated face he wore anytime he talked with his family.

"I didn't know you were there too—" he continues but is cut off before he can finish, and I hear his mom's animated voice on the other end. "I'm sorry, it was an unexpected trip, and when I get the situation handled at the station, I'll rent us that cabin outside Nelworth. The one with the spa and skiing trail you liked?"

There's a pause on the other end and then a reply too quiet for me to catch. Heath is one of my oldest friends — the self-proclaimed leader of our trio, although Logan would never admit it — and I respected him deeply. However, when it came to his family and soon-to-be-wife, the man acted like a puppet on finely crafted strings. They tugged the strings, and he obeyed. Each bow and nod is carefully orchestrated by the invisible hands of expectation and reputation. Apparently, his station as a rider meant nothing when his family owned half of Venovian land.

"Love you too," he murmurs and then ends the call.

"Trouble in paradise?" I tease.

He sinks back into the seat, weariness tugging at the corners of his eyes. "Jess called her after we left, and she's angry that I neglected to invite her too."

A tight knot of pity forms in my stomach. "She'll get over it. You just have to distract her with the wedding planning stuff."

He sighs, and the knot tightens further. I can't imagine what he's going through. The feeling of being trapped in a future you didn't want. "Jess isn't the worst you could do, you know," I say. "I give her shit, but she's not *that* bad."

He rubs a hand over his eyes. Between meeting people over drinks and catching them at their houses, neither of us got much sleep last night. "I know," he finally says. "She's fine."

"That's the spirit. Fine keeps your parents off your back for not being their good little boy to take over the company, *and* you get to play house when your tenure is up at the station."

Heath peers between his fingers at me and doesn't respond.

It's a line of bullshit, of course, all of it. Riders fulfilling their full ten-year service and receiving a discharge is a myth. A legend. In the past, maybe, but now, flaring out is the only future a rider can expect.

Only one rider is the exception: Marshal.

Heath takes a deep breath, his shoulders rising and falling with effort. "She's trying to get me transferred, Carter. The Drakefords have some connections, and she's been trying to pull strings to get me moved and my services shortened."

I'm taken aback, my eyes narrowing. "Are you serious? She *does* know it doesn't work that way, right? You're bonded, numbnuts. That's not something you can just cut short."

"I've tried explaining it to her," he says, sighing. "But she just doesn't grasp the depth of it. She thinks if we get a house near

Blackhawk, it'll somehow make things easier. That being closer to her will weaken the bond. And she's dead certain that once we start a family, it'll break."

I widen my eyes at him. "Oh, shit, Heath. You haven't told her." Irritation floods my veins, not at Heath, but at Jess for not understanding and thinking *she* knows what's best for him.

Heath looks down, avoiding my gaze. When he finally speaks, his voice is thick with emotion. "No."

I want to lecture him, tell him *he's* the one being selfish for keeping a secret like that from her, but I bite my tongue. Even without his guilt seeping through the bond, it's clear it's eating him alive right now. I'd be no better than Jess if I tried to interfere with his choices. I have to trust he knows what he's doing.

I lean forward, placing a hand on his shoulder. "You can't protect her by keeping her in the dark, Heath. She needs to know. This is your life, and she's a part of it. She deserves the truth."

Heath nods slowly. Strain, tugging at the corners of his eyes. "I know, Carter. I just... I just wanted to give her some hope, you know? Besides, I can only handle one problem at a time."

I exhale sharply. "You're right. So, speaking of the other problem, what *do* we know now that we didn't before?"

"We know a group took it," Heath says. "And Venovia is small."

"You know we did the best we could. If we pressed them for more details, the more it would only make them suspicious."

Heath frowns. "I'm afraid you're right."

I tap my fingers against the armrest. When I'd first moved to Meridian, I'd taken every shuttle I could, wishing to spend my free weekends in Delford. Dance at the clubs, eat at the restaurants. But now, the more time I spend away from the city, the more I realize I like the quiet seclusion the station provides. Well, and the fact that it felt like my skull was about to split into two the longer I was away from Ember.

"Perhaps Logan and Brigid had better luck than us," Heath says.

I laugh, causing Heath to arch an eyebrow. "If they didn't kill each other while we were gone."

"True. But I doubt it with a bonding ceremony and all."

I sit up straighter in my seat. "What the hell? You didn't tell me a bonding happened." I stammer. "Who was it?"

"Keven Danner and Wraithwind."

"No shit." Dammit, I'd been really working Danner. I should have been there. He's smart but his instincts are spread a little thin, and I can only imagine the lack of guidance Master rider-not-my-problem Logan dished out. "Any bets who fucked who?"

A slight smile appears on Heath's face. "As station manager, it would be inappropriate for me to invest myself in the personal lives of the staff."

"Petyr and Sandra, for sure," I continue. "And that the new tour guide, Tim? He and his husband split, so I bet he was down to get frisky."

"Carter," Heath groans.

My thoughts race ahead, feeling the overwhelming disappointment that I'd missed the rare event on the station. The last one had been with Logan and Galaxian. The night had been a blur, and I'd awoken with the two guests and the traveling nurse in my bed. It had been three days before any of us could walk normally again. A bonding night is like catnip to riders if catnip is mixed with steroids and gives you a raging boner that just won't quit.

My mood instantly sours. Brigid is there. And Logan.

No way they did. I pound my fist against the seat, causing Heath to flinch.

"There will be more," he says, misinterpreting my anger. "Nytheria and Stefensen are close. I anticipate it in the next month or so. I have already reached out to Vanguard for another novice assignment."

Heath leans back and closes his eyes.

Suddenly, the two hours left of the ride feel like an eternity. I can't sit still, and my leg starts bouncing up and down restlessly.

"What is it," Heath asks, keeping his eyes closed.

"You don't think Logan and Brigid?" The question, half-formed, trails into the air.

Heath sighs before opening his eyes. "Don't ask questions you don't want the answers to."

I shake my head. "There's no way, right? Brigid would never. And Logan? He probably drowned himself in a bottle and blacked out."

"Mhmm," Heath says.

"Dammit, Heath. Answer me."

Finally, he opens his eyes and leans forward. "It's a bonding night. People make choices. Miss Corsair is an adult. Logan is an adult. As long as the station is secure, I'm okay with it."

A dry laugh erupts from me. "Don't tell me you're *honestly* okay with her and Logan fucking?"

Heath's eyes burn with intensity as he leans closer. "Jealousy is a dangerous game, Carter. The three of us are bound by something greater. Logan is our bondmate. Don't let a woman tear that apart."

I nod begrudgingly, knowing he's right but still feeling a surge of possessiveness towards Brigid.

"Talk to her," Heath continues, his voice softening. "You want answers. She's the only one who can give them."

I tighten my grip on the arms of the seat and take a deep breath before releasing it slowly.

"Now," Heath says. "I'd like to get some shut-eye. We have a long day tomorrow."

I doze off and on for the rest of the flight. I'm awoken when the pilot announces our descent onto the island that Meridian sits on. From the window, the rising sun casts a brilliant glow across the morning sky.

Heath stirs when a notification chimes from his wrist comm interrupts the silence. His eyes light up as he scans the screen. "The scientist at the private lab I paid off got back to us. They tested the samples from Galaxian's legs."

I lean in, anticipation tightening my chest. "And? What did they say?"

Heath's face falls as he reads. "They said it's inconclusive."

"Inconclusive? What the hell is that supposed to mean?"

"It means they are required by law to report it."

"Of course they fucking do."

Heath swipes away the notification on his comm, and his face looks even paler than usual. "We're about to have the entirety of Circuit's environmental investigations unit come down here and swab anything that moves."

"Well, shit."

Heath makes a sound of agreement. "Yeah, and it means we need Miss Corsair more than ever."

Twenty-Four

BRIGID

"The fundraiser is in two days," Carla says, waving her hands for emphasis from where she sits at the end of the conference room table. Heath called a meeting for us as soon as he and Carter had returned from Delford. Apparently, their contacts had been a bust, and unfortunately, the samples of liquid taken from Galaxian had caught the attention of Circuit health and safety officials.

"We can't have Circuit crawling around here with traps trying to catch wild animals," Carla continues. "We have guests arriving. They've booked tours and are expecting catered lunches on the grounds."

"I'll handle it," I cut in. Public relations *is* my domain. And with so much else I can't control: Sharice's disappearance, the strange way I'm drawn to the druadan barn or the confusing feelings I have toward three of the men here, this—I can control this. "I'll reach out to Circuit. Make sure whoever they send is briefed on discretion and that they can only perform tests with designated escorts from the security team." I glance at Logan. His jaw is tightly set, eyes forward. It's so obvious he's avoiding looking at me.

Good. Serves him right.

After the bullshit he pulled in the barn, he should feel guilty. If it hadn't been for Galaxian coming to my defense—which I still hadn't entirely figured out why he'd done that— Logan might've gone further. Not hurting me. Sure, he scared the shit out of me, but Heath seemed to have him on a short enough leash. No, it had been how he'd looked at me.

Like *I* was the threat.

But why? What was it about me that he hated so much? Maybe I'd never know. Maybe he was just that much of an asshole, and there wasn't an explanation.

No doubt, he must be worried that I'll end up telling Heath what happened. I didn't have much authority there, but Heath seemed to be the only one who could control Logan's outbursts, and while I wasn't a tattle-tale, I wasn't going to let some jerk try to push me around.

"My team is available," Logan says, looking to Carla. "We can ensure the investigators don't interfere with the tours."

Carla doesn't look convinced, but she gives a reluctant nod. "Fine."

The door opens, and one of Logan's other security officers enters wearing the black uniform. Her honey-blonde hair is braided into a low bun, and she has striking green eyes. A surprising tang of jealousy coats my tongue as I watch her throw heated glances toward Carter when she thinks he's not looking.

What had Logan said? That Carter was mine?

Maybe there's some truth to that. He hadn't come to see me when he'd returned, and I still felt like there was so much left unsaid between us.

I can't deny I like him. But things are different now that everything is out in the open. I'd assumed it'd make things easier. Clearer. But I'd been wrong. Instead, it'd made everything even more confusing.

I was now privy to the secret they shared.

A secret I know they'd never let leave the station.

So, where did that leave Carter and I? If I wanted to leave, would he side with me or his bonded riders?

I hoped I'd never have to make him choose.

Heath folds his fingers on the desk, his eyes scanning the room before settling on me. "How about we move some of the early VIP guests to the main house guest rooms for now? We can say the guest cottages are being deep-cleaned or that there's a plumbing issue. Then, once the Circuit officials clear the area, we can transfer them back."

Carla leans back, considering it. "It's an idea. But we'd need to sell it as an upgrade, not a downgrade. Brigid, I need you to pitch this."

"No problem," I say, already mentally drafting the idea in my head. Luxury experience, exclusive personal touch—the works.

Carla turns to Logan. "How long will it take for your team and the Circuit officials to comb through the area?"

Logan double-taps the tablet on the table, and a 3d projection of the station appears in the space above it. He flicks his wrist, and the image shrinks, showing a top-down view of the station and the desert landscape beyond the walls. The shimmering image slowly twirls. "With my team escorting them, at least a full day to cover the North end. Maybe two, depending on how far out they want to go."

Heath rubs his forehead. "We don't have that kind of time. The gala is the day after tomorrow."

It's then that Carter— who's been uncharacteristically quiet — finally speaks. "What if we find the proof ourselves? Like whatever creature that blood is connected to. If we can show them it's some sort of unclassified hybrid animal, they might back off. There are all sorts of weird frogs and reptiles on the island."

The room falls silent for a moment, then Logan says, "He's got a point. If we find the creature first, it could work to our advantage. I'll take security to check the perimeter outside the grounds."

I seize the chance. "I'm coming with you."

Logan starts to object. "The fuck you are. It's too dangerous."

"You'll be there, plus three other armed security," I fire back, "You protect me from whatever it is, and I'll do my job taking photos and documenting it. You want to control the narrative? Fine. Then you need me."

"Logan's right," Carter says to my dismay.

I stuff down the bitter tang of betrayal. *Guess that answers my question about whose side he's on.*

Then adds, "We can't risk you getting hurt again."

Absently, I rub my wrist where the burn is still not entirely healed and look to Heath, hoping that *he* agrees with me. He's the boss. He's the one I should be trying most to convince. I give him my most pleading look, but a swift shake of his head snuffs out all hope.

"I refuse to have anyone else put in harm's way than is necessary. Logan and his team are trained. I'd feel better if you were safe behind these walls."

I nod. "Understood," I mumble, trying to keep my composure even as I'm seething with frustration. Their concern for me felt like a cage, their own idea of safety. The holographic display of Meridian twirls lazily between us as my thoughts race ahead. Are they really protecting me, or are they afraid of what I might find out there? That I'll stumble upon another one of their secrets that they're sworn by some rider code to keep?

"So, it's settled then. Logan and Carter will do a quick scout of the perimeter and report back anything we think can be used to delay Lannett from sending people here during the gala. And in the off chance you don't find anything, Brigid and Carla will have accommodations set up for the guests. That way, they can hopefully be kept in the dark about the investigation going on." Heath pauses, his eyes passing between us. "I'll be available to assist if I can."

Finally, his dark eyes grasp mine. "Are we clear?"

"Crystal," I affirm.

I LEAVE THE MAIN HOUSE. THE AIR OUTSIDE IS CRISP, A WELCOME change from the stifling tension in the meeting room. I make my way to my cottage, feeling a mix of relief and restlessness. The weight of their decisions is like a shroud over my shoulders.

"Hey," Carter's voice catches me off guard, causing me to halt. I turn, finding him approaching with that all-too-familiar swagger of his.

"I was hoping we could talk," he says.

"About what?" I say sweetly.

His eyes scan my face, and I realize he's not in his usual playful mood.

"Dr. Rajesh cleared me," I blurt. "No infections and no lasting damage."

"That's good," Carter says, sounding forced.

Wow. Why was this so awkward? It was never this awkward before.

I shift the weight on the balls of my feet.

"I heard about Waithwind and Danner," he says. "Did you get a chance to watch?"

First, my injuries, and now a bonding night. Boy, are we good at avoiding the elephant in the room. "Yes. Carla and I went, actually."

The crease between his eyes eases as relief washes over his face.

"Pretty wild, huh? I won't miss the next one." Then, almost as an afterthought. "The energy can make everyone wired. Did you sleep all right?" His attempt at casualness doesn't mask the underlying root of his question.

I'm momentarily caught off guard, debating whether to divulge what happened with Logan, Galaxian, and me in the barn. Nothing *had* truly happened, and a part of me kind of liked the subtle flare of jealousy from Carter. It's an aspect of him I find as unexpected as it is endearing.

I reach up, cupping the side of his face. My thumb rubs on the stubble, and almost imperceptibly, he leans into my touch.

"I slept alone if that's what you're asking.

He lets out a deep breath, and a smug smile materializes on his face. "It'd been no big deal if you hadn't. You know. I get it, I just wanted to—"

"Master Rider James," Logan calls out from where he's standing at the bottom of the main house. Even at this distance, I can see him glance at me before staring at the ground and kicking the dirt off the toes of his boots.

I drop my hand to my side and Carter's expression changes. The vulnerability in those green eyes of his fading. "I'm glad to see you're recovering. I was worried about—," he starts to say but is interrupted again by Logan's voice, now filled with frustration.

"We have shit to do."

Carter frowns. "If I'm free, maybe I'll come by later?"

I grin. "I'd like that."

His face alights with hope, and then, with a final look, he turns, jogging back to Logan.

I continue the rest of the way through the courtyard and down the path to my cottage.

Inside, I put a pot of water on the stove and toss in some instant noodles. The simplicity of the task is oddly comforting. I add a package of freeze-dried veggies, watching them rehydrate and mix with the noodles. It's not gourmet, but it's mine.

Still riding the high that Carter James was jealous of me sleeping with anyone, I grin to no one in particular. I didn't want to put pressure on this...whatever this was. Still, it felt good to have someone care about me. Worry about me.

Especially someone like Carter.

Eating my noodles, I pick up my personal comm. The light from the screen casts a soft glow in the dim room. Opening the group chat, I see a message from Laura and Vince, along with a photo of them at my favorite seafood restaurant, Salty John's.

Laura: *Guess where we are? Miss you, Brigid. How are you?*

A wave of nostalgia and affection washes over me.

Brigid: *Doing fine. Sorry, I haven't responded. Just been crazy busy here with the fundraiser.*

Almost immediately, Laura's next message pops up, filled with her usual curiosity.

Laura: *Any luck with Sharice?*

I hesitate, my fingers hovering over the screen. What can I tell them? That some mysterious gang or terrorist group coerced her into stealing a druadan egg? And that I'd been left with crumbs of answers? They're my best friends, yet I'd sworn to keep the station's secrets.

I sigh, deciding to split the difference.

Brigid: *A few small leads. Nothing concrete, though.*

Vince jumps into the conversation.

Vince: *I'm personally offended you haven't sent us any photos of the riders. Btw, Carter's shirtless spread in that cologne ad has been my go-to these days.*

Laura's response is a swift, gagging face image.

I chuckle, imagining their expressions. If they only knew the truth about Carter and me alone in the spa, in my shower. A delicious heat settles in my core, and I'm instantly distracted.

The blinking cursor showing they're awaiting my response pulls me back to the present.

Brigid: *Haha, you guys are too much. I'll send some pics soon. Promise.*

I set down my comm, a grin still playing on my lips. The noodles are done now, and I sit down to eat, savoring the herb-infused broth.

Slurping my noodles, the conversation with my friends, and the normalcy in their lives cause me to drift into the sea of what-ifs that is often aligned with guilt. Is this where I'd thought I'd be at twenty-two? On an isolated druadan station? My mind wanders to the life I left behind. I think of the potted plants perched on the windowsill of my old apartment, silently hoping Laura remembers to water them in between her hectic schedule as a personal assistant to a Delford fashion media editor. Those plants were my little oasis, a touch of green amidst the stone and steel buildings.

I remember the window in my bathroom, coated in pink paint that had faded over time. Every morning, the sun would peek through, casting a rosy hue over the room. It bathed my furnishings in a soft, pink light, a daily reminder of the charm and quirks of my old life.

I miss Triton Strategies. The bustle of creativity at the firm while working with politicians and business owners navigating their scandals. The challenges and payoff that came with each project. My old boss's encouraging words echo in my memory, reminding me of a different kind of fulfillment. It's strange to think of how much has changed since then.

If, by some miracle, Sharice appeared on my doorstep right now, what would I do then? Once I knew she was safe and alive, would I still belong here at Meridian Station? What would my purpose be? Would she return with me to Delford if I asked? Surely Circuit would keep her busy with their multitude of questions, but what about after? She couldn't be held responsible, right? She'd been threatened. She had no other choice but to do what she did. So, say they let her off the hook, then what? Before she worked here, she'd been a PR intern at Lannett. She'd often commented about how they made their intentions obvious, that they intended to hire her once she'd finished her internship and graduated.

Surely, they'd be happy to see her return. A warmth spreads across my chest as I imagine my sister excelling at her job. Living her life. Maybe even marrying and giving me little nieces or nephews.

I twirl the noodles around my fork and slurp it down. The sound is exceptionally loud in the quiet space, and I can't help but giggle. It feels good after everything to laugh at something silly. Sharice wouldn't glare at me for the rude noise, but I know deep down she'd think it was funny, too.

As I eat, I double-click my wrist comm, allowing the projection to hover above the table, and swipe through the Network site of the station, confirming the updates I asked Carla to have an IT person do before the gala. On the roster page, the nine riders and novices are listed. The top three spaces reserved are for the Master Riders, and the three men are dressed in their formal riding jackets. I nearly have to wipe drool from my face as I let my eyes linger on them. Heath's professional photo is on the left, then Carter's crooked smirk, followed by a grim-faced Logan that had undoubtedly left the photographer frustrated.

Despite myself, I've grown attached to the people here. Carla, with her experience and work ethic, puts mine to shame. Heath, with his intense loyalty to the station. Carter, with his...

well, Carter. And Logan is literally the biggest asshole here, but I can't help but respect his fierce commitment to the safety of everyone here. There's a kinship I feel with this place, an unexpected connection that's hard to ignore.

What would my life look like if I stayed here past my original intention? Carla has been here for five years and has maintained a long-distance relationship. Could I do the same? Maybe I'd meet someone back in Delford, take Laura up finally on one of her many offers to set a profile up for me on the Network dating app. The idea seems almost laughable now, with everything else that's at stake.

The truth is, this has become more than just a job; it's my passion. Living myths surround me. Strong, beautiful, and dangerous horses who form an invisible and powerful bond with a human.

I'd witnessed it at the bonding night. It'd been as close to magic as anyone could have ever hoped to see in their lifetime. How many people would live their whole lives and never get that experience? Never get to see a druadan disappear and reappear with their rider. Feel the air hum as the riders talk to their stallions in their own secret language.

This strange, unpredictable life at Meridian Station has woven itself into the fabric of my being. For now, this is where I need to be and where I *want* to be. I refuse to let anything happen to jeopardize that.

As the afternoon wanes, I immerse myself in my work designing the digital graphic we'll use to promote the main house as overnight arrangements for the gala guests. Graphic design has never been my forte, but today, it's a welcome distraction. I pull up photos of the main house's luxurious rooms from the station's stock database. Each image speaks of elegance and comfort, perfect for our high-profile guests.

Sitting at my desk, I lose myself in the process of manipulating images, adjusting colors, and playing with layouts. After about an hour of meticulous tweaking, the design starts to take shape. It's not perfect, and I'm certain Laura would have a few things to say about it, but it'll have to do.

Next, I focus on the text. Using bold, eye-catching lettering, I highlight the allure of choosing the main house over the guest houses. I want the guests to feel the exclusivity and luxury we offer. For good measure, I add a note about private dining access in the main house, a detail sure to entice those seeking privacy and a unique experience.

Satisfied with my creation, I send a quick message to Carla, giving her a heads-up about the idea and hoping she'll see the potential in it to charm our guests. It's a small contribution, but one that ties me back to my roots in marketing.

As evening falls, the sky outside transitions to a canvas of deep blues and purples. I take a moment to appreciate the view before heading to the shower. The warm water is soothing, washing away the day's worries and leaving me refreshed.

Climbing into bed, I switch on the latest Parnian reality show. It's a group of rival vineyard-owning families, and the drama is delectable. It's terrible, but we all need our guilty pleasures. Vince had gotten me hooked in college as a way to unwind and escape into the dramas of a life far removed from mine, filled with late-night cramming sessions and research projects that ate up every second of free time.

As the show plays, almost inevitably, I think of the three men who have become inexplicably intertwined in my life.

I move my tablet to the nightstand and position myself on my side. Closing my eyes, I slip my hand under my silk pajama bottoms. I can almost feel their presence as I rub a slowly growing warmth surrounding me. I imagine their hands joining mine. First Carter's, then Heath's, and then Logan's. The feel of the fingers rubbing, stroking, slipping in and out. I close my eyes and take in a deep breath, filling myself with the image of Carter caressing my breasts. The soft feel of Heath's hair between my fingers, the heat of Logan's breath along my thighs.

Wave after wave of desire courses through me. My body trembles and my skin aches to be touched. The memory of Logan's lust-filled gaze in the barn during the bonding ceremony returns to me. He'd been so hard. Everywhere. An unyielding presence I wanted so desperately to tear down. I remember his hands on my neck, my arms, my face. Finally, I crest over, pleasure flooding my body as I succumb to the sensations. I draw in a shuddering, satisfied breath as the world fades away.

IN THE GRAND BALLROOM OF MERIDIAN STATION, AMIDST A SEA of elegantly dressed guests, I stand in my golden yellow evening gown. The light catches the fabric, making me shine like a star amongst the crowd. The music, a gentle melody, weaves through the air, mixing with laughter and the soft chime of glasses. I feel like a princess in a fairytale, lost in a moment of enchantment.

But suddenly, something changes. An unexplainable shiver runs down my spine, and a feeling of dread settles over me. It's as if a shadow has passed over the sun, turning my moment of magic into one of unease. I look around, trying to find the source of my discomfort, but everything seems normal. Still, the feeling grows stronger, urging me to flee. With renewed determination, I run. My mind races with questions. What is chasing me? Why can't I see it? Confused and scared, I listen to my instincts and start running.

The hallways of the station stretch out endlessly, a maze of turns and twists. My breath comes in quick, shallow bursts, each one sounding loud in my ears. My heart thumps wildly, a frantic drumbeat echoing my fear. I can sense something behind me, an unseen pursuer that's always just a step away. It's terrifying, not knowing what chases me, yet feeling its presence so close.

My panic reaches a terrifying peak as I trip. The sound of my heel snapping is like a gunshot in the silence. I fall to the ground, hands scraping against the cold metal floor. Desperation grips me. I can almost feel the eyes of my unseen hunter on me, waiting to pounce.

I lay there on the cold metal floor of the station, my heart slamming against my chest. My breathing is fast and shallow, and I can feel the sweat trickling down my neck. Fear has taken control of my body, making it hard to move. Then, voices pierce through my fear. Logan's voice, strong and commanding, urges me, "On your feet!"

Heath follows, his tone filled with urgency. "Don't stop, Brigid!"

Then it's Carter, his voice a distant but distinct. "Keep going!"

Their words are like a beacon in the darkness, giving me the strength to stand up and discard my broken shoe. Something inside me rises up and gives me a burst of strength as I push myself up off the ground and start running again.

But this time, I'm not running away from something - I'm running towards it. I have zero clue why but I'm no longer afraid of what's behind me as long as I keep running. The key to my salvation, my safety, the key to everything is just ahead. My pulse ratchets another beat higher, as my bare feet slam onto the concrete.

There's something waiting for me at the end of this hallway - something more powerful than the overwhelming fear. The need to reach my goal intensifies, and then I see it: the druadan eggs seated on their marble pedestals.

As I approach the voice, I am filled with a mix of emotions.

Fear still lingers in the back of my mind, but it is overshadowed by curiosity and an unshakable feeling I need to get closer. This must be why I am here. Something to do with these eggs?

The end of the hallway looms closer. The pair of eggs beckon me. An overwhelming sense that I need to be closer. I'm here for a reason.

I extend my hand, about to touch them, when a large shadow obscures the light, plunging the room into darkness. A cold chill wraps its icy arms around me, threatening to suffocate me. My breathing, loud and panicked, is the only sound in the void.

"Hello?" my voice echoes, small and frightened. "Is anyone there?" I plead, desperation bleeding through. "Please! Someone!"

Alone in this dark, empty space, I sink to my knees, overcome by a sense of isolation and despair. *So alone. So dark.*

Then, abruptly, I awake, sitting bolt upright in my bed. It takes a moment for me to recognize my surroundings - my bedroom, safe and familiar. The darkness of the night peeks through my window. I pause, breathing heavily, trying to calm my racing heart. Usually, my dreams involve warm sandy beaches or playing hide and seek with my sister back home at the research station. Never anything like that. It'd felt so *real*. I had been scared. Fearing for my life over something unseen. Yet I knew it was there. Chasing me. Stalking me. Hunting me. I shiver, wrapping my arms around myself, and realize I'm cold and damp with sweat.

I glance at the clock. 5:00 AM. The fear from the dream lingers, clinging to me like my pajama top clings to my chest and making the thought of returning to sleep unappealing.

I'm wide awake now. Tomorrow is the gala.

Twenty-Five

LOGAN

oday is going to be the fucking longest day of my life.

Master Rider and head of security at the station, and I get assigned to babysitting duty. The group of scientists encircles me and my team. Two men and two women, all dressed in sterile white lab coats courtesy of Lannett Research Corp — the environmental research division of Circuit — are already giving me disdainful looks. Their chief scientist is a skinny man with a pressed blue coat who looks like he's never stepped foot in nature.

"Logan McCeleroy. Head of security here at Meridian."

He merely glances at my outstretched hand before turning his attention back to his tablet. "Dr. Thomas Langley, Lannett Chief scientist. These are my assistants, Dr. Rebecca Chelsea, Beth Harwell, and Garrett Reeves. We've been brought on to examine the environmental conditions of this station."

Don't fucking care. "Great, here's the deal. My team will be your shadows. You don't go anywhere without us. You can start on the east side of the station today, then work your way north. Clear?"

Langley raises an eyebrow, obviously irritated. "If we don't feel like we've made a thorough assessment, we'll have to report it back to Lannett."

"Then be thorough."

His lips thin. "We know how to do our jobs."

"Good, then you won't mind the added security to ensure you do them right." I turn to my own team of four as well, including Carter. "Alright, listen up! I know this is different from our usual patrols, but I needed all your eyes peeled for any potential threats that may endanger us or the scientists on board. We are not there to assist or interfere in their investigations in any way." I give a side-eyed glance to Langley, and his grim expression is answer enough that he heard me. "We are there to provide protection and security. That means always keeping watch and paying attention to our surroundings. Necks on a swivel. Keep an eye out for anything out of the ordinary."

We mount our druadans, me on Galaxian, and Carter on Ember. Both as a means to cover ground faster and to benefit from their heightened senses of hearing and smell. Roberts is down with a cold, Ve'Loth had his annual review with Marshal at Blackhawk, and Nelson, well, I didn't have a good excuse for not inviting him except he annoyed me. The hell if I needed more of a reason?

As soon as I'm seated, the constant ache in the bond evaporates. A quietness dulls the sounds as if I'd put them in earplugs. Carter settles onto Ember's back. The faint lines of worry on his face he'd had since his brief chat with Brigid melted away.

The bond. It's a drug, an addiction. They try to explain it to you at the academy, but nothing comes close to compare it to. They try to prepare you for the insatiable need, the relentless drone in the base of your skull if you're away from them for too long. The blurring of thoughts, feelings, and impulses. The yearning to be physically near your stallion.

"We'll start at the east end of the station first," I call out, both to my team and the Lannett researchers. "Everyone heads behind the training building, then work your way northward."

As if to remind me that this is one of the last days of the season, a cold wind cuts across my face as I guide Galaxian alongside the towering stone wall. The winter is milder here. However, shuttles run into snowstorms, and in two months, the off-season will begin at the ranch. Three months to allow the druadan and their riders to relax, repair damages done to the buildings, and discuss the details of the program starting in the spring.

Carter rides beside me on Ember, the red stallion's hooves stamping on the hard-packed dirt in tandem with mine.

I feel the weight of his eyes on the side of my face and the question dangling on the tether between us. "What?"

"You know, for a moment there, I thought I saw a smile," he says. "If you're not careful, people might start to think you're not a robot."

"Fuck you. Maybe I don't smile when you're around. Ever think of that?"

Carter laughs, throwing his hands up in a mock gesture of surrender. "I'm just calling it as I see it, man."

I set my jaw. It's an instinctual response, this overwhelming sense of joy and purpose when I'm riding Galaxian. The feeling that I can conquer any mountain and tackle any situation. When I'm on him, I can fight the fucking world.

The offroad vehicle driven by the newest member of my security team, Elena, passes us, carrying two of the scientists, Dr. Chelsea, and one of the other scientists whose name I didn't bother to learn.

I grip Galaxian's reins, bracing myself for Carter to make some comment about Elena since she's a female and breathing, but to my surprise, his eyes don't drift over to her.

"She's married, you know."

"Who is?" he says, sounding a little defensive.

"Elena. The security officer with the nice ass."

"It didn't even cross my mind—"

"The hell it didn't."

Carter shakes his head and laughs dryly. "I'm taking a break, anyway."

When I don't respond, he continues.

"I plan to use the off-season to better myself and allow Ember and I to reconnect. Maybe visit a retreat on the southern coast."

I scoff. "Really?"

"Yes. Really."

"Does this sudden self-reflection have anything to do with a certain silver-haired, blue-eyed staff member?"

Carter doesn't look at me, instead keeping his gaze on Ember's ears, which is answer enough. I chuckle as a tremor radiates in the bond between us. It's too subtle to detect precisely what Carter is feeling but amplified by our nearby druadan. It's caught somewhere between lust, no surprises there — there's always *that* as an undertone with him— and a hint of... apprehension.

Wait.

Carter James is rattled because of a woman?

The irony is too good, and the chuckle turns into a full laugh, spilling from my throat.

He glares at me as I wipe a non-existent tear from my eye. "Promise me one thing. When you come clean to Heath, I want to be there."

Carter lets out an exasperated sigh. "There's nothing to come clean to Heath about."

"Mmm-hmm," I say.

"Fine. You want to play this game? I'll come clean to Heath about the feelings I may or may not have for Brigid when you come clean to him about you and Galaxian."

"There's nothing to tell," I say, through gritted teeth.

Carter raises an eyebrow. "Really? Because to me, based on the last demonstration practice and Galaxian's refusal to pirouette alongside Gemindusk, there is definitely *something* to tell."

"He said Gemindusk snores at night. I've rearranged their stalls, and he's fine now."

"Uh huh," Carter says before adding, "Gosh, I love our little chats, Logan. We should do this more often."

AS WE LEAVE THE STATION, FOLLOWING THE ROAD, THE VAST desert spreads out before us, its reddish-brown sand seemingly stretching into infinity. Sun-bleached in shades of beige and umber, broken only by the reds and yellows of the rock formations in the shapes of arches and pillars.

"The DNA you sent over from the sample suggested the creature was nocturnal, and the genome sequences match that of cave slugs or worms. I'd assume there are caves out here?" Dr. Elms shouts, pointing toward a towering rock formation.

We stop as the road splits, one segment going to the ocean in the West, the other deeper into the desert in the north.

Carter and I follow behind them, guiding our stallions cautiously through the uneven terrain.

"Yeah, there is one not too far from here, actually," Carter says. "This way." He pushes his stallion into a rocking canter, and the four-wheeled drive buggies hum as they start off down the ridge, a plume of dust billowing in their wake.

Within thirty minutes, Carter and I pick our way down a slope, and an icy dread creeps over me as we approach an opening nestled in the rock's shadow. I dismount. Holding Galaxian's reins, I move to the cave entrance. I survey the narrow gap that leads into the darkness. The walls of the cave converge and are just wide enough for a person to squeeze through.

Glancing back at Carter and the rest of the survey team, I say, "It'll be too tight for all of us. Dr. Langley and Carter come with me. The rest of you will wait out here. Dr. Langley can take samples and bring them out to you, Dr. Chelsea."

She purses her lips, pinning Dr. Langley with a hard look as if he should intervene and force me to change my mind.

But I won't, and I'm pleased Dr. Langley tilts his head slightly, signaling to her to back down.

I turn to Galaxian. He swishes his teal-colored tail, already anticipating what I'm about to say. "You'll need to stay here too, with Ember." I brace myself for his argument and worry Carter will sense my stallion's defiance through the bond. I'd worked too damn hard to keep the tenuous nature of my bond under wraps to have it fall apart now.

However, even though Galaxian's eyes flicker with annoyance, he snorts and steps back to take a position beside Ember.

Finally, a fucking win. The muscles in my shoulders relax. "Alright then, follow me." I watch for a moment as the two other scientists drop their bags at the mouth of the cave and begin removing various pieces of equipment. Elena leans against the rock wall, and next to her, Stephen lights a cigarette, elbow resting on the pistol at his hip.

Ensuring everyone is set and is following my command, I turn my attention back to the cave. Carter and I exchange a glance, and he gives me one of his signature smart-ass grins. I shake my head, stepping inside.

Dr. Langley follows me, his expression unreadable, and Carter behind him.

Soon, stalagmites and stalactites line the walls like a twisted maze, and pools of phosphorescent liquid bubble in stony outcroppings on the wall.

Instantly, shadows swallow us. Even with the use of our

flashlights, the darkness is overwhelming as we venture deeper into the narrow cave. Our footsteps echo against the damp stone walls while globs of luminous liquid bubble up from the jagged floor. The acidic stench burns my nostrils with each breath. The rock walls glimmer with a strange, luminescent substance, eerily similar to the liquid I'd seen on Galaxian.

The glow pulses like a heartbeat, casting a sickly green hue across the dark cave walls.

"What the hell is this place?" Carter's voice sounds small and hollow in the oppressive darkness.

"Fascinating." Dr. Langley pauses, sweeping his flashlight over the glistening rock formations. "The mineral composition appears similar to —"

"I don't give two shits about the rocks," I snap. "I want to know why there's a goddamn cave full of this glowing shit out here in the first place."

Langley flinches. "I'm afraid I'm at a loss. My purpose here is merely to study the unique environmental conditions, not speculate on their origins."

I suppress a growl of frustration. "Dr. Langley," my voice echoes against the damp stone. "You need to see this."

Boots scuff the loose gravel as the doctor picks his way toward me. I keep my eyes trained on the viscous liquid, watching venomous green droplets branch and split. Do rocks excrete like this? Or some freakish algae.

"Good gracious." Langley raises his eyebrows as he collects a sample, sealing the swab in a sterile case.

Langley senses my unease because he murmurs, "It's most likely harmless, but I'll do a rapid tox test outside the cave to be sure."

As we move further into the cave, I click on a flashlight. I spot what I assume is an odd-shaped rock, and then as I step closer, realizing it's a small shipping crate like the kind we store dry goods in.

What the hell?

No one should be out here. This is miles away from the station. There is a possibility someone could've hired a private shuttle and landed out here without us knowing, but this is Circuit protected property. They'd be violating about a dozen laws by not checking with the station first. Researchers or adventure seekers had to register and pay for a permit with the station before heading out on their backpacking trips, so records were kept. Should any fail to return, search and rescue could be sent out. Ashburn Island is isolated and remote. Sure, the air is clean, but there's nothing out here. It's a wasteland of desert and rocks.

I wave Carter and Dr. Langley over.

"Maybe it's one of ours?" Carter asks, squatting beside the body. His flashlight passes over it, revealing a label for a canned fruit company. "It's odd. It doesn't look very old?"

"Any missing staff?" Dr. Langley offers, his voice woven with an accusatory tone that makes me curl my hands into fists.

"No. All our staff are accounted for. We keep strict protocols in place to prevent any unauthorized trips out from the station perimeter."

"It's possible someone rented a private shuttle without our knowledge," Carter says.

I stand and rest an arm on the strap of my rifle. "It's possible, but then I would've detected it on the scanners." I kneel to examine the crate more closely. It didn't look familiar, and with all its markings scratched out, I can't even tell where it came from. "There were two gates out of the station, and no one entered or left without seven different cameras recording them. I'd know if one of our own had been out here."

Dr. Langley purses his lips. "If you insist."

A sound slices through the air, sharp and relentless. For a split second, it resembles fireworks, but my gut tells me otherwise. It's rapid gunfire coming from behind us, outside the cave.

A few feet from me, Carter collapses. His flashlight slips from his grasp, hurling wild shadows across the cave walls. He writhes on the ground, his body contorting in agony, his face twisted in a silent scream. Adrenaline floods my system.

His pain is tangible, a raw, searing presence between us.

Tears stream down Carter's cheeks, his screams of pain echoing off the cave walls. He's inconsolable.

Dr. Langley hovers nearby.

"Go!" I shout at him. "Get the hell out."

The scientist scoops up his bag of equipment and darts toward the entrance.

I drop to my knees and place my hands on either side of Carter's face.

The bond tethering scorches my insides like lightning coursing through my veins. Excruciatingly sharp, painful, and heavy. It's so damn heavy. I brace against it, stiffening my shoulders, knowing what the pressure means. I've felt it before. When I lost Galaxyla, but this is different. It's not originating through my bond with Galaxian; instead, it's coming from Carter, which means...

FUCK.

Ember is hurt. Alive. But very much hurt.

I know what I need to do. I roughly shake Carter until he meets his eye. "Shut it off."

Carter blinks, confusion clouding his face. "What?"

"The bond," I growl. "Shut off the bond. You have to. It's the only way, or you'll be dragged down."

"I can't," he stammers, shaking his head. He hunches over as a fresh wave of pain seems to wrack his body. "I don't know..." His words trail off.

"You can," I say, my words hard. "And you will. If you want to save Ember, you need to block the bond."

"How... do... I," He stammers, his teeth chattering as he begins to shiver.

I ball my fists, remembering the way I'd managed to survive, keep breathing even as part of my soul was ripped from my fucking chest. "Feel the bond." Carter squeezes his eyes shut as his body curls into a fetal position. "That's it. Good. Now, imagine a cube of ice forming around it. Crystallizing with the cold. Numbing it."

Carter nods slowly. "Okay,"

"Good. Now focus on that and stand."

Carter rolls onto his side, his body still shaking. I help him up. Half carrying him, half dragging, I pull him out of the cave.

Outside is fucking chaos.

Dr. Chelsea and another scientist emerge from where they'd been hiding behind the off-road vehicle. Stephen and Elena stand with guns pinned on the third scientist, clutching a shaking pistol a few feet away from the body of Ember lying on his side.

"I'm sorry," he begs. "I didn't mean to. Please don't shoot."

In a burst of energy, Carter hurries over to Ember, collapsing beside him.

Red rims the edges of my vision as my eyes narrow, zeroing in on the Lannett scientist who's now holding the pistol like it's a live grenade. The world around me blurs; all I see is *him*. A high-pitched ringing drowns out the others' voices. My blood feels like lava in my veins, a hot surge of fury that is preparing to detonate.

I stalk toward him, my hands clenching and unclenching. The ringing in my ears climbs to a fever pitch.

"It was an accident! He didn't mean to!" another scientist yells, but his voice is distant, smothered by the piercing screech in my head.

"An accident?" My voice is a feral snarl, barely recognizable even to myself.

He's shaking now, eyes wide with regret, but it only fuels the inferno inside me. My hands tremble with the urge to rip the pistol away and beat him senseless with it.

"We didn't see it," he stammers. "I didn't have a choice. I had to...to save us."

The world around me moves in slow motion as I close the distance between us. My body trembles with rage, my muscles coiled and ready to strike. The Lannett scientist's eyes widen in fear as he takes a step back, his grip on the pistol tightening.

But I'm faster.

With a roar, I launch myself forward, tackling him to the ground. The gun flies out of his hand and skids across the floor. We roll on the cold concrete, my fists raining down on him like a storm. He tries to fight back, but I am fueled by an uncontrollable anger.

"Stop it! Stop it!" the other scientists shout, trying to pull me off him.

My hands wrap around his neck, squeezing tightly. The pain radiating from Carter's bond, even muted, encases me, and I'm reliving Galaxyla's death over again. The agony as my lungs were ripped from my chest when he collapsed. The blood oozing from his nose. The glow fading from his eye as I cradled his head on my lap.

"Logan! Get off him!" someone screams behind me.

But I can't stop now. The betrayal and pain coursing through me have taken control of my actions. In this moment, all that matters is making this man pay for what he has done.

Suddenly, strong arms wrap around my waist and lift me off of the scientist. I thrash and kick against whoever is holding me but find that I am no match for their strength.

My two security guards lock their arms around mine. One-on-one, I am stronger, but not with them combined. I growl but finally quit struggling.

My eyes don't leave the scientist still sprawled on the ground as I shrug my arms free. They release me but stay close.

"You have five seconds to get the fuck out of my sight." Each word is clipped, my voice vibrating with rage. "Before I take that gun and shove it down your throat." My eyes bore into him, promising violence. Every muscle is coiled tight, ready to lunge should he argue. Every fiber of my being hopes to fuck he does.

He's shaking now, his eyes wide and full of regret. The pistol slipping from his grip, he turns to run, but Galaxian's hulking form materializes in front of him.

He's cut off. The scientist lets out a choked scream as Galaxian lunges. Fanged teeth close around the cowering man's throat before he is lifted off the ground.

I should stop him. Command him.

But I don't.

With a satisfying crunch, Galaxian squeezes the life from him. His feet dangle helplessly, and his screams turn to gurgles before going silent.

Snorting, Galaxian hurls the lifeless body to the ground. Then he turns to me, teal eyes glowing. A single word rumbles through the air to me. *"Kill."*

The oxygen freezes in my lungs. His anger radiates off him, tainting the air with it.

He's a loose cannon. He's lost all sense of self-control, and I'm not an idiot. I know that if I even take one step toward him, he will attack again.

I might not even be safe. Not anymore.

A chill races down my spine as I gaze into his glowing eyes across the space. I always knew he was powerful, unpredictable, and dangerous, but in that moment, it finally sank in.

He's broken. Just like me.

Sometimes, a druadan is born that's never meant to bond, never meant to be shackled. Somehow, I knew this was going to happen. It was simply a matter of not if but when.

Time stops. Elena and Stephen are speaking, but I can't understand their words. It didn't matter, anyway. Galaxian has killed a human. He's a dead druadan walking, and by the time he's punished, I'll no longer be a rider. He was my second and last chance.

My life is completely and utterly fucked.

"Logan," Elena's frantic voice pierces my thoughts. "You know what you have to do." She presses a laser pistol into my hand.

I take it, my eyes never leaving the stallion. Galaxian's nostrils flare and his eyes lock with mine. My whole world is defined by this creature standing before me. His fate was sealed the second he ripped that scientist's throat out.

I raise the gun and point it at him, and he takes a step back. Tears prick my eyes. This is how things have always been. Dangerous druadan cannot be allowed to roam freely. As I rest my finger on the trigger, I grind my teeth together so tightly I fear they might crack. Unbearable guilt seizes my heart like razor-sharp claws, squeezing it until I can barely breathe.

"*No. Kill,*" his voice echoes in my mind, unemotional yet begging for mercy. He knows what he has done, and while his will to live is strong, he has no remorse for his actions.

"*Man. Hurt. Ember. Kill. Man.*"

"*I understand,*" I answer him back.

With a swift motion, I aim the pistol at the night sky and pull the trigger.

The laser cracks, shattering the silence.

Galaxian disappears from sight for a moment before reappearing ten feet away from me on my left side. He looks at me with a bewildered expression on his face. He knows I won't kill him.

Not this time.

"*Fucking, go,*" I yell in my head, "*Run and never come back!*" He bares his teeth before his body fades away, and all that's left is the sound of hoofbeats disappearing into the distance.

Twenty-Six

*E*mber.

Exhaustion permeates every cell in my body.

Ember.

Fatigue gnaws at me, threatening to suffocate me, but I shove it away. Ghostly echoes of pain radiating from my right shoulder. I've never felt pain like this before. The excruciating sensation of muscle being torn from the bone was awful, but worse had been the fear. The fear of losing Ember.

I rub my eyes. I refuse to sleep. Refuse to relax while my stallion is hurt. Hurting. Not while the acrid smell of burnt flesh still lingers in my nose. I should have protected him. Should have been there to stop it.

I sit on the cot outside of Ember's stall, resting my hands on my knees.

Dr. Gideon has been here since the moment we got back. He had sedated Ember to keep him from attacking anyone while in pain and to allow him to examine him more thoroughly.

He steps out of the stall and closes the door.

He gives me a reassuring smile as he slides off the insulated gloves. "Ember will fully recover, but his shoulder will take some time to heal. Luckily, the laser missed any vital organs or major arteries."

I nod or think I do. I'm too fucking tired to know anymore.

"I'll be contacting the specialist at Blackhawk station," he continues. "I'll send over Ember's scans and lab reports to get a second opinion and see if they have any additional recovery recommendations."

"What can I do?"

"Rest, just the same as Ember." Dr. Gideon regards me with concern. "You should go home and get some sleep."

I shake my head firmly. "I'm staying here."

Dr. Gideon sighs but doesn't argue further.

As he leaves, I lower myself onto the cot, exhaustion threatening to drown me. My body feels worn out like I haven't slept in weeks.

My comm buzzes with a new message.

Brigid: *Heath told me about what happened. I'm so sorry. They're restricting everyone except riders and Dr. Gideon from the barn. I promise I'll come see you ASAP.*

I type a reply: *Thx*

I pause, my mind shuffling with all the dirty jokes I can make, but I don't have the energy.

Brigid: *Thinking about you and Ember.*

She finishes the message with a heart-shaped icon.

I'm plunged into near darkness as my comm screen goes dark. At some point, sleep overtakes me, coming in fits and starts. Images haunt my dreams of Ember's wounded body, the sounds of his labored breathing, and the unbearable pain as if it had been I who had been shot.

"You awake?" I hear someone say. I squint open my eyes to see Heath's outline looming over me.

"How are you?" he says and moves to my side.

"I've been better," I grumble.

His hand rests on my arm. Awakening the connection. He

pours comfort and reassurance into it. More than I've ever felt him do before.

I desperately need it.

A long pause passes between us.

Ember stirs in the stall and pain shoots through my shoulder, and I can't stifle a sharp intake of breath.

"Logan told me you shut it off."

I hang my head between my legs, controlling my breathing.

"I did."

"Doesn't look like it."

"It came back, okay?" I hiss between my teeth. "I'm not like you. I'm not like Logan. I can't just fucking shut my emotions off."

"Circuit's launching an investigation," he says, his voice low. "As soon as our security guard's gun was fired, it sent an alarm to Blackhawk. They called me to check on our well-being, but we both know it was to confirm what Dr. Langley had already reported to Circuit."

I narrow my gaze. "Galaxian is his second."

Heath's reply is solemn. "I know."

"This will break him."

"I know."

A mere two years as a rider, and he's done. Finished. The loss will strip him of his identity, strip him of his future. Heath and I both have families we can return to and support us if our careers are cut short for some terrible reason, but Logan has no one. His parents long shifters at the plant, and his grandfather, who mostly raised him passed away while he was at Vanguard. Heath and I are it. We're all he has.

No one truly knew Logan, but Heath and I understood him enough. We'd learned how to navigate his mercurial temperament. We'd nearly lost him, too, after Galaxyla died.

He'd been seconds away from leaping off the edge before we'd pulled him back. The month after, until he'd bonded again with Galaxian, had been one of the worst they'd ever experienced. Tempers flared. Extended bouts of drinking led to broken furniture. Arguments breaking out. The only reprieve was that it had been in the off-season, and there were no public performances, which would have spelled disaster.

Gradually, the pain in my shoulder eases, and the soft snores of Ember tell me he's finally asleep. I sip from the bottle of water Dr. Gideon had left me.

"How are you doing?" I ask, attempting to change the subject. "You should've stayed longer with Jess."

Heath rests an elbow between the bars, watching Ember. "I'm fine."

"I'm not in the mood for your bullshit."

"I've been making it a priority to ride Shadowmane every other day and visit him at least once, and it seems to be helping." Heath's hands flex on the bars, and the artificial light reflects the silver sheen of the scar.

"Did Dr. Rajesh confirm?"

"No. But I don't need him to. I can feel it." His head swivels in my direction. "I'm cooling. I'm better."

A tendril of anxiety trickles through the bond. "Good. You should still have him check it out, though. You know how brimming can—"

"Enough worrying about me when you have bigger things to worry about right now."

I frown. "The health of the bond is only as strong as the riders that share it." I didn't dare say the truth, however, that the bond was only as strong as the weakest rider because I wasn't in the mood to see smoke pour out of Heath's ears.

He wasn't weak. I didn't believe that. But he was spread too thin. The weight of the bond was just one of many he was burdened with. While Logan and I need only worry about the welfare of our mounts and performances. Sure, I had a few guided tours tossed in, and Logan patrolled, but they were walks in the park compared to Heath's budget meetings and staff hiring and firing.

He moves away from the stall and looks down at me. "I'll clean this up. As I always do. You have my word. I'll do everything I can to protect you and Ember."

Not Logan.

A sharp jab forms between my shoulder blades. He didn't say it because he can't promise it. Even with all his connections, all his power his position provides him. There's no recovery from when a druadan kills a human.

"Thank you," I murmur.

"It's been a long day. You should get some rest," he says, and then he's gone.

I get to my feet and enter Ember's stall. He's lying on his side, eyes closed. His chest rises and falls in a steady rhythm. He doesn't need to see me know I'm there, just as I can sense him, too, through the bond.

I lower myself into the corner of the stall and lay my head against the stone wall. I doze off and on for some time, listening to the steady rhythm of Ember's breathing when footsteps rouse me.

Dr. Gideon's face appears over the stall door. "Just here to reapply antibiotics and do a wound check," he says.

My right foot has fallen asleep from the weird sleeping position, and it takes me a second to stand.

The door rattles as the vet slides it open.

Carefully, Dr. Gideon examines Ember's shoulder, his hands moving with practiced ease. He takes out a bottle from his bag and applies medicine to the wound. The hiss of the medicinal spray is a soft sound in the stillness of the barn, but Ember doesn't flinch. Whatever he'd given to sedate him was pretty damn powerful. However, the bond between us hums as I send wave after wave of assurance.

"The wound is healing nicely," he says, standing. "I'm not

concerned with infection but will do a final check tomorrow. Come find me if he seems to be favoring it or if you notice any changes."

I squint in the dim light at his shoulder and can just make out the edges of the injury already knitting together. After Dr. Gideon leaves, I move closer, and I lean my head against his neck. The heat sears my cheek, but with the bond regulating my body temperature, it's no more uncomfortable than pressing it against pavement warmed by the sun.

Finally, Ember stirs, and his eyes open.

He struggles to stand, and I press my hands against him. "*No. It's okay. It's better if you stay down.*"

He pushes back against me, and I force reassurance through the bond until he relaxes.

"*Galaxian.*" Ember's voice resonates in my mind. He's never been a big talker, but I hadn't heard him speak since the accident, and hearing his voice causes my heart to soar.

"*He's gone, buddy,*" I respond. "*Logan told him to run away. I think he's okay. I don't think he's going to come back, though.*"

"*Galaxian trouble.*"

"*Yes, he is. He killed a human.*"

"*You trouble.*" His words are less of a question more of a concern.

I laugh and gently scratch his withers. "No. I'm fine. Just worried about you, is all."

"*Carter sad. Snow woman happy.*"

Holy shit. Get the boy some drugs, and suddenly, he's a talker. A laugh escapes me. It's one of the longest god damn sentences he's ever spoken. It might as well have been a whole novel.

"*Snow woman?*" I say, just as the realization sinks in. "*Brigid? Is that what you call her because of her hair?*"

Ember snorts and flicks an ear. "*Brigid. Yes.*"

"*Reckon, you're right about her, boy,*" I say, stroking his nose affectionately. *"Brigid might just be the best thing to happen to Meridian in a long while."*

The name sends a sharp twinge of pain between my ribs, but it's not from me. I care for Brigid, probably more than I should allow myself. No, the sensation is coming from the bond. From Ember.

"What is going on?" I murmur. *"Are you in pain? Do you need Dr. Gideon?"*

No. Doctor. Worm. Hate.

I tilt my head. *"Worm?"*

There's an affirmation in the bond. Fine. I'll play along. *"Sure. I hate the worm, too. Is that what attacked us at the cave?"*

My pulse races as a blast of fury and indignation enshrouds me. This level of rage is almost overwhelming, causing me to lean back against the wall of the stall for support. I've never experienced this intensity of emotion from him before. Sure, there have been moments of hunger at feeding time, excitement when I'd visited him after some time away, arousal during bonding ceremonies, and pride during demonstrations, but nothing like this.

It floods through me in pulsating waves, threatening to drown me. The edges of my vision bleed with red. *"It's okay,"* I gasp, trying to calm him down. *"You're going to be fine."*

Despite my words, I can feel his anger seeping through our bond, causing me to shudder with its intensity. My mind races, trying to come up with a way to calm him down before he does something rash like Galaxian. I take a deep breath and push back against his emotions, channeling my own calmness towards him. Slowly, I feel his anger start to dissipate.

He chuffs in frustration.

I get the sense there's more he wants to tell me, but the limited vocabulary is proving to be a barrier. *"Keep trying, I'm listening."*

The bond hums again with the anger I'd felt before, although more in control this time, tiny currents instead of tidal waves.

New. Danger. Not Sleep.

I press my lips together, growing more and more concerned that I might never understand what he's trying to say.

"You can't sleep?"

He moves to an upright lying position and shorts while shaking his head.

No.

"You're no longer sleeping?"

His nose flares, and he swivels his head. His golden eyes blaze with irritation.

'No longer sleeping'. I puzzle over the phrase, then try, *"You're awake?"*

A cool ripple rushes between us. Relief, I understood. *"Yes."*

More questions burn inside me, but I hesitate, not wanting to overload him while he's so agitated. This is the most he's ever communicated with me, and I need time to process what this revelation means.

I should tell the others what Ember said, see if they have any insight, or if Shadowmane has told Heath the same.

I should place a call to Marshal instead —if anyone can shed light on interpreting druadan, it's him. Ember nudges my shoulder as if encouraging me to seek answers.

"Don't worry, boy. We'll get to the bottom of this," I assure him.

After he drifts back to sleep, I stand and stagger to the cot.

I lay down, and within seconds, I'm out.

Twenty-Seven

HEATH

I step into Logan's dimly lit cottage, and the overpowering scent of alcohol fills the air.

I feel for a light switch on the nearest lamp and turn it on. My eyes sweep over the small cabin. Jackets tossed haphazardly over chairs in the dining area, bottles piled up in the trash can, and dirty dishes stacked in the sink.

I sigh. He hasn't been letting maintenance in to clean. I add to the list to deal with.

The previous head of security left the dated furnishings of rugs and curtains, and the only personal touch is a cross-stitched heart made by his mother before he'd left for the academy hanging on the wall in the entryway.

"Logan?" I call out, worry creeping into my tone. He's probably drunk himself into a stupor. I can't blame him, and it's his typical reaction to dealing with stress. I remember the few times during our academy days when Carter and I'd drug him out of some of the bars when he'd failed an exam at the academy and thought the best choice was to drown the brain cells in liquor as punishment.

I make my way toward the back of the cottage. As I pass by the trash can, the overpowering scent of whiskey emanates from the empty bottles within. I quicken my pace.

"Logan!" I call out again. To my relief, a grunt comes from the bedroom. I go to it and find him sitting on the edge of his unmade bed, gazing vacantly at the floor. His eyes are bloodshot, and fatigue weighs heavily on his slumped shoulders. An almost empty whiskey bottle dangles loosely from his fingers.

"Sorry," Logan mutters from where he sits in the armchair. "I don't think my legs are working."

I sigh, torn between annoyance and concern. I gesture angrily at the bottle. "This has to stop. I need you clear-headed if we're going to have any hope of fixing this mess before Circuit arrives."

My brief flare of frustration fades as I take in his disheveled state. I soften my tone. "When's the last time you slept, anyway? Or had a decent meal? You look like hell."

I grab the bottle from his limp fingers, and he puts up little struggle. It's empty anyway.

After setting it firmly out of reach, I crouch down to meet his lowered eyes and squeeze his shoulder. "Circuit authorities are on their way here. They're going to want to talk to you."

"Talk, talk, talk," he says, slurring. "That's all anyone wants to do. It's all bullshit."

A knot of frustration tightens in my chest, but I press on. "They've agreed to keep this incident discreet and let the fundraiser continue in three days."

Finally, Logan shifts on the bed and stands. "He was going off fucking instinct, you know!" He jabs a thumb at his chest. "This is our fault. We've bred them for hundreds of years to be warriors, fierce and protective. He was reacting to protect me as he should have."

Logan's face contorts with anger as he struggles to keep his balance. I take a deep breath and reach out to steady his arm, which he abruptly shrugs off.

"I know he was," I say. "But there are rules in place for a reason. Laws dictating what happens to druadan who turn." For Logan's sake, I don't finish my train of thought. Turned druadan; dubbed rogues are fairy tales, fantastical stories from the past about those stallions that can no longer be controlled by the bond.

I hesitate. Rogues were the stuff of legend, nightmares told to young riders. But the rules still stood— if a druadan ever slipped beyond the grasp of the bond and their rider... there would be consequences.

Logan's face pales. He may be drunk, but he grasps the severity of Galaxian's actions.

"We'll bring him back, Logan," I say firmly, as much to convince myself. "But you need to find him, and you need to prepare yourself for him not being the Galaxian you knew. There's a chance he's becoming something else, something we might not understand."

He swivels his head toward me. "You can't fucking know that."

"You're right. I can't know that for sure, but Circuit will be here. I don't see any way this doesn't end with him killed, and you disbanded from the station."

Logan's eyes reflect a haunted look from the soft glow of the solitary lamp on his nightstand. My mind races with one useless strategy after another, each more futile than the last. Finally, Logan is the one to shatter the quiet, his voice low and resigned. "There might be a way."

I sigh. "No, there isn't." I turn away and start out of the room.

"I'm serious."

I linger on the threshold. "Look, Logan, you're drunk, and Circuit will need you sober. I'm going to make some coffee."

He pounds his fist on the table. "Would you just listen for one goddamn second instead of dismissing me like one of the other staff?"

I hesitate, seeing a spark of his old intensity behind the drunken haze. This isn't just the ramblings of impaired judgment. Logan truly believes he has a solution.

My shoulders slump. We're out of options, and time is running short. What could it hurt to hear him out?

"Alright, fine, you have my full attention."

Logan slides open the drawer on his nightstand and steps back, gesturing toward it. "Here's your fucking proof."

Skeptical, I peer into the drawer. Slimy tendrils lay curled up in the drawer like a clump of translucent spaghetti. The lamplight glints off the rows of tiny snakelike scales.

I lean in for a closer look. "What is this?"

"This is it. This is the thing that attacked Brigid and Galaxian in the barn, I'm sure of it. This the fucking creature Lannett was out there looking for and what got the jump on us."

I narrow my eyes. "How did you end up with it?"

"It was caught in between Ember's teeth when we brought him back to the barn."

I purse my lips in thought. Logan and I butted heads, but I trusted the man. Memories flash through my mind - the first time we'd met at the academy, he'd stepped in to defend me when a second year had stolen my shoes as a prank and tossed them in the sewage pond. Logan had strong-armed the second year into diving in to get them if he wanted to keep all his teeth. Then, later, the midnight meet-ups Carter, he, and I had at the Gauntlet, a hellish obstacle course we'd been required to pass our first quarter or be dismissed.

We'd snuck out of our bunks—and thanks to Logan's experience growing up underground at a filtration plant that meant navigating scaffolding, slippery stairs, and endless corridors of low-hanging pipe — had coached us on how to tackle the various hazards. All of it eventually led to my decision as station manager to appoint him head of security despite his lack of formal credentials.

"Fine. Yes. I believe you, and I'll stand by you when the Circuit investigators arrive. We'll have to make a case that it was an unfounded occasion that caused Galaxian to act as he did and that extreme circumstances should be considered." I sigh and stuff my hands in my pockets. Lives hang in the balance, and I can't afford another misstep. "We need help with this. I want to loop Ms. Corsair in."

Logan groans, and I hold up a hand, stopping him from arguing more. "You want help or not? She's the expert. I trust her expertise. If anyone can spin this to make you look good, it's her."

His jaw tightens as he crosses his arms like a petulant child. "No fucking way."

Desperation propels me to try again. "Logan, if you would just listen for one goddamn—" I start to say, but he interrupts me.

"No. Why don't *you* listen?" he spat. "What is it with you guys and blondie? She bats those pretty long eyelashes, and both of you lose your minds. I don't want to involve her. Unlike you and Carter, I'm not so quick to forgive and forget that it was her sister who took the egg."

"No one said anything about me forgiving her," I say, my voice tinged with annoyance. My patience is rapidly declining. "Yes, her sister made a choice that affected the whole station. However, since we brought her into the loop, she's been nothing but professional in her role. Did you know she didn't want to file anything with the station or Circuit when she was injured in the barn? Carla finally made her write something down for our own records, but she was adamant that she was fine and didn't want to do anything that would cast a bad light on the station."

Logan's jaw flexes, and he glances away for a moment before speaking. "This situation is way beyond her experience, Heath. We can't afford to bring an outsider into this mess. It could complicate things further."

I consider his words and open myself to the bond. He's drunk, so the emotions are muted, but I can detect the faint shades of anger, sadness, and worry. He's worried about Galaxian. We all are. But what if he's worried about Brigid? About what would happen if she became more linked to his rogue druadan than she already is."Logan, I trust her judgment. If anyone can navigate the Circuit investigators and spin this to make you look good, it's her. We need all the help we can get right now."

Twenty-Eight

BRIGID

 y fingers chatter on the keyboard as I respond to a barrage of emails.

This is all I do now. Send and receive messages through Network.

It's all I can do.

I'm not allowed into the barn to see Ember and Carter. I'd messaged him and unsurprisingly received a clipped response. I'm not a rider and could only guess what they're going through now.

Heath told me earlier he'd check on them, and for once, I didn't argue.

So, what can I control? Emails.

Emails to Circuit officials. Emails to long-time patrons of the station. Emails to fan groups. Emails to anyone I think will raise awareness about the gala, *and* when the time comes for authorities to deal with Logan, take the station's side.

Once I hit enter, I reach up, stretching my arms and neck.

I'm seated at the polished mahogany table in the main house. The meeting room is bathed in warm, late-afternoon sunlight, and across from me, Carla is in front of her own laptop with her headphones. She sips from a straw in a can of soda, discussing logistics for the landing pad schedule. "I don't see how that will work if the Bennington's shuttle arrives at 9 am tonight." She waits for a response, and then she nods at the three other faces on the screen. I can't hear what they are saying, but from the exasperated look on her face, they are struggling to find times that won't interfere with each other's "most esteemed" families' arrivals.

My comm dings. The interview with the Delford broadcast station is going to happen in thirty minutes. I press my lips together, pressing down at the anxiety bubbling up inside me.

To fill the time, I move to Heath's office to set up the interview space. I organize and reorganize the two chairs and position a small square metal table between them, before swapping it for a round marble one. Carla brings me the flower arrangement from the entryway downstairs, silk flowers but still pretty, and I place them on the table.

I fluff the greenery and smooth down the petals. The flowers need to look elegant and chic but not over the top. We are trying to garner sympathy that the station needs money and a real floral bouquet isn't *it*.

Carla joins me shortly after, having finished her meeting, and places herself where the camera would be on the tripod, directing me so the spacing of the furniture is even. Heath and I will need to be close to fit in the frame but not too close, or we'd run the risk of bumping knees or elbows. I've chosen an all-black jumpsuit with a maroon scarf that I think will translate well on the camera, and Heath will wear his blue rider coat with gold embroidery, black riding pants, and knee-high boots. *Where is Heath?* He'd promised he'd be here a little before so we could go over some practice questions, plus any curve balls the interviewer might throw at us.

I send him a quick 'Where are you?' message, then start to the door to go. When I open it, I see him coming down the hallway. I bite my tongue, willing myself not to snap at him about being late, and judging by the way his forehead is pinched together and the hard line of his jaw, it is a good decision on my part. Whatever has kept him hasn't been good.

"Sorry, Miss Corsair," he says, walking past me into the room. "I was held up with something."

"How's Carter?" I ask.

"Carter is resting. Ember is healing fast and will recover." I suck in a sharp breath of relief.

At his wardrobe, he takes out one of his riding jackets from the closet and puts it on.

Out of the three guys here, Heath is the hardest for me to read. Logan is obviously, an arrogant asshole, and Carter is a playboy with an ego as big as his, well I can't say yet of knowing exactly how big, but from the privileged few seconds I ran my fingers over it through his shorts in the hot springs, I'd venture a guess they're equally well above average.

When it comes to Heath, however, he keeps me at arm's length, distancing himself from me like I am a contagious disease he doesn't want to catch.

Heath checks himself in the mirror hanging on the back of his wardrobe, plucking off invisible pills from his shoulders and straightening the golden buttons so the Meridian station insignia is facing right side up. With his dark black hair and broad shoulders filling out the coat, he reminds me of the generals I'd read about in the Venovian history books. Leaders who led others into battles no matter what the odds were.

I clear my throat. "So, uh, the first interview will be with Carine Anderson from Delford public broadcasting, then we'll do a quick swap over, and Geff Sanchez from Venovian Central

News will get another twenty minutes. All in all, it shouldn't last more than an hour."

Heath smiles, but it doesn't reach his eyes. "Sounds good."

"I gave them clear instructions that this is to discuss the fundraiser and that we will pass on any personal questions."

"Excellent," he takes a step toward me before finally meeting my gaze. The intensity of his stare grips me, and I quickly gesture to the empty chair on the right. I know Heath to be left-handed and figure if he gestures anything, it'd be with his dominant hand, and I wouldn't want it off camera. Yes, I am good at my job.

"We have about ten minutes; you want to go over a few questions?"

He sits in the chair and then moves forward slightly so his back is straight. "Yes."

I take the seat next to him, then open up the notes on my tablet screen. "The Meridian Station annual gala is…"

"An important function the station is hosting. Its purpose is to ensure the continued support of Venovian founding families so the heritage and legacy of our past can be upheld for years to come."

A perfect response. Holy hell, what have I been so worried about? He is born for this.

I drill him with a couple more easy ones. The number of druadan at the station. Eleven. The number of riders. Nine. The impact on the ecosystem on the island. Numerous scientists have been through this, and all have been determined negligible. Although his eye does slightly twitch when he responds, I hope the camera won't pick it up when the live interview comes.

My comm beeps with the one-minute warning.

"Okay." I shift in the chair and plaster a smile on my face. "Here we go."

Heath inhales, straightening further, and folds his hands on his lap.

The camera light turns from red to green, and on the small monitor next to it, a dark-haired woman in a plaid blazer appears.

"And now we're joined by Meridian Station manager Heath Lockwood and Brigid Corsair, head of public relations at the station. Good evening, how are you?"

"We're doing well, Carine. Thank you," Heath answers.

"Glad to hear it. I know you both have a very busy schedule, so diving right in, many of our viewers have never been to a druadan event. Could you please explain what exactly is a druadan and what a day is like at the station?"

Heath, not missing a beat, relays a practically perfect response that I couldn't have drafted better. He hits all the right notes. Heritage. History. Future generations. Remembering our past to protect our future. It is a sight to behold, and as the interviewer keeps tossing questions toward him, he nails them one after another. I grin and nod, playing the attentive assistant, and while we'd discussed me answering a few questions for balance and transparency, it doesn't seem like Heath is going to let that happen.

I don't get the sense that he doesn't trust me to answer, more than his controlling nature won't let him do anything but control the narrative.

Ten minutes into the interview, Carine calls for a brief break. Her makeup assistant powders her cheeks and reapplies lipstick.

Heath and I both sip from our bottles of water and Carla hovers by the doorway, ready to help with any technical issues and to ensure no other staff members interrupt us during the interview.

Three, two, one...

"In the current election cycle at Circuit," Carin says, once the stream is live again. "The Penswell Historical Society has struggled to keep a bill from reducing funding to the stations. Are you aware the Drakeford family is one of the committee's biggest contributors?"

"Apologies, Carine," I say, cutting in to save Heath. "But how is any of this relevant to the annual gala?"

Before she can respond, however, Heath answers. "Yes. I am aware of that information. The Drakeford family has a long history of supporting conservation efforts for not just druadans but other endangered wildlife as well."

"That is true. So then you do understand that your fiancé, Jess Drakeford, could be seen by many to be a conflict of interest involving the Circuit bill surrounding druadan conservation funding?"

My heart shutters in my chest.

Fiancé?

I bite the inside of my cheek to keep my face a mask of composure, even as my insides somersault. He's *engaged* to Jess Drakeford. Why hasn't he told me? Why hasn't *anyone* told me?

Frustration rises inside me for him not thinking it relevant for me to know, and the twinge of jealousy along with it, which is silly. Heath is a Lockwood. Which means the daughter of a scientist, even as respected as my mom, would never meet the standards his family certainly has for a life partner. There aren't royal families technically anymore, but if there were, the Lockwoods would be the closest to one existing in Venovia, which would make Heath their prince.

Swoon. Yeah... *okay*, so I have thought more than a little about this.

"Of course," Heath replies. "I understand how some people might interpret that as the case, however..."

"An interpretation that many beyond myself have speculated has meant the Drakeford foundation is seeking to acquire sought-after land under the guise of 'protecting Venovian heritage.'"

"Those claims are unfounded." Heath's voice is laced with venom.

I stare at the side of Heath's face, feeling like I am trapped on a shuttle that has lost control and is rapidly descending into the ocean.

I need to salvage this interview before it devolves beyond something that permanently blemishes Heath and the station's reputation.

"I believe what Master Rider Lockwood is trying to say is," I jump in, interrupting Carin as she starts in with what I am sure is a rebuttal. "There has always been a connection between druadan stations and esteemed families in Venovia, but it is a byproduct of the tradition for firstborn sons to enroll in the academy. Circuit legislation is certainly aware of this frequent situation, and as such, I'm confident that any decisions made regarding druadan station funding would be made entirely under unbiased pretenses. Do you not agree Circuit has Venovia's best interest at heart?"

Carin's mouth forms a silent 'O'. It's the tiniest of cracks in her facade, but undeniable. She is backed into a corner, and she damn well knows it. Beside me, Heath shifts in his seat, and I catch the faintest sound of a chuckle, which he quickly tries to cover with a cough.

"Well," Carine finally says. "I believe that's all the time we have for today. I want to thank you for taking the time to chat with me, and best of luck with the fundraiser event." She then turns to another camera we can't see and begins her segue into her next interview, which involves a woman shuttle pilot surviving a crash landing on one of the western continents, but I don't catch the rest of it before the screen when black, leaving Heath and I sitting under the lights.

When Heath turns to look at me, my pulse quickens. His dark brown eyes dance, and his perfect lips are curved into a smile. Holy hell, if I thought he was good-looking before, he is gorgeous when he's happy. It occurs to me I've never actually seen him smile before. Whether it is from the rush of adrenaline from having to combat the journalist or the way the lights reflect off the hard line of his jaw.

In that instant, there is nothing else I want to do more in my life than make him happy. See this side of him. His true face behind the guarded mask.

"Brigid," he says.

A thousand butterflies flit in my stomach as I hear him call me by my first name.

"You were... brilliant." His voice is thick with emotion.

I laugh, tossing my hair over my shoulder at the compliment. "Just doing my job, is all."

He laughs a warm, husky sound that seeps into my bones. "Well, I appreciate it."

The air feels charged between us as our gazes hold, and I can feel the heat radiating from his body. His eyes search mine and like he is looking into my soul for *something*.

He must have found it because he laughs again and whispers. "As soon as you set foot into my office, I knew you were something special." A wave of excitement goes through me as we stand there in silence—the only sound being our shallow breath mingling in the air.

"And why is that?"

"I, too, am very good at my job."

He inches closer and brushes a lock of hair away from my face with gentle fingers. The contact sends a trill of electricity skittering over my skin. Time slows as his hand lingers on my cheek before cupping it softly—as if he has been waiting for this moment forever and needs to savor every second of it. His deep brown eyes are hooded as he moves closer, and I lift my chin, anticipating the kiss.

But then something shifts in his gaze, and he pulls back as if I'd shocked him.

"Fuck," he curses under his breath and stands so abruptly that the chair tips over backward and lands with a thud on the carpet. Heath stares at me with a pained expression on his face, and for a moment, I think he might reach out and touch me instead. He grabs the chair and rights it before turning away from me.

"Dammit," he says louder, running his hands through his hair.

"It's okay," I say, standing too for some reason.

"No, it's not okay. I'm engaged, remember?"

Oh. Right. Shit. Wait, I was supposed to be pissed about that. "Uh yeah, way to blindside your PR person. You didn't think you soon to be married to the Drakefords merited me knowing?"

He stares deeply into my eyes for a long moment before finally speaking. "It slipped my mind."

I scoff. "Slipped your mind?" I cross my arms and roll my eyes at him. "Wow, what a lucky girl to have a guy like you."

He winces, and I know I've dealt a low blow. Instantly, I'm filled with regret and the realization that I lashed out not just cause I'm angry with him but with myself. I had methodically researched this station and any information and backgrounds on the staff I could find before coming here.

So, how had I not known? Perhaps his family had kept it secret for fear the pending nuptials would affect stock prices or business negotiations.

"How did the reporter know?" I ask, keeping my tone neutral. This is exactly in my skillset, and so I should approach it as part of my job. Own personal feelings be dammed.

He shakes his head. "Probably leaked through one of the caterers or florists. I don't know."

He sighs, running a hand over his face. "I'm sorry, Miss Corsair, truly. It's complicated."

And just like that, I am back to Miss Corsair. "Complicated how?" I ask. "You're going to get married. End of story."

"This marriage has been planned by our families for a long time before I..." He pauses, his jaw working as he formulates his words. "Before I knew who I was. What it was I wanted."

In a woman, a partner. That's what he's trying to say. Before he knew who he would love.

"I see." I lick my lips, noting his eyes dipping quickly before coming back up to my face. "So, breaking it off is out of the question?"

He nods.

"I'm sorry."

"Don't be." He shakes his head. "There's nothing you or anyone can do."

My cheeks burn with embarrassment as I remember how close we'd come to kissing earlier—how badly I'd wanted it to happen—and that I would have become the other woman.

A mistake. A lapse in judgment.

I sicken at the thought. That is something I will never do. If, in some alternate reality, Heath and I do end up together, it will be only when no one will be hurt in the process. I won't settle for anything less. I need all of a man or none at all.

"You're right," I say quietly after several moments of watching him pace. "There isn't anything any of us can do about it."

Heath nods slowly and then looks me in the eye. His expression softens for just a brief moment before he speaks again, his voice low and rough around the edges. "Glad we are in agreement."

The layers of meaning are obvious in his statement, and I tip my head enough to imply that I do understand the two-fold message. No more, whatever that had been. Maintain a professional distance at all times.

Check.

The next interview blessedly goes much better than the first. And while Heath is hiding it well, I can tell he is shaken from the previous interview. However, his fear is unfounded as the questions are all druadan particularities related, and Heath handles them deftly with his exhaustive amount of knowledge and expertise. Geff has a cousin who had been a master rider, who sadly passed away a few years ago, and comes armed with a multitude of questions regarding feeding schedules, custom bridles, and himself is one of the founding members of a fan-led website that he proudly plugs not once, but twice during the interview.

Just when it feels like we are wrapping up, Geff asks about the Meridian station's upcoming anniversary.

"Yes, it's true," Heath says. "The station is approaching its two-hundredth anniversary, and we're proud of the strides we've made. However, it's essential to acknowledge the challenges we face. We currently have only twelve stallions at the station, a significant decrease from a decade ago when there were twice as many. Pressure from animal activist groups has caused several labs to close, and with fewer applicants in the academy, means fewer druadan being born."

Geff suddenly perks up, his eyes alight with curiosity. "Do you suppose it was one of them that caused a fire at Lannett East last month?" He asks, leaning forward in his chair.

Heath and I exchange a look of surprise as our minds race to try to make sense of what Geff has just said.

"I'm sorry," Heath says slowly. "What break-in?"

Geff adjusts his headphones. "A contact of mine heard there was a break-in at the lab last month. They suspected one of the extremist groups was responsible. Do you know anything about it?"

Heath glances at me before shaking his head. "No, I don't know anything about it."

"Ah," Geff says with a slight smirk, obviously not believing him. "Well then, I guess you do now."

Heath clears his throat before continuing with the interview. "It is obvious Lannett security should be enhanced, then."

Geff nods. "My source said the oddest thing: nothing seemed to be stolen."

"Small blessings," Heath says solemnly, but I can tell he is rattled by Geff's question. Who had broken into the lab? And why? Was it connected to Sharice's disappearance somehow? Or were we dealing with an entirely separate issue here?

Before he can rattle Heath further, I segue the conversation back to the fundraiser and assure Geff that a ticket for his media team is available.

Once the camera is switched off, Heath sighs and buries his face in his hands.

"Well, that's that, I guess," I say. "Do you feel happy with just the two? I can see if Carla can squeeze one in one more this evening if you think it'd be beneficial?"

Heath rubs his face wearily. "No. Two is fine."

I study him for a moment, thinking back to his smiling face that was soon followed by our near kiss. It seemed like a distant memory that I'd imagined him ever looking happy. The air around him seemed weighed down by the enormity of the pressure surrounding him. Managing the station, managing a powerful and connected family, and, as I'd so abruptly learned, soon to be married to an equally powerful family.

He'd kept me on here when he so easily could've done otherwise, and I wished I could provide some comfort. I owed him that.

"You're right. Besides the fundraiser tickets have completely sold out," I offer brightly. "And we've already raised double our goal just from pre-donations alone. It's really shaping up to be a very successful event."

Heath manages a weak smile. "That's good to hear."

But he still seems preoccupied, lost in thought, and I don't know what it is, but I swear my intuition is on overdrive these days. Like the pull to the barn every time I walked past it or the way I'd sensed the druadan colt in the dust.

More secrets. He is keeping something from me.

I speak the dreaded words. "What is it, Heath? Please talk to me."

He shakes his head dismissively. "It's nothing... most likely all for nothing at this point, anyway."

I furrow my brow, confused. "What are you talking about?"

He hesitates before finally speaking again. "It's Logan. He's gotten himself into some major trouble, the kind that could take down the whole station."

My heartbeat races just as swiftly as my thoughts. My eyes widen. "What? What kind of trouble?"

"The not recoverable kind," he says grimly. "Very soon, none of us will have jobs." He stands, waving his arms around and laughing a little manically.

I stand up in alarm. Losing my job means losing my connection to the last place my sister had been. The door to finding out whether she is alive or dead will slam firmly shut. "You need to tell me right now what is going on."

"Nothing. Its rider matters."

"Dammit," I curse. Hadn't we just had this discussion? "You have to trust me. I can't protect you or the station if I don't know things like this. Important things."

Heath sniffs. After a long few seconds, he finally locks eyes with me, almost a little defiantly. "Fine. You're right. You need to know everything. Follow me."

Twenty-Nine

LOGAN

$\mathcal{A}$s I stand near the window, I can make out the distant lights of the barn, where I know Galaxian is safely sleeping in his stall.

No! A voice screams in my head. That's wrong. He isn't.

He's somewhere out in the dark desert. Alone. Is he hungry? Cold? Afraid? I open myself to the bond I have all day, hoping to catch a taste of his emotions, but there's nothing. The bond is still present, the tether whole, but where there's the usual heat, it is just numbness like a rubber band drawn too tight until it's lost all elasticity. My hands grip the tumbler of amber liquid, and I put it to my lips, already working to stave off the oncoming brimming.

Galaxian is strong. He'll find a way to survive.

I hope I can, too.

Throughout the day, I've drowned my thoughts with alcohol to stave off the sense of emptiness, a void that I'm not sure how to fill. If I sober up too much, I find myself contemplating my life, confronted with questions about purpose and choices I don't want to deal with.

Gazing at the horizon outside, I am reminded of the world

beyond my isolated existence. A world where my parents spent their days toiling in filtration farms. It's a path I could choose for myself, guaranteeing a longer life and protection from the harsh desert conditions. However, it would also mean a life deprived of natural light and a meager income compared to what I earn now.

I glance at the expensive bottle of scotch on the table, worth 780 in credits. It's my parent's monthly income combined. But for me, it's nothing—a fraction of my weekly salary as a master rider.

As if its walls are closing in on me, the cabin suddenly feels suffocating. It dawns on me that I've been chasing an unattainable dream and living on borrowed time.

What purpose did my existence hold now? The mission, the pursuit of the egg, had been everything, a cause that had driven me forward.

But now, I'm left adrift in a world that suddenly seems uncertain.

After Heath left, Carter enters. No one knocks.

"I need a drink," he says.

I gesture to the bar cart. He pours himself one and then collapses on the couch.

For a long time, we sit in silence, letting the bond do the talking. The rage, the fear, the regret.

"If you hadn't been there," Carter says, swirling his drink. "Fuck Logan."

I sigh and rub a hand over my chin. "You okay?"

Carter sighs and leans his hands on his thighs. "No. But I will be."

The sunlight turns from yellow to orange outside.

We're on our second round of drinks and sitting in silence when Heath's body appears in the living room doorway and behind him, blondie herself. What the hell is going on?

In the two years I've been here, before today, Heath had set foot in my cabin exactly two times. Once, when I'd been sick as a dog from the flu that was going around the station and had slept past a meeting, and the second when he'd given Jess a tour of the station. Personally, I think he'd hoped I'd scare her off and make her want to end the visit short, but he'd been shit out of luck. I'd been on my best behavior and even going so far as to offer to take her coat. If he wanted to break off the engagement, he'd have to do it on his own.

"Drinks?" Carter offers, heading to the wooden bar cart I keep stocked.

"I'd love one, thanks," Brigid says from where she stands behind the chair.

"Vodka soda," Heath says, taking a seat in the armchair next to the fireplace. "Looks like the first guests are arriving." He looks down at the alert on his wrist comm. In the distance, I can hear the hum of a landing shuttle in the direction of the pad and peer out the window, trying to catch a glimpse of the blinking lights on the engines as it lowers itself down.

Carter groans but takes the bottle of vodka from the back of the shelf.

"If I never have one of your signature 'frog in a basket' ever again, it still won't be long enough," Heath says.

"Don't fancy another midnight swim in your shoes, do you?" Carter says.

Heath's eyes narrow on me. "Those were *very* expensive shoes."

Brigid laughs, a light sound, and I'm not the only one's attention it draws.

My eyes linger on the side of her face before drifting down to her neck, shoulder, curve of her breast, and thighs under her short skirt. She'd smelled so fucking good in the barn.

Fuck me. I shake my head and drain the rest of my glass. The strain from Galaxian putting miles between us is doing some wild ass shit to my bond right now. I need something stronger.

Something that'll overwhelm my senses. Block out the drone of silence that has replaced the comforting hum of Galaxian's consciousness.

Carter pops the cork from the spiced brandy and pours the lime green liquid into a cocktail shaker.

"How's Ember doing?" Brigid asks, moving to sit on one end of the loveseat.

Carter's face visibly relaxes, and he squeezes the slice of lemon into the shaker.

"Dr. Rajesh says he'll be sound to ride in a week or two," Carter says, squeezing the slice of lemon into the shaker. "He's a fast healer."

The bond between the three of us has gone cold, and it's like dipping my face into a bucket of ice water. I can still feel them, but I don't want to stay submerged too long. It's a telltale sign that either a rider or druadan isn't feeling well. With the flu season last winter, it had been a goddamn nightmare. No one had escaped the wrath of the bond energy in flux, riders and staff alike. Everyone had succumbed to the constant numbing sensation like their fingers and toes were trapped in blocks of ice.

Carter hands me one of his signature cocktails, then passes Heath a vodka soda. Then, retrieves his and Brigid's. He bends over, handing hers first before he takes a seat next to her on the loveseat. Heath's gaze follows Brigid's every move, though she seems oblivious as she smiles warmly at Carter.

Satisfaction unfurls within me—my gut never betrays me.

She'll be the ruin of us, I'd warned him.

Brigid sips from her glass and giggles as a droplet spills on her chin. Carter's hand is instantly there, wiping it away, and I steal a look at Heath.

His dark eyes are fixed on the contact.

How fucking interesting. If we don't watch our asses, our trio is rapidly transforming into a quartet.

"I've drafted a formal statement," Brigid says, cradling her drink on her knee. "I'll send it to the presses tomorrow. Hopefully, it'll help to shield the station from too much scrutiny. The key in these situations is to be proactive, stay one step ahead of the media, before they sensationalize the situation and make things messier than they are."

Carter and Heath both nod, seeming to buy into her reassurances.

I'm not so easily convinced. Do they actually believe this bullshit?

"For fuck's sake," I scoff. "Not make it messier? Blondie, this is as messy as it gets. We're now classified as a station with a rogue druadan, which means we've skyrocketed to the tippy top of the list of stations on the slate to be shut down. Galaxian tore a guy's throat out. My career as a rider is over. Done. Which in turn makes these two on edge as well."

Brigid's face pales. Clearly, Heath hadn't told her everything. "That may be true, but—"

"It is."

She frowns. "You didn't let me finish." Her blue eyes flash with anger.

Blondie has fire. I see the challenge in her eyes, and I like that.

A lot.

I'd lost all tolerance for pushovers when I'd gotten my mark. Life was too short for bullshit. When I first met her, I'd assumed she was just another overeducated Delford socialite - polished, poised, but ultimately soft. I expected her to be consumed by Venovian gossip like the rest of high society. But perhaps I was wrong.

I set my jaw, not daring to break my gaze. Fine. If she thinks she can convince me there is some magical way to fix this, I'll hear her out. What the hell did I have to lose? It will all be gone in a few days, anyway.

"What I was *trying* to say was," she continues carefully, "Heath told me you found something in Ember's teeth. A piece of the animal that attacked you and the scientists?"

I hesitate as my suspicion flares. Heath is normally as secretive as fuck. The words 'telling staff on a need-to-know-basis' should've been tattooed on his goddamn forehead. And yet, Brigid has been here barely a week, and he's told her about this. What is it about her that has turned Carter into an eager-to-please puppy and Heath into an open book?

I puff out my cheeks. Well, shit. The cat is out of the fucking bag now. Even if I don't trust her, I don't have a choice. Grumbling, I reach down and grab the old coffee can by my feet and then set it on the table. I pry off the lid, and the aroma of seaweed that has been left out in the sun too long permeates into the room at once.

Brigid wrinkles her nose and covers her mouth with her hand. "Oh my god. That smells awful."

"Maybe it should be kept in the fridge?" Carter suggests, even as he moves to peer inside.

Before I can stop him, Carter tips the can over and dumps the contents onto the table. Brigid yelps in protest, but it's too late—the dark, slimy tendril lands on the wood with an obscene squelch.

"And there it is," I say, gesturing to it.

"There *what* is?" Brigid asks.

"The thing that was in Ember's teeth. I don't have a goddamn clue what it is, but I can tell you the scientists seemed pretty keen on taking samples in the cave."

"You think they knew this was out there?" Carter asks.

I shake my head. "Knew? No. Suspected is more like it."

Brigid holds up her wrist and swivels her hand with her pointer finger outstretched, preparing to take an image.

Carter rests his hand on her arm, gently stopping her. "I

think it's better we keep this limited to just who's in this room, at least until we know more."

Her mouth parts slightly, and I get more than a little thrill at the anticipation of witnessing her tell him off, but then she slowly lowers her hand.

"All right." She twists her comm to face her and speaks the search command into it. "Venomous wildlife in Venovia."

"Don't bother," I say. "There's nothing on the web that fits it. I already talked with the scientists when they came here, remember? That was the whole reason they were here. Because the samples didn't match anything in their system."

Carter stands, takes a metal stirring stick from the bar, and then returns to where we're gathered. He studies it and pokes and prods at the lump of flesh.

"You know what this looks like? The holograms of the monsters we fight during demonstrations."

"Mystyl?" Heath supplies. "They're extinct. Have been for centuries."

"Obviously not," I say.

"So, then that means they're back?" Carter asks. "But how? And why now?"

I scoff. "Does it matter?"

"Of course, it does," Heath adds. "It means the station is in more danger than we realized."

Carter screws up his face and swipes his hands through the air. "Okay, so let's just assume the extinct poisonous jellyfish-like aliens that poison you and are nearly invisible *are* back. What are we supposed to do about it?"

"It's easy. Shoot any of those fuckers we see," Logan says.

"Come on, Logan," Heath says. "It's not that easy. We can't go around shooting at them if we can't even see them."

Brigid sighs. "Okay, Heath is right. The station is in danger, and I can offer no advice on how to protect it. But I know we'll have less of a chance defending the station and everyone in it if Logan is in handcuffs."

"Very well," Heath says. "So, what do you propose?"

"All of you said that the Mystyl hasn't been around for centuries. This means this is something no one in our lifetime has ever seen before. An outlier." Brigid's voice raises an octave higher just as her eyes widen. "This is it. You're right. This is the answer." She looks at me, delight dancing in her eyes, and my head swims.

Fucking success. I've finally reached the level of intoxication that I think words are dancing in someone's eyes.

"What do we need to do?" Heath asks.

Brigid's teeth dig into her lower lip and my drunken gaze lingers on the movement.

"The laws of druadan being euthanized and their riders being discharged from service were written a long time ago," she says after a minute. "Which means any instances where the law has been enacted had to go to trial, they used to expedite the ruling. There has to be a record showing the procedures to enact the law." She licks her lips with excitement, and heat clouds Carter's eyes.

The man is so fucking gone. He thinks he's out for a nice swim and doesn't realize he's lost sight of the shore.

"And while I'm not a lawyer, I do know they can't enact the law without previous cases to draw their arguments from. With no one knowing what this animal was that was involved, it translates into this particular case being unique. There are no previous rulings they can draw from. This is an outlier. They'll have no choice but to take it to a trial."

The realization grips me, searing hope into my veins that I thought I'd never feel again.

A trial. I have a goddamn chance.

"Holy shit," I breathe, watching her.

Her full lips twist into a sly smile. My cock twitches.

Her authorial attitude is stunning, and I want to see more of it. There's a fiery creature hidden underneath that she keeps locked away, and I'm determined to coax it out.

"A trial will delay things," Heath says. "The court system might push it forward, but with the election and Galaxian missing, it could be weeks before they can set a date."

Carter punches me in the shoulder. "Maybe you get to stay being a rider after all."

"We'll see," I say, refusing to give in to the optimism.

"We'll have to play our cards right," Heath says, setting his drink on the table. He's barely touched it. Maybe his quick jaunt to Delford has proved successful with his brimming, at least if nothing else.

I'd be the most romantic mother-fucker alive if it meant I'd rarely sleep in an empty bed and a near-constant way to temper brimming effects. But that'd never happen. Ladies were always available for a quick fuck, but marrying a rider was a totally different matter. No one married riders for obvious reasons. Heath was a rarity—another outlier.

"Circuit authorities will be here tomorrow," Heath says. "You'll have to play nice. Keep your mouth shut, and keep demanding a lawyer. The station has one on retainer that they can contact. I'll make sure he's oh so conveniently off the continent for a vacation, which should buy us a little more time. I refuse to give up. If they shut down the station, any clues Sharice might have left me will go with it."

Carter bumps her with her shoulder. "Even if that does happen, we'll still help you find her."

She nods, although her eyes darken.

"But that's tomorrow's problem," Carter says. "Let's enjoy tonight. Who needs another drink?" He claps his hands. "Let's enjoy tonight. Tomorrow will come soon enough, so let's fucking cut loose."

I raise my glass in a silent toast, conceding to the camaraderie.

As the hour passes, my eyes keep drifting back to Brigid. Her laugh, the way she moves, the way she looks at Carter with those big blue eyes of hers.

That unexpected attraction I'd experienced at the barn last night stirs, feeling like a pulling sensation. I needed to be closer to her.

Touch her.

I grind my teeth together, resisting the feeling that was too bond-adjacent to be normal. This is wrong. It's the stress messing with my brain.

She isn't like the girls Carter usually parades around; more like the lilies that struggle to grow in the crevices of the perimeter wall. They look like delicate white flowers but are resilient little shits. Their roots somehow manage to cling to the wind-battered cliffs, and when they bloom, their sweet scent wafts for days across the island. And guessing by the way Heath and Carter can't take their eyes off her, they notice it also.

Still, she just isn't a rider. No matter how much she tries to worm her way in, she'll never share what we share.

Carter raises his glass again. "To stopping these slimy fuckers and Circuit shutting us down."

"To the gala being a success," Heath says.

"To finding my sister," Brigid adds.

I raise my glass in a final salute. "To what is most likely my last night as a rider." Without waiting for the others to respond, I tip back the glass, draining it. The alcohol scorches my throat deliciously. For a few seconds, the tightness in the bond eases, and I feel like I can finally inhale. But then it passes, and I'm left again, gasping for air.

Thirty

BRIGID

onight is the night.

Days spent prepping, organizing, and scheduling have all led up to this.

The gala is here. The exhibition hall is fully decorated, the caterers are busy in the kitchen, and already people are mingling and dancing to the orchestra on the stage.

It's perfect.

Its grandeur, the shimmering chandeliers, and the continuous drone of chatter feel almost oppressive. I steel myself as I prepare to step into the crowd. No more hiding in the wings doing the behind. the scenes stuff. It's time for me to be the 'face' of the station.

Maybe champagne first? I mean, Carter never fulfilled his

promise, so I might as well see what the fuss is about by myself. I smooth the front of my dress, flick a loose lock of hair over my shoulder, and stride in.

The stakes for this event could not be higher. I have to have faith that everyone knows their job and is doing it. We're all assuming our roles. And if we play our cards right, we can all work to keep Logan out of jail, Galaxian alive, and Heath from losing the station.

The lawyer had agreed to cooperate just as Heath had anticipated. Our statement had been sent out that morning to the media, and while we'd assumed some guests would request to leave early, no one had. None of them wanted to miss a chance to be a part of the salacious scandal or perhaps glimpse a rider being led out in handcuffs.

And indeed, the murmuring of whispers during the hosted brunch and guided tours often were led by the thrill of seeing a rogue druadan racing through the sands outside the perimeter wall.

A delicious heat settles in my core as I watch Heath—dressed in his formal blue riding jacket—mingle with the guests. Carter will be performing, and Logan remains on house arrest for the time being.

Heath is cornered by a group of equally well-dressed men and women, and I recognize several of the faces as politicians and real estate investors. I swipe up on my comm, summoning up the guest list Carla and I had compiled with names matching the profile photos. We'd distributed them to the other riders and waitstaff for reference. I'd received a notification two seconds after sending the message that Logan had deleted it, unopened.

I'd been determined to call him out on it, but then, with everything that had happened with Galaxian, I'd let it go. What was the point since he wouldn't be at the gala, anyway?

My chest tightens as I notice Heath's face drain of color, his shoulders hunching as if trying to collapse in on himself. His eyes are wild, pleading silently for escape.

Jess, in her off-the-shoulder black velvet gown, approaches with that familiar, sickly-sweet grin. "Heath," she purrs, "You must meet the Thompsons. They're crucial for our endeavors when we see to it to grow the Drakeford and Lockwood family tree."

As she loops her arm through his, that's when I see it.

His fingers flex beside him. His breathing is shallow and rapid like a hunted animal trying to stay silent. Sweat beads on his forehead, glistening in the chandelier light.

Despite his efforts to maintain composure, I notice the small subtleties, the tiny details no one else in the room seems to. Either because they aren't looking close enough or because they simply don't care. It's in these details that I realize Heath is teetering on the edge of a full-blown meltdown.

A fierce rush of protectiveness swells inside me, and my nails dig painfully into my palms. I have to get to Heath's side before his panic completely consumes him.

Swiftly, I approach the group. Time slows as I near Heath. I angle my body slightly, gently easing between him and the other guests.

Heath offers me a timid smile, and I turn to the man nearest me.

"Mr. Thompson," I begin brightly, willing my voice to remain steady despite the adrenaline coursing through me. "I've heard so much about your ventures in the East. Truly ground-breaking."

Mr. Thompson smiles, clearly pleased. "Why, thank you, Miss...?"

"Brigid. Brigid Corsair," I supply, keeping my tone calm and even. "Meridian's public relations manager."

I subtly position myself between Heath and Jess, widening the physical barrier and giving him space to breathe. "Actually,

Heath and I needed to go over the last-minute details regarding the list of items for the auction."

I gently touch Heath's arm, an electric yet gentle grounding sensation. His muscles seem to relax under the comforting pressure of my hand.

Heath's mouth gapes as his eyes bore into mine.

"Surely, you've got it covered, Ms. Corsair," Jess says.

"I wish I could say I do, but you know how Heath gets about wanting to oversee everything." I tilt my head back and giggle. "The station would fall apart if it weren't for him overseeing it all."

Jess arches an eyebrow, her gaze shifting from me to him.

"I agree," she says, running her lips over the rim of her champagne glass. "Heath does like to be in control."

Ignoring the pang of jealousy, I refuse to let her get under my skin. She is Heath's fiancé. The five-carat rock on her left hand gave her access to parts of Heath I'll never have.

Heath clears his throat, clearly conflicted.

I hold my breath, peering up at him with the most passive mask of professionalism I can.

The brown in his eyes swirls with indecision, and I will myself not to back down. I knew what I'd seen. He needs help. A break from these people. But I can't force someone to be rescued that didn't want it.

After what feels like an eternity, he nods. "Yes, absolutely. Please excuse me, Mr. and Mrs. Thompson. We shall continue this conversation later?" The couple both tilt their heads and back away.

Then Heath turns to Jess. "Sorry. Ten minutes at most. Go have fun. I'll find you."

Jess's face tightens, her lips pursing slightly. "Fine. Go. Do your station manager thing. But I expect at least three dances when you return."

"Of course." He presses his lips against her forehead. I can feel the chill radiating off of his kiss, devoid of any emotion. But even so, it makes me feel uneasy to witness it. Like I am staring at something I shouldn't be.

We make our way out of the ballroom and away from the bodies, and the air instantly cools.

As we reach the balcony, Heath hurries to the railing, practically collapsing against it. His hands grip the marble balustrade, knuckles white as if it is the only thing tethering him to the ground.

"Just breathe. Okay?"

He nods, not meeting my eyes. I study the side of the face, taking in his haggard expression. The sheen of sweat on his brow, the haunted look in his eyes. He has been barely keeping it together in there.

He hangs his head, taking a few shaky breaths as he focuses on steadying his breathing. After a moment, he lifts his face. He looks utterly exhausted and at his breaking point.

Against my better judgment, I reach for him, wrapping my arms around his shoulders in a fierce hug. He stiffens in surprise before melting into my embrace.

"It's okay," I murmur. "You're okay now."

"No, I'm not fucking *okay*. I'll never be okay."

His breath hitches, and his shoulders shake under my hands. He's succumbing to the panic attack again.

I refuse to let him crumble.

My hands slip free from where I'd had them on his back and move to the sides of his head. I pull his face to mine, crushing my lips against his.

The kiss is brief, only a second, but it's enough. Our bodies press against each other, the sensation of his hands on my lower back.

Then I step back.

He stares down at me. His shaking ceases. His breathing

slows. The storm has lightened in his eyes. "How.." he whispers, looking as confused as I feel. "How did you do that?"

"I have no idea," I murmur. "It's like I knew what you needed, and so I did it."

His eyes search mine like I might reveal more answers there, but he's out of luck. I reacted on instinct. An innate desire to help him. Calm him.

As much as my conscience would want me to believe otherwise, it was for selfish reasons that I kissed him. While that might carry more than a little weight to it, I mean, look at him, with his jet-black hair that demands my fingers to twirl into it. How could I not? But if I'm being completely honest with myself, I would've done it for anyone I cared about.

He shifts, and hooded eyes peering down at me. "I need to tell you something, and you have to promise me you won't tell another soul."

"Okay. I promise," I say, a little hesitant. I hate promising things before I know them. They always end up biting me in the ass in the end, but desperation clouds his eyes, and I make an exception.

"You know about brimming?"

I nod. I know a little. Aside from what he'd told me, Carla had told me more to help fill in the gaps.

He lets out a long sigh. "There's more to it. When a druadan bonds with you, your body temperature rises. The bond allows you to survive what would kill most people, but the constant stress is what shortens our lifespan. We're not meant to be this hot forever. Endure this constant fever." He pauses, drawing in a shaky breath. "But there's more…"

My lips parted, air seizing in my throat.

"Haven't you wondered why there are no children of druadan riders?"

I frown, wondering where he is going with this. I've never

really thought about it that hard. I knew they didn't live long, so I'd assumed they didn't want to bring a child into a world where they couldn't leave the station or their druadans, and then since they died so young, they'd barely get a chance to know their father.

"Because of their lifestyles, I guess? They're so busy at the stations, it'd be unfair to a wife and kids."

Heath shakes his head. "That's part of it, yes. But there's more to it. The strain of the bond on our bodies makes it so we *can't* have children."

I blink, thinking I'd misheard him. "What do you mean? Like you *can't*?" I tilt my head and make a pointing finger with my gesture. Carter had seemed to be more than capable of that physical act, so to be fair, I had a right to be confused. Maybe Carter took a special medication, or maybe Heath was different?

Heath sighs, amusement flickering briefly in his brown gaze. "I assure you, Ms. Corsair, that works just fine." A flush warms my cheeks as he continues, "It's because of our temperature rising. We're infertile the instant a druadan marks us."

"That's..." I trail off, unsure what to say. While I didn't have anything against children and contemplated having them when I found the right person in the future, they weren't something I thought about often. "I'm sorry." It sounds weak, the two words not doing nearly enough to comfort the hurt I see reflected in his face.

Heath moves, freeing himself from my arms. "It is what it is."

"Does Jess know?"

His eyes narrow, the rings of brown darkening to almost the same as his pupils. "No."

I want to tell him he should tell her that it's wrong to keep a secret like this from her, someone he will share his life with, but I don't have the heart. He'd nearly passed out in front of everyone at the gala. He was so much more fragile than anyone seemed to know.

"Thank you," he says, although I'm not sure why. He's so close now I can smell the champagne on his breath, and where my hands grip the sleeves of his jacket, I can feel the incredible heat radiating from his biceps.

"You fascinate me, Ms. Corsair. You know what I need, what to say before I do."

My cheeks flush with heat, and a small laugh escapes me. "I'm just good at reading people, I guess."

Our eyes lock again, and I'm overwhelmed by the want, no, the *need* for him to kiss me again. It'd been wrong. In every possible way, it could be.

But oh god, then why had it *felt* so right?

"I feel like all I'm doing lately is thanking you," Heath says, "and it's still falling short." He pauses, and his knuckle presses gently against my cheek, and he traces it down to my jaw, leaving a trail of tingling electricity in its path. "You are the most incredible and surprising woman I have ever met." His voice is husky as if he'd just woken up.

I can't move, and I inhale a series of shallow breaths, feeling like I'm on the precipice of a very high, very *dangerous* ledge. His gaze is all that tethers me, anchoring me so all the rest of the world fades, leaving only his face.

God, his face. This close, I want to absorb every detail. Memorize the layers of brown in his eyes, chocolate, sand, rust. Colors I can't find the names of but how I want to. I need to name them. Spend every second peering into them until I know them as I know my own.

"I want to kiss you again," he says. "But I can't." His throat bobs as he swallows.

"Jess," I murmur, and her name tarnishes the purity of the moment. I hate this sour taste of jealousy her name elicits. She had Heath first before he even knew I existed. He'd made a promise to marry her. No matter how much it hurts, I won't be the reason he breaks that promise.

His nod is nearly imperceptible.

"You should go," I say.

Neither of us move.

He lowers his hand to just above my shoulder, and I feel his fingers gently caress the lengths of my hair. "I should."

"They'll be starting to announce the winners of the silent auction and need you there."

"Indeed."

I swallow the walnut-sized lump in my throat as his fingers continue to move, fanning the flame of heat low in my belly. I inhale, breathing him in. The sweet and spicy scent of leather. Of *him*.

Every second we linger, I fear, is a second we cross into the uncrossable. The line that had been so firmly drawn is beginning to blur.

"Nothing can—" I begin to say; however, before I can finish the thought, the door opens, and I startle as if I'd been stung by a bee. Heath doesn't flinch, instead casually turning to address whoever barged in.

Carter.

He sees Heath first, and then green eyes focus on me. A crooked grin materializes on his face. The tops of my ears burn, and I slam my lips together.

"Everything alright?" Carter says. "I thought I saw you two scurry in here." Without waiting for us to answer, he shuts the door.

"Yes," Heath says. "Ms. Corsair was helping with something."

"Was she?" Carter raises a curious eyebrow in my direction, sauntering closer. He's dressed in the same blue rider coat as Heath, although he is missing the manager emblem on the right shoulder.

"Yep. That's me," I reply, hurrying to walk past Heath. "Helper Brigid. Always doing what I can when—"

Carter moves toward me, but Heath sidesteps, blocking him.

Hold on. What is happening? Why do I feel like a helpless prey trapped between two predators? I swallow down the lump in my throat.

"Care to enlighten me on the specifics with which you're helping?" Carter pauses, then adds, "Ms. Corsair?"

Heath grits his teeth. "What is it, Carter?"

A crooked smile appears on his face. "The guests just want to talk about the election candidates and interest rates. Figured whatever you two were doing was much more interesting."

Okay, I've had enough of whatever this is. I move around Heath, having to scoot past one of the armchairs, feeling like I'm escaping.

"Ms. Corsair," Heath says, not looking at me but maintaining his focus on Carter. "You should go first," he commands. "I'll wait a few minutes, then leave after."

I sigh and reach for the door handle. The sinking sensation intensifies as I start to leave, feeling more and more like the 'other woman'. The very thing I'd wanted so desperately to avoid.

I swing the door open and glance back at the two of them, still stuck in this uncomfortable stand-off.

Could they be fighting over me? No way. Heath is engaged, so why would Carter see Heath as a threat? I push the thoughts aside, reassuring myself that the kiss with Heath had been to help him. A one-time favor to a friend in need. He had been seconds away from hyperventilating, and I'd done the only thing I could think of to stop it.

It won't happen again, so there's no need to tell Carter.

Besides, since I'm not a member of their boys-only rider club, I'll always be in the dark, left to wonder what's happening between them. Despite how much time we spend together and how much we learn to trust each other and help one another, there will always be a part of them that remains closed off to me. No matter how long I live or how long I work beside them,

I will never truly know Heath, Carter, or Logan, for that matter, and for some wild reason, it annoys the shit out of me. I have no choice, however, but to accept it. Make peace with the secrecy and the lies.

It's just the way it is. I'm a woman, and therefore, I can never be a rider.

It's how it's always been and always will be.

Thirty-One

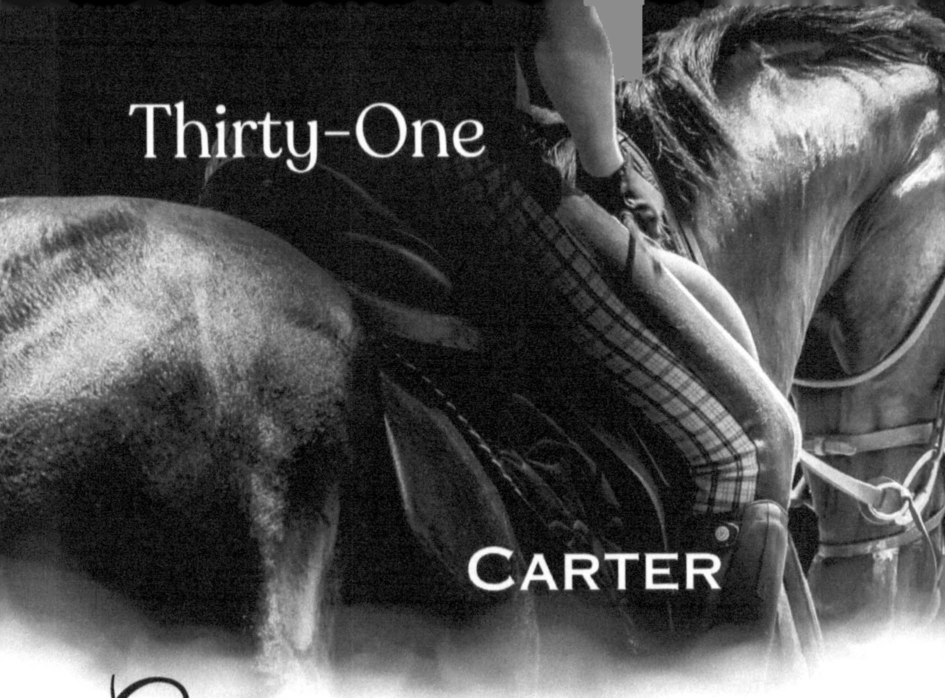

Carrying a flute of champagne, I glide through the crowd of the most influential people in the city. I'm doing the dance. The small talk. The smiling for pictures. The ignoring of napkins with comm numbers slipped into my pocket.

I'd been disappointed upon reading the guest lists that Marshal wasn't listed.

But after two phone calls and a comm message later, I'd learned from Blackhawk's manager that he was off the continent and wouldn't be returning for three more days.

Any answers I wanted regarding Ember's mood shift would have to wait.

The demonstration, led by Heath and the other three riders, had been decent enough, even without Ember and me out there in the spotlight. I swallow down the feeling of being left out, but there was no other choice since Ember is still recovering.

There will be more performances. I should enjoy myself. This is a party, after all.

I swap my empty glass from a server's tray for a full one and approach a trio of ladies clustered around a tower of shrimp and crab legs that was supposed to resemble the Meridian station logo. They're all around my mom's age.

The one wearing a red dress with her tits pushed up to her chin greets me. "Master Rider James, is it?" she says, playfully biting into a shrimp.

"In the flesh," I tilt my head in a mock bow. "And who might you lovely ladies be?"

She beams. "I'm Elizabeth Jameson, and these are my dearest friends."

"Penny Fairfax," the one to her left says. She's attired in a similar style dress, but it's a dark bronze color.

The third, in a purple silk jumpsuit, has black hair with streaks of gray along her forehead. "And I'm Gwendolyn Harrington." She extends her hand, and I take it, choosing to kiss it gently on the knuckles instead of shaking it.

The three-giggle confirmed I made the right decision.

"What did you think about the performance?"

Penny presses a hand to her mouth. "Incredible. Truly. I'm kicking myself for never attending one before."

"I went many years ago and treated my daughters recently."

"Was that before or after they were escorted out of Le Chez Rondeau?" Gwen teases, plucking another shrimp from the bed of kale shaped like an M.

Penny giggles, and the two exchange a conspiratorial look.

"Those allegations are completely fabricated. My girls simply had a row, is all, and the waiter overreacted when Alliya spilled her drink."

Penny lifts her eyebrows. "She threw a bottle of Champagne de Rouge, Betty."

Betty pulls a tube of lipstick from her jeweled clutch and reapplies it, staring into a compact mirror. "Exaggerations of the truth," she says, dabbing her lips together. "The restaurant seized the chance to fan the flames of a scandal in the media and tarnish a reputable family's name. My Robert is keen to press charges for slander should they refuse to back down."

Robert Jameson. *Senator* Robert Jameson. I swallow the rest of the champagne, quenching the awkwardness. I knew she looked familiar. I'd been seconds away from banging both of her daughters recently.

Elizabeth squints slightly. "So, help us settle a bet," she says. "We haven't had the privilege of meeting many Master Riders in person. Is it true about how you..." She stops in the middle of her question, and her eyes sweep from right to left, then, sure no one is within earshot, says, "Have exceptional stamina?"

A smug smile plays on my lips. "While I can't speak for all riders, however, I'd say it's safe to assume that we have a bit more endurance than your average man."

I take a sip of my champagne, enjoying the feeling of the bubbles in my mouth.

All three laugh.

"I told you," Penny says triumphantly. "I knew those rumors had to be true."

I give them both a sly smile and rest my elbows on the table so I'm a little bit closer. "Well, you know what they say: the secret to perfection is practice."

Gwen bites her lip and leans closer to me. "Speaking of practice... would you be willing to give us a demonstration?"

These women are bold. I'll give them that.

Before I can respond, however, a movement of bodies by the backdrop display with the Meridian station logo repeating over the black banner catches my attention. Brigid is there directing the group of novice riders with some guests to take a photograph.

Even from this distance, my eyes drink her in. The sapphire blue dress—a shade darker than her eyes—hugs her curves. The satiny fabric highlights the gentle slope of her waist and the swell of her breasts. Waves of her silver-blonde hair cascade down her back, making her stand out against the sea of black attire. In front of her, Keven flexes his arms in a mocking pose, and her smile reaches her blue eyes.

I can't help but feel drawn to her. Like wherever she is in the room, I can sense it.

"As tempting as that offer is, ladies," I say, swiveling my gaze to the three women. "I'm afraid I don't think it would be appropriate in this setting." I gesture around at the party.

Disappointment flickers across Penny and Gwen's faces as they nod slowly.

Elizabeth's gaze lands on something behind me. "My apologies, Master Rider, but it seems we've kept you far too long."

Penny and Gwen look to Betty, annoyance creasing their foreheads, but they follow her as she leads them along the perimeter of the buffet tables to where the quartet is playing a lively melody. I spot Senator Roberts awaiting them, along with two other men whom Penny and Gwen quickly join.

I shake my head, and step away, seeking out another glass of champagne.

As I weave through the crowd, my gaze inadvertently lands on Jess's parents. There's no sign of Jess, though, and part of me wonders if Heath is with her, a smart move on his part. A little rendezvous in one of the storage closets would certainly help him temper the brimming tension that's so evident in his demeanor. The guy needed to get laid desperately. After everything he'd dealt with in the past twenty-four hours, god, did he deserve it.

Barely an hour has passed since I'd stumbled upon him and Brigid on the balcony. I caught them standing together, looking rather cozy with one another.

Hell, I'd been surprised more than anything. I'd even joined them if they'd asked. Damn, that would have skyrocketed this party into interesting territory.

Catching them alone together had *not* been on my list of

things I'd imagine seeing tonight, and the brief flare of jealousy had quickly passed the second I'd felt the strain saturating our bond. The panicked expression on Heath's face had confirmed it.

His brimming was out of control, and the poor fucker was spiraling.

After Brigid had left, Heath had confessed that she'd noticed him struggling. The excess energy in the bond, combined with the stress of the party, had triggered a panic attack.

He'd refused to give me details on *how* she'd helped, the dick. But I'd pieced together enough to learn that her presence, in some strange way, had been enough to help him. While I didn't have any answers for him, I was grateful he'd got a handle on it.

I make a mental note to seek her out and thank her, and more than a few ways come to mind.

Among the guests, Jess' parents catch sight of me and wave. There's no escaping. Politeness dictates I greet them. Pushing thoughts of Heath and Brigid aside, I make my way over.

"I'm telling you," a middle-aged man with a large belly and nearly bald head says. "The shareholders won't be happy with these numbers. We're going to have to make some tough calls come spring."

I rarely read the news unless it's about celebrity gossip or Circuit military updates since my younger brother, Derrick, was deployed off-continent to help with the recovery efforts from the hurricanes. But I'd heard from Logan that his parents were one of the few whose jobs were still safe due to their need for engineering skills. Many filtration plant workers, however, were not so lucky, and the impending layoffs hung over the conversation like a dark cloud. To lighten the mood, another man in a black suit and gray striped tie chimes in, "Maybe I should sell off one of my beach houses down on the southern coast, eh?"

Laughter ripples through the group.

"Oh, that'll be pried out of your cold, dead hands, and you know it," the first man retorts, and they all nod in amused agreement.

"Ah, speaking of cold, dead hands," Mr. Drakeford says. "How's that filtration plant outside Blackhawk doing?"

The newcomer chuckles. "Still standing, Drakeford, despite your best efforts."

"Well, when you decided to toss in the towel, you know where to find me."

I step closer, and Mrs. Drakeford's eyes crinkle as she smiles up at me.

"Mr. and Mrs. Drakeford, a pleasure to see you both this evening."

"Indeed," Mr. Drakeford says and motions toward me. "This is Master Rider James. He's close friends with our soon-to-be son-in-law, Heath Lockwood."

Close friends. Sure, whatever you say, bud.

The others all murmur in agreement and tell me their names, but I only half listen, my attention waning from the slowing effects of the champagne.

"Did Heath decide on making you his best man yet?" Mrs. Drakeford asks. "I know it's not up to me, but you fill out a suit, don't you..."

Senator Darrow clears his throat. "Speaking of pending nuptials, how's the family, Carter? Heard your mother was promoted to Brigadier General."

"That's right. My dad's handling her having a higher rank than him about as well as you'd expect."

They both laugh.

"I can imagine." Mrs. Drakeford says. "It must be quite a change at home not having your brother there either anymore. But I'm sure they're managing just fine. Your family has always struck me as remarkably resilient."

It's a compliment but laced with the undercurrent of an

insult. As a Master Rider, I've reached the pinnacle of my career, but it's a bittersweet victory. I'm acutely aware that while I soar through the skies, my time is finite, my path inevitably leading to an early end. In contrast, my brother's life stretches out before him, filled with possibilities I'll never know. I am the limb of the family tree that will never branch.

Over the loudspeaker, the quartet stops playing, and Brigid announces the live auction will be starting. Our group bids farewell, returning to our tables.

Thousands of dollars in credits are shouted for the next forty-five minutes. Brigid and Heath give the winners cards so they can collect their pieces of original art, lunar retreat certificates, and an antique druadan rider manual signed by one of the first Master riders here at the station.

Once the auction is finished, I get swept onto the dance floor by the music. Then am pulled into a photo op with the biggest donors, which leads to an awkward dodging of the wife of a Circuit commander that I *did* give a private demonstration to a few months back. Finally free of my obligations, I make my way to where Brigid is handing out drink tickets to guests in line for the bar.

"Looks like congratulations are in order," I say with a smile, gesturing to the bustling room. "Everyone seems to be having a great time."

She looks up, a hint of relief in her smile. "Thank you. It's been a lot of work, but it does feel like it's paying off."

I lean in slightly, lowering my voice. "So about what I saw earlier..." I begin, watching her reaction closely. Her eyes flicker up to mine, a trace of nervousness, maybe even fear, dancing in their turquoise depths.

"Don't worry," I add quickly, my tone light but reassuring. "My lips are sealed. Heath is like a brother to me, and I love the guy. I just wanted to thank you for doing whatever it was you did."

A visible tension releases from her shoulders, and she offers me a small smile. There's a glimmer of something more, a connection that goes beyond mere words, and I'm desperate to reach out for it.

Reach out for her.

"You're welcome," she says. "I care about Heath, too."

Suddenly, Brigid's head whips to the entrance into the hall. "Hey, can you finish this? I gotta go." She shoves the roll of tickets into my hands.

"What? Where are you—"

She doesn't wait to answer. Instead of darting through the tables of seated guests, she holds the lengths of her dress as she weaves through the people toward the archway leading outside.

I'm left standing there confused and holding the tickets.

After a brief moment of indecision, I set them down on a nearby table. The thought of being anchored to this spot to hand out tickets is fucking ridiculous. I'll find some novice to do it. I've got more schmooosing and drinking to do, and I'm pretty sure I saw them roll out the dessert cart.

As I start walking away, the buzz of conversation suddenly dulls as if I'd muffled it with earplugs. A commotion on the stage ceases the music abruptly.

Someone nearby curses, and a series of gasps follows it.

A single ear-piercing scream erupts from the direction of the food tables. Adrenaline floods my veins just as shared murmurs of confusion and fear ripple through the crowd. I bolt for the buffet table.

People dart past me, eyes wide with terror, moving away from one particular direction. I weave through the chaos, heart racing, as I push through the fleeing guests.

Guests scramble in every direction. An older woman in a sequined gown stumbles, her pearls scattering across the marble floor. There's a clatter of overturned chairs and the heavy thuds of hurried footsteps as security rushes in, pushing their way through the terrified people.

"What the hell is going on?" I shout, scanning the overturned table and shattered glass scattered on the floor.

A woman with freckled skin and dark red hair is sprawled on the ground. She winces as I crouch beside her—angry streaks of red crisscross the back of her hand and wrist.

My stomach plummets. I've seen these marks before on Brigid.

Fuck.

I shout for security, my voice barely cutting through the noise. "Security! We need help here!" But even as I call out, I'm unsure if they can hear me over the commotion.

"I reached for a crab puff," she says with a shaky voice. "and something burned my arm. See?"

The revelation slams into me as if Ember kicked me square in the chest.

The Mystyl.

They're *here.*

Thirty-Two

BRIGID

I've seen a ghost.

The chill of the night seeps into my bones as I bolt out of the exhibition hall. The cloaked figure darts ahead, a silhouette against the moonlit courtyard outside. My heels click on the stone walkway, and my breath forms misty clouds in the cool air. Each exhale is sharper than the last. Giant potted cacti and shrubs dot the edges of the pathway, their forms eerie and elongated in the dark.

I'd only glimpsed the side of the person's face, but it'd been enough.

"Stop, please!" I shout into the night, but the figure's pace quickens. My heel catches in one of the cracks between the stones, and I trip.

The split second before my face hits the ground, I catch myself. Gritting my teeth, I regain my footing before kicking off my heels angrily into the bushes.

I charge ahead barefoot. I've lost valuable time, and

when I look up, the person is disappearing around the south outside corner of the hall. I curse under my breath and break into a jog, but before I can cover more than ten feet, I'm yanked into an alcove between the pillars that hold the massive building's roof. The rough texture of the wall scrapes against my back and arms as I'm slammed against it.

An oppressive weight pins me, and I'm engulfed in the smoky scent of whiskey. Panic erupts inside me, a wild, primal instinct to fight for survival at whatever is holding me captive. I lash out, my fists connecting with what feels like a solid chest. Every strike is an explosion of fear and desperation.

"Fucking hell, Brigid," a man says.

My heart is like a bird trying to escape its cage as it takes a moment for me to match a face to a voice. "Logan?" I say. He places a calloused hand over my mouth.

His face inches closer. I strain to get a better look, but we're too far away from the security lights, and I can only make out the general shape of his jaw and nose.

My chest heaves against his, each breath shallower than the last. The hard lines of his body push against me. He shifts the weight from where his hips are, pinning me against the wall. I nearly gasp from the heat radiating off of him.

"They're attracted to movement," Logan whispers.

"*What* is?" I say, but my voice is muffled by his hand. His hand releases where it had been on my lips, and he lowers it slowly. His knuckles graze the front of my dress, teasing my nipples to harden through the thin layers of fabric. My traitorous heart hammers against my ribcage so loud I'm sure he can hear it.

I swallow, forcing past the lump in my throat. He's an asshole, remember? The one who had been Captain of the "Kick Brigid off the station" team.

From somewhere above me, I hear a low, hissing noise like

steam escaping. The memory is hazy, but I've heard that noise before. The night I'd been attacked in the barn.

Time stretches, and still, we stand there. Him covering me with his body, and my breathing shallow and nearly inaudible.

Finally, he moves, and I feel the relief of his weight. The heat of his body is gone, too, though, and goosebumps prickle my arms.

"They're gone," he says.

"How do you know?"

"I just do." His hand slips into mine. The rough callouses and warmth are surprisingly comforting. "We need to get out of here." He pulls on my hand, and I jerk it free.

"No. I can't. My sister, I saw her here. She's in danger."

There's a long pause in the dark before he says. "I saw her too."

My breathing quickens. "You did? Then you know I have to talk to her. She needs my help. I need to find out where she's been. What's happened to her?"

"No."

"No?" I retort. "Last I checked, you *wanted* to find her just as bad as I did."

He doesn't reply.

I shake my head in frustration. "Dammit, Logan. I don't have time for this." I pivot on my heel to leave, but Logan's iron grip locks around my bicep.

"You're not going out there."

"Let go of me," I say, trying to break free again, but it's no use. His hand stays firmly clamped.

"Please," I beg, my voice cracking. "Please. She's my sister."

From the shadows, I hear Logan curse as his grip loosens.

I wrap my arms around myself. The night air feels colder now, and I shiver, not just from the temperature but from the realization of the danger hundreds of people are in. My sister included.

"The whole station is crawling with those fucking things," he says.

I clench my teeth to stop them from chattering and say, "I don't care."

"You will care when one of those tentacles wraps around your pretty little neck. This isn't brave, Blondie. This is being stupid."

He's right. I know he is. But I refuse to give in. Not now. Already, I can feel the hope of seeing her again slipping through my grasp. "I can't lose her." My voice cracks. "Please. Not again. Not when she's this close."

He curses again. "Fine. But I'm going with you."

"What about the guests?"

"My team is in there. They'll handle it."

He could stop me if he wanted to. Throw me over his shoulder, fireman carry style, and haul my ass back to my cottage. I'm not stronger than him, and I doubt I'm faster. If this is the only way he'll let me go, then so be it.

We set off together, our footsteps quick and quiet as we hurry toward the shuttle pad. Logan leads, alert to every sound, every shift in the shadows.

As we near the shuttle maintenance building, a piercing scream shatters the silence. We freeze, and Logan places a hand protectively in front of me.

In the low light, I watch as he presses a finger to his lips and then silently draws his laser pistol.

A scream echoes off the walls, and Logan and I sprint toward it. My breath is ragged in the still air when we reach the small building used for storage.

Its door is open, and my eyes scan the pitch-black interior for any sign of movement. Logan maneuvers in front of me, blocking the inside from my sight.

Something metal clatters inside, and a jolt of adrenaline floods my veins.

Logan raises his pistol, holding it in front of him. His deliberate steps are cautious as he vanishes inside.

I stay rooted at the doorway, my heart pounding in my chest, every sense heightened.

I hear the crack of the laser pistol and dart to the entrance. A shimmering tentacle creature, its skin glistening in the faint light, leaps out of the rafters.

"Logan!" I scream.

He fires his gun again, the sound deafening in the confined space, and I clamp my hands to my ears. The creature recoils, its body shifting in mid-flight, narrowly avoiding the laser.

From the rafters above, two more of the creatures attack, their bodies twisting and contorting like many-legged serpents as they fall from the ceiling, landing on Logan's shoulders.

He's a flurry of movement, furiously trying to fend off the whip-like tentacles as they wrap around his arms and neck.

"Run!" he yells.

I hesitate for a split second, torn between the instinct to flee and the desire to help.

"Get the fuck out of here!" he snarls, and I obey. I dash away from the building, my bare feet pounding against the ground. Behind me, the sound of gunfire and the creatures' eerie hums fill the air.

As I run, the cold night air burns my lungs. The shuttle pad's security light casts long, ominous shadows. I glance back, hoping to see Logan following, but there's only darkness and the distant sounds of shouting and laser fire elsewhere on the station.

Panic cinches my gut tighter, twisting and turning as if a serpent coils within.

Logan is fighting those creatures by himself.

The thought propels me faster.

He's a good fighter and has a gun, but what if there were

more of them? More hiding nearby that the sound of the gunfire had attracted?

I'm no expert, but I'm fairly certain laser pistols have a limited number of charges.

He's going to die if I don't get help.

I skid to a stop by a shipping container when the shuttle pad comes just into view. A shuttle sits on it with its lights on, and a fueling truck next to it. I count at least two dozen people in formal attire huddling around it.

I release the breath I didn't know I'd been holding. They're evacuating guests. That's good, at least.

Indecision rages like a battle inside me.

Logan is in danger. Sharice is in danger. The whole goddamn station is in danger.

So, who do I pick? Who do I choose to save?

Before I can decide, I see Heath and Carter helping the group up the ramp.

I cup my hands to call out to them when I'm suddenly surrounded by four figures wearing hooded jackets. Each points a laser pistol at me.

"One word, and we'll see how pretty that dress is with your blood on it."

Confusion swirls in my head. I don't know who these assholes are or what they want, but the only chance I have to live through this is to cooperate.

"Fuck you," I spit, lowering my hands. They're yanked behind my back with ruthless efficiency.

"Good girl," a man sneers, chillingly close. A fresh wave of fear washes over me, leaving me breathless and disoriented.

"Take her comm," says a woman with a voice as cold as steel.

I feel the familiar weight of my wrist comm being removed, severing my last chance at helping Logan or telling Heath and Carter I'm in danger. A desperate whimper escapes me.

"Who are you? What are you doing?" My voice is shaky, barely audible over the pounding of my own heart.

"We need her alive," the woman says.

With my wrists bound, they begin to drag me away, and sharp rocks bite into the tender soles of my feet. I stumble, and firm arms haul me upright.

The biggest of the cloaked figures presses the butt of a pistol into my side.

"We're just going for a walk," he says in my ear. Desperation claws at my throat as we draw near the idling shuttle.

Heath and Carter are no longer here. My one hope that they were just hidden in the crowd is snuffed out.

I silently plead for someone, anyone, to notice that I'm being taken against my will—a guest, a station worker, anyone who might be able to help, but no one appears. The pistol is shoved harder into my side, and I grimace at the jab in between my ribs.

We stick to the shadows of the buildings. Several security light poles along our path are dark. Burned out, or perhaps deliberately disabled. This attack, or whatever it was, was planned. That much is obvious. These aren't some disgruntled gala guests who smuggled pistols in their suitcases or purses. These are soldiers.

Rebels.

The word surges to the front of my mind. At any given time, there were a handful of revolutionary groups torching Circuit-owned buildings and holding protests all over Venovia. The government always downplayed their actions as a nuisance or an annoyance.

Obviously, that had been wrong.

The shuttle pad comes into view, a stark, open space that feels like a stage under the glaring overhead light poles. A line has formed of guests in formal attire, each with a bag over their head, handcuffed and being herded like cattle. A pang of horror grips me. I'm not the only one.

"That makes four of them, including the judge," a man's voice cuts through the air, matter-of-fact.

"Good." The response sends a chill through me. No matter how much time has passed or distance, I'd know that voice anywhere.

A figure steps forward from the group wearing a long, green coat. They're about my height, and as they lower their hood.

An icy dread solidifies my blood.

Sharice.

My sister's skin is pale, and she has a nose piercing and a new tattoo of a rose with thorny vines curling around her neck. But it's definitely here. Her blue eyes hold me captive, cold and calculating.

This is my sister, but she has changed...different. More than I'd expect to see in a year.

"Hello, baby sister," she says. Her tone is foreign, laced with a mixture of amusement and disdain. There's no doubting it's her, but her words carry none of the warmth I remembered.

"Sharice," I stammer, my voice breaking. "Where have you been? Who are these people? Please, tell me what's going on?"

The sister I thought I knew doesn't flinch. "I'm sorry, truly I am, but I need you."

My pulse rages in my eardrums, and I clench my teeth so hard I fear they might break. I'd been wrong. She hadn't been coerced or blackmailed by a rebel group. She wasn't a captive at all. She was *the* leader. The one who planned this attack.

"I promise I'll explain everything soon. For now, it'd be best if you quit struggling, or I'll have to have Dalk here give you a little something extra to calm you down."

A cold shiver trickles down my spine as if icy fingers were trailing along it.

My throat tightens as Dalk looms closer. The needle he holds — a menacing sliver of metal that glints in the dim light — fills me with dread.

My sister's words are cold and alien in the night air. "It's just a sedative, but I don't want to use it unless I have to. So, are we going to cooperate?"

My lips slam shut. My pulse pounds in my eardrums at the sight of the needle, yet my mind races ahead, calculating my chances of escape. Consciousness is essential if I'm to make it out alive—I need to be alert and aware.

They start loading a crate, and I sense my window of escape narrowing by the second. Suddenly, I spot something: two rounded shapes obscured under tarpaulins. And then, almost miraculously, one slips ever-so-slightly to reveal a bumpy pale blue shell of a druadan egg. Holy shit.

They've taken the other two. During the panic at the party, they must've snuck in and stolen them. I hadn't been imagining things. I really *had* seen her at the gala.

Panic seizes the air from my lungs. "Wait. What are you doing? Why are you taking the eggs?" My voice breaks the silence, but my sister might as well be a statue for all the attention she pays me. She turns away, dismissing my plea with a cold shoulder.

I'm desperate now, thoughts racing. I need to contact Heath or Carter. My comm device rests in one of the rebel's pockets, out of reach. Outnumbered, unarmed, barefoot, and wearing nothing more than a stupid silk dress, my options are— let's just say— limited.

Helplessness crashes over me, followed by a creeping tide of sadness and despair.

I came here for her—for my sister. I had found her, yes, but at what cost? Everything has spiraled so far from what I had planned. This isn't how it was supposed to end. Not like this. I feel a deep, aching sorrow at the thought of leaving without saying goodbye to Heath, Carter, or even knowing if Logan is still alive. If any of them are.

Maybe I should've fought back took my chances against the sedative she'd threatened me with.

The ramp leading into the shuttle is frigid cold against my bare feet, and I hang my head, the weight of defeat heavy in every step.

A blinding flash of light illuminates the ramp, followed a split second later by the loud crack of splintering metal as a laser pierces the hull of the ship. The smell of burning rubber and hot steel fills the air. The engine erupts in flames and chaos ensues as rebels shout and scramble around, realizing we are under attack.

One of the guys who jumped me falls to the ground, a smoking hole between his forehead between his eyes, frozen in a blank stare. My heart leaps into my throat, and I choke on a scream. I try to scurry away, but my hands are still tied behind my back, and I lose my balance and fall.

My diaphragm seizes, and I gasp for air as I twist over to crawl on my belly.

Laser blasts from both sides whiz over me. My shoulders strain as I army crawl inch by inch to hide behind a stack of supply containers.

Once safely behind them, I twist myself into a sitting position as panic grips me. I see Heath, and for a brief, bittersweet moment, our eyes meet. So much is conveyed between us without saying a word. But then he's forced back behind the storage shed. I can't see Carter anywhere. Did something happen to him? Is he hurt?

Bodies lay scattered on the ground, some moving, others not. The sound of gunfire fills the air, and my heart races with fear.

The sharp staccato of laser fire from every direction is relentless. Dust and the acrid smell of burning filled the air, stinging my nostrils. The ship's engine groans a tortured metal is consumed by fire. Heat washes over me.

The ground shakes as another explosion rocks the ship. Shrapnel flies, a deadly hail, and I duck, feeling the heat of a passing laser fire inches from my left ear.

A jagged piece of metal lands a few feet from me. I scoot over and twist my shoulders so I can cut whatever is binding my hands. I clench my teeth at the protesting muscles in my shoulders from holding them at the odd angle.

Frantically, I work them back and forth before I feel the bonds loosen, and I free my hands from the coarse rope. I rub my sore wrists, the sensation returning to my hands, and peek around the corner of the crate. A hundred feet away from me, Heath, Carter, and four other security officers are trading shots with the rebels.

In the mayhem, I've lost sight of my sister. Two rebels scramble up the ramp while a third covers them with rapid blasts of their pistol.

Soon, they emerge carrying the crate with the eggs and hurry sideways to the fueling truck. Fire engulfs the shuttle, and I hear a series of small explosions inside the cabin before the engines catch, too. I haul myself up on my knees and shuffle across the dirt to get further away before the fuel takes ignite and the concussive wave throws me forward. Dust coats the inside of my mouth and nose, and I cover my mouth, coughing at the acrid smell of smoke.

I cover my head and duck as a laser blast flies past my ear. I'm too exposed out here. I abandon my path and dart to another stack of containers. Smoke clogs my throat and nose, and I stifle a cough.

Beside the shuttle pad, two men charge each other with wild intensity, tossing their spent pistols aside and throwing punches at him.

The left sleeve of a blue riding jacket is torn completely off, revealing his bare arm, and blood splatters his neck and cheek, but from the glow of the explosion, I recognize his face: Carter.

Relief crashes over me as I see he's alive.

Carter dodges the other man with an agility I wasn't aware a person could possess. It's incredible to watch. He swerves, lands a blow on one guy's jaw, then pivots to hit the other one in the gut. The man grunts and doubles over but doesn't go down. Carter seizes the moment by kicking the first guy in the knee and then shoving hard so he falls backward.

The ground shudders again. The large fuel truck has been started. A stranger sits in the driver's seat, coaxing the engine to idle, and great black puffs of smoke erupt from the exhaust pipe.

"Get to the south cove!" My sister shouts. Her face is coated in soot, she has a cut on her right cheek, and blood drips down her left arm where a laser had caught her in the shoulder. Quickly, she moves to the cargo hold of the shuttle. She tears a piece of shirt from a body, too severely burned for me to tell if it's one of ours or theirs, and wraps it around her hand to keep it from being burned by the heat of metal. Then she grabs a hold of the latch and lifts it up. I recognize the crate she removes as the one with the druadan eggs.

The thought hits me—this is my one chance to retrieve the eggs. Around me, the firefight continues. At once, I'm on my feet and moving. Sharice calls to those nearest, urging them onto the truck as she hurries to carry the crate to it. Other rebels are either distracted by their own fights or are choosing self-sacrifice for Sharice and the eggs' chance at escape.

I sprint towards the truck, bare feet pounding the cement and gravel. If they have a boat waiting for them, then they're as good as gone if they breach the station's gate. With the main shuttle destroyed and the limited options for vehicles we have, I can't guarantee they didn't sabotage those.

I pause, crouching behind the stack of plastic tubs, and watch as Sharice secures the crate in the back of the truck with straps, then jogs to the cab.

Adrenaline fueling my veins, I close the distance to the truck and leap into the back of it. I land with a thud near the crate with the eggs. Sweat clings to my neck and back as I grab the straps, trying to loosen them. I've barely gripped them when the truck lurches forward, and I'm forced to let go and grasp the side of the truck or tumble off the back.

The driver guns the engine, bouncing over the rocks on the maintenance road that leads to the southern gate.

Shouts and cursing trail behind me, and I search the moving bodies for signs of any of the three men. The barrels of fuel beside the shuttle ignite, and the shuttle pad is rocked by explosion after explosion. I wrap my arms around the crate, trying to shield the eggs from being too jostled as tears stream down my cheeks.

Thirty-Three

HEATH

I've lost all control.

The entire station is under siege, and I'm helpless to stop it.

Frustration permeates every fiber of my being as I watch the crate with the eggs loaded into the truck.

It had been a planned, calculated assault on the station. Meridian Station was facing a crisis we were never prepared for. We were trained to handle dust storms, disgruntled guests, and the occasional wild cat or coyote that tunneled under the wall.

Not this. Never this.

When the hall had been attacked, I'd rushed to get the guests, Jess and her parents included, to safety into the basement under the exhibition hall. The two empty niches I'd passed by had been proof that the Mystyl attack had been a mere diversion.

They'd left the fake one. They knew it was fake because *they* were the ones who had the real one. It was the same people that coerced Sharice and forced her to take it.

And now they were here for the others.

I sprint towards the truck, leaping over the injured and dead, military training from my academy days pulsing through me, a guiding light in this unexpected storm.

Combat training from my academy days coursed through me, and honed instincts took control of my body. We'd been trained alongside the Circuit military cadets, but it had never been meant for us to put it into live practice.

We were performers. Our skills are used for demonstration only.

However, it had given us an advantage. An edge that I prayed like hell it would be enough. I dodge a barrage of laser blasts and the screams and shouts of the rebels to flee and leave the injured. Twenty yards from the truck and shuttle, the fuel barrels detonate, sending waves of heat and force crashing over me. Instinct takes over; I shield myself, feeling the scorching heat skim my skin. Around me, everything spins with noise and confusion. Something painfully burns the inside the side of my thigh and calf, and my knees buckle.

Through the blur, I see a guard go down, struck by flaming shrapnel. Close by, a rebel, trapped under the shuttle wing, struggles in vain.

My ears fill with a sharp ringing sound, drowning out everything else.

Struggling to my feet, I call for Carter, but my voice is hoarse, and it comes out garbled. It's too loud. Too confusing. Everyone is covered in blood and dust. There's no way to know who is on my side and who is against it. *Get to higher ground.* The combat lessons drilled into us at the academy echo in my skull. *If you fire at nothing, you hit nothing.*

I adjust my grip on the laser pistol and see the indicator light on the side showing a five-percent charge left.

The bitter taste of defeat presses down on my shoulders, but I shrug it off. This is my station. And whoever these people are, hurting the guests here and trying to steal the eggs, are not going to succeed so long as I draw breath.

Logan's still MIA. His absence gnaws at me. Why isn't he here? Did they catch him in his house asleep? No. Logan sleeps with one eye open. There's no way they got the jump on him.

So, where the hell is he?

I hadn't seen Brigid anywhere either. Carter had told me she ran out before the incident, and the first place I'd checked after evacuating everyone had been her cottage. The lights had been off, and it had been empty. I hoped she had found somewhere to hide and was staying the hell put.

I'm standing but feel myself swaying. Suddenly, Carter's face comes into focus, his mouth forming urgent, silent commands. Slowly, the sound trickles back until his voice matches his face.

"Did you hear me?" he yells. "Brigid is on the back of that truck." He gestures with his pistol to our right. "They have a goddamn boat and hacked the code on the south gate. We have to fucking stop them!"

My eyes follow the direction of his gun at the truck's fading taillights. A sense of dread gnaws at my gut. There is no way we can catch them on foot, especially with my injured leg.

"Follow me," I say, and limping, head to the maintenance shed.

Carter keeps behind me, covering me with a few well-placed shots of his gun. Soon, we're behind the cover of the machine shed, and we hurry inside the pair of four-seater off-road vehicles.

"Fuck," I hear Carter cuss. "Look."

I follow his gaze. The front tires on all of them have been viciously slashed. A wave of anger and helplessness surges through me.

"Damn it!" I hit the cold metal fender of the one nearest me, my frustration echoing in the hollow space.

"What do you want to do?" he says.

I ball my hands into fists, feeling the shirking list of options growing smaller by the second.

"We can ride," Carter says.

"Ember's shoulder?"

Carter smirks. "My boy took the feed bucket from a novice this morning. He's feeling better." Carter gestures to my leg. "Honestly, I'm more worried about you."

The black tux pants are torn over my knee, revealing a six-inch-long bleeding gash on the lower part of my thigh. The skin's edges darkened, sung from the heat of the laser.

"I don't have a choice," I say.

"Doing this puts them at risk."

"I know."

"What they did to the quads. We don't even know if they went to the barn too."

"Yes, we do," I reply and tap the back of my hand. The bond is still *very* much present and connected.

"Fine," Carter says, nodding. "Let's do this."

***

EACH STEP TO THE BARN FEELS LIKE AGONY, AND I GRIT MY TEETH against the pain. We pass by the exhibition hall, and to my relief, I see the doors are closed and hear nothing from inside. I can only hope the guests, Jess included, are still safely barricaded in the basement where I'd left them.

The closer we get, however, the louder a low hum in my ears. "*Shadowmane?*" I call out mentally. We're close enough now he should be within earshot.

I'm slammed with a forceful reply, and the humming intensifies.

Worms. Many. Hide.

I curse and force myself into a half-jog. Carter matches my pace, no doubt getting similar messages from Ember.

At the barn entrance, we slow. Cold sweat trickles down my neck as Carter and I exchange a tense glance. Something is wrong.

He starts forward first, creeping towards the half-open doors. I follow him inside. The vibrations hum louder now, penetrating the soles of my boots.

Silhouettes of sleek and glistening tentacles drape over the rafters, barely visible under the starlight. They move languidly around the barn, bending and twisting over the walls of the stalls as they slowly glide through patches of moonlight. It's as if they're waiting.

Predators lying dormant as unsuspecting prey stumble under them.

Carter points his gun at one, but I press a hand on his and shake my head when he gives me a questioning look. I put a finger to my lips. There are dozens, too many for us to take on. We have no choice but to sneak past.

I hold my breath as one slithers down the wall nearest us, its mirror-like scales reflecting the night sky, as it scurries across the stone floor and ascends the wall of Galaxian's empty stall.

Carter and I sidestep almost silently down the aisle way, laser pistols gripped in our hands, eyes glued to the overhead beams. The barn creaks under the wood, complaining against the rapid drop in temperature.

Carter's jaw is set with determination as he approaches his stallion's stall. He knows him better than anyone, and I have to trust his judgment that he wouldn't ride Ember if he thought it'd further injure him. However, this is Brigid and the eggs we're talking about, and I can't be certain his judgment hasn't been affected.

My thoughts drift to our kiss on the balcony. Even I'm not safe from her influence.

Carter murmurs soothingly to Ember as I head to Shadowmane's stall. He snorts with a greeting when I step into his stall.

Heath. Alive.

"Yeah, I'm alive," I whisper.

I run a comforting hand down his trembling neck. *"There are bad people here. They took a friend of mine and stole the eggs from us. I'm going to need you to help me get them back."*

It's hard to tell with druadan's glowing, cat-like eyes, but I can sense he's peering at me, tasting the urgency in our connection.

Shadowmane wears his leather halter, and I grab the lead rope from the hook just on the outside of the door. There's no time for a saddle. No time for the safety helmets or vests we usually wear. Carefully, I slide open his stall door and see Carter and Ember already stepping out of theirs further down the aisle.

I lead Shadowmane out, then grab hold of his mane and swing myself up and over. I grunt with the sharp stab of pain in my right leg as the intense heat radiates from him into the wound. Without the saddle leathers to shield me from him, my riding pants are all that insulates me, and I'm certain I'll have red welts on my legs tomorrow.

If I live to see tomorrow, that is.

I settle onto his broad back, and a rush of energy through our bond reverberates inside me. My back arches, and my vision goes black, and for a second, I'm terrified I've had a stroke, but then I see my surroundings again. The barn, the stalls, the single light above each stall. But there's more.

An awareness of other *beings.* Minds.

Worms. Shadowmane says in my head. *Show them. Feel them.*

Holy shit.

These creatures are invisible in the dark. Fighting them at the gala felt like grappling with the wind. Fighting ghosts.

You can't fight what you can't see.

I can't see them, but Shadowmane can. Hundreds of them. Lurking in the rafters, clinging to the walls.

The whole barn is swarming with them.

I look at Carter ahead of me, and the frantic swinging of his head confirms that Ember, too is sharing the feeling through the bond.

Our druadans *can* see them. Before I can get lost in the hows and the whys, my wrist comm chimes with an alert. *"Nelworth officials have been notified of your emergency. ETA of protective personnel is twenty minutes. Please seek shelter until authorities have secured the area."*

The dispatcher's automated warning shatters the tense quiet, and before I can even process the words, the creatures attack.

They surge from the shadows. I feel the air move as their tentacles unfold. One by one, they drop from the rafters.

Shadowmane screams as several lands on his back. He rears, hooves striking blindly at the air, trying vainly to dislodge the creatures. I cling to his mane as he thrashes, my legs clamped around his barrel. His panic bleeds through our connection.

Ahead, Ember squeals, echoing Shadowmane's rage and terror. Translucent tentacles run slickly over his hindquarters. Carter curses, firing his pistol toward the corner of the ceiling.

In the stalls, the other stallions panic, and the air is alive with their hums. Each calls out in desperation to their rider for help.

I fight back the urge to cover my ears, my eyeballs rattling in their sockets at the combined voices of the druadans. The other riders will be here soon, none would ignore their stallion's alarm.

"Go!" I shout, and we bolt out of the exit, charging past Carter and Ember. Tentacles drag at their legs, threatening to topple them, but my stallion leaps and dodges the attack.

We break free onto open ground, the hoofbeats of our mounts thundering on the pavement and gravel roads. I guide Shadowmane to the south gate, the air whipping at my face and whistling in my ears.

Ember streaks alongside, Carter leaning low over his neck. Behind us, I can hear the swarm giving chase, gaining by the second.

Hooves thundering, teeth bared against the darkness, we run.

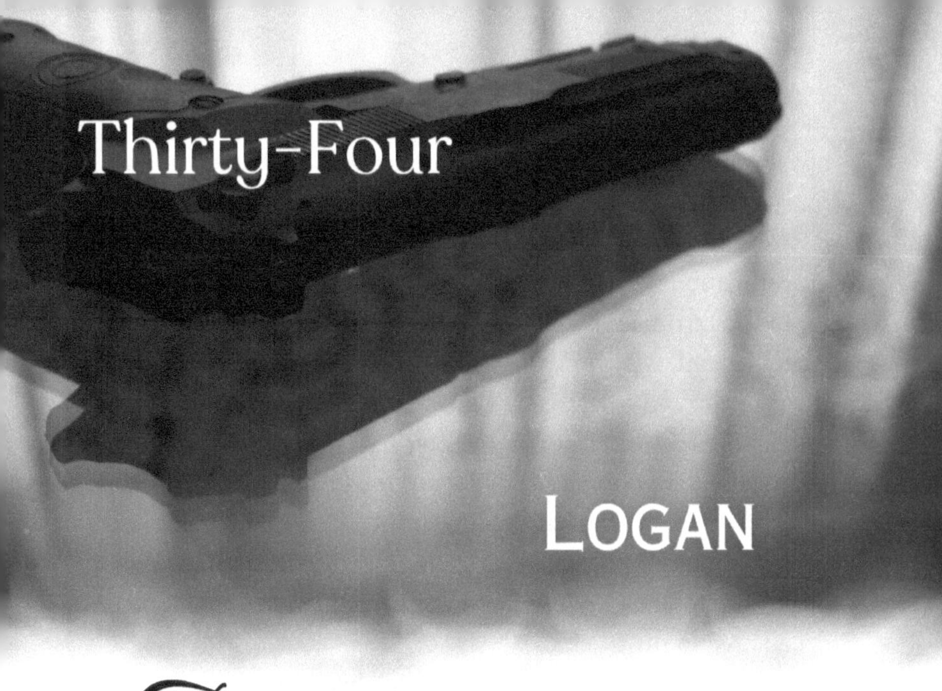

Thirty-Four

LOGAN

The roar of the shuttle's engines thunders overhead.

They do little, however, to drown out the shrieks rising behind me from the burning storage shed. I grin, even as the pain radiates from my dislocated shoulder.

Those slimy fuckers almost had me. I'll give them that, but they have nothing to do to save themselves from locked doors, a gas can, and a match.

I move away from the burning building and the billowing black cloud of smoke. The clatter of hooves grabs my focus, and I catch sight of Heath riding Shadowmane and Carter beside him on Ember. They're galloping full-tilt after a truck driving down the maintenance road into the desert.

Fucking dumbasses.

I let out a heavy sigh and followed after them. My singed clothes reek of smoke and sweat as I jog in the direction of the gate. I'll never catch them on their stallions. I gnash my teeth in frustration that Galaxian decided *now* was the time to go rogue.

If I ever lay eyes on him again, I swear to god I'll…

I trail off, knowing it's an empty threat. The bond prevents me from ever harming him. I cut across to a man's door instead of the main gate and find the old motorcycle I'd stashed in there for just such occasions. The truth was I was fixing it up. Restoring it was a great way to pass the time when I took the graveyard shift.

I kickstart it, and while the brakes aren't tuned and the back wheel is bent, it'll work for what I need it for. I slam down on the throttle, and it leaps out onto the road. I can just make out the flailing tails of Heath and Carter's stallions in the dark, but judging by the bobbing headlights of the truck, it looks to have gone off-road, tearing hell-bent over the dunes and rocks.

My shoulder spasms as I steer the motorcycle around a broken crate, then another. I squint in the dark, gaining on the druadans and the truck.

A figure stirs in the back of the truck bed.

Soon, I'm flanking Heath and Carter.

The idiots are bareback. Another shuttle passes, closer this time, overhead.

It's a Circuit authority craft. Probably the one that was supposed to be here for me, but then the emergency alarm switched their mission.

I rev the engine and push forward, the darkness offering some semblance of cover.

"You're alive!" Carter yells, his eyes focused between Ember's ears.

"It appears that way," I shout over the galloping hooves and drone of the motorcycle engine.

"They took the eggs," he shouts. "Brigid is with them. They have a boat."

I look ahead to the truck and spot the pale silver hair whipping in the wind. Relief and fury pound through me in equal measure. What the fuck, blondie? Irritation burns through me as it occurs to me that she is escaping with the eggs. I hate that I'm right.

Anger burns away my pain. If I had those traffickers in front of me right now, I'd tear them limb from limb for what they've done. Heath leans low over his heaving druadan, eyes fixed on Brigid. I follow his gaze to see her slumped weakly against the crates.

She'll be the ruin of us all.

It bothers me more than it should that she's in danger, and a fresh wave of protectiveness washes over me.

Twice, I'd pinned her against me. Every time I turned around, I was having to put myself between her and danger. As much as I wanted to deny it, the gentle curves of her body against mine had turned me on. And even now, I longed for that sensation again, of being near her, keeping her safe. The feel of her rapid heartbeat had been like a bird trying to escape its cage.

I need, no, *crave*, that feeling of being close to her, protecting her.

The invisible fuckers had crawled along the walls and corners surrounding her, waiting to strike. If I hadn't been there, standing guard while she'd been chasing after her sister— I shoved the thought away.

And now here she is on the back of a damn truck.

No sense of self-preservation whatsoever.

An idea occurs to me – what if those creatures were after her? What if they were targeting her specifically? Stalking her. It would explain why they were able to get so close to her before anyone else noticed them.

My mind races with different scenarios as we continue our pursuit of the truck.

For a few moments, the truck disappears out of sight. Only when we crest the hill does the truck come into view again, a dark silhouette against the moonlit horizon. It's veered off-road, cutting a treacherous path across the rocky desert. I know where it's heading, and my gut tightens with a grim certainty.

The cove. It's the only safe passage for a boat to navigate along the island's coastline.

In between strides, they'll phase and momentarily jump ahead of me before I catch them. Heath pushes Shadowmane to run faster, and Ember grunts as he attempts to keep up. Inky blood oozes down the stallion's right shoulder. Carter shouldn't be riding him.

If we all survive this, it'll be a fucking miracle.

My motorcycle growls in protest as I push it to the limit and swerve off the gravel road. We're closing the gap, but with rocks and bushes obscuring my path, there's no room for error.

The truck's tires kick up sand and dust as it races forward, its speed unchecked. Brigid is there. I can see her now. Her torn evening gown flutters out behind her as she clings to a crate.

Above us, the shuttle hovers, and its spotlight pierces the darkness, a blinding beam that focuses on the truck ahead. "Stop now. On behalf of the Nelworth Circuit Authorities." A loudspeaker blares. But the truck doesn't slow down, and I know what's coming next.

A visceral sensation constricts the air in my chest. It's a Class Eight shuttle, the kind that comes armed to the teeth with guns powerful enough to blow a guy apart.

Or a truck into pieces.

A second later, the laser fires and bright flashes of deadly light cut through the night and strike the metal cab and doors. The truck swerves wildly as it tries to evade the attack.

I can feel the heat of the beams as they streak past, too close for comfort.

I watch in grim silence as the truck weaves and dodges.

"No!" Carter yells at the sky. "Stop shooting!"

Heath repositioned a galloping Shadowmane between Carter and me. "Cease fire. Cease fire." He shouts into his comm, but there's no response, and two more laser blasts strike the truck, hitting the rear tire with deadly accuracy.

The tire explodes in a shower of sparks and debris, causing the truck to pitch to the right before rolling. My heart clenches as I lose sight of Brigid, and the truck tumbles one, two, three times before coming to rest on its side in a crumpled wreck.

The shuttle's engines roar past us, preparing to double back and confirm its strike. I slam down the accelerator, jumping a dune. The sand shifts beneath my wheels but I keep my balance. Fifty feet from it, I leap off the bike and sprint in the direction of the truck.

My heart is in my throat as I run, the fear of what I might find clawing at my chest.

The truck erupts in flames, an inferno of heat and fury, and I'm forced to stop. I shield my face against the blinding heat. I pace in front of the flames, roaring in frustration. My hand scoops up a handful of dirt, and I throw it at the truck.

I'm too late.

I wasn't fast enough to save her.

Heath and Carter stop their stallions beside me and slide off their backs. The three of us stand shoulder to shoulder in silence, our eyes fixed on the burning wreckage of the truck.

"I didn't see her jump," Carter says, his voice barely audible over the roar of the flames.

"Fuck!" I yell at the truck. Then, glare at Carter and Heath. "Fuck everyone. Fuck you for thinking you could control her. Fuck *me* for believing you that she could be trusted."

"She could be trusted," Heath's words are thick with emotion. "She was trying to save the eggs."

I swallow the lump in my throat, the heat of my anger barely ebbing. "Yeah, and look where it got her. "

Carter turns to me and jabs a finger at my chest. Fury blazes in his eyes. I've never seen him like this before. "No," he says, "Why don't *you* fuck off. She risked her life for those eggs because she knew how important they were to us."

I don't move, our eyes pinned on each other.

Beside me, Heath lets out a sigh. "Where were you, Logan?"

His tone is full of disappointment. "We needed you, and you weren't there."

Carter's lip curls in a sneer, and he jabs a finger at my chest. "If only you had been there, maybe we could have saved her. But you weren't, and now she and the eggs are gone."

The weight of guilt crashes down on me, and I drop my eyes from Carter's.

I spin away from him, walking a few feet away. "Fuck," I curse. They were right. She wasn't even a rider and yet, she'd sacrificed herself for the eggs.

Sacrificed herself for us.

Guilt coats my tongue, and I curl my hands into tight fists. "What do we do now?"

"We find out who was behind this," Carter says, "and make every one of those fuckers wish they'd never been born."

Thirty-Five

BRIGID

I've lost all sense of direction.

Up from down is all the same, as my body tumbles in every direction, leaving me nauseous and disoriented. The ground beneath me seems to shift and move as if it were alive. I reach out to grab onto something, anything, but my hands find only air.

Finally, with a thud, I stop rolling. A sharp rock stabs into my ribs. Ignoring the ache, I quickly wipe dirt from my face and mouth, spitting out the taste of blood and dirt. I start to push myself up, wincing as pain shoots through my chest.

The truck's engine grumbles, and the metal frame protests under the weight of tires and axles. Pain sears through my left ankle. I muster every ounce of self-control to yank it free from whatever pinned it. Once freed, my racing thoughts try to catch up. The crate. The eggs. I squint through the haze, scanning for them. Panic tightens my chest when I spot them overturned. The crate is empty.

"Oh no. No, no, no," I shout, crawling towards it on my hands and knees. I flip the crate as if to convince myself it's not empty. My eyes dart around, searching for signs of the eggs, but I can't see more than a few feet ahead through the dust and smoke. The drone of a small engine, perhaps a motorcycle, mingles with the familiar whoosh-whoosh of a hovering shuttle above.

Circuit police. It has to be. They'd probably already been on their way here to deal with Logan anyway and then learned that the station was under attack by rebels.

My breathing comes in ragged gasps, and I force myself to give up searching for the eggs. I wipe the grit from my face, attempting to clear my vision, and crawl in what I assume is the direction of the overturned cab.

My sister is in there. Is she alive? Injured? I can't bear to look but wrestle with the urge to turn away. I need to know if she's okay. She was stealing the eggs and was somehow involved with this rebel group that attacked the station, but I couldn't simply shut off my feelings for her.

As I draw nearer, I pull a tarp aside that had blown off the bed of the truck, and my heart catches in my throat. Two eggs are half-buried in the sand.

I hold my breath as I carefully pry the first one free, swiping away loose sand at its base. When three-quarters of it is exposed, I gently pull it free. Inky black liquids oozes from the base, a six-inch crack staining the ground.

I choke back a sob as the sand is stained black. "No...please, no," I murmur, pleading as if I can reverse the unreversible. My vision blurs as my throat constricts. I've failed. The little innocent creature is gone.

Tears choke my words. "I'm sorry. I'm so sorry." I should have held onto them tighter. Taken longer to find a way to cut the straps. I never should've let them on the truck.

I should have pushed aside my personal feelings and stopped my sister.

Carefully, I set the broken egg down. There's nothing I can do now.

The soul within will never see the light of day, never draw a breath, because of me.

I'm sure the other egg met a similar fate. The last two druadan eggs in existence, protected for centuries at the station, and I failed them. I failed the station. Heath, Carter, Logan – how could they ever trust me again? Forgive me for my failure? I couldn't blame them.

I push on, moving in the direction of the overturned truck cab.

The driver is dead, his head twisted at an unnatural angle, vacant eyes staring back at me. My eyes shift to the passenger seat, release a sigh, seeing it's empty. Lightheadedness overtakes me as I stumble back from the truck, black spots dancing in front of my vision.

The smoke is too intense, and each breath is agony. I cough, trying to clear my lungs, but it only makes it worse. Crawling away from the cab on my hands and knees, I try to put some distance between me and the fire. The world spins and darkens around me as I struggle to stay conscious.

The smoke is too intense, and each breath is agony. I crawl away from the cab on my hands and knees, the world spinning and darkening. I'm not going to make it. Fatigue weighs me down, tempting me to lie down and close my eyes. I picture my fluffy pillow back at my apartment in Delford.

I caress the sand. It's so soft and round, but then my fingertips catch on evenly spaced ridges. I blink, clearing my vision, and see the oblong side of what I initially guessed was a rock.

It's too perfectly round and smooth. It's the smaller of the three. I squint to see the pale blue one with white speckles in the dark.

I bite my lip, hoping that it's okay. My hands are incredibly gentle as I spin it on its side and lift it. I shut my eyes, using only my fingers to feel along the surface for any cracks or breaks. Nothing. It's intact. I check it again just to be certain, then pull it close into an embrace. It's okay. By some miracle, this one survived. Whole. Alive.

I hang my head, ignoring the approaching footsteps and voices shouting at me to stand and raise my hands. Still kneeling, I refuse to move. If they want to take me, fine. I deserve whatever punishment they have in store.

"Get up," a gruff woman's voice commands. "Slowly," she adds.

She's not Sharice. This woman sounds older. I peer up at her. She's wearing a cloak, but curls of red hair frame her face. Refusing to stand, I hold the egg against my chest, overcome by an intense protectiveness.

If they want it, they'll have to kill me for it.

A gentle sound thrums through my chest, arms, shoulders, and back.

It's the egg. It's doing something. My stomach flips with excitement.

It's alive.

The rebels' startled shrieks draw my attention. The air shimmers like heat in the desert in the middle of the group, and Galaxian— sandy-colored hide is matted with splashes of blood — materializes. He bares his teeth and lowers his head, snaking back and forth at the group surrounding me. The rebels scramble back, their eyes wide with fear and confusion.

They lift their guns, but I know it's all a ruse. After what they'd done to get it, they wouldn't dare risk damaging the egg I'm carrying.

The humming from the egg grows louder, and carrying the

egg, I move him. Eyes never leaving the group, he lowers his front legs, allowing me to climb on. His hide is hot, but I feel no pain.

I cling to the egg as I straddle him, and he stands upright. I catch a quick glimpse of shocked faces before I feel my ears pop from the sudden change in pressure, like riding in a high-altitude shuttle.

Then we're alone somewhere else in the shadowy dark of the desert. It's not too far since I can smell the smoke from the burning truck and the Circuit shuttles hovering over the station.

The egg continues to vibrate, and I feel Galaxian's body tense. I grab a handful of mane, and he takes my cue, breaking into a gallop. The most experience I had riding something was a stationary bike Laura let me borrow.

With one hand firmly gripping the egg, I can only cling desperately to his mane with the other, hanging on for dear life. His hooves pound against the sand, creating a steady rhythm that matches my heartbeat. It feels like we're flying, our bodies moving in perfect harmony.

The exhilaration floods my senses. Holy shit, I'm riding a druadan. An excited whoop, tears free from my throat.

I can't help it.

This is incredible. More than that, it's impossible.

I'm not bonded. I'm not a rider. I'm a woman. This can't be happening. Maybe I'd inhaled more smoke than I thought, and there's a chance I'm still lying unconscious by the truck, imagining all of this.

But then I feel the warm shell of the egg against my chest and the flutter of movement inside. This is no dream.

The wind whips my hair behind me, and tears stream from my eyes as Galaxian races across the desert. His powerful legs propel us forward. The humming grows louder, and adrenaline surges through me, heightening my senses. As I straddle Galaxian's back, feeling his muscles flex beneath me. I steel a look over my shoulder. The Circuit shuttles grow smaller in the distance, and I can barely make out the pillar of smoke.

My mind lingers on the three men I'd left behind: Heath, Carter, and Logan. I pray that they're alive. Safe. Even as it feels like I'm abandoning them.

My ears pop as we arrive somewhere else, and Galaxian halts. I slide off his back, landing on knees that feel like jelly.

As the sun rises in the distance, painting the horizon with shades of yellow and orange, I take a deep breath and look around at our new destination. He's taken me to a flat stretch of land surrounded by towering sand dunes. But there is something else here – a small oasis in the distance.

A pool of crystal-clear water shimmers under the first rays of sunlight, surrounded by lush green palm trees and vibrant flowers.

Galaxian trots towards it without hesitation, and I instinctively lean forward to shield the egg from any potential danger. But there is none here – only tranquility and beauty.

Galaxian nuzzles my hand as if sensing my concern for the fragile object. I stroke his neck, grateful for his saving me from capture and allowing me to ride him and not come away with third-degree burns on my legs.

My body is spent, exhausted from the night of adrenaline and fatigue burns at the backs of my eyeballs.

I find a spot that obscures anyone passing by from seeing me in the shade of one of the trees and sit in the sand. I cross my legs. My dress is stained and torn, but I'm able to fit it over my knees and make it into a makeshift hammock to cradle the egg. "You're safe now," I say. "I'll protect you."

The vibrations ease. I had grown so used to them that I hadn't even realized it was still happening. A soft glow of light radiates from me onto the egg like someone had pointed a pair of car headlights at it. My head swivels, but I see no one behind us. I glance down and realize it's my hair that's having the effect. It's glowing, like moonlight.

My fingers brush the soft curls of my hair as it lays over my right shoulder. The silvery tendrils, each individual strand, are glowing like the fiber optics I'd had in the dress I'd begged mom to buy me for a school formal.

I sigh, adding it to the list of unbelievable things that had happened to me today.

The morning sun warms my face as I lean my head against the trunk of a tree, and drift in and out of sleep. I hear Galaxian's footsteps in the sand and his labored breathing close by. The tension leaves my body as I realize he's standing guard. He's protecting me as I'm protecting the egg.

The rebels that didn't leave on the boat will find us soon enough.

Even with his sporadic phasing, Galaxian still left tracks behind. But until then, I can take a moment to rest.

Just when I begin to doze off, the whir of Galaxian's voice vibrates in the air. I open my eyes to see three men peering down at me the rising sun silhouetting them. Behind them are their magnificent stallions, glowing eyes glinting in the morning light.

"Its…you," I murmur.

Heath is favoring his leg, and Logan looks like he got in a fight with a thorn bush and the bush won. They focus their gazes on me, and they all smile, even Logan.

"It's us," Carter says, softly.

I shift, preparing to stand, when Heath's voice stops me. "Wait. Look." I peer down at the egg cradled in my lap. A small crack forms on the top, and I gasp. A stirring sensation, like a gentle pull, resonates within me. My hand trembles as I reach out to touch the egg's surface.

The men's gazes are a mix of awe and disbelief as if the

impossible is unfolding before their eyes. Which, in all honesty, it is.

In a rush of movement, all three of them drop to their knees, encircling me. My face flushes with embarrassment as I feel the weight of their stares.

Carter's voice trembles as he speaks, finally breaking the silence. "This is impossible."

Eyes never leaving the egg, I say, "I agree. But it seems the impossible has just become our reality."

Continue the journey with SOULBOUND: Druadan Legacy Book Two

The hidden history of the druadan is emerging from the shadows...

During the attack at Meridian, a shocking truth was revealed: my sister leads a rebel group hellbent on stealing the last druadan egg. By sxqheer chance, I managed to save one, but as it begins to hatch, the three Master Riders—Heath, Logan, and Carter, with whom I've developed undeniable feelings—and I must surrender the egg to Circuit officials.

To keep the egg's survival a secret, Circuit shuts down Meridian, forcing us to relocate to Blackhawk Station. There, ancient secrets await, holding the key to understanding the rebels' desire for the druadan foal, my connection to it, and the bond I share with the three master riders and their stallions.

However, tensions escalate as Logan finally faces trial for his rogue stallion, and civil unrest engulfs Venovia, with strikes and violent protests pushing the country toward war. I must tread carefully. The long-buried truths I unearth at Blackhawk could prove the world's salvation—or the catalyst for utter ruin.

Keep up to date with the latest book announcements from Amelia by subscribing to my newsletter (no spam, I promise!)

Visit my website at: www.ameliacolebooks.com

Questions/comments?

Email me: contact@ameliacolebooks.com

ACKNOWLEDGMENTS

Thank you so much for reading Shadowbound!! This book was such a labor of love. Starting with the first page, I poured myself into it, pushing it to be the perfect version you see today.

It was one of the most challenging stories I've ever written, and there were times I didn't think I was worthy enough to craft it into what it was destined to be.

This book never would have seen the light of day if I hadn't been surrounded by many supportive people in my life.

To my editor, Hina. Thank you for understanding and adoring my characters as much as I did. Your suggestions and our chats are the reason this book is as brilliant as it is today.

To my Llamaquad pals, you guys are always my rock, my center, my go-to friends when I feel like the words aren't wording and I need a boost of encouragement to get my butt in the chair.

To my beta readers, Katelyn, Jo-Anna, and Morgan. You are the cream to my cheese. Your first reads helped me shape this story into something truly spectacular.

To my family, you are my whole world. Thank you for being my people I bounced ideas off, listened to me talk plot on long car rides, and drew pictures of my characters for inspiration.

I love you all very much.

ABOUT THE AUTHOR

Amelia Cole is a fantasy, sci-fi author for adults. She always includes romance and speculative elements and takes inspiration from myths and historical events. She is a short story contest winner and has been published in magazines and anthologies.

She lives with her family in Washington state.

www.ingramcontent.com/pod-product-compliance
Lightning Source LLC
Chambersburg PA
CBHW051302130726
47987CB00004B/1632